"I'm the only thing between you and ten thousand lifetimes of emptiness and pain."

Knowing there was nothing he could say, Alex just grunted derisively. T-Bone smiled, almost sadly, then shoved Alex against the truck and turned to his gang of road pirates.

"No," he told them. "This one's too dangerous to play with. We'll just give him to the darkness."

He stepped back as the others closed in.

Seeing death coming for him, Alex ignored the pain in his side and tried to fight his way clear, but there were too many of them at once, and they were strong, and he was hurt. Weapons, fists, and feet pummeled him for blinding, hectic moments before he managed to stagger through the circle and away from them, into the high weeds.

But there was nowhere to go. Figuring his karma from the *Markham* had finally caught up with him, he turned, faced his assailants, and spat blood onto the dry grass.

"It takes all of you," he growled with a bravado he didn't really feel.

Billy-Bob thumbed back the hammer of one of his .45s, but Yvonne pushed his arm down.

"No," she said, her tone no-nonsense. "This beefcake is mine." She looked at Alex, her smile broad. "You're wrong, beefcake. It only takes one to party."

She raised her .357 and cocked it with deliberate slowness, staring Alex right in the eye.

"And now the party's over, and I'm gonna have to break your heart."

Ridiculously, the last thing to go through Alex's mind was that he was going to be very late this time, and it really pissed him off.

By Christopher Dow

Fiction
Effigy
>   Book I: Stroud
>   Book II: Oakdale

The Books of Bob
>   Devil of a Time
>   Jumping Jehovah

The Clay Guthrie Mysteries
>   The Dead Detective
>   Landscape with Beast
>   The Texas Troll Unlimited
>   Darkness Descending, Insatiable

Roadkill
The Werewolf and Tide, and Other Compulsions

Nonfiction
Lord of the Loincloth (nonfiction novel)
Book of Curiosities: Adventures in the Paranormal
Occasional Pilgrimage: Essays on Film, Literature, and Other Matters
Living the Story: The Meandering, True, and Sometimes Strange
>   Adventures of an Unknown Writer (Vol. I & II)

Martial Arts
The Wellspring: An Inquiry into the Nature of Chi
Circling the Square: Observations on the Dynamics of Tai Chi Chuan
Elements of Power: Essays on the Art and Practice of Tai Chi Chuan
Alchemy of Breath: An Introduction to Chi Kung
Leaves on the Wind: A Survey of Martial Arts Literature (Vol. I–VI)

Poetry
City of Dreams
The Trip Out
Texas White Line Fever
Networks
A Dilapidation of Machinery
Puzzle Pieces: Selected Poems

Editor
The Abby Stone: The Poetry of Bartholo Dias
The Best of Phosphene
The Best of Dialog

ROADKILL

ROADKILL

Christopher Dow

Phosphene Publishing Company
Temple, Texas

Roadkill
© 2010 by Christopher Dow
ISBN: 0-9796968-4-4
ISBN 13: 978-0-9796968-4-8
Published by:
Phosphene Publishing Company
Temple, Texas, U.S.A.
phosphenepublishing.com

2.1

ROADKILL

PROLOGUE

THE *MARKHAM* HAD BEEN BUILT for pleasure, but now the ship's decks and passages reeked of death. As the squad—what was left of it—moved tensely through the gangways that led toward the ballroom, distant gunfire from fore and aft announced that the mayhem was not yet over.

As if they didn't know it already. One of their own had bled out not three minutes earlier, but they'd sent four of the pirates to hell in return.

Just ahead and to the left, another passageway intersected the one they were in. Thomas, on point, gave a quick peek around the corner then signaled that it was clear and only one door opened in that direction. Lieutenant Jackson consulted his hand-held, tapping quickly at the keys with long, dark fingers.

"It's one of the entries to the ballroom galley," he whispered to the other three. "We sweep it first then take the ballroom. Thomas on point, Brant second, I'm third, Albarado last." He gave Thomas the go-ahead, and Thomas, crouching, hurried down the short gangway. Brant and the lieutenant arrived at the door at the end just behind him, and by the time Albarado joined them, Thomas already had pushed the door open a crack and surveyed what he could from his low angle. Looking at Jackson, he shrugged.

Jackson pointed to each of them in the same order that they'd come down the hall then counted down from three to zero on his fingers.

Trigger fingers tight, they went through the door, Thomas to the left, Brant to the right, Jackson and Albarado spilling in after them.

Only silence greeted their entry. A dead young man in a waiter's uniform lay in a pool of blood on the floor, but otherwise, the room was unoccupied. "Check the pantries," Jackson ordered, then paused as Albarado gestured toward the door of the walk-in freezer. A spoon was jammed in the latch, and the door was riddled with bullet holes.

Jackson jerked his head, and he and Albarado crept forward, the other two covering them. Albarado eased the spoon out, levered back the handle, and jerked on it. The door stayed closed. Something was holding it from the inside.

Jackson rapped on the door.

"Inside the freezer," he called out as loudly as he dared. "Open up. We're American soldiers. We're here to help."

"Yeah, right," came a man's muffled reply. "How do we know you're not pirates?"

At that moment, the muffled boom of an exploding grenade sounded from somewhere in the belly of the ship.

"We don't have time for this," Brant said, and Jackson nodded.

"Put the spoon back," he told Albarado. "They'll be safe enough in there, and we don't want 'em coming out at the wrong time."

Albarado complied, and by now Thomas and Brant were at the twin swinging doors that led to the narrow hallway flanking the ballroom. The doors had windows, but all that could be seen through them was the bulkhead on the other side of the hallway.

Brant carefully pulled the left door back while Thomas eased his head through to scope out the hall. He quickly looked one way then the other, but not quickly enough. A burst of automatic weapon fire came from the second direction, and he jerked and fell against the door, wrenching it from Brant's hand. More bullets scored the doors, and by the time Brant and Albarado had pulled Thomas back into the galley, half his head was gone.

The remaining squad members didn't look at the corpse. They couldn't afford to. Brant wiped the sweat from his combat-grimed face then pulled the door open again. Albarado and Jackson both tossed grenades in the direction of the gunfire and Brant quickly shut the door. A moment later, two explosions left a rattle of debris then silence in their wake.

Brant thrust his head through the doorway and pulled back, but he'd seen what he needed to: a shredded body lying akimbo across the flimsy barrier of an upturned table.

Suddenly, gunfire erupted from the ballroom. A lot of gunfire, accompanied by screams, the trample of feet, and sounds of furniture being overturned.

"Move!" Jackson snapped, and the three of them dashed into the hall. There were two doors: one by the body of the dead pirate and one in the other direction. Jackson pointed to Brant and the door beside the dead pirate, then he and Albarado ran toward the other. All three paused, before bursting into the ballroom, and a scene from hell.

There were maybe a hundred people left standing in the room and an equal number down, either wounded, dying, or dead. The eight pirates in the room were simply machine gunning anyone standing as fast as they could.

There was no time to think, only act. Brant sent a short burst into the chest of the pirate nearest him, and another, about thirty feet away, turned and fired. Brant flung himself to the side, rolled, and came up shooting. His bullets, not well-aimed, cut across the pirate's upper thigh, nearly severing one leg. But as the man went down, Brant saw, to his horror, that a part of his burst had missed the pirate and slammed into a portly middle-aged woman, who simply collapsed in a heap.

He heard firing from the other end of the ballroom as Jackson and Albarado fought, but he didn't have time for more than that as a burst stitched across his body. Two rounds caught him in the chest and flung him backwards to the floor, a third pierced his right arm, and a fourth shattered his assault rifle.

A groggy moment later, he cautiously raised his head. The pirate who'd shot him was standing near the bar, not realizing the American was wearing body armor and was far from dead. By now, no one was left standing, and the pirate was simply spraying fire from his Uzi into the bodies that lay around him on the deck. Just behind him a young woman, her face covered in blood, crouched over a the crumpled body of a slender, middle-aged woman. She tried to drag the woman behind the bar to shield her from the pirate's sight, and she'd just about made it when the pirate, swinging around as he emptied his Uzi into the bodies, saw her.

Face a distorted mask of rage and blood lust, the pirate aimed at her and pulled the trigger. A single shot kicked up the floor next to the young woman, then nothing. The pirate was out of bullets. But not out of magazines.

Brant, seeing him eject his spent magazine, surged to his feet and lunged toward the man, ignoring the pain in his wounded arm and fumbling awkwardly with his left hand for the pistol at his right hip.

The young woman finished dragging the older woman behind the bar just as the pirate slammed his mag home and stepped behind the bar after them. He let loose a burst, then seeing Brant rushing toward him, he lifted the snout of his Uzi. By now, Brant had the automatic half out, but he could see that he'd never get it off safety and aimed before the pirate shot.

An abrupt look of pain shot across the pirate's maniacal face, and the Uzi's barrel jerked upward as he pulled the trigger, sending the bullets harmlessly into the ballroom's ceiling.

Suddenly, the young woman rose behind the pirate, a bloody paring knife in her hand, and she plunged the short blade into his neck. Dropping the Uzi, the man clutched at his throat, and in an instant, the young woman had the gun in her hands. She was obviously inexperienced, but a close-range Uzi burst is forgiving of the shooter, not the one shot. The pirate's chest caved in, and he fell behind the bar.

A second later, Brant reached the young woman, just as she was aiming the Uzi in his direction. He caught her before she could pull the trigger and disarmed her efficiently. As she tried to beat her fists into his face, he noticed that she might have been pretty, but right now, her stark eyes stared wildly from her blood-covered face, her lips pulled back in a feral snarl. She was terribly strong for someone so slender.

"I'm an American soldier," he said into her blood-matted hair as he clutched her writhing body close. He wanted to say it calmly to help sooth the frightened young woman, and he tried to, but the words just came out in a harsh rasp. "I'm an American."

Suddenly she went limp. Sobbing, she turned toward the dead woman behind the bar. Brant let her go, and she fell on the dead pirate and tried to pull him off the woman's body. Brant grabbed the man by the belt, dragged him from behind the bar, and cast him aside.

Only then did he glance around, noticing that the gunfire in the room had ceased. At the other end of the ballroom, he could see Albarado standing and looking dumbly around. Of Jackson, there was no sign.

"Beta," crackled a voice in his com set. "This is Alpha. What's your status."

"We need help," Brant said, leaning tiredly against the bar and trying to staunch the blood flowing from his wound. "The pirates are down, but we need medical down here, fast."

Albarado came across the room toward him, pausing once to put a short burst into a pirate who was still alive.

"Jackson?" Brant asked, and Albarado shook his head.

"Those stupid fuckers," Brant said, staring at wounded, dead, and dying, unable to do anything, unable to help even himself.

ONE

THE BLOOD RED DISK OF the sun quivered in the atmosphere as it touched the rim of a rumpled and barren ridge of hills. Ragged shadows cast by the ridge inched darkness across the desert toward a desolate two-lane blacktop that ran parallel to the hills a mile to the east. As the night line moved inexorably from rock to cactus to creosote bush and rock again, night creatures emerged from their burrows to scuttle across the desert floor. One, a lizard, darted across the pavement and barely missed being squashed beneath the tires of a battered decades-old Chevy pickup that rattled down the road toward the west.

The pickup's scarred, dull-green body had lost its luster long ago, and each dented fender was a different color, as if some joking back-yard mechanic had attempted to give the old hulk an air of clownish festivity. To the casual eye, the old clanker was at least trying for a colorful comeback, and the patchwork look went a long way toward masking several incongruous additions, such as the shield of heavy welded pipe protecting the grill and headlights, the CB antenna on the roof, the silvery window tinting, and the fat, heavy-treaded tires with flat black wheels. Those and the smooth, throaty roar that rumbled from twin mufflers seemed seriously out of place.

The truck ambled on down the pavement at a moderate speed befitting its apparent age, kicking up occasional clouds of dust from pools of sand where the desert was trying to reclaim the roadway. Its single occupant, a shadow in its darkening interior, steered it over a short rise and around a curve, and it disappeared from sight. As soon as it had, the lizard who'd nearly been squashed scurried back across the still-hot asphalt, looking for a bug to eat, a lady lizard to molest, or, perhaps, in fear of some larger predator behind him.

The sun sank several more degrees, until only a fraction of its circumference still arced above the torn hills. Another vehicle rolled down the road, also heading west but otherwise as different from the battered pickup as the desert day was from its night. It was a shiny new Lincoln Town Car, paint glistening a chic pearl gray. It sped along at a fashionable clip, and though this sleek bullet emitted nary a rattle, it, too, kicked up desert dust as it gleamed for an instant in the last rays of the setting sun then dipped into a shadowed arroyo and whizzed around a curve.

The man at the Lincoln's wheel glanced at the sun as its last drop oozed behind the ridge. He switched on the headlights, and though he performed the action perfunctorily, his movements were almost too nonchalant. His jaw was set in a tense line.

His wife, sitting next to him, was pissed. He shrugged inside his Eddie Bauer jacket and settled back in his seat. As if his show of relaxation had been a signal, she harrumphed at him.

"What, Phyllis?"

"I hope you're comfortable."

He smiled grimly to himself and, knowing better, let the words out anyway.

"Sure. I'm comfortable."

"Well, I'm not," she cracked then plucked at the shoulder harness binding her to the seat, moving it so it wouldn't chafe her breast. "We've been in this damn car all day, and now we'll be in it all night. And look at Heath. He's asleep back there."

The man glanced into the back of the sedan. The last ambient light of the fading day revealed the form of his son stretched out on the seat.

"Let him sleep," the man said, turning again to the road and studiously avoiding his wife's glare. "If we keep arguing, we're going to wake him up."

"I just wish you'd stopped like I asked," she went on anyway, still peeved but with her voice subdued. "That was a perfectly good motel back there, but no, you just had to push on."

"Don't worry about it," he hissed curtly. "I can last a few more hours, and then we'll be home."

Phyllis yawned and stretched and pulled with renewed distaste at the shoulder harness confining her. She moved the strap and massaged the sore spot between her breasts. Sensing her husband watching her, she looked over at him. He was hungrily eyeing her body. Two weeks in a string of motel rooms with a twelve-year-old boy hadn't been conducive to love-making. She smiled coldly to herself. At the age of thirty-five, she was, she thought, even more attractive than she'd been when they'd married. She knew her husband thought so, too. Stretching sinuously for his benefit, she let a smile ease enticingly out.

"We could be in bed right now, Rob," she said seductively and arched her breasts toward him.

He grinned and reached eagerly for her but jerked back abruptly as she bridled indignantly and slapped his hand away.

"Asleep," she hissed.

He looked so hurt, she almost felt sorry for him. Even if he could be damn inconsiderate, her anger really wasn't fueled by anything more than tiredness and the fact that she was feeling bitchy and claustrophobic.

"Aw, Phyllis, it's only a few hundred miles. There won't be much other traffic on this road. We'll be there by midnight. One at the latest."

"We'll get there exhausted," she said, unswayed. "We should have stayed in that motel."

Rob shifted uncomfortably in his seat and rubbed a hand over his midriff bulge.

"My back can't take another night on those crummy motel mattresses," he complained. "In a few hours, we can sleep in our own bed." He turned and winked at her. "Heh, babe?"

He reached out for her, and she glowered at him again, but in a moment, the frown eased from her features. She never could hold a grudge long, at least not against Rob. Unfastening her seat belt, she sighed with relief then scooted over and snuggled up against him. He slid a hand along her thigh.

In the back seat, the boy raised an eye and wrinkled his nose as he saw his mother nibble on his father's ear. Did parents fight just so they could make up and then make out? He shook his head, shifted to a more comfortable position, and tried to settle back to sleep.

Just at that moment, light flashed over the backs of his parents' heads as a car topped a hill half a mile behind them. Heath saw the light through half-close lids, but it seemed to drive all sleep from him, and he woke completely.

He sat up, groaning for his parents' benefit, and stretched. High shreds of clouds in the sky ahead of them were still tinged with reds and golds, but to the sides and rear, the sky was turning to star-spangled pitch except where a gibbous moon had risen a hand-width over the eastern horizon. He turned and peered through the rear window at the approaching headlights. They were still some distance off, but gaining rapidly. Then his mother's voice drew his attention, and he looked forward again.

"Some other fool on the road besides us," she said sourly, pointing ahead at a dim pair of taillights.

The family in the Lincoln couldn't see that the taillights belonged to the battered old multicolored pickup that had passed along the road a few minutes ahead of them, and had they known, it would have meant nothing. All that mattered to Rob was that the vehicle was going slow and the road ahead was snaking into a series of curves as it wound up through the hills where there'd be almost no chance to pass. His lips tightened with annoyance.

"A slow fool," he said. "Probably a local."

He eased off on the accelerator, and the sedan lost speed.

In the back seat, Heath peered intently at the slowly moving taillights ahead of them. Then he scrambled around and knelt on the seat, staring at the headlights approaching from behind. He couldn't articulate the feelings that rose suddenly in his gut and chilled his spine and, in fact, didn't even really want to acknowledge them. After all, he was twelve—almost thirteen—and it hadn't been that long since the shadows in his room had sometimes seemed more than shadows.

He twisted to look at the slow-moving taillights ahead, then back at the all-too-rapidly nearing headlights. Articulate or not, acknowledgement or not, he couldn't contain himself. He turned to the front again and reached out to touch his father's shoulder.

"Don't slow down, Dad." He meant to sound concerned but was surprised at the flame of panic searing the edges of his words.

His father started slightly at the boy's touch, and his eyes sought his son's silhouette in the rearview mirror.

"Eh?" He seemed surprised at the boy's tone, but whatever thought that might have generated was lost as he saw the headlights behind them closing the gap between the two cars. "And a fast fool coming up behind." He stared again. "That guy must be going ninety."

"Don't slow down, Dad," Heath repeated, this time blunting the edge of fear in his voice. It was an effort, for the feeling seemed to crush down on his breathing with viselike pressure.

His mother turned to glance at the headlights then said to her son, "Now, Heath, let your father drive." To her husband, she said with a heavy dose of sarcasm, "Good thing there's no other traffic."

The boy looked again through the rear window. The car following them now was right on their tail, so close he could see the chrome grill glitter through the glare of the headlights. He craned around. The taillights in front of them were discernible as belonging to an old pick-up, off-color fenders showing in the beams of the Lincoln's headlights. The pick-up seemed to be going slower than ever, now.

Heath felt the vise of panic screw tighter as the Lincoln was pinned between the two vehicles. Abruptly, all three rounded a curve and entered a short stretch of straight road.

Rob pressed on the Lincoln's gas pedal and twisted the wheel, accelerating into the left lane.

The boy, struck dumb with fear, watched as the battered pickup swerved waveringly in front of the Lincoln.

"Shit!" Rob barked as he hit the brakes and dropped the Lincoln back into the right lane. "Goddamn drunk redneck!"

The boy swiveled around, seeing the car behind edge closer.

Why couldn't his father understand what was going on? The question had barely penetrated the rushing sound in the boy's head when he was plunked down onto the seat as his father, seeing another opening, jammed on the accelerator. The Lincoln veered into the left lane as Rob tried to pass the truck a second time.

Moving like a slow-motion nightmare, the truck weaved across the centerline, nearly slamming one of its party-colored fenders into the Lincoln. Rob cursed again and fell back but this time hit the horn, sending an obnoxious blast into the quiet desert night.

"Get the fuck out of the way, you dead-beat drunk!" he yelled.

"Rob, don't curse in front of Heath," his wife scolded half-heartedly.

"Why the hell doesn't he get that crate out of the way?" Rob demanded angrily of no one in particular. Then he nervously eyed the car behind them. It had drawn so close that its headlights were nearly hidden by the curve of the Lincoln's trunk. He quickly looked forward again. "The bastard's blocking traffic."

At that moment there was a break. Rob whipped the wheel and tried to speed around the pickup. With predatory quickness and speed belying its aged and ramshackle looks, the old truck lunged forward and sideswiped the sedan. The Lincoln careened off the road.

Inside the car, Phyllis shrieked as the car lurched across the shoulder then into the desert, Rob grimly wrestling with the jerking wheel. Only instead of sand and cactus and boulders, there was a wide metal gate blocking their path.

As the Lincoln's jouncing headlights washed across the gate, Phyllis screamed again, and Rob cursed. In the back seat, Heath just gasped and stared wide-eyed at the strange-looking, cavorting man who quickly operated the latch and swung the gate open just in time to let the sedan speed through into the darkness beyond. In that fragment of time, the boy had burned into his memory a vision of frizzled, windblown hair, a shouting rictus grin of triumph, and glittering chains draped and wrapped around the man's leather-clad body. Then the wild man flashed by, and the Lincoln was roaring and bouncing down a rutted dirt road.

The chain-festooned man at the gate howled and jumped up and down as the battered pickup raced through the gate after the Lincoln, followed closely by the fast car that had come up behind the Lincoln—a heavy-bodied old Pontiac.

As soon as they passed, the man slammed the gate and leapt onto a Harley that squatted, idling, beside the dirt road. He jammed the motorcycle into gear, gunned the powerful engine, and rooster-tailing dirt, sped through the dust cloud raised by the three vehicles in front of him, his voice trailing whoops.

Out in front, headlights cutting through the night, the Lincoln bounded and swerved as Rob fought to stay on the narrow, rutted road.

"Slow down!" Phyllis screamed.

Rob, through some automatic reflex, obeyed, and instantly the Lincoln jolted as the pickup, armed with its pipe-work grill, rammed it from behind.

"Rob!" the woman shrieked.

Rob stomped on the gas and tried to speed up, but the old pickup leapt forward again, not so much crashing into the back of the Lincoln as shoving and urging it on to greater speed and more erratic guidance.

As the Lincoln swerved around a bend in the dirt road, Phyllis was flung against her husband. He shoved her away, but not before he'd lost control long enough for the sedan to miss the next curve. In a split second, the road was gone, and the Lincoln was jolting across raw wasteland.

"Mommy!" wailed Heath. He tried to climb over the seat, but the pickup rammed the Lincoln again. Grip jarred loose, he was thrown to the floor of the back seat, where he lay stunned.

Phyllis screamed again as the pickup pulled along one side of the Lincoln and the Pontiac on the other and narrowed the gap, squeezing the Lincoln between them. Rob shouted curses as the Lincoln was herded for another hundred yards. Then, with a slamming and crashing, the other two vehicles forced the sedan to a halt in a cloud of dust. A moment later, the motorcycle roared up and stopped nearby.

Before the two adults in the Lincoln could recover their wits, the doors were yanked open, and they were dragged screaming and yelling from the car. Their captors hauled them a dozen yards from the Lincoln, into the glare of the pickup and Pontiac's headlights.

Phyllis and Rob clung to each other as they stared at the people surrounding them. There were seven of them, menacing stances backlit by the headlights, faces obscured by shadows.

"W-what do you want?" Rob stammered.

The circling figures remained silent with frightening stillness. Frustrated, angry, and afraid, Rob shook off Phyllis and took a step toward one of the figures. Suddenly, brilliant light flared from one of the figures, blinding Rob. Frightened as he was, he realized the person was holding a video camera.

He raised a protective hand across his face, trying to block out the searing light, when a metallic jingling sounded behind him. A length of chain snaked out from the far side of the circle, wrapped around his legs, and jerked taut, tripping him. He fell heavily to the ground. His wife cried out and tried to rush to him, but a massive bald man with a brushy black beard stepped quickly out of the circle and grabbed her by the arm.

She kicked and struggled, but he was too large and much too strong. He just wrapped a meaty arm around her waist and held her against his side like a child. She bent frantically and tried to bite his pinioning arm, but a small chrome ball-peen hammer appeared in his other hand, flashing in the light from the cars. With a flick of his wrist, he rapped her on the head. The blow wasn't hard enough to do more than raise a lump, but she cried out and stopped trying to bite.

As if that was a signal, the other assailants laughed, suddenly and raucously, and it was obvious that one of them was a woman. A big woman, tall as most of her companions, frame hung with lean muscle.

She stepped forward, into the light, and Rob saw her clearly for the first time. She was pretty, in a rough sort of way and looked like she might have American Indian blood. But whatever good looks she had were almost completely submerged in her fearsome appearance. Wild, wind-teased blonde hair topped a face heavy with exaggerated makeup. Metal-toed cowboy boots shod her feet, her legs were sheathed in denim, and her torso was clad only in an unbuttoned black leather vest that did nothing to hide the globes of her breasts as she bent over him.

A glitter at the brown tip of her left breast drew his eyes. The nipple was pierced crossways with a slender golden rod. From the rod ends pended a loop of gold chain. The nipple was straining erect.

Rob looked up from the glittering aureole into her eyes. There was a glitter there, too, colder than gold, hotter than fire.

A mean smile creased her makeup, and she reached out and caressed the fallen man's cheek, almost lovingly.

"My name's Yvonne," she said. "My, you're such a handsome gentleman. So well dressed. You want to have a good time?"

Rob pulled back fearfully.

"I...I...."

Yvonne smirked and nodded as if in agreement.

"Me, too." She turned her eyes to gaze slyly at Phyllis. "Your wife won't mind."

Suddenly Yvonne hauled back and slapped Rob hard with her open palm and followed that with a back hand to the other side of his face. As he collapsed, she guffawed in a loud, obnoxious bray.

"Let's party!" she bellowed. The others laughed derisively and, except for the video cameraman and the one pinioning Phyllis, moved in on the fallen man. As the ring of tormentors tightened and the five of them began to beat and kick Rob, the big man's thick, rough fingers sought the front of Phyllis's blouse. With a brutal, clumsy jerk, he ripped it open. Phyllis cried out and writhed futilely in her captor's grip, and he dropped her to the ground, grabbed a handful of her hair, and cuffed her alongside the head. As she slumped to her knees, he yanked her bra down to her waist.

Unnoticed by the mob, the rear door of the Lincoln eased open, and Heath crawled out and scurried away into the darkness. He halted in a crouch behind a creosote bush a hundred feet away and looked back, breath heavy with terror.

Silhouetted against the dust in the combined lights from the vehicles and the video camera was the tight knot of assailants beating his father, while off to the side, his mother struggled weakly as the big man tore off her clothes. With the sound of fists and boots striking flesh came crude laughter and words much worse than his father ever used.

Suddenly, his father broke free from the knot, staggering and reeling. Heath's heart surged with hope as Rob ran a dozen steps from the group, mindlessly trying to escape. He would get away! He would....

But then, horribly, one of the assailants, a pudgy, pasty-faced man wearing fancy cowboy clothes and a cowboy hat, smoothly drew a silver-plated, pearl-handled Colt .45 from an ornately tooled holster and shot Rob in the back. Rob fell heavily in the dirt, squirming and moaning in agony, still trying to crawl away.

"Finish him off, Blade," called one of the others, a huge man with bulging muscles and a commanding stance backlit by the headlights.

A lean whip of a man with dark skin quickly stepped forward, a slender knife glittering in his hand. He bent over Rob, grabbed his hair, jerked his head back, and with a quick twist of the blade, slit his throat. A fountain of blood, blackened by dust and moonlight, splashed onto the dirt as Rob thrashed and convulsed. The others looked on, sniggering. At last Rob lay still in the mud of his life. The only other sounds were Phyllis's gasping sobs as she watched her husband die.

Then the sobs turned to screams as her mammoth captor dragged her over to the Pontiac and pitched her inside. The rest of the gang got into the pickup and the Lincoln, except for the chain-looped motorcycle rider, who mounted the Harley. Together, the four vehicles roared off into the darkness, heading back to the highway, leaving the boy staring after them in bewildered shock.

As the taillights disappeared, Heath emerged from his hiding place, staggered over to the body of his father, and fell down beside it. He tried to call, "Daddy," but the word collapsed in his throat, blocked by sobbing grunts of pain and terror.

He didn't know how long he knelt there nor how long the boot was in his field of view before he actually saw it. Suddenly, though, he was aware of it, roughly worn and scuffed, topped by a threadbare khaki cuff. Startled, the boy looked up, renewed terror wiping away his tears.

Standing over him was the gaunt figure of an older man. The moonlight illuminated a weathered, grizzled, and gruff but not unkind face set in grim lines. Had the boy known the phrase, he would have called him a desert rat, but right now he knew only fear, shock, and empty pain.

The man stood over Heath and the corpse of the boy's father as he and the boy stared at each other, unmoving in the moonlight. Then the boy threw back his head and wailed his anguish into the night. He toppled forward, seizing the old man's leg with a grip of iron desperation. The old man bent over the boy and enfolded him in his embrace.

TWO

THE WAIL OF THE ELECTRIC guitar soared over the insistent drive of the drums and propulsion of the bass. With a smile tipping the corners of his mouth, Alex Brant let the ascending notes carry him up and up then release him in a long glide of feedback that warped the strain of music into another dimension. A moment later, in a chatter of staccato notes, the music twisted again, returning to this time, this place. The bass line reasserted itself, and the guitar fell in for the finale.

Alex's eighteen-wheeler reached a short upgrade. He downshifted with expert non-attention, arm muscles rippling beneath tan skin, then he turned up the volume on the stereo. He really liked the next piece.

While it played, he surveyed the countryside through the windows of the truck cab. Hot, dry, rugged. Not much else to be said for Arizona. He'd just left Globe, heading northeast on U.S. 60, which he'd picked up just east of Phoenix, en route from Los Angeles to Dallas.

Sure, it wasn't the fast way. I-10 or I-40 would have gotten him there quicker, but Manny hadn't said anything about speed for this cargo. Electronics didn't spoil if they weren't kept on ice, though considering the rapid rate of development in the electronics industry, this load might be obsolete by the time he arrived.

Hell, probably already was when he picked it up, if he knew Manny.

At this stage of Alex's life, speed wasn't as important as the scenery, and besides, the interstates were so congested they seemed little better than urban freeways creeping between cities and littered with idiot drivers going too slow or too fast. No, right now, freedom was all he needed, and he found it on the old U.S. routes. That was the main reason he put up with Manny and his bullshit and having to collect his fees in cold hard cash before he released a load to Max Electronics. As long as he got the load to the warehouse in a reasonable amount of time, Manny wouldn't complain, and that gave

Alex the chance to take the longer scenic routes—an opportunity he might not have if he hauled perishables or leased himself and his rig to a larger, more time-conscious company.

In fact, the only reason he'd taken I-10 as far as Phoenix this trip was to gain a little time so he could make that necessary stop in Lubbock, unpleasant as it might be.

He'd learned the trick of traveling the old U.S. routes through a curious set of circumstances. Following the debacle on the *Markham*, his career in the Marines was finished. Not that anyone had held him accountable—he'd just been one of the grunts. No one could have said they failed, either, since they did achieve their objective. But the collateral damage had been too great, and he and the other eight Marines who'd survived the assault were unpleasant reminders that the Corps didn't always do the best job, even at the top levels. They were given their token medals and each sent off to a dead-end assignment that spoke as eloquently as any court-martial.

Acutely aware of his status as scapegoat, Alex mustered out at the first opportunity, anxious to get on with life and put the nightmare of the *Markham* behind him. And the guilt. Scapegoat or not, a lot of innocent people had died. In fact, he knew he'd killed at least one himself. Watching the older woman go down, inadvertently pierced by his bullets, was seared into his cortex for life.

He'd spent his first couple of weeks as a civilian with his sister and her family in Houston, then, as soon as he found work, he moved into a tumbledown little garage apartment owned by a woman named Nora. Nora, somewhere in her late fifties, was a sculptor who actually managed to sell enough of her large, mystically abstract work to make a living, and she occasionally asked Alex to help her move pieces in his Nissan pickup.

More important, she saw him practicing his tai chi form in the backyard and learned that he'd been in the military. One day, she approached him and told him about a friend of hers named Simone, who had problems. Not money problems, exactly, though money was at the root of the difficulty. Simone's ex-husband, scion of a wealthy industrialist family, had left her when she was forty for a trophy wife twenty years younger. The divorce settlement included a batch of blue-chip stocks in addition to a hefty cash settlement— enough to let Simone live in modest style for the rest of her life.

Simone had resided for a time in Houston, where she met Nora and bought one of her sculptures, which she donated to the city. But Houston, unsurprisingly, wasn't cultural or mystical enough for Simone, and she'd moved out to the San Francisco Bay area. One thing led to another, and she wound up involved with a low-grade cult of Satanists who realized her blue chip stock dividends could keep them in food and drugs almost indefinitely.

They kept her drugged and locked up for nearly four years before they grew careless and she escaped. Stealing one of their cars, she hot-footed it to the home of her only living relative, where she thought she could find sanctuary.

Unfortunately, things weren't all that different there. The guy was her uncle, though in fact only a few years her senior. Uncle ran a Christmas tree farm just south of Portland, Oregon, and that wasn't so bad, but he was a Mormon. He did not comprehend a woman of Simone's temperament, and she couldn't take the subservience demanded of her. Nor could she stand watching while uncle and wife waited, hoping for her to die before they did so they could inherit her blue-chip stocks. Finally, she began to suspect that they weren't content to just wait.

She had to get out. Somewhere. Anywhere. But there was a problem.

Through years of abuse, neglect, and confinement, Simone had developed a strong case of agoraphobia. She couldn't stand to be in public places, and she couldn't tolerate public transportation. She found a place to go—a contemplative retreat run on an old farmstead by an American guru. This guru, self-styled as Brother Chester, was a leading American disciple of a powerful guru from India. The old Indian guru, it was claimed by some, used his power for dark purposes, but Simone had heard good things about Brother Chester. And she was desperate. She decided he was the one to help her reintegrate into society. Chester's farm, however, was in the hills of Virginia, and she was in Portland, with no friends aside from agoraphobia.

She managed to get in touch with Nora, who said she knew someone who could drive her from Portland to Virginia. Someone she could trust to protect her. And then Nora suggested it to Alex, saying it was just the thing for an ex-Marine with military assault training who was at loose ends. It would almost be like a paid vacation.

Out of one frying pan and into another, Alex had thought as he flew to Portland, though he wasn't sure if he meant Simone or himself. He rented a car, drove the two hours to the Christmas tree farm, and pulled up in front of the house. Simone, a matronly woman in her mid sixties, was waiting for him, but it seemed that uncle didn't want her to leave. He pulled a shotgun on Alex, and Alex had to take it away from him and throw it and the shells, separately, out into the weeds bordering the yard before he could drag Simone's two heavy suitcases to the car and take her away.

The cross-country drive had been pleasant enough, though nearly three solid days of corn fields through the north-central states had been pretty tedious. He and Simone had gotten along well, and he hoped that he was doing his own small part in helping her find a comfortable place in society.

But the days on the road with Simone had done him good in a couple of ways that had nothing to do with her. Psychologically, it had helped him get out of himself and his preoccupation with the events on the *Markham*. Even better, it pointed the way to his future. The long drive made him realize that he liked to drive long distances—something he'd never really done before. He liked the feeling of movement and the ever-changing panorama of nature that he passed through and the way that the scenery pulled out his grief and left it strung across the landscape behind him. And after the claustrophobic terror on the *Markham*, he had developed, it seemed, an almost bottomless predilection for freedom. By the time he'd delivered Simone to Brother Chester, he knew that he was going to give professional driving a shot. Sure, things had been tough in the beginning, and he sometimes had tight schedules. But now, five years later, he had his own rig and no boss staring over his shoulder tapping an impatient foot. He could afford to be somewhat choosy in the jobs he did take.

And almost as important as inadvertently pointing the way to his freedom, Simone had shown Alex the best way to enjoy it. Perhaps because she'd spent her youth before the great network of interstates had been built, and even more because of her agoraphobia, she'd insisted that they stay off the interstates as much as possible and keep to the old U.S. routes.

She's paying, he'd thought as they started out from the Christmas tree farm, but even before they checked into a motel for the night, he realized that the old routes had a lot of advantages. There wasn't as much traffic as on the interstates. And there weren't as many cops waiting to give tickets. Even better, you could still go sixty or seventy between the towns and make damn good time. Maybe not quite as good as on the interstates, but almost. And the countryside was a hell of a lot more interesting to look at away from the generic swaths the big highways cut across the landscape.

So now, here he was, chugging across Arizona on U.S. 60, enjoying relatively relaxed driving, taking in the sights of the countryside instead of staring down the seemingly endless double-wide ribbon of cement that was I-10, with its shuttling steel and glass bugs, alert to the momentary flicker of brake lights that said the drivers ahead had tapped off cruise control because traffic was once again slowing down for construction, a wreck, a cop, or just another bad driver.

God knew where Simone was now. About a year after he'd left her in the questionable care of Brother Chester, she escaped from him. Seemed that all Brother C wanted out of her was the dividends from her blue-chip stocks.

Surprise.

She'd called Alex from a motel in Maryland. Would he please come and drive her to Bar Harbor, Maine? He did, skirting New York City and taking U.S. 1 up the coast. He left her in a bungalow apartment in Bar Harbor and never heard from her again.

But even if she had tried to get in touch with him, it would have been difficult. During the year between their trips together, he'd gone to truck-driving school, and soon after delivering her to Bar Harbor, he put a down payment on his own rig and left the settled life behind. Though he maintained a post box and a rented room from his sister in Houston, the truck was his home, the road his backyard. And, for the time being, that was all right with him since he had no romantic attachments to keep him fixed. He traveled and got to see a lot of the country. He worked for himself, was well paid, and hoped to retire before either taxes or hemorrhoids did him in.

Best of all, five years of scrubbing by the countryside and the incessant wind blowing by his truck window had, if not purged the stain of his guilt, then at least made him feel clean once more.

The music finished, and Alex selected another album on the iPod—this time of softer music.

He was making good time, and it looked like he'd easily reach Springerville, just this side of the New Mexico state line, before dark. He'd never been this way before, but he'd heard that there was a truck stop there with showers and tolerable food. By tomorrow night, he'd be in Lubbock.

That thought darkened his brow, but he managed to suppress the emotion. Life was too good to dwell on the negative. He'd finally paid off his rig last month, so from here on out, he was in the black. Thanks to the contract with Max Electronics. It was a godsend and should be sufficient to keep him in the money for the next year or two. Or at least as long as Manny kept shy of the IRS. Plus, Alex was picking up some good money on the return runs to LA, too. Maybe he could even start saving for that house in the country he kept thinking about.

Or, he thought, as Dad would have said, that place in the sunshine. Too bad he never found it for himself.

And that brought him again to Lubbock. Always to Lubbock. Frowning, he shook his head. How to begin? What to say? It was a little late to be starting over, or even to let bygones be bygones. The bastard lost that chance years ago—gambled it away like every damn thing else. If he hasn't changed by now, it's never going to happen, Alex thought. Not in this lifetime.

He gave a snort, thinking how lame it sounded when, for years, all he really wanted to say to the old bastard was, I don't forgive, I won't forget, and kiss my ass when the reaper hauls your measly carcass to the deepest circle of that hell reserved for bastards who tear and trample their children's dreams.

The time was past for that, though. Their relationship had gone astray for too many years, and now, all that was left was for Alex to finish it right. He shrugged with a wry smile. And how else to do that but jump right in? It's not like there was any other way. The *Markham* had taught him that—and more. He'd seen too much death on that ship not to know how final it is. Maybe his dad didn't deserve any kind of acknowledgement, but Alex knew he'd kick himself for the rest of his life if he didn't grab this last chance to say goodbye.

But for the moment, he was saved from further thought on the matter when, through the windshield, he saw a sign that warned of a truck weigh and inspection station just ahead. The old fashioned, manually-operated sign was flipped to the "open" position.

"Shit," he muttered, glancing at the clock on the dash. It read 4:18 p.m. He certainly didn't want to lose time at a weigh station—it was still another hour to Springerville. But he shrugged off his impatience. Inspections went with the job.

Turning the wheel, he exited the highway.

"Good," he muttered as he pulled onto the scale, seeing that no other trucks were in front of him.

Alex got down from the cab and handed his manifest to the state trooper on duty, a big man gone thick with inactivity. His name tag identified him as Hobbs. While the scales registered the load, the trooper examined the paperwork.

"Making pretty good time?" Hobbs asked, eyeing Alex sideways. Alex shrugged.

"Pretty good."

"You left LA this morning. 'Bout reached your legal limit. I trust you'll be stopping soon."

"Yeah. At the Pleasant Haven in Springerville."

"Nice place," the trooper commented absently as he looked over the manifest. "So you're carrying electronic gear?"

"That's right," Alex acknowledged. "A few computers and video games. Stereo equipment, mostly."

The trooper leaned over to look at the weight reading on the scales. He looked at the manifest again, then peering at Alex over the manifest, he shook his head.

"Looks like you're a mite over, son."

Alex was surprised.

"That's impossible...."

He reached for the manifest to check out the recorded weight, when he noticed that the trooper was standing on the scale. Alex dropped his hand and looked the trooper in the eye. The trooper grinned back with the nonchalance of a man who is in a position to abuse power and knows it.

"Yep," the trooper went on. "Just about two-sixty over. Looks like it might just be about the weight of one of them video games you got. Maybe you got a couple extra stashed in there. Why don't we just take one out and see if that's the problem?"

Alex stared at the trooper for a moment and flexed his hands, trying to decide what to do. The trooper's eyes grew hard, and he dropped a hand to the butt of the pistol strapped to his thick gut.

"Now, son."

Alex shrugged and turned. Why get into something unnecessary? Max Electronics would just have to consider the loss a sort of extra road tariff. He went to the back of the trailer and opened the large doors. The trooper half relaxed, smiled unctuously, and followed a few steps behind, keeping his hand close to his pistol. Alex climbed into the truck and, in a moment, found a box containing a video game system. He jumped down and dropped the box at the trooper's feet, listening carefully as the box hit the pavement, hoping to hear even a faint hint of something breaking. But the trooper's voice interrupted his concentration.

"And a VCR, too. Won't nobody miss it."

Alex complied.

Hobbs, oily smile in place, nodded and initialed the manifest. Alex closed the truck doors and took the manifest as the trooper handed it to him.

"Take it easy with that load, son," the trooper advised. The phony smile remained unbroken.

Alex stared back without humor, then he walked with deliberate steps to the truck cab and climbed up into it.

"Asshole," he muttered as he put the truck in gear. He accelerated and pulled back onto the highway.

Behind him, the trooper went to his car, carrying the video game and VCR. He opened the trunk and dumped the boxes inside. The smile vanished as he reached into the trunk, switched on the short-wave radio there, and made a call.

"This is Hobbs," he said into the mike. "T-Bone there? I got something he'll be interested in."

"Just a minute," a crackly voice came back.

While he waited, the trooper stared with hard eyes after Alex's departing truck.

THREE

ALEX'S KNUCKLES LOOKED BLEACHED AGAINST the black of the steering wheel as he pulled out of the weigh station. He watched in his side view mirror while the diminishing figure of the trooper carried his pilfered pittance of Alex's former cargo toward the back of the patrol car. Then Alex was on the highway, accelerating away.

Gradually, the tightness went out of his fingers and his gut. He loosened his grip on the steering wheel and realized with a rueful smile that he'd been gritting his teeth so hard his jaw hurt. Thoughts about the trooper's neck in his hands flashed through his mind, but he sighed and shook his head.

Fantasy, he thought. Let's keep it strictly realistic. There was nothing else you could have done. After all, the guy had the law on his side.

That elicited a mordant chuckle, but even though the flush of anger was already draining out of his limbs, he couldn't easily calm the roiling stream of his consciousness. He ruminated on what he could have done, given the situation. True, he'd had no choice about stopping at the weigh station, even had he known what would transpire. And how could he know that? He'd stopped at such stations thousands of times, and this was the first time that anything like this had happened.

So now that the damage was done, what could he do? Report the fucker? Sure. It was his word—the word of a transient trucker—against that of a law enforcement official. If push came to shove, he'd just be accused of slipping the stuff into the sleeping berth of his cab to pad his own pocket. Like as not, *he'd* be the one looked on with accusation, not the trooper, and it might have adverse repercussions down the road.

Not that he was worried about his reputation with Manny. He'd known the owner of Max Electronics a long time and had made plenty of runs for him. Besides, Manny understood legal shenanigans and would believe the story about the trooper when the cargo came up missing a couple of boxes. But the irritating thing was that Manny wouldn't really care as long as the cargo was 99.9 percent intact. He'd just jack up the prices a few cents more per item on everything else in the shipment, and that would be that. The customers would pay the deficit. Corruption was just part of the cost of doing business.

It looked like that asshole trooper would go scot-free. Alex shook his head again, just as pissed as before, but now a sadness was worming its way into his consciousness, upsetting his self-righteousness. It was sadness for himself and for all the trooper's victims, for surely there'd been others. Sadness for all the world of victims who'd found it necessary for one reason or another to bite the bullet and go on, remembering the moments they were victimized but unwilling, or unable, to exact retribution.

And that brought memories of the *Markham*'s passengers—those who'd lived to have the terror become a part of their lives.

Shit! He pounded the wheel with the heel of his hand. He couldn't afford to think like that. It dredged up too much of the past, too much he thought already finished. Yeah, it was a crappy world. What could he do? He'd already tried and failed. The greedy always turned plenty into want. And the pity was that victimizers almost always chose victims as bad or worse off than themselves—those whose only crime was a desire to make their own way. Shit! Not just greedy bastards but lazy as well. And weak for using their power to prey on the powerless.

He fought the churn in his mind, trying to still his indignation and anger. Thinking music might help blanket his feelings, he switched on the iPod, but the first album—some driving hard rock—only accentuated the violent surge of thoughts, and the second—something softer and more melodic—just tinged the strain of reflection with bitterness. At last, he shut off the iPod and settled for the muted, steady roar of the diesel and the hiss of the pavement beneath his tires.

By the time he saw the sign proclaiming that the Pleasant Haven Truck Stop was just ahead, he'd managed to wipe away most of his pensiveness and was returning to his normal state of contemplation, trusting things to turn out as they damn well pleased, whether or not he put in his two bits. He knew he would have to crap out and let this incident die into the shadowy discomfort of a half-submerged resentment that would, in its own turn, sink into the undercurrents of his subconscious.

In any case, the growling in his belly and the needle nearing the E on the fuel gauge informed him that this was, indeed, a pleasant haven and certainly the place to stop.

He decelerated, downshifted, turned the wheel, and pulled into an empty lane in the fuel plaza. As he swung open the cab door, the mixed odors of sour diesel and truck stop food assailed his nostrils. Wincing and salivating at the same time, he dropped to the ground and stretched the residue of anger out of his cramped muscles.

"Time for a workout," he muttered to himself as he surveyed the Pleasant Haven and its surrounds.

The restaurant squatted adjacent to the fuel plaza, a low brown brick building as nondescript as any roadside restaurant hunkering beside any back highway in the U.S. The wide windows plating two sides of its rectangular shape were shaded from within by faded orange Venetian blinds to keep the lowering afternoon sun off the diners.

Behind both the restaurant and the fuel plaza sprawled a two-acre truck park. Eight or so trucks already were situated on the expanse of lumpy, stained asphalt, along with a couple of RVs and one pick-up pulling a camper trailer. Beyond the asphalt rose a low hill whose raw face was mute testimony that half the asphalt flatness had once belonged to it. Mouths of gullies sprawling red deltas across the edges of the pavement proclaimed that the hill was trying to take back its own, inch by inch. Past the hill were others, just as ragged and strewn with scrub. The Pleasant Haven was on the outskirts of Springerville, and those hills masked the outlying homes of the town.

Dry, hot, dusty, he thought. Just like I like it.

With that in mind, he headed toward the office door. When he finished fueling a few minutes later, he moved his truck to the truck yard and found a spot next to a cross-country cab pulling a refrigerated trailer. He climbed into his sleeping berth and, without further ado, swiftly changed into loose pants and tennis shoes.

Muscles tingling with anticipation, he headed toward the hill behind the truck yard, thinking of the anger, sorrow, and frustration of the last couple of hours. Work it out, he told himself. Take the bad and make it something good.

At the top of the hill, he found a relatively flat, clear spot the size of a living room floor. One by one, he rolled all his joints, one way then the other, and stretched, loosening up. Then, after standing still for a few moments and sinking inside himself, he began to move. Slowly.

At first, it seemed as if he was waving or trying to catch something—an insect perhaps—out of the air. But his slow movements didn't stop with that leisurely grab. Leaving his right hand in space as if he'd caught what he was reaching for between his fingertips, he pivoted his body to the left, bringing his left hand in a gradual sweep, face high, across the front of his body. The hand ended almost fully extended to his front left, but then, without discernible pause, it moved again. Indeed, Alex's entire body moved in unison as he brought his limbs and torso in slow speed to another posture, which, in turn melted into yet another.

All tension was forgotten as he wove through the tai chi chuan form. Smooth and sure and slow with a pace of effort and deliberateness rather than laziness, he waved and swayed as if in an unknown wind. But a wind with purpose. Here was a punch and there a block and now a kick. These were followed by a movement so convoluted that it blended multiple purposes.

Alex had learned a number of martial skills in high school and later in assault training school, most based on strength and speed. But then his instructor, Captain George Selter, had taken him aside.

"You're good, Brant," Selter told him. "But you could be better."

"I thought I was doing pretty good," Alex said, trying not to bristle at the implied insult. It wouldn't do any good, anyway. Selter was way out of Alex's league.

"Don't get your hackles up," Selter soothed. "We both know you can take just about anybody in the battalion. I can help you take just about anybody in the regiment."

He had Alex's attention—if anyone could take anybody in the army, it was Selter.

And that was Alex's first real introduction to tai chi. He'd heard about it in the past, of course, and seen old folks and New Agers floating through the movements. Like many karate enthusiasts, he'd disparaged the art's probable effectiveness because the movements were so slow and without visible effort or strength. But his condescension quickly gave way to interest when he learned that it was the basis of Selter's personal practice. And then Selter showed him how those seemingly soft and gentle movements could snap bone, bounce an opponent across the room, and do crushing internal damage.

So Alex had learned what Selter could teach him in the short but rigorous two years they spent together. He still practiced a few of the more vigorous katas he'd learned in the past for their aerobic effect, and he topped off his workout with thirty minutes of stretching and strength and conditioning exercises.

At last he was done. Sweating and tired but feeling relaxed and stable once more, he stood for a few quiet minutes, taking in the stillness. The sun was still a couple of hand widths above the ridge line, and he breathed deeply of the heated air. The desert might be hot, he thought, but he loved the uncluttered atmosphere, devoid of the weight of humidity and the cloying scent of vegetable rot and other less-specific odors that humidity inevitably carried.

But humidity could be a good thing too, he grinned, getting a whiff of himself. Thinking of a good, hot shower, he descended the hill to his truck.

As he approached the door to the showers a few minutes later, his kit bag slung over his shoulder, a movement attracted his attention. Off to the side of the building stood the large brown metal bin of a dumpster. What caught his eye was the tow-headed kid squatting atop the metal box next to the opening revealed by the thrown-back lid. The kid was twelve or so and looked pretty disheveled and dirty. Then Alex saw a thin arm reach out of the dumpster toward the kid. Alex started, flashing that some sort of creature was going to haul this ragged child into a minor pit of hell.

But no, the arm gave the kid something that the kid stuffed into a brown pack looped over one shoulder. Alex relaxed and watched, not without fascination, as the arm retracted then reemerged again with another item for the pack. It disappeared again and came back, this time followed by the gaunt, grizzled figure of a man who appeared to be in his mid sixties. The old man put something into the pack then dived once more into the dumpster.

Alex shook his head, not so much with pity for the bum and the lost child as with a resurgence of all the thoughts that had plagued him since his encounter with the corrupt trooper at the weigh station. The old man and boy were like the capper to his reflections, and it wasn't a pretty sight—as if all the world was lost, not just those two. In fact, the old man and kid didn't even count; they were just society's detritus, as cast aside as the trash they were foraging from the dumpster.

Alex stared at the pair for a moment longer before realizing his fists were tightly balled.

How quickly we revert, he thought ruefully as he loosened his fingers with conscious effort. And life goes on. He turned from the old man and boy and entered the showers.

Alex wasn't the only one who'd noticed the desert rat and Heath. A ratty brown conversion van had pulled up at the gas pumps, and while one of the four scruffy young men inside jumped out to gas up, his boss, riding shotgun, spotted the pair. A sadistic gleam in his eyes, he elbowed the driver and gestured toward them.

After the desert rat came up from his last dive, he clambered out of the dumpster, hopped spryly to the ground, caught the pack as Heath tossed it down to him, then helped the kid to the pavement. The two of them went around the corner to the side of the office, where a blank wall would let them examine their scavenged booty in peace.

Right away, the desert rat pulled a pair of sunglasses from his pocket, handed them to Heath, and motioned for the boy to put them on. The boy did and gave a big grin.

"Those look real good, kid," the old man said approvingly. "They'll protect your eyes. When you're old like me, you won't have all these crow's feet around your eyes."

He made a humorous, squinty face, and Heath laughed. That did the old man a world of good. It was about the first human reaction he'd gotten from the boy since taking him under his wing the week before.

"Sumpin' funny?" asked a harsh voice.

The desert rat and the kid turned to see the four toughs from the van coming around the corner. In seconds, they surrounded the old man and boy, shoving and harassing them.

The old man tried to put up a fight, and though he was wiry and strong in a way that belied his years, he was only one against four. Then one of the thugs pulled a knife, grabbed the old man from behind, and held the blade to his throat. One of the others snatched the pack from his hand and began rifling through it while his boss amused himself by bullying Heath. He pulled a knife of his own and gestured with it to Heath's pants.

"Take 'em off., kid. Let's see what kind of equipment you got."

The one holding the knife to the desert rat's throat said, "Bet it ain't even enough to bother cuttin' off."

"Leave him alone," the old man said, and the thug holding him pricked his neck just enough to draw a trickle of blood.

"Shut up, old man."

"I'll bet your ole thing ain't even worth cuttin' off, either," the leader sneered at the desert rat, and this brought a laugh from his companions.

Suddenly, Heath wriggled out of the leader's grip and tried to get away. But the leader easily knocked the boy down then grabbed him again. As he was dragged upright, Heath cried out a single syllable of anger and fear.

Alex was brushing his wet hair inside the shower room when the boy's cry echoed through the tiny vent window set high in the wall. Thinking that something had happened to the old man or boy, he hurried out of the shower room and around the corner.

"Beat it, fuckface," the leader said as Alex came into view.

Alex stopped, but he didn't beat it. Silently he stared with deceptive nonchalance at the leader.

Anger clouded the leader's face, and he shoved the kid into the arms of one of his cronies and came at Alex, knife up.

"You know how many people I killed, you stupid fuck?" the punk leader snarled.

"You haven't killed me," Alex said.

"Fuck 'im up, Jerry," said the one holding the boy.

"Won't be enough left to fuck," Jerry said, then he lunged at Alex.

Alex sidestepped and almost casually raised his hand, and Jerry stumbled away, clutching at the side of his jaw.

"Git 'im, Jerry!" yelled the third thug as he rose from the pavement where he'd been going through the desert rat's pack.

Jerry did his best to stab Alex, but this time, Alex took away the knife and knocked him to the ground. The one with the pack leapt forward and met a similar fate. The one holding Heath let the boy go and stepped in more cautiously, giving Jerry and the other fallen thug time to recover and join him. For several moments, Alex was the whirling center of a brawl that seemed to leave him untouched but inflicted considerable punishment on his antagonists. Then suddenly Jerry drew a pistol, but as he raised it to fire, Alex disarmed him. Tossing the gun to the ground, Alex delivered a blow that left Jerry stretched out on the ground, unconscious.

Alex turned to the punk who was still holding his knife to the desert rat's throat.

"Don't come no closer, or I'll do him. I swear."

Alex took a step, and the punk drew another trickle of blood from the desert rat.

"I'll do him!"

Suddenly, there was a loud thunk as a rock the size of a grape-fruit slammed into the side of the punk's head. With a groan, he collapsed, dropping the knife.

Alex and the desert rat looked to the side, where Heath was proudly dusting his hands.

"Good work, kid," said the desert rat, putting a hand to his throat. Alex stepped toward him.

"You okay?"

The old man merely grunted.

"Glad to hear it," Alex said.

The desert rat picked up one of the knives, went over to the thugs' van, and punctured all four tires and the spare bolted to the rear doors. Then he broke the blade and tossed the knife aside, disposed likewise with the other knife, and picked up Jerry's pistol and pocketed it.

"You sure you want that?" asked Alex.

"It's better than letting him keep it." The old man gestured toward Jerry, who was twitching as consciousness crept back into his dull brain.

"You have a point," Alex conceded.

The old man began gathering the scattered contents of his pack, and he gave a sidelong glance at Alex. "I saw you up on the hill earlier," he said. "Looks like you were practicing patience."

"Yeah," Alex smiled. "I guess that's what it is."

"Didn't work so good," the old man said, glancing around at the fallen thugs. "Seems like you're still a might testy."

"I'll just have to practice some more," Alex replied, chuckling good-naturedly. He went over to the boy, dug out his wallet, and handed him two $50 bills.

"Here, kid. Buy your grandpa a decent meal."

He glanced at the desert rat again, and the old man wrinkled his nose with distaste.

"Sure, kid," he said sarcastically. "Come on, let's go find us a health food store."

Alex chuckled again, and the desert rat smiled back sourly. Alex winked at the boy, then left them and returned to gather his things from the shower room. When he came out again, the old man and boy were nowhere to be seen, though the punks were beginning to stir. Ignoring them, Alex walked to his truck.

40

FOUR

AS THE DESERT RAT AND Heath moved away from the Pleasant Haven Truck Stop, the old man looked down at the boy striding beside him, and the boy stared up from behind his sunglasses and smiled. The old man returned the smile, gratified. Now if the boy would only talk. Not that the desert rat could blame the kid for not saying anything. What he'd experienced was enough to curdle any man's tongue. Yes, the smile was nice and spoke more eloquently than words.

The encounter back at the truck stop seemed to have done the boy good. It taught him that while the world may be full of low-life scum, there were good people, too, who'd look out for you even if they were strangers. And he was proud of the way the kid had hefted that rock and taken a hand in his own salvation. Life wasn't always about loss, and even if the odds seemed stacked against you, sometimes you won.

Sure, he thought. One step forward for every three back. Then he shook his head. Forget it. There's more important things to think about now.

He lifted his face to the rising night breeze as if scenting unseen currents. Yes, there's work to be done. The boy had learned one valuable lesson today, and now there were other things to teach him before the night was over.

"Come on, kid." The old man poked his young companion. "Smells like Springerville's ripe for the pickin'."

Half an hour of walking brought them to the outskirts of a residential neighborhood of older, sun-baked, and weathered frame and brick ranch-style homes. The sun was just minutes from union with the hot horizon when the desert rat pulled the kid into a patch of scrub brush, weeds, and mesquite growing in a ditch at the side of the road.

The boy squinted at him through the sunglasses and smiled.

"You're like the sun, you shine so brightly," the old man said, smiling back. "But night's coming on, so don't think you have to wear those sunglasses every minute."

The boy showed some more tooth and levered the shades back up onto his head.

He sure does look miserable, the old man thought, surveying his young companion with compassionate and knowing eyes. He's not complaining, but a growing young animal needs a good meal—food for the belly and food for thought as well. Time for another lesson in acquiring power for the powerless.

The boy looked at the old man, eyes trusting.

"You're hungry." It wasn't a question.

The kid nodded numbly, and the desert rat smiled gently.

"You want something to eat?"

The kid nodded again, more vigorously.

"But we don't have anything." The old man shrugged, as if helpless.

The kid made a gesture for the old man to look, and he pulled out the two fifties the trucker had given him. The desert rat stared at the boy, consciously willing himself to remain steady and not flinch, weeping, from the expression of shy selflessness in the boy's eyes. After what the kid had been through, the old man wouldn't have been surprised to see cunning and covetousness there instead of open generosity.

Why were people so complex? he wondered for another un-countable time. It shocked the old man's sensibilities to be con-fronted with such powerful proof as this boy that his own view of practical reality was unbalanced. Life would be so much simpler if everyone could be neatly categorized, their words and actions and attitudes compartmented off in easy structures.

But life, damn it, never seemed to stand still. It couldn't afford to. If the lizard ever stopped moving, the ever-moving desert sands would bury it in the drowning clutch of dry humor. If....

He felt a tug at his sleeve, pulling him from his reverie. The kid's shining eyes were boring into the desert rat, his fingers trying to press the bills into the old man's hand. The desert rat pulled his hand away, slowly and gently so he wouldn't startle the kid, though he could barely keep himself from jerking back to keep from sully-ing the boy with his age and personal demons. The boy's innocent bounty was almost too much for him.

"You're sure generous, kid, but naw." The old man shook his head. "He gave it to you. That was real nice of him. You keep it. You might want it for something later. Besides, sometimes you gotta survive by your wits. Suppose we didn't have it. What then?"

The kid looked sad and rubbed his belly.

"Stay hungry, is that it?

The boy nodded, and the desert rat laughed. Then, seeing a hurt expression cross the boy's face, he quickly stifled another outburst. He patted the boy on the shoulder.

"I'm not laughing at you," he said. "I'm laughing at the situation, and you'll be laughing, too, before long. Put that away," he gestured to the money. "I'll show you how to get something to eat without spending anything but a little time and effort."

Heath brightened, curiosity obvious in his eyes, and he stuffed the bills into his jeans.

"You gotta work for it," the desert rat cautioned.

The curiosity was still there, and the old man suddenly felt very good. It was fun showing this apt young pupil a few tricks of survival. That the boy was needy only added rightness to the enjoyment. He dug in his pack and pulled out a large tin can he'd found in the dumpster at the Pleasant Haven. The label proclaimed it once held peaches, but only a crusted brown residue lined it now.

"Look." He pointed to the picture of peaches on the label. "Sure look good, don't they?"

The boy nodded, a bit sadly, the desert rat thought.

"I'm gonna show you some magic," the old man said. "I'm gonna show you how to turn this empty peach can into a real peach cobbler. You wanna see that?"

The boy nodded again, but he didn't look convinced.

"Here." The desert rat handed the can to the boy and said in conspiratorial tones, "Now, listen to me. You take this can and kick it all the way to the other end of that street." He pointed to the residential street that led away from where they were concealed.

The kid took the can and looked up to the far end of the street, three quarters of a mile or so away, puzzled. He looked back at the old man.

"What's the matter? Got no faith? Go on. Kick it. Take your time and don't be shy. Make noise. Lots of noise." He grinned with what he hoped was bright invitation.

The kid tentatively returned the grin, nodded his head, and slithered out of the brush. In a moment, he was on the road, and after looking uncertainly left and right, he threw the can to the pavement. It's noisy rattle seemed to spur him on. He swung his foot and kicked almost too carefully at the can. With a bang and a clatter, it skittered ten feet across the asphalt.

The desert rat watched, a hard knot of humor tinged sorrow forming in his chest. From the way the kid swung that kick, it looked like he'd spent some time playing soccer. The desert rat thought of the ragged bundle of blood, meat, and bone that he and the boy had buried in the desert, and he thought of the man, alive, kicking around a ball with his son in the backyard of some nice suburban home. Too bad the kid's old man wasn't here to see how far his son had gone—sports hero to street trash in one easy lesson.

With effort, the old man swallowed the dregs of anguish and let the cream of humor rise to the surface of his mind. Things are going to be tough enough, he reminded himself, without letting useless bathos clutter the picture.

Out on the street, the kid approached the can again, swung his foot, and sent the can on it clangorous way. This time, the desert rat let a chuckle escape from his lips. He watched for a moment longer as the boy walked down the street, getting into the fun of noisily kicking the can along. Then he crouched and sniffed the air like a hound on the scent. A second later, he darted around the other side of the brush and was gone.

The boy progressed down the street. As he passed the first house, he began whistling loudly the only tune he could remember—the Popeye cartoon theme music. The can reminded him of Popeye's spinach can, and he kicked it, falling into a rhythm that was easily punctuated, he found, if he zigzagged back and forth down the street, banging the can against opposite curbs every second or third kick. Suddenly, a loud barking startled him, and he jerked his head around, looking. But when he spotted the dog, he relaxed, seeing it was safely trapped behind a hurricane fence at the rear of the first house. Smiling, he whistled louder and kicked the can again, not harder but clumsily so it would clatter all the more. The dog swallowed the bait, its yapping rambunctious and strident.

Inside the house, Louella Babtree was just taking a roast from the oven and placing it on top of the stove when suddenly Tim began barking.

"What's that fool mutt barking about, now?" she wondered aloud.

Wiping her hands on her apron, she left the kitchen to investigate. From behind the front screen door, she watched the raggedy, dirty boy pass by her house, whistling and kicking, apparently with vicious delight, a big tin can. She shook her head, both at the noise and at his obviously unkempt appearance, and she pursed her lips and shook her head indignantly.

"That boy's parents ought to be shot," she muttered, folding her arms above her thick middle.

Then the boy was past, though Tim kept on barking like he was right up in the yard. Louella shook her head again as the clattering of the can diminished. Then she returned to the kitchen. She still had to whip up that rich meat gravy her husband, Jim, liked to spoon over his biscuits. It took her several blinking moments to realize that her roast had vanished from the stove as if it had never been, though the greasy pan proved that she had not dreamt its cooking.

At the third house down the street from the Babtrees', a pair of hands reached up and took a cooling pie from a window sill, and at another, some boy's clothes were snatched from a clothesline. All the while in the background was the howling and barking of dogs overlaid with a whistle and the reverberation of the old peach can clattering across the pavement.

At last, Heath reached the end of the street. He gave the can one last hearty kick that sent it skittering off into a culvert. As its final clank vanished on the early evening breeze, a hissing sound whispered in his ear. He looked around and saw nothing but heard the hissing again. It came from a clump of nearby brush and mesquite. He scurried into it, and there, waiting for him, was the desert rat. The old man's pack was bulging suspiciously, and a delicious medley of aromas assaulted the boy's nose. He stared at the pack, his mouth watering.

"Pretty good magic, even if it ain't peach cobbler, eh?" the desert rat grinned at him. The boy looked up, the hunger in his eyes reflecting the emptiness in his belly. The old man grinned wider and poked the kid in the ribs with his finger.

"Come on, boy, I hear the dinner bell ringing. But we'll have to wait until we get away from here, or we'll have a posse of hungry townsfolk breathing down our necks."

Off they went into the deepening dusk.

FIVE

ALEX DUMPED HIS THINGS INTO his truck, locked it up, then headed over to the restaurant to eat. He was feeling good. The workout had burned the tautness out of his muscles, the shower had washed its residue down the drain, and helping out the old man and kid had assuaged the helpless anger of the afternoon. Maybe he couldn't save the world, but occasionally good deeds were possible that made someone's life a little better.

Inside the restaurant, he found a booth, and a minute later, a bleach-blond waitress with ample thighs and buttocks left him with a glass of water, spotted silverware tightly wrapped in a paper napkin, and a dog-eared laminated menu. He stared at the bright color pictures of the restaurant's offerings gracing the front of the menu, doubting that the actual contents of the plate would live up to the photos. He shrugged. So what was new?

A couple of minutes brought the waitress back, and Alex ordered. After she left, ripping his ticket off her pad, Alex pulled out the paperback he'd been reading and opened it, but he'd barely gone past a page when his cell phone beeped. He pulled it out of his left inside jacket pocket, thumbed the talk button, and lifted the phone to his ear.

"It's Beth," his sister's voice said to his hello. She sounded strained.

"Dad?"

"He collapsed about an hour ago. They've got him in intensive care. He...." Her voice caught, and there was a pause while she regained control. "They say he might not last past tomorrow."

"He's got to," Alex said, the intensity of the emotion in his own voice surprising him. "Tell him I won't lay over tonight. I'll drive straight through. Soon as I get a bite to eat."

"I'll tell him," she said. "But hurry."

They said goodbye, and Alex took a moment to get hold of himself, then he quick-dialed another number. There came the distant click of connection.

"Max Electronics."

"Manny, it's Alex."

"Hey, boy, how's it swinging? You in town yet?"

Alex rolled his eyes, smiled faintly, then shook his head.

"What do you mean am I in town yet? I'm only in Arizona. Just west of New Mexico."

"Oh, shit. I was expectin' you in Dallas tonight."

"Tonight! Who the hell told you that? I just picked up this load in LA this morning."

"Listen, Alex," Manny said in a worried voice. "You gotta get that truck here ASAP. We gotta big warehouse sale this weekend, and I can unload everything you got, but it's gotta be here."

"And I bet you'll make a big fat profit on it, too. That right, Manny?"

"Well…."

Alex shook his head. He knew better than to believe anything Manny told him when he heard that hedging tone in the guy's voice.

"Look," Alex said firmly. "Nobody said anything about a straight-through run when I picked up this load. Besides, I have personal business to take care of in Lubbock."

"Can't it wait a day or two," Manny whined. "You can go through Lubbock on your way back. Look, I'll up your ante 20 percent."

"Not this time, Manny. I just talked to my sister. It's my dad. He's got terminal cancer. He's only got a day or two at the most."

"I thought you told me you two had a falling out," Manny said, for once the weasel dropping from his voice.

"That was a long time ago. I need to see him while I still have the chance."

"Okay, okay," Manny soothed. "I'm not heartless."

Alex smiled to himself.

"Fuck the sale. We got a bunch of crap left over from the last one, anyway. We'll use that. Go see your dad. Take as much time as you need." "Thanks, Manny," Alex said. "I just need a couple of extra days. I'll see you before the weekend."

Alex hung up, slid the phone back into its pocket, and sighed. He'd driven all day, and now he'd have to drive all night, too. He wasn't troubled by the strain—he'd made worse runs. But it offended Alex's sense of the rightness of things to be late—late to a meeting or movie, late to an appointment or date, late in bringing in a load. And now he might be late to his father's last moments. It reminded him too much of the ill-conceived order that had resulted in the *Markham* fiasco, and it made him feel trapped. That was a feeling he didn't like.

And he'd have to watch it for cops if he was going to drive overtime. Now he wished he'd taken the interstate all the way from LA. If he had, he'd nearly be in Texas by now instead of a huge state away. But he couldn't have known his father would collapse so suddenly. And hell, at least he'd gotten in a good workout and kicked some assholes silly. Something good had come of it.

The waitress brought his food, and he ate quickly but not hurriedly. The night was going to be long enough without heartburn hitching a ride. When he was finished, he went to his truck, skirting around a beat-up old pickup with multicolored fenders and a heavy iron grill welded to the front that had parked nearby.

The desert was cooling rapidly as it usually did at night, and Alex was glad for the jacket as he grabbed his thermos to take it to the restaurant to have it filled. Returning to his truck, he got in and laid the thermos on the shotgun seat.

He sat for a few moments in the dark cab before he switched on the interior lights and pulled out a map. He was pretty far from either I-10 to the south or I-40 to the north, and driving to either of them would take two or three hours and put him hundreds of miles out of the way. If he stayed on 60 to Socorro, he could jog down to U.S. 380, which would take him just south of Lubbock. Then he could head southeast on 84 to I-20 near Abilene, and that would take him the rest of the way.

It was his original route and, from here, still the most direct. But if the route was the one he'd have taken anyway, there was a difference—he'd be driving across scenic New Mexico at night, and dawn would find him on the drab high plains of Texas. About the only scenery he'd be seeing until then would be the headlighted stripe down the middle of a dark road. Wrinkling his nose and sighing, he threw the truck into gear and pulled out of the Pleasant Haven.

An hour and a half of driving saw Alex crossing the Continental Divide near a small bump in the road with the unlikely name of Pie Town. For the next forty minutes, the terrain sloped generally downward, and the traffic was light, so he took the opportunity to pull out the cell phone and give his sister a call.

"Beth? It's me. How's he doing?"

"He's still here," she said, sounding washed out. "But it won't be long. I told him you're coming, and I think he's just stubborn enough to hang on until you get here."

"Stubborn is something he's had a lot of practice at."

"I hear the apple doesn't fall far from the tree," she said gently.

"Yeah," he laughed. "I suppose you're right. You tell him to hang in there. I'll be there by morning."

A sudden flash in his side view mirror attracted his attention.

"Hold on." He lowered the phone and peered at the mirror.

A car was coming up behind him, flashing its brights. He'd first spotted the headlights a couple of miles back, and since then, the vehicle had made good time, closing the gap in just a few minutes. Must be going eighty or ninety, Alex thought.

The car jerked into the left lane and started to pass, lights still flashing.

"Listen Beth, I gotta go. I'll see you in a few hours."

He hung up, dropped the phone back into the inside jacket pocket, and kept a steady foot on the fuel pedal, holding his speed at sixty-five. As the car came up on his cab, he threw it a glance. It was a Lincoln Town Car, some sort of neutral color whose exact nature was masked by the night—it could have been powder blue, gray, or even silver. Though it was a new model, large patches of sanded bondo marred its fenders and doors.

A few more feet, and the Lincoln was abreast of Alex's cab. Then, unexpectedly, it slowed to keep pace with the truck. Alex shot it another look. The passenger window slid down, and a slender, good looking young woman in her mid twenties leaned out. Shoulder-length brown hair whipped in the wind. She was dressed in some sort of formal evening gown and wore a worried expression. Jabbing her finger urgently toward the back of the semi, she shouted something, but her words were torn away by the slipstream.

Puzzled, Alex looked in his side view mirror. He didn't see anything unusual, but the woman continued to wave and point. Then the Lincoln accelerated, and the woman slipped back inside. The sedan passed on and sped off into the night, its taillights becoming a distant glow that vanished around some unknown curve in the darkness ahead.

Alex was a little concerned since, in his haste to leave the Pleasant Haven, he hadn't checked out his rig as thoroughly as usual. He didn't know what might be wrong, but it could be anything. Though nothing seemed amiss in the side view mirrors, nor was the truck handling any differently than normal, the woman's warning was unmistakable. Something was wrong.

He began scouting the road ahead for a place to pull off. Luckily, just a few moments later, there appeared a blue road sign proclaiming the presence of a rest stop one mile ahead.

Handy, he thought with a grin, some of the tension in him easing off. He geared the truck down and let it crawl into the dirt and gravel dent in the roadside that masqueraded as a rest stop. A dingy cement picnic table and filthy cement box that had once been a grill but now was just a useless eyesore filled with garbage squatted beside the pull-off. Nearby, a green barrel overflowed trash and stench in equal proportions. A line of small cottonwood trees flanked the rest stop, and apparently, the highway department hadn't mowed the tall weeds between them and the road for about as long as the trees had been there.

Alex reached behind the seat and pulled out a crowbar and a powerful flashlight, then he opened the door and hopped to the ground. Walking along the trailer, he pounded the tires with the crowbar and flashed the light on the treads and up into the undercarriage. He reached the back of the rig without finding anything wrong, and he looked over the rear trailer doors, the taillights, the tires. Still nothing.

Mystified, he shook his head and started up the right side of the trailer, pounding the tires and checking the undercarriage. About half way, he paused to check the moorings for his spare tire. They bound it tightly in place, and he straightened then recoiled a step as his flashlight beam raked across a stark, lean black man.

The way the man appeared silently out of the darkness, the nasty grin on his face, and his menacing, cocky stance made Alex thankful for the reassuring drag of the crowbar in his hand.

"Who the hell are you?" he ground out.

"My friends call me Blade." The man hissed the words as much as spoke them, and in emphasis, he reached across his body and drew a machete from a scabbard at his belt. The yard of steel gleamed in the glow of Alex's flashlight. "But you ain't one of my friends."

The man's grin widened, and he took a step toward Alex.

Alex sucked in his breath and backed off two paces. With vicious suddenness, the other leapt forward and slashed with the machete. Alex dropped the flashlight and wrenched the crowbar up fast enough to ward off the hissing blade, but the man came at him again, quick as lightning. Only Alex's reflexes kept him from being split open by the brush hacker.

Metal clanged on metal as the two struck and parried and struck again, each looking for advantage. Blade was fast and agile and expert with his weapon, but Alex's training, strength, and heavier weapon quickly turned the tide in his favor. Swinging the crowbar like a two-handed sword, Alex forced Blade to retreat until the man stumbled and sat with a thud and puff of dust. Alex's next swing was a solid swipe that tore the machete from Blade's grip and sent it spinning in a glittering arc into the nearby weeds.

Abruptly a metallic ringing sound whipped through the air behind Alex. A chain lashed out of the darkness, wrapped around the crowbar, and jerked it from Alex's hand.

As if by magic, a slender throwing knife appeared in Blade's hand. With a flick of his forearm, it was gone from his hand and protruding from Alex's abdomen.

Gasping, Alex staggered back against his truck. He jerked out the knife, and as it clattered to the ground, Blade lunged to his feet, a butterfly knife in his hand, chrome tongue licking open with expert flicks of the knifeman's wrist. Blade took a quick step forward and stabbed at Alex, who clutched his gut with one hand and warded off the blow with the other.

A second man, no taller than Alex but stockier, with wild hair and a thick, dark mustache, loomed over him. A heavy length of chain wrapped around his wrist snaked off into the darkness like a metal whip. Other chains of various sizes looped his black leather jacket and body like bandoleers, belts, and bracelets.

"Meet Chains," Blade breathed, backing off. He pointed with the butterfly as a third man stepped out of the darkness. "And Billy-Bob."

Blade snatched up Alex's flashlight and went off into the weeds to retrieve his machete, but Alex wasn't about to try to attack either Chains or Billy-Bob—not because of the pain lancing from the knife wound but because of the silver-plated, pearl-handled Colt .45 casually but steadily balanced in Billy-Bob's right hand. The pistol's twin sat on the other side of a double holster of ornately tooled black leather that slouched beneath Billy-Bob's protruding gut.

Even in the dim light, Alex could see that chubby Billy-Bob was dressed like a very fancy rendition of a ten-year-old kid's idea of a Wild West gunfighter, from the black cowboy hat down to the black boots. It would have been laughable if it wasn't for the .45s and the merciless gleam in the man's eyes.

As Blade came back, machete swinging from his hand, a massive man, well over six feet, wearing a full black beard and sporting a shaved skull, followed him out of the darkness. The bald brute dangled a baseball bat that looked childish in his ham-like fist. Almost immediately after him came a woman dressed in tight jeans and a leather vest. Spiky peroxided hair haloed her head like Medusa's snakes. She looked part Indian and was swinging a .357.

"This is Mallet," the woman said huskily. "And I'm Yvonne." She paused and peered hard at Alex. Her nearly black eyes had a sort of shallow, metallic sheen. "Yvonne the Terrible. And this," she waved casually behind her, "is Flix."

Flix was wearing a wild, colorful Hawaiian shirt and holding a video camera. A bright light on top of the camera flared on, and he aimed the lens at Alex and depressed a button.

"Flix is my fan club," Yvonne said, as if that explained everything.

Alex leaned against the truck, nursing his wound and staring at his assailants. Anger surged through him, but it was overlaid with a fatalistic fear as they crowded in on him, jeering and threatening.

And then hope swelled in Alex as headlights flashed across the tableau. Maybe the presence of the newcomer would frighten off this fearsome crew. But the hope shrank into a leaden lump in his gut as the car drove up to the group and none of them so much as flinched. Alex realized that the car was the same one that had flagged him that something was wrong—the Lincoln. He could see that it was pearl gray. And now, he also could see what was wrong.

The good-looking woman who had motioned to Alex from the window got out. Though the top half of her clothing seemed to be an expensive evening dress, one of her long, shapely legs was sheathed in skin-tight black leather, while the other was completely bare all the way up to the hip. Black spike-heeled knee boots completed her picture of decadence.

But it was the man emerging from the driver's side who arrested Alex's attention.

"It's T-Bone and Jojo," Blade muttered. The awe in his voice was unmistakable.

Alex watched as T-Bone came around the Lincoln. The man was bare from the waist up, and heavy slabs of muscle hung on his big frame as naturally and easily as outcrops of rock hung on the face of a cliff. And they looked just as hard. But no harder than the empty, penetrating blue eyes he turned on Alex from beneath heavy brows. Above the brows bristled close-cropped sandy hair, and below them a strongly aquiline nose ended over a wide, thin-lipped mouth.

Those lips twisted in a cruel sneer as T-Bone caught Alex's eye. The circle opened up to admit him, while Jojo remained on the periphery, acting bored, as if the whole affair was a bit beneath her.

T-Bone stared at Alex for a moment as the trucker slumped against the the rear wheels of his trailer, holding his bleeding side. The cold eyes cut into Alex like an inquest, taking in his physique, his resolution, and the rage in his eyes. The cruel sneer widened, but some of its sardonicism melted into ironic approval, though his eyes remained vacant of anything but finality.

A scrawny, sharp-faced man hurried up to T-Bone, carrying a flashlight and Alex's manifest.

"What's he got, Rat?" the big man asked without taking his eyes off Alex.

"Check this out, boss," Rat replied. "Electronics. Just like the man said."

Rat held the manifest out to T-Bone. Only then did the big man look away from Alex. He took the book, and Rat shone the flashlight beam on the pages as he checked them over. Then, with a nod, he handed the manifest back to Rat.

"Professor Sledge will be pleased."

T-Bone turned his attention once more to Alex.

"And what shall we do with you?" The sarcasm was back like a heavy prophecy.

"Looks like he's hurt," Blade sniggered. "Maybe he wants to go to the hospital."

T-Bone laughed.

"Maybe he wants to see a lawyer," Mallet put in.

They all laughed.

"Give him to Yvonne," Chains suggested.

Yvonne stepped forward eagerly to cries of "Yvonne the Terrible!" But T-Bone, examining Alex like a bug under a magnifying glass, waved her back. He stepped close to the wounded trucker, grasped him tightly by the jacket, and dragged his face close to his own.

"I'm the only thing between you and ten thousand lifetimes of emptiness and pain," his taunting and dangerous whisper breathed into Alex's ear. Amazingly, his breath smelled of peppermint.

Knowing there was nothing he could say, Alex just grunted derisively. T-Bone smiled, almost sadly, then shoved Alex against the wheel and turned to his gang of road pirates.

"No," he told them. "This one's too dangerous to play with. We'll just give him to the darkness."

He stepped back as the others closed in.

Seeing death coming, Alex ignored the pain in his side and tried to fight his way clear, but there were too many of them at once, and they were strong and experienced. And he was hurt. Weapons, fists, and feet pummeled him for blinding, hectic moments before he managed to stagger through the circle and away from them into the high weeds.

But there was nowhere to go. Figuring his karma from the *Markham* had finally caught up with him, he turned, faced his assailants, and spat blood onto the dry grass.

"It takes all of you," he growled with a bravado he didn't really feel.

Billy-Bob thumbed back the hammer of his .45, but Yvonne pushed his arm down.

"No," she said, her tone no-nonsense. "This beefcake is mine." She looked at Alex, her smile broad. "You're wrong, beefcake. It only takes one to party."

She raised her .357 and cocked it with deliberate slowness, staring Alex right in the eye.

"And now the party's over, and I'm gonna have to break your heart."

Ridiculously, the last thing to go through Alex's mind was that he was going to be very late this time, and it really pissed him off. Then Yvonne fired, and the bullet slammed into his chest. Staggering back, legs giving way as his consciousness fled, he tumbled into the patch of weeds.

Mallet and Flix rushed forward. The light from the video camera illuminated Alex's body. Blood pumped over the front of his chest, and his mouth gaped open. A fly, already attracted by death, was exploring the slack face.

"You're a real heart-stopper, all right, Yvonne!" Mallet called out as he straightened. "You got him right in the ticker. He's deader 'n shit."

The others cheered and slapped Yvonne on the shoulder and back. Her brutal lips twisted with a satisfied grin that pursed to blow smoke from her gun barrel. She twirled the pistol into its holster then shouted to the man with the camera.

"I hope you got that, Flix. I want a replay as soon as we get home."

"I got it, Yvonne," he assured her, then licked his lips in anticipation. "I'll play it back for you real slow."

Yvonne's smile grew wider.

"You know I like it slow."

The pirates laughed wickedly before a shout from T-Bone cut them off. "Let's get moving!" He waved them on. "Back to the compound!"

He and Jojo returned to the Lincoln, and it roared off in a cloud of dust.

Yvonne and Flix went off into the darkness to find the Pontiac, while Rat and Billy-Bob followed, looking for the battered, party-colored pick-up. Blade and Mallet got into Alex's truck, Blade behind the wheel, and in seconds, they pulled out onto the highway, followed by Chains on his motorcycle.

Behind them, as the sound of the vehicles diminished in the night, dust raised by their leaving settled quietly onto Alex's body, scumming the blood that seeped from his chest. More flies, drawn by the scent of blood and the breath of the reaper, buzzed like miniature vultures over him. One by one, they lit at the edges of the pooling blood like thirsty creatures around a desert oasis.

Six

PICTURE AN OASIS IN THE desert. But from this oasis springs not the waters of life that irrigate and flower. This oasis is not a haven for the parched and travel worn. There are no palms, no cool, colorful tents. Picture this oasis as an island of ragged, torn metal in a sea of blistering earth, sand, and harsh rock.

This was T-Bone's compound, a junkyard, roughly circular and about half a mile in diameter. Surrounding the perimeter was a stockade of corrugated sheet metal twelve feet high. The top edge of the sheet metal was cut into sharp, ragged-edged spikes that in turn were draped with coils of razor wire. Not that any innocent passersby would venture far enough out into this wasteland to try for a peek over the walls.

Inside the perimeter, the majority of space was filled with heaps of wrecked cars and trucks, assorted odd machinery, and unidentifiable disjuncted metal, all laid out in deranged rows. A labyrinth of canyons ran helter-skelter between the heaps and piles, mazing the filthy, oily ground. Thousands of vehicles were stacked there, each attesting to terminal old age, neglect, or that final lethal encounter.

Just inside the wide front gate was the first of two cleared areas. This one contained a rude and greasy dirt parking lot and a large, windowless metal building painted a dingy gray. The building, which was ninety feet long and fifty wide, had two large garage doors and a personnel door at one end and, at the other, just a single personnel door.

The other clearing lay at the rear of the compound and held the working components of the junkyard—a small bulldozer, a car crusher, and a crane, a large electromagnetic disk dangling from its arm. An avenue about fifteen feet wide wound through the center of the junkyard, connecting the rear clearing with the front gate. It was sinuous enough that neither clearing could be seen from the opposite end.

The junkyard had not originally belonged to T-Bone. He had acquired it as he acquired everything—by force and domination. His discovery of it had been pure accident bred of desperation. That had been ten years ago, long before he'd hatched his present plan after the way to make it real had miraculously fallen into his grasp.

Back then, he'd been Walter Haines, a tall, rangy young hoodlum on the run after a bloody debacle at a bank in Phoenix. He and his partners had robbed the bank of just under three hundred grand, but it wasn't the law he was running from. It was his erstwhile partners.

As soon as they had the loot bagged and were heading for the door, Walter found himself the focus of his partner's guns. And he understood in an instant of crystal clarity that they'd set him up to help rob the bank but not to help bring home the loot. And in that instant, he grabbed the middle-aged woman customer cowering beside the teller's counter, knowing her matronly breasts would shield him from his partners' lead.

He managed to shoot Thompson before the woman's dead weight, at least a pound heavier from the lead she'd absorbed, dragged itself out of his grasp, but by then, Miller, ducking Walter's fire, had fled through the door.

Walter grabbed the sacks of cash and went out after him. There was nothing else to do unless he wanted to sit in the bank until the law came.

Miller and Fredericks, who'd been waiting at the wheel of the getaway car, fired at him, but Walter flagged down a passing Toyota with a shot through its windshield. He dragged the terrified young woman out of the driver's seat, threw her aside, and got in. Several of Fredericks and Miller's rounds hit the car before he could speed off in the opposite direction. He found his way as quickly as he could to the highway, knowing he'd have to leave the city fast before the cops had a chance to revive the young woman and get a firm description of the car. And he'd have to stay ahead of Miller and Fredericks, who wouldn't be more than a few minutes behind him.

And they'd know which way he would go. Back to Vegas. What else could he do? Brooks had Gwen and Andy, and the only way for Walter to get them back was to pay off the bookie. But right now, he couldn't afford to think about his wife and son. He had to get away if he was going to save them, and that was going to be tough. Tough as hell.

Most of the hits his car had taken were nothing more than holes in the trunk and sides, but one had penetrated to the engine, and by the time he reached Wickenburg, he knew something was seriously wrong. He wasn't going to make it to Las Vegas. Not in this car. Already its speed was reduced to fifty, tops, and at that rate, Miller and Fredericks would catch up before he made another thirty miles.

Twenty minutes past Wickenburg, he left the highway and took a state road, thinking to evade Miller and Fredericks long enough to steal another car or get this one fixed. Another half hour or forty minutes convinced him he'd been an idiot to leave the main road. There was nothing out here but nothing, and not only was he losing precious time, the car's engine was rattling and shaking like it was running on kerosene.

Had he been going any faster, he might have missed the small sign, so weathered it was almost illegible. "Car Parts Cheap," it read as it pointed off into the desert.

The obscure dirt road didn't look like whatever was down there did much business, which suited Walter fine.

What he found at the end of the dirt track, nearly ten miles from the blacktop, was a junkyard, though that begged the comparison. It certainly couldn't have been called an operation, just a ratty, tumbled accumulation rotting and rusting out in the desert. But he knew when he saw it he'd found a perfect place to hole up.

Perfect, that was, except for the old man who owned it.

The old geezer squatting out there didn't care if the junkyard was nothing more than a collection, for he was more of a collector than a purveyor. He'd amassed the assorted rummage out of a compulsion to hoard and surround himself with metal walls to shut out others rather than out of a misguided sense that some of it must be worth something to someone.

Certainly he was no mechanic. The dilapidated sign out by the road hadn't brought any business in more than ten years, and by now, there was nothing left worth salvaging. That suited the old man fine, for he lived in the wasteland to get away from other people. In that, he'd largely succeeded for three decades, so he didn't appreciate T-Bone rattling up in a cloud of dust and plainly told him so from behind the barrel of an old Winchester.

T-Bone had made as if to get back into his car, but that was as far as he planned to go. This deserted locale had everything he needed, and he wasn't about to leave.

The old man lowered his guard as T-Bone got into the car, and that was all the opportunity T-Bone needed. Seconds later, the geezer lay with his skull and chest shattered by three rounds from Walter's .45.

T-Bone dragged the corpse two hundred yards into the desert behind the junkyard and left it. It was a lot easier and quicker than burying the body, and the coyotes and buzzards would dispose of the remains quickly enough. Then he went into the junkyard's metal building, found the keys to the geezer's beat-up old Chevy pickup, and headed back to the highway. He took with him only enough of the loot to pay off Brooks and secure the release of his family; the rest he stashed in a rusted wreck in the middle of the junkyard.

He drove the battered old Chevy to I-40, then on up to Vegas, wondering where Miller and Fredericks were. Stopping at a pay phone on the outskirts of the city, he called Brooks to let him know he was coming in with the loot and to have his family ready. Brooks gave him a meeting place on the west side of town, but somehow it was too easy. Brooks was too high up in the mob to be easy, and he'd said yes one too many times. Something was wrong, so before Walter went to the meeting, he stopped by Gus Marks' house for a friendly chat.

When he burst in, Gus was getting ready to go out, and he was loaded for bear. After half an hour and the judicious application of a pair of pliers, Walter learned that Brooks had called Gus to help kill Walter. What about Gwen and Andy? Well, Gus admitted, since Brooks hadn't expected Walter to come back from the bank robbery, Walter no longer had a family. They were pushing up cacti somewhere out in the desert.

Walter strangled Gus, slowly, staring deeply into his eyes as they bulged and died. Then he went to the meeting place set by Brooks. Or, rather, he sneaked up on it.

Brooks was there, all right, and so were a dozen of his boys, hidden in various locations. Two of them were Miller and Fredericks.

The entire double-cross settled into place in Walter's mind: Brooks, Miller, Fredericks, the money. His family. He saw the whole stinking conspiracy that was Las Vegas and how it lured you in, chewed you up, and spit you out then dangled another lure for the next sucker. He almost laughed aloud at the popular notion that Vegas was a fun place to bring the family and have a good time, but the memory of his own family and how he'd brought them here and what had happened to them stopped the laugh in a grunt of dead pain.

Walter's heart was hot with revenge, but his mind iced with calculation. He could go in, and maybe he'd get Brooks and even Miller and Fredericks, but probably he wouldn't get any of them. Brooks was too well protected. He and his kind were Las Vegas and always had been. Walter didn't want just Brooks and the hirelings he used to keep from dirtying his own hands, though certainly his hands were dirty. He wanted the whole damn lot of them—Brooks and his bosses and their bosses, all the way to the top—and he wanted them so badly he was willing to wait.

So he didn't go in because he wasn't ready for his revenge to be only partial and forever incomplete. Instead, he went back to the battered old pickup, drove out of Vegas, and returned to the junkyard.

Somehow, he promised himself, he would have them all, and it wouldn't be pretty. He had plenty of money, now all he needed was a plan—something grandiose, something appropriate to the ambition that was growing inside his hatred that in turn fired his need for vengeance. And all of them—vengeance, hatred, ambition— were like the successive shells of a Chinese box that hid from him the single kernel of terror that was his awareness of how his wife and child had suffered because he had no self-control.

But seeing it or not, he vowed never again to lose control of himself, of others, or of any situation. He began to reforge himself in the furnace of the desert, on the anvil of the junkyard. At first, using his own muscle and carefully portioned amounts of his stolen loot, he built the junkyard into a working concern, expanding and fortifying it and all the while planning. And along the way somewhere, Walter Haines ceased to be, and T-Bone was born.

T-Bone knew that Las Vegas wasn't really a city. Not the way Phoenix or Chicago or LA were cities. Vegas was, pure and simple, the largest and most successful money laundering machine the world had ever seen. In a place where huge amounts of cash are thrown around and won and lost, large sums can easily be hidden and manipulated. That was why the mob built Vegas in the first place and why it endured. But if illegal finance and mob control were Vegas's strengths, they also were its Achilles heel. T-Bone knew that if there was any way at all to hurt such a city, it was in its hidden pocketbook. He was going to peel back a few layers of that onion of illicit finance for himself, not because he gave a shit about the money, but to make the bastards cry.

And when they'd cried long enough, they'd give him not only the money he demanded but Brooks and Miller and Fredericks and more and be glad to get off so cheap.

Knocking off one of the casinos was out of the question as well as not ambitious enough, so while he waited for something bigger and better to come to him, he settled on road piracy and hi-jackings to get the ball rolling. Before he'd graduated to strong-arm work for Brooks, with a little out-of-state armed robbery on the side, he'd driven trucks for mob-controlled truck lines, and he knew who to hit and where.

And so, with his first scheme in mind, he began to gather a gang to carry it out. Five years went by while he initiated it and found the men and women to help him. It had paid well and consistently, and after a while, they branched out to take anything they wanted off the highways, mob-controlled or not. For a long time, it seemed enough—the pickings were easy and, judging by the morale of his gang, the work rewarding. Fun, even. He, at least, thought so.

But though he'd acquired a castle, warriors, serfs, and a queen, T-Bone felt something lacking in his kingdom. The need for expansion and conquest and major vengeance touched him with acquisitive fingers. He dreamed of something big—really big. But what, how, where?

Then one day, while he was passing through Mesa, New Mexico, he'd run across Professor Sledge. Sledge was trying to hitchhike to Roswell after being kicked out of the National Labs at Los Alamos, or so he said. He was looking for the aliens, who might be the only persons in the universe able to appreciate him. Instead, he found a bunch of rednecks in a roadhouse, and they appreciated only that he was a freak and a prime target for a little fun. But T-Bone was looking for a little fun, himself, or at least a way to blow off steam. He beat Sledge's tormentors senseless—not because he gave a shit about the freaky scientist, but because he was bored and feeling thwarted in his desire to inflict the kind of pain on Las Vegas that would hurt it as much as it had hurt him and his own. As it was, his hijackings were little more than a mere annoyance, and if there was anything that T-Bone didn't want to be, it was mere. But when the fight, all too short to be really sweet, was over and he took Sledge to Roswell and questioned him along the way, everything became as clear to him as a desert noon. So clear, it seemed ordained.

Night now hung over the compound, cooling the blast of harsh, heated metal and deepening the shadows in the labyrinth of canyons. Both of the clearings, the avenue, and several other spots in the maze of junk were lit by the sickly green glow of mercury vapor lights. Off to one side, near the northern perimeter, the steady but subdued chug of a diesel generator attested to the source of power for the lights and the building.

And the beauty was, T-Bone didn't even have to purchase fuel—he just hijacked a few tankers a year from the eight-state area prowled by his pirates, and that was that.

The compound's front entrance was barred by an electrically operated chain-link gate nearly as tall as the corrugated metal stockade. Like the stockade, its top was draped with coils of razor wire. Just to the right of the gate was a raised platform that gave a commanding view of the dirt track leading to the junkyard. A man in his early thirties perched on the platform, peering over the stockade.

At first sight, especially in the darkness, the man might have been mistaken for black or East Indian, but on closer inspection, his pigment, gleaming with highlights thrown by the mercury vapor lamps, proved to be a heavy coating of oil and grease. They called him Slick for a reason. Every part of him—his skin, hair, overalls, and work boots—had a uniform, gray-green, plastered look. Even his eyes seemed to have an oily sheen as they anxiously scanned the dark desert.

T-Bone had told him to keep working on the *Granola Gray*, and he'd tried. He really had. But the absence of the warrior pirates made Slick nervous. It wasn't that he feared for their safety. They were too mean and tough to fear for. But still he was anxious. Those two freaks down there in the garage were bad enough, but he felt lost when T-Bone wasn't there to tell him what to do. And he missed the others. Even if they weren't particularly nice to him, they respected and relied on his skills as a master mechanic. Without him, he thought with some pride, they'd be like a cavalry without horses.

But even the pride didn't keep his hands from shaking so much he couldn't fit a wrench over a bolt or keep a screwdriver blade in its slot. At last, he'd put away his tools and left the garage to climb up to this platform, smoke cigarettes, and wait. He'd been standing here for hours, fidgety, smoking, and waiting.

When he finally saw headlights jouncing across the desert floor, the high of his elation was almost drowned in his fear. What if it was strangers, or worse—the police? What if...?

But in a moment, he recognized the headlights of T-Bone's new Lincoln, followed soon after by the Pontiac, the old pick-up, and Chains' bike. And his elation ballooned to near choking because that final set of headlights could only be the tractor–trailer rig they'd gone out to get. And now, they'd brought it back to him to play with. He whooped loud and long. Man, but he loved this place. There was enough work here to keep a master mechanic like him in nuts and bolts and engine oil to his dying day.

The greasy man slid down the ladder like a monkey, scurried over to the gate control, and pounded the big red button. The motor hummed, and the gates slid back almost soundlessly on well-oiled tracks. Everything mechanical around here worked real good, he thought with pride. He was the one made sure of that.

Slick forgot his pride as T-Bone's Lincoln roared through the gate, followed quickly by the Pontiac, the pick-up, Chains, and the new semi. He pounded the control again, and even before the gate began to close, he was running toward the new truck as it ground to a halt near the metal building.

"Boy, oh, boy!" he chortled gleefully as his lope covered the final distance to the truck. He reached it just as the pirate warriors emerged from their vehicles, whooping and hollering like wild savages after a successful raid.

Billy-Bob waved pudgy hands in an expansive gesture toward the semi. "Look, Slick. We brought you a new toy."

Slick immediately climbed up onto the truck's bumper, opened the hood, and dived into the engine compartment. Things looked good in here. Real good. This trucker had known how to take care of his rig. Well, Slick chuckled, I'll be the one takin' real good care of it from now on.

Meanwhile, the others began to ransack the truck. In minutes, they'd ravaged the cab and sleeping berth, removing everything that wasn't fastened down and soiling everything else in the process. In moments, Alex's clean, neat truck was in shambles.

Just then, two men emerged from a door in the metal building. One was a disheveled, middle-aged man with wild gray hair and a hefty spare tire of flabby gut around his midriff. He was wearing a rumpled and grimy white lab coat, splotched with multicolored stains, and wire-frame glasses perched lopsidedly on his blunt nose.

The other man, though younger, made the wild-haired man look positively clean and beautiful. Grubby, dark rags clothed his body. He might have been as tall as the wild-haired man had not the significant hump on his back bent him over and dragged him toward the ground. Around the hunchback's waist was an elaborate tool belt loaded with fancy tools. The tools were sparkling clean in shocking contrast to his personal squalor. He trailed the wild-haired man like a dog, fawning at his feet.

T-Bone and Jojo emerged from their car, and the big man leaned against the Lincoln, watching his gang plunder the truck, a smile on his face.

Everything is just dandy, he thought, popping a peppermint into his mouth. Just dandy.

"Ah, my dear Mr. T-Bone," the wild-haired man ebulliently greeted the pirate leader. "What goodies have you brought me this time?"

"Electronics, Professor Sledge," T-Bone told him, giving the truck a perfunctory wave. "That's what you asked for, isn't it?"

"You hear that, Bulge?" Professor Sledge asked the hunchback. "He brought us electronics. We like that, don't we?"

The hunchback nodded enthusiastically and fondled the tools hanging from his belt. His slender-fingered hands, like the tools, were surprisingly clean, the nails ungrimed and neatly trimmed.

Rat came up and handed Alex's manifest to Sledge, who ran his eyes over it and smiled, a bit insanely, Rat thought. Rat didn't entirely trust Sledge and liked him even less. One of his fondest hopes was that T-Bone would squash the renegade scientist as soon as the *Granola Gray* was finished.

Sledge looked up at T-Bone.

"Excellent, excellent," he proclaimed. "These computers and stereo components should be all we need to complete the mechanism for the *Granola Gray*. Bulge and I shall begin work immediately."

He gestured toward Bulge, who was busy leering at Jojo, a blatant gleam in his eyes as he ran his gaze down and up the long, bare leg. He licked his lips, and she glared back, nose wrinkling with disgust.

T-Bone noticed how Bulge was looking at his woman, and he kicked him. The hunchback whimpered and scuttled behind the professor.

Sledge looked from T-Bone to Jojo, admonishment in his eyes.

"You mustn't mind poor Bulge," he said in a hurt tone. "He means no harm."

"He may not, but I do," T-Bone said with certainty. "Just keep him away from Jojo, or I'll personally feed him to the coyotes." The big man gestured imperiously toward the truck. "Now, get to work."

"Yes, sir," Sledge said quickly. "Right away."

The scientist bowed obsequiously then hurried over to the truck, dragging Bulge behind him. T-Bone turned and, trailed by Jojo, headed toward the metal building. Just as she followed T-Bone through the door, Jojo glanced back at Bulge, who sent her one more lecherous leer and waggled his tongue. Shuddering, she haughtily tossed her hair, entered the building, and slammed the door shut.

SEVEN

AT THE REST STOP, THE cool darkness beyond midnight blanketed the ground. A few night creatures stirred among the shadows, but their movements ceased as the shadows were washed by a swath of light sweeping across the gravel pull-off.

A new powder-blue Cadillac Fleetwood crunched to a stop on the gravel, and almost immediately the front passenger door was flung wide. Courtesy lights came on inside the car, and there was the desert rat, reaching for his pack. A second later, the door immediately behind him opened, and Heath scrambled out even before the old man had swung his legs to the ground.

Millie Parker ducked her head so her tastefully lavender bouffant wouldn't brush the headliner and watched from behind the wheel as her passengers debarked. Her anxious gaze slid from the man to the boy. Such a tragic thing, she thought, feeling her heart bleed. So young to carry so much pain. And a smart little whipper-snapper, too, though he hadn't let out so much as a peep since she'd picked up the two of them at that truck stop back there.

She blinked to herself, as if only at this moment realizing, now that the potential for danger was almost over, just what she'd done. She'd picked up two total strangers, two tramps. At a truck stop in the middle of the night, for God's sake! And here she was, carrying a month's worth of receipts from the cosmetics sales force she had spread throughout Arizona. Millie was on her way to Socorro to visit her sister, Marileen, before heading home to Albuquerque. My God! What could have possessed her?

What, indeed?

Her gaze moved to the old man as he levered himself out of the car. He wasn't as old as he first appeared. Nor as scruffy. He was weatherworn and rough like the desert, but underneath it all, he certainly seemed like a gentleman with education and breeding, even if his speech was deliberately rude and insulting.

There just had been something about the two that said to give them a ride. But now that they were getting out, she was feeling the same sort of panic she should have when she first offered them a ride and they got in. Why were they leaving? She would gladly take them home if they asked. If they had a home. Marileen could wait another day.

The old man stood up out of the car, stretched, then leaned inside the open door. Why was he leaving?

"It's so dark," Millie said in a quick, almost pleading voice before he could speak. "We're miles from nowhere." She looked at him, but couldn't hold his intense gaze. Her eyes turned to the boy. "Will the child be all right?"

The desert rat smiled at her. It was a slightly sarcastic smile, but the shadow and the woman's worry masked it's edges.

Ah, he thought. Once again I have wormed my way into the heart of Middle America. He shook his head.

"This is it, my dear woman," he assured her with a tone of finality. "This is perfect. This is where we are, and this is where we wish to be. Thank you so much for getting us here on time."

Stepping back, he slammed the door a trifle too hard. At least he hoped it was a little too hard—not enough to be obnoxious, just unsettling.

Millie looked at the man and boy through the windows for a moment longer, then shaking her head, she pulled the Cadillac onto the road and drove off.

"But it's miles from nowhere," she muttered in a baffled voice to the empty and suddenly lonely interior. "And it's the middle of the night."

The desert rat and Heath watched the Cadillac's taillights retreat, then the old man turned to the boy.

"Bet you're hungry again. Growing boys are always hungry."

Heath nodded, and the two of them went over to the cement grill squatting off to the side of the pull-off. The old man dropped his pack beside the firebox, poked the boy, and gestured around them.

"Lots of cottonwood trees," he said. "They like to drop branches. Why don't you collect some for firewood?"

The boy nodded and scurried off. The desert rat stared after him for a second then squatted in front of the firebox and, using a stick, scraped out the garbage. It took him a few moments to separate the real garbage from the trash, and he put the latter back into the firebox to serve as kindling. By this time, the boy had returned with an armload of dry sticks, and the desert rat carefully arranged them on top of the trash. Then he produced a disposable butane lighter and winked at the boy.

"Found this in that dumpster," he said. "Still works pretty good. Amazin' what folk'll throw away."

With that, he flicked the lighter into a flame that he applied to the trash. For several minutes, he and the boy fed sticks to the hungry, youthful flames, but it was obvious that the boy's first armload wasn't enough.

"See if you can find some more wood. The bigger the better."

As the boy disappeared from the circle of light cast by the fledgling fire, the old man began rummaging in the pack and pulling out the leftovers from their supper.

Leaving the desert rat beside the fire, Heath moved off through the dark weeds beneath the scrubby trees, kicking his feet to feel for branches. He'd found half an armload of smaller ones when he stumbled over a really big one. Knowing the old man would be pleased, he reached down, grabbed the branch, and picked it up. The texture told him it wasn't wood almost immediately, but he didn't react until he'd dragged an arm up into the dim light from the distant fire. Eyes widening in shock, he dropped the arm.

Suddenly, a horrifying, blood-covered figure sat upright out of the weeds and reached out to him, moaning hoarsely. Heath shrieked, dropped his armload of sticks, and ran.

Back at the fire, the old man was arranging the remains of the roast on the grill when he heard the boy's cry. He surged to his feet as the kid ran up and cowered behind him. As he stared into the darkness beyond the light of the flames, the old man dropped his hand into his jacket pocket and pulled out the pistol he'd liberated from the thugs at the truck stop.

Hearing the rustle of weeds and the shuffle of uncertain steps, he cocked the pistol before he saw the blood-covered man staggering toward them, one hand clutching his chest and the other reaching out limply.

"Help...," the man croaked.

The desert rat jammed the pistol back into his pocket and leapt forward just in time to catch the man as he collapsed.

EIGHT

THE SUN HAD RISEN FORTY-FIVE degrees over the compound, which lay like a metallic sausage patty in a frying pan valley. The earth outside the ragged walls was heating up but wasn't sizzling. Yet.

Inside the walls, though, the heat was already on. In the open area between the metal building and front gate, the rowdy pirate warriors were gathered around, cheering and goading on a fistfight between Chains and Mallet. From their yells, it wasn't certain who they were rooting for—they seemed to be cheering the fight itself.

The antagonists battered at each other for several minutes, but Mallet, far larger and stronger, at last wore Chains down. After Chains sluggishly ducked a hammer-like blow aimed at his head, Mallet snagged him by a loop of chain dangling around his shoulder, jerked him forward, and slugged him low in the gut, three times in quick succession.

As Chains gasped then retched, Mallet let go of the loop of chain and shoved him backward. Chains fell on his ass, and Mallet loomed over him like a threatening thundercloud, arms hanging loosely, watching him choke back bile. Reaching down, Mallet grabbed Chains by a lapels of his leather jacket and dragged him up, flush face close to his own.

"The name's *Mal-A*," he grated, voice still inflamed despite his victory. "It's French. Not *Mal-It*. *Mal-A*! Got it?" He shook Chains until the smaller man's links jingled like sleigh bells.

Chains nodded numbly, and Mallet contemptuously shoved him aside. Chains staggered, but this time, he didn't fall.

"Hey, Chains," Billy-Bob jibed. "I got a buddy wants to fight you. Says you called him Hong Kong when his name's really King."

"Yeah, Chains," Blade chimed in. "Then we'll talk to Godzilla."

Chains spit a red-tinged glob onto the oily dirt and turned away. Their cat-calls didn't mean anything, really, since he could easily kick all their asses, except T-Bone and Mallet, and they knew it.

Mallet, ignoring his defeated foe, turned on his heel and went to a nearby wooden shed sitting on cement blocks. He wrenched open the door, revealing a cowering figure crouched in the corner of the empty, dingy room. The figure turned blinking eyes away from the harsh light. It was Phyllis, dirty and disheveled, her clothes in tatters, barely concealing her body. Mallet reached for her with predatory quickness and brutally dragged her by the arm out into the sunlight.

"Hey, Mallet," Yvonne called out, exaggeratedly pronouncing the name "Mal-It." "Don't make a mess of that sweet stuff. I want some later."

Most of the other pirates laughed nastily, and Mallet turned on them, anger swelling the bulk of his massive body.

"The woman is mine!" he thundered, shutting off all the laughter.

Without waiting for a reply, which wasn't forthcoming anyway, he dragged Phyllis over to a bench that sat in a wedge of shade from the building, and pulled her onto the seat next to him.

"You do what I say, bitch, or I'll pulverize you," Mallet rumbled in her ear. He wrapped a meaty left arm around her waist, leaned close to her, and jerked down the stained remains of her bra. She gave out a whimpering cry and cringed away, but the enveloping arm drew her closer. The ham-like left hand fumbled for then found and gripped her left breast, calluses rasping her nipple.

Groping at his belt with his free right hand, Mallet drew out a small chrome ball peen hammer. He held the gleaming hammer to Phyllis's cheek, then with a malignant smile and deliberate slowness, lowered it, running its slick coldness down her neck, along the swell of her right breast, and over the aureole of her nipple.

To her horror, the nipple crinkled from the cool metal. Even worse, Mallet noticed. He squeezed her left breast painfully, then looked with greedy, coarse eyes at the fold of her crotch, hidden by her crossed legs.

Mallet whipped the hammer in an abrupt arc that ended on her knee. She jerked, crying out in pain, but he held on, the grip on her left breast growing more crushing.

"Open your legs, slut," he rumbled at her. "Always open your legs when you're with me. Keep 'em open."

Phyllis nodded and forced her knees apart. Mallet drew the chrome hammer slowly along the skin of her inner thigh, and she shuddered as the metal touched her.

Across the clearing, Blade poked Flix, who was shooting video of the proceedings.

"Huh?" Flix grunted without taking his eye from the viewfinder.

"That woman'll be tenderized before *she*," Blade jerked a thumb toward Yvonne, "gets hold of her."

Flix chuckled and aimed his video camera at Yvonne. In the eye-piece, a tiny black-and-white Yvonne stared at the woman in Mallet's grip and licked her lips. Watching the Amazon, Flix wet his own.

Blade turned from the cameraman and sauntered over to a stack of hay bales. A crude human form was spray painted on the face of the pile, and sticking out of the target were a dozen throwing knives. He pulled them out, walked a dozen paces from the target, and proceeded to throw them with whizzing snicks into various vital areas of the painted human form.

Meanwhile, Chains left the group for the part of the cleared area to the far left of the front gate, where he began swinging and whip-ping his chain around. The metal links snaked from his hands like a living thing as he whirled and lashed at a man-shaped target made of rusty, rudely welded iron pipe planted solidly in the ground.

Near the back of the clearing, Billy-Bob and Yvonne turned to the narrow curving avenue that lead toward the car crusher and crane at the rear of the compound. Yvonne pointed at the gleam of a side view mirror protruding from a wrecked auto near the top of a stack of rusting hulks. The target was about sixty feet away. Billy-Bob nodded, and the two of them squared off, facing the target. There was a moment of stillness, then they both exploded with movement as they whipped their pistols out of their holsters and fired at the mirror. Billy-Bob's bullet smashed the mirror to frag-ments a full half-second before Yvonne's gun bucked in her hand.

"What's the next target?" Billy Bob asked, spinning his six-gun back into its holster.

"Why am I always the one picking the targets?" Yvonne groused.

"Loser picks the target. You know that," Billy-Bob said with a snide lift of his upper lip.

Yvonne twisted her face in a sour look, hawked, and spit.

"Practice makes perfect, Yvonne," Billy-Bob told her. "I guess I just practice more than you."

"So you're perfect. Is that it, fat boy?"

"Well...." He let the word hang in the air.

Yvonne just snorted and searched for a new target.

"There," she pointed. "See that gauge?"

About fifty feet away, on top of a six-foot pile of scrap, the two-inch-diameter disk of a pressure gauge jutted from a corroded compressor tank. He nodded, and the two of them faced off.

A moment later, they both moved, beginning almost exactly together.

The air cracked with the sound of their guns firing. Again, Billy-Bob's bullet reached the target first, whisking it away with shattering impact. Yvonne's bullet struck slightly lower on the heap of scrap and ricocheted through it. A yowl of pain split air already nearly deaf from the gun blasts.

Yvonne and Billy-Bob looked with surprise at each other then back at the target just as Bulge emerged from behind the heap of scrap. He was clutching a solenoid trailing wires in one hand and holding the other hand to a superficial scalp wound. Blood was beginning to run across his fingers and down his temple and cheek, and he winced with pain as he pulled his hand away to look at it. When he saw the blood on his fingers, real panic crossed his eyes. Feeling faint, he stumbled toward the two gunslingers.

"You win, Yvonne," Billy-Bob laughed. "I don't know how I could have missed *that*."

An expression of concern crossed the cowboy's face as Bulge neared. "Sorry, Bulge," he called out.

Bulge, pressing his hand to his wound, stopped about fifteen feet away and looked up at Billy-Bob, hopefulness in his eyes.

"Sorry I missed," Billy-Bob sniggered.

Bulge cowered as the gunman causally raised his pistol to aim at him. "Don't you worry, Bulge," he promised. "Next time, I'll take care of all your problems for you."

He ripped off several shots, and the bullets whizzed by Bulge all too close for comfort. He stood frozen until the last reverberation died in the jumbled aisles, then he shuddered and hurried toward the metal building. The warriors jeered and called him names until he reached the bench where Mallet sat fondling the woman and caressing her with the ball peen hammer. As Bulge tried to pass, Mallet stopped him with an outstretched leg.

"Pretty nice stuff, eh, Bulge?" Mallet asked, gesturing to the woman.

Bulge eyed the woman. Her bared breasts swelled from the rags of her clothing, luring his gaze. Gawking with lust, he dropped his glittering eyes to the slit between her open legs. She instinctively started to bring her knees together, but Mallet smacked her on one with the hammer. She gasped but kept her legs open. Mallet gestured with the hammer to the fruit of her crotch.

"Maybe I'll let you have it when I'm finished. Would you like that, Bulge?"

Bulge grinned, eyes bugging. The woman shrank back in disgust.

"Don't you worry none, honey," Chains called out from across the clearing. "He'll give you a real good time."

"Yeah," Blade put in. "You don't think we call him Bulge because of that lump on his back, do you?"

The warriors broke into unanimous laughter, and Bulge grinned even more stupidly. He reached for the woman and gently touched her bare knee. It was the first time he'd ever been this close to the real thing, and he was just inching his manicured fingers down her thigh when Mallet suddenly leaned forward and cracked him smartly on the forehead with the hammer. Bulge grunted and staggered back, holding his head.

"I said when I'm through, Bulge," Mallet rumbled. Then he gestured toward the metal building. "Now, get the fuck outta here."

Bulge stumbled toward the metal building, still holding his head. He opened the personnel door next to the garage door and went inside.

The cool quiet inside the building was a sharp contrast to the rowdy pirates and hot sun outside. Bulge breathed a sigh of relief as he closed the door and hastily wiped a ragged sleeve across his forehead, smearing the blood as much as cleaning it off. The lump from Mallet's hammer hurt. Guiltily, he looked around, hoping Professor Sledge hadn't seen. He hated it when Sledge admonished him for being the butt of the warriors' jokes, but it wasn't as if he could help it. Fortunately, the scientist wasn't in sight.

This section of the building was outfitted like a cross between a garage and a scientific laboratory. Electronic instruments lined one rack of shelves, mechanic's tools another. Parked in the center of the space was an over-sized gray Chevy cargo van. Painted on the front end in crude, garish red letters was the name *Granola Gray*, and gathered around the van's side door were T-Bone, Rat, and Jojo. Slick was jammed under the hood, tinkering with the engine.

Giving his forehead another swipe, Bulge joined the group at the side of the van. Inside, Professor Sledge labored over a complex wiring harness strung out of an open access panel in a large black metal cabinet that took up most of the space inside the van. On top of the casing was a control panel with a number of switches, instruments, and LCD readouts in place and several holes where controls had not yet been positioned. Jumbles of wires and other components were visible through other openings.

Bulge handed the solenoid he was carrying to Sledge, who impatiently snatched it from him.

"What took you so long?" Sledge snarled.

Bulge's features contorted with shame. Waving his arms, he grunted and bubbled half a dozen indecipherable syllables. When Sledge saw that Bulge was sufficiently cowed, the scientist reached up and patted his head like a puppy.

"That's all right, Bulge," Sledge said lightly. "You're forgiven."

The hunchback looked happy, then he glanced surreptitiously toward Jojo. His eyes barely grazed the woman when he noticed T-Bone's glower. Afraid to look longer, he quickly cast his eyes at the floor and scuttled around the van and out of sight.

As the hunchback disappeared, Sledge looked at the solenoid, only then noticing that some of Bulge's blood was on his hand. He stared blankly at the blood for a moment then absently wiped it off on his lab coat, leaving one more unidentifiable stain among the many others.

"I don't know why you have to keep that disgusting freak around," Jojo sneered to Sledge.

The scientist frowned at her from beneath beetling brows.

"That disgusting freak, as you so gently put it, is my brother."

Jojo snorted with amused amazement.

"You're brother! Looks like you got the best end of a short stick. Or did you just get a short stick?"

Sledge started to retort, but T-Bone's laugh cut him off. Sledge looked at the pirate leader and saw that, though the man's mouth laughed, his eyes were black pits of warning. He quickly forgot what he'd been about to say and turned back to the interior of the van. As he did, T-Bone pointed toward a door in the wall of the garage area.

"We got business to discuss, honey bunch," he told Jojo, patting her on the rear with his other hand. "Why don't you go make yourself beautiful."

Jojo bristled and pushed his hand away.

"I'm already beautiful."

"Shit, woman. Then go cook me something to eat."

Jojo pouted at him but obeyed and exited from the garage.

As soon as she was gone, T-Bone laid a heavy hand on Sledge's shoulder and pulled him around, out of the van. The renegade scientist winced and cringed under the pressure.

"How long, Professor?"

"It's practically ready right now, Mr. T-Bone," Sledge temporized. "All we need are a few specially machined parts for the triggering mechanism. And the reactive materials." His thin smile reeked of insincerity. "By the time you manage to acquire those, I'll have the rest of this finished." He waved over the interior of the van.

"Are you certain it will work?"

T-Bone's voice was harsh, but the scientist seemed not to have heard the dangerous tone, only the implied insult. Instantly, Sledge's countenance grew rigid. With a jerk, he shrugged from under T-Bone's grip.

"Work!" he shouted indignantly, spitting saliva all over the front of his lab coat. "Why, I have more scientific training than you have junk cars out there." He waved his arms wildly. "I am the most brilliant theoretical physicist in the country. For me, making this," he waved at the van, "is child's play, and you ask, 'Will it work?' You sound just like those morons at Los Alamos and Caltech. They questioned my work, too. Their petty jealousies made it impossible for me to get research grants. They took away my laboratory facilities. Well, we'll see what they have to say after this." Sledge smacked the side of the van with his hand. "We'll see if they're so smug then."

He looked at T-Bone, his eyes beaded with madness, a sheen of unhealthy looking sweat glazing the skin of his cheeks and forehead.

"Of course it will work, Mr. T-Bone," he said, voice quieter but no less febrile. "If you get me the parts for the triggering mechanism, and most importantly, the reactive materials."

"You'll get what you need," T-Bone assured him then crooked a finger at Rat. "Come on, Rat. We've got plans to make."

Rat nodded, and the two of them left the garage through the same door Jojo had departed. Sledge glared after them for a few moments, then turned back to the van.

"Bulge!" he shouted. "Bring me my spanner!"

Bulge cautiously eased around the end of the van, spanner in hand. Seeing that the others had gone, he gained courage and scurried over to Sledge. As the scientist took the tool, his gaze held for a moment that of the hunchback, and silent pain exchanged between them.

"Ah, my dear brother, it seems as if we must pay our dues once again." Sledge sighed. "The things we must do to get funding."

Sledge returned his attention to the black console inside the van.

NINE

ALEX WAS WITH HIS FATHER. Funny how he didn't look like he was dying of cancer. Instead, he seemed the same as when Alex last saw him. No, better than when Alex last saw him. His cheeks didn't sag grayly, and there weren't dark circles under his eyes. His breath didn't smell of alcohol and cigarettes. But his fancy string tie was in place, and his white Stetson was on his head, cocked at a jaunty angle.

"It's fine, Son," his father said. "I know you got tied up and couldn't make it, but it's okay. I just want to apologize for the way I neglected you and Beth."

"It's all right, Dad," Alex said.

"Thanks, Son. It's not, but I appreciate your sayin' so. Now, it's time to wake up."

The dream faded and Alex opened one gummy eye, then another. The sky was above him.

No, he thought, as his vision cleared. It was a ceiling. A blue ceiling. But as he stared, the ceiling suddenly seemed to recede away in the middle, and he blinked, trying to make it flat. But it kept receding, so he quit looking at it and tried to sit up.

The dull ache in his chest, which had dragged him out of unconsciousness, suddenly laced his chest with fire, and he groaned, shut his eyes, and fell back.

"Awake at last."

He cracked his eyelids again. Standing over him was an unsmiling but attractive woman of medium height, with short, dark brown hair. She looked to be in her early thirties.

"Are you a nurse?" Alex tried to ask, but the words came out as a croak.

"Try this," she said and held a cup of water so the protruding straw touched his lips. He drank, washing the dryness of his mouth down his throat.

She didn't seem to be a nurse, unless nurses in New Mexico dressed in faded jeans and tan T-shirts.

"Where am I?" he managed to get out.

"Little Paradise," she replied flatly, and when she saw the look in his eyes, she said somewhat dourly, "Wrong paradise. You're not dead, yet. Hold on."

She wrapped his hands around the cup, and he felt so weak that holding it was an effort. Then she went to the door, opened it to a world of bright sunshine, and went out, shutting off the light behind her. Alex sipped some more water and scanned the small but pleasant room. Now he realized why the ceiling had keep receding—the room was conical, its round base about fifteen feet in diameter and the tip of the cone a little more than that above the floor. Except for the odd shape, it looked like a clean, cut-rate motel room. Certainly it wasn't a hospital room. Subdued light filtered between the slats of the venetian blinds covering the single window, and the air conditioner in the wall gave out a steady hum.

A few minutes passed, then the door opened again, admitting bright light and three people. The door shut, and as the glare faded, Alex saw that the woman was back, and with her were the desert rat and kid he'd helped out at the Pleasant Haven. Both the old man and boy were considerably cleaner than when he'd last seen them, and they wore fresh clothes.

The old man leaned over the bed and said, "On meeting a friend after a long journey, of what should you be certain?"

"I don't know," Alex said.

The old man leaned closer in a confidential manner. "That he's still a friend."

The desert rat and the kid chuckled, and Alex joined in with a painful snort. Behind the man and boy, though, the woman remained stony-faced, arms crossed.

"Well, boy, how you feeling?" asked the old man, straightening.

"I...I was shot in the heart." Now that things were coming back to Alex, he was amazed to be alive.

"Not quite," the old man said, a twinkle in his eye. He raised a clear plastic food bag containing a shattered and bloody chunk of black plastic and circuit boards. "You were shot in the cell phone. It deflected the bullet just enough to save your life. Probably the best use anyone ever thought of for one of these abominations."

He tossed the remains into the trash can.

Alex reached carefully toward his chest, but the desert rat gently restrained him.

"You're lucky. Not much debris in there. Just a few transistors and.... No, no, my boy," he assured Alex as the trucker's eyes widened with worry. "Just kidding. You've lost some meat and blood, but you'll be okay, and the stab wound isn't serious."

"This isn't a hospital."

"Awake only minutes and fully cognizant," the old man said. He bent over Alex and gave a somewhat fiendish grin. "Now why would you want to go to a building full of breeding germs to get well?"

"I need a doctor."

"Well, so you do. Got my diploma mail order last week and my black bag of tricks from a Cracker-Jack box. Besides," he waved offhandedly as he straightened up, "your wounds aren't life-threatening, just painful. It'll be a lot cheaper and friendlier here than any hospital. I ought to know."

"Cheaper, at least," said the woman, sarcasm in her voice.

Alex suddenly remembered more and tried to sit up. Pain lashed through his chest, and he flinched, hissing.

"What day is it?"

"Friday," the woman said. "You've been out most of two days."

"Oh my God...."

"What is it" the old man asked.

"Is there a phone? I have to make a call. Long distance. It's an emergency. I'll pay."

He tried to sit up again, groaning, but the old man pressed him back to the mattress.

"Here's a phone," he said, pointing to the bedside table. He looked at the woman, "Molly, go patch him through."

The woman frowned as if she wasn't happy with what was happening, but she left, and a minute later, the phone rang once.

"What's the number?" the old man asked.

Alex told him, then accepted the receiver. Beth answered on the fourth ring.

"Beth," he said. "It's me."

"What happened to you, Alex?"

The woman, Molly, reentered the room, but Alex didn't notice.

"Is it too late?"

"He's gone, Alex. What happened? You were supposed to be here."

"God, Beth, I'm so sorry. I tried to make it, but I got...held up." He stopped, not knowing what more to say, suddenly realizing that his father was dead.

"Held up?" she asked, worried. "That's not like you, Alex. Tell me what happened. I know something happened. Were you in a wreck?"

"I was hijacked."

"Hijacked?" Beth breathed. "Are you all right?"

"I was shot," he told her, then quickly said, "I'm okay."

"Shot!" He could hear the fear in her voice. "Where are you? I'm coming...."

"No," he said. "You don't have to come here. I'm okay. Really. You've been through enough watching over Dad." He hesitated, then went on. "Did he miss me?"

"He went into a coma right after we last spoke. I tried to call you, but you must have been out of the service area."

Yeah, Alex thought. I was out of the service area. Or was I? he wondered, remembering the dream.

"I don't think he knew anything," Beth went on. "It was all over pretty quickly after that. He didn't even last until morning. You wouldn't have made it here in time, anyway." She was quiet a moment. "Alex?"

He couldn't answer. Something was rising in his throat and he couldn't stop it, couldn't keep it down. But he choked most of it back, and what came out sounded like a gasping cough instead of the sob it should have been. But he couldn't stop the tears.

"Alex?"

"Yeah," he managed. "I'm here. Look, I gotta go."

"Don't go, Alex. Tell me where you are."

"I'm okay. I'll call you back. Tomorrow. Okay? I'll call you tomorrow." He hung up the phone and covered his face with his right hand. He'd have used both, but he couldn't flex his left shoulder.

The others in the room looked on, expressions mixing bewilderment and sympathy. After a few minutes, Alex stopped crying, and he felt a gentle touch on his shoulder.

"Here," said the desert rat, holding out a large white caplet. "Take this. Hydrocodone. It'll take care of most of the pain."

Alex doubted that it would, but he swallowed the pill anyway and took a sip of water. As the desert rat put the cup on the bedside table, Alex noticed that the kid was watching him with solemn eyes. He gave the boy a wan smile.

"Your turn to save me," he said. "Thanks." He wanted to hold out his hand, but he was too weak. The kid seemed to understand. He moved closer and took Alex's hand.

"Okay, enough socializing," the old man said. "You two, outta here."

Molly and the boy obeyed, and after the door shut behind them, the desert rat pulled a chair over next to the bed.

"What's your name?"

"Alex. Alex Brant."

"What happened to you out there, Alex?"

Alex didn't want to talk. But he recognized that the old man was trying to pull him back from death, psychological and emotional as much as physical, and he was too stunned and too weak to resist, so he let the old man lead him along.

"A car pulled up next to me and the woman passenger seemed to be telling me something was wrong with my rig. I pulled over in the rest stop to check, but the only thing wrong was this gang that attacked me."

"Can you describe them?"

"Pretty well, but everything happened fast. And it was dark." Alex did his best, and when the old man nodded, eyes narrowing, he asked, "You know them?"

"Not personally. But I've seen 'em. Word has it an interstate gang of road pirates has been operating all over the Southwest. There's nothing definite—just road rumor. I don't even know if the cops are wise."

"It's no rumor. I know they're real."

"You and the kid, both. The same bunch killed his parents just a week ago."

"Jeez. He tell you that?"

"He doesn't say much," the old man said, casting sad eyes away. "No, I saw it happen. The gang didn't see him. They shot his father and carried off his mother. They're nothing but vicious animals. She's probably gone by now, too. I helped him bury his dad, and here we are."

"You didn't take him to the police?"

"Nor you," the old man pointed out. "What's the point? So they can traumatize him more and send him to a foster home or an orphanage?"

"He might have family...."

"Yeah," the old man admitted. "And all he had might be out there under the hardpan. Anyway, I have absolutely no faith in the system. I know what it's like out here, and the kid's as well off with me as with anyone. Probably better."

"I don't know...."

"Maybe not," the old man interrupted, "but you're in no shape to argue. We'll talk about it later." He paused, looking thoughtfully at Alex. "I couldn't help but notice you've been shot before." The old man touched the circular scar on Alex's upper right arm.

"Yeah."

"So you know the drill. Rest and more rest." The old man pointed to the phone on the bedside table. "If you need anything, just pick it up and dial nine. Somebody'll answer eventually."

With that, he left Alex alone in the dim room, where sleep came like a weight.

TEN

EARLY MORNING'S FIRST LIGHT GLEAMED on the metal jewel of the compound in its setting of barren earth, sand, and stone. The air outside the jagged walls was quiescent as if in anticipation of the heat that would soon be pouring down in scalding waves, bringing a different sort of torpor. But inside the walls, just in front of the metal building, limbs flew in a flurry of activity.

Slick and Bulge were there, scuffling in the oily dirt, grunting and panting as they fought over something. Slick clung to Bulge's back, pounding on the hump, but Bulge just shrugged him off, threw him to the ground, then pounced on him and popped him in the eye with an indecisive fist.

Slick retaliated by kicking Bulge in the crotch. As Bulge fell back, eyes bugging, Slick landed on him and started pummeling his chest and face. Bulge raised limp defensive hands and heaved, trying to topple the flailing mechanic.

Unnoticed by the struggling antagonists, one of the doors in the building opened, and T-Bone emerged into the reddish dawn light He stretched, reaching as if to grasp the sky, muscles rippling and bulging beneath a bright red tank top.

He loved this god-forsaken life, he thought for the thousandth time since he'd taken over the junkyard. Especially these cool mornings after fucking a willing and energetic bitch all night. And Jojo certainly was willing and energetic. Just thinking about her lithe body writhing atop him made his cock stiffen. Nothing else came so close to being wonderful for him.

Then he saw the two men fighting, and his eyes lit.

Well, maybe nothing came so close to wonderful as fucking, but kicking ass sure came in a near second.

He stepped up to Slick and Bulge and brutally booted them apart.

"What the hell's going on here?" he demanded as Slick and Bulge hurriedly scuttled to each side, leaving something fluttering and colorful in the dirt between them. They both looked fearfully up at T-Bone.

Ignoring them, T-Bone bent and picked up the rumpled piece of paper. It was a lurid, full-color pinup of a young and busty but not really pretty woman. She was lying on her back on a bed, legs spread, fingers at her crotch. Her mouth rested in a slack, supposedly lustful pout, but the moue was more ludicrous than seductive.

As he scrutinized the pinup, T-Bone's own mouth twisted into a caustic leer. He studied Slick, then Bulge, both still cowering in the dirt, apprehension and desire mixing comically on their features. T-Bone's sardonic regard widened into a broad, gloating grin, and then he let out a belly laugh. The two hesitantly and inanely did likewise, still apprehensive of T-Bone but unwilling not to follow his lead. Their weak sniggers stopped abruptly, though, as T-Bone, with an agonizingly slow flourish, ripped the pinup into a dozen pieces then cast the tatters into the morning breeze.

As the pieces scattered like confetti across the ground, T-Bone swaggered away from the two, toward the interior of the junkyard. Behind him, Slick and Bulge, moaning with thwarted desire, scurried after the dispersing particolored shreds of the pinup, trying to gather them. Fierce contention raged once again in front of the metal building.

But all that was behind T-Bone. He'd had his morning fun, now it was time to get serious.

Five minutes later, he entered a thirty-foot-diameter clearing in the interior of the junkyard. The area was surrounded by fifteen-foot high walls of stacked and rusting hulks of cars. To one side of the clearing sat a lone, mostly intact junk car of Japanese make, and near the car, an automobile axle with wheels and tires attached rested on the oily, pounded soil.

The other side of the clearing was occupied by a heavy-looking cubical framework of welded iron struts, eight feet to a side. Cables snaked through pulleys, suspending iron ingots in the middle of the framework. This was T-Bone's exercise machine. He'd personally designed it, and Slick had put it together. As with everything mechanical that Slick worked on, it operated with maximum efficiency.

When T-Bone had first come to the junkyard, he hadn't been the proverbial ninety-pound weakling, but he hadn't had the powerful physique he now did. That had come later, after he'd seen the need for physical power to back up his plans for fucking the shit out of the Vegas mob. It was hard to lead violent men and women if you weren't stronger and more ruthless than they were.

The ruthless part had come easy after Brooks had killed his family, but the physique had taken a little longer, though he was already strong and, at six-four, had the height and the frame to build on. By the time he'd gathered his gang, he had grown from a tall, rangy thirty-year-old into a muscular titan whose physical proportions matched both his need to dominate and his ambition. Well, perhaps not his ambition. That was unbounded.

Behind the metal framework sat a stack of thick, rough boards cut into foot-square sections. T-Bone picked up one of the squares, went straight to the exercise machine, and slipped the board between a pair of vertical slots about head high. Then he walked around the metal framework, seated himself on a worn wooden bench at the front. Grasping a pair of handles, he leaned into them, lifting the weights on their cables.

As he worked, T-Bone thought of the trucker Yvonne had scratched a few days ago. Too bad they had to kill the guy. T-Bone knew from personal experience what an effort the trucker had gone to to keep himself in such fit shape. And the guy owned the truck, too. An enterprising son of a bitch. Reminded T-Bone a lot of himself, though on a smaller scale, of course. A real shame to have to waste it all.

T-Bone couldn't help but feel a touch of admiration, and even what might have passed for regret. But then he thought of that final look in the guy's eyes as he faced death. Not without fear or loss, but defiant and pissed as hell. And the way he'd growled when T-Bone promised him death, T-Bone knew he'd killed before and would have killed any of the gang given the chance. Probably could have, too, if he hadn't been wounded and overwhelmed. Almost enough to make even the pirate leader nervous. If T-Bone had nerves, and if the guy was alive. But he'd been too dangerous to let live, so they'd given him to the darkness, and that was just as well. No loose ends. No hitches in T-Bone's perfect plan.

The weights and mechanism of the exercise machine clanged in the morning air.

At the same time, a hundred yards away in the junkyard, a barrage of rumbling snores reverberated from the interior of a mud-brown

'72 Cadillac Eldorado with a crumpled front end. Mallet sprawled on the dimly lit back seat, the raucous wheeze issuing from his gaping mouth and wide nostrils. A thick rivulet of slobber oozing from the corner of his mouth trembled among the coarse black hairs of his beard. One outstretched hand clutched the neck of an empty whisky bottle, the other rested heavily on Phyllis's thigh.

Phyllis was completely awake, wincing at the gurgling snorts grating from Mallet's facial orifices. She gazed longingly at a large ball peen hammer slung in Mallet's belt and eased his hand off her leg. She started to reach for the hammer, but the hand that had been on her, needing something to grip lovingly, flopped onto the hammer.

Eyes shining with equal portions of disappointment and hatred, Phyllis crept carefully out of the Cadillac into the morning light. Looking around fearfully, she darted off between two rows of wrecked cars.

In his exercise clearing, T-Bone finished his workout on the exercise machine. He got up from the bench and strode over to the car axle. Sweat ran down his face and dripped off his hawk nose as he squatted over the axle. Flexing his muscles, he hefted the axle as if it was a barbell, first jerking it to his waist, then pressing it over his head.

Phyllis, winding her way through the maze of metal corridors, had unknowingly skirted the walls of T-Bone's exercise yard as she headed for the perimeter. A couple of minutes later, she arrived at the corrugated stockade surrounding the junkyard. Gazing wide-eyed at the height of metal and the jagged spikes at the top adorned with their ringlets of razor wire, she knew she'd never be able to climb over it, though the thought of digging under occurred to her. But before she did, she needed to know what lay on the other side. A nearby stack of cars offered an adequate vantage, and she quickly climbed to the top.

As she stared out over the desolation that lay as far as she could see, disappointment and apprehension washed the last dregs of hatred from her face, and her shoulders slumped.

Suddenly, a muffled roar and the sound of grating metal galvanized her features. She scrambled to the ground and stared around but saw no one. The roar and ripping metal sounds came again. Curiosity didn't exactly overcome her fear, but she wanted—no, needed—to know what made that sound. If this was to be her hell, then she had to know what monsters inhabited it in order to understand how to cope and survive. Warily, she moved off toward the sounds.

In T-Bone's clearing, the big man was still working out, but this was the fun part. He'd abandoned the barbell axle and now faced the junk car. His large, heavily callused hands grabbed one of the car's fenders, and he roared like a bull. Muscles twisting and bunching with tremendous strength, he began to rip the fender right off the car, and the grating shriek of tortured metal blended with his roar in a nightmarish cacophony.

With a last twanging thunk, the fender pulled completely free. Grunting and growling, T-Bone bent and wrenched the fender with his bare hands, crumpling and twisting it into a shapeless mass. Then, with a ferocious snarl, he cast the wadded fender across the clearing, where it whanged into the clearing wall.

Cheap shit cars they make these days, he thought contemptuously. Nothing but plastic and aluminum that was little better than tin foil. He could never have done that to anything made in America before 1970.

Turning to the car again, T-Bone moved predatorily around it, planting large dents all down its length with smashing front and side kicks. At the rear end, he sprang around to the other side, jerked open the passenger door, ripped it off its hinges, and cast it aside. The door sailed fifteen feet before crashing into a wall of wrecked cars. Even before it thudded to the ground, he leapt to the front of the car and raised both hands in tightly balled, heavy lumps of bone, gnarled sinew, and callus. Venting a bellow that boiled up from his gut, T-Bone slammed both fists down onto the hood, embedding twin concavities in the metal.

Immediately, he whirled in two quick, practiced steps toward the homemade exercise machine, whipping up his right hand sharply in a back fist. Flesh and bone made lethal with strength and precision smashed against the board he'd placed there earlier, shattering it. As the broken pieces of wood snapped out of the holder and clattered to the ground, T-Bone grinned with savage, almost fiendish satisfaction at the ham of his balled fist.

He did not see the pair of eyes watching his actions through a niche in the stacks of cars surrounding the clearing. From the other side of the wall of cars, Phyllis peered through the hole, watching

T-Bone, eyes wide with horror and fatalism. How could she possibly cope with such people, much less survive?

Suddenly, a heavy hand fell on her shoulder and whirled her around, and her fear-widened eyes were staring right into the blood-shot rage of Mallet's piglike orbs. Mallet raised his other hand and swiped Phyllis on the side of her head, and she stumbled and fell full length to the ground. Nausea flooded her throat, and she strove to see again through the lights and colors flickering inside her skull.

"What the hell you think you're doing, sneaking off like that?" Mallet growled. "I'll teach you, you stupid bitch."

He reached down and snapped one end of a pair of handcuffs painfully tight around her left wrist. Holding the other loop of the cuffs, he dragged her limp body off through the dirt.

Eleven

"How are you feeling, today?"

Alex winced as he reached for the bowl of soup Molly handed him and felt the tender edges of his wound pull.

"Still pretty tender." He spooned some of the soup into his mouth. The hearty, thick broth was filled with chunks of chicken and fresh vegetables. Obviously homemade. "This is good."

"Dad made it." She turned to leave.

"What's with your father?" he asked quickly, not wanting her to go. He'd seen only the curmudgeonly old man and the silent but expressive boy since he'd awakened three days before, and she was a heck of a lot nicer to look at than either of them. "Is he really a doctor?"

"How do you feel?" She brushed back a few strands of her short, dark hair that were clinging to her cheek.

He looked quizzically at her.

"Like I said, sore but basically fine."

"I guess he doctored you all right, then."

Alex laughed, as much at her vinegary disposition as at the lack of information in her reply.

"That's not what I meant."

"Does he have a medical degree?" She shrugged. "Yeah. He has a license to practice, if that's what's worrying you. He used to be chief medical officer in one of the big hospitals in Albuquerque."

"I don't understand. If he's a doctor, why's he running around the desert like some kind of hobo?"

"He says its more rewarding than his old job."

"You seem to think differently."

"Dad lost it a long time ago. Way before he came out here."

As if that explains anything, thought Alex as he chewed. And what about you? What's a cultivated flower doing growing wild and thorny out here in the desert? Looking at the way her trim body packed her Levis and T-shirt, he felt a thrill of desire that was blunted only a little by her bitter attitude. Then, a little embarrassed by this turn of thoughts, Alex stared into his half-empty bowl, as much to keep Molly from seeing his eyes as to concentrate on his next bite.

But the truth was, Alex had a strong hankering to reach out and touch her. It wasn't just that she was good looking, though she was that. She reminded him of someone, though he wasn't sure who. Maybe it was something in her manner, in the way she held herself like a wounded animal trying to conceal its hurt from potential predators. Maybe it was the way that hurt resonated with his own.

"He tells me you saved his hide," she said.

It was Alex's turn to shrug.

"He got it backwards. He saved mine."

"Well," she said, "That would be a first."

"What about the boy?"

"Okay," she granted. "A second."

Alex finished the soup and handed her the bowl. She took it and turned for the door.

"Do you rent these rooms?"

"Yeah, we rent them, but hardly anybody ever stops. About all we get is an occasional UFO nut who thinks he can drive around the perimeter of White Sands and Fort Bliss and spot a UFO or a super-secret military aircraft." She chuckled, and it was the first real mirth Alex had seen in her. "I guess it's just as well. Sure is easier to maintain when you never have guests to clean up after."

"How do you earn a living if no one ever stops?"

"When Dad quit the hospital and sold his house, he had plenty of money. He bought this place outright, and we don't really have to make anything to get by."

"What's the rent for the room?"

"Twenty-five a day plus tax," she said, pausing. "But Dad doesn't want you to pay."

"I appreciate his hospitality, but unpaying guests are like fish—after a couple of days they begin to smell. Besides, I don't mind pulling my share, even if I'm flat on my back."

He opened the drawer of the bedside table and pulled out his wallet. The road pirates hadn't even bothered to take it, and it had his credit cards and a few hundred in cash. He handed her one of the cards.

"He doesn't have to know. Put me down for two weeks," he said. "Retroactive to the time he brought me in. And include the meals." He smiled. "You'll have to bring me the receipt to sign. I don't think I'm quite up to walking that far, yet."

His smile didn't thaw her chill, but she seemed to take a new appraisal of him.

"And something else," he said, gesturing toward the phone. "I need to make a couple of long distance calls."

"The cops?"

"For one."

"Don't bother. Dad already called them."

"What did they say?"

"They're sending a couple of officers out this afternoon."

"Good. But I still need the phone."

"Give me a minute to get to the office, and I'll patch you through."

With that, she was gone, leaving Alex to contemplate just how he was going to tell Manny that the load was permanently late. And he'd have to call his insurance company.

"Hey," he said when Manny answered. "It's Alex."

"Alex! I figured I'd be hearing from you today. How's your dad?"

"He died."

"Sorry to hear it. But I guess it was good to see him, huh?"

"I didn't make it."

"Oh, man. That's tough."

"I've got some bad news, Manny." Alex took a deep breath. "I won't be bringing that shipment in."

"Oh, hell, whatever. Bring in tomorrow or the next day."

"No. I mean I won't be bringing it in at all."

There was a moment of silence on the other end, then a brief nervous chuckle.

"I know you're pulling my leg...."

"I'm afraid not. I didn't make it to Lubbock because I was hijacked."

"Oh, shit!" Then Manny said something that stunned Alex—he didn't think the manager of Max Electronics was human enough. "You're sounding a little faint. You're okay? I mean, they didn't hurt you did they?"

"They shot me, but I'll live. It's just a flesh wound."

"Oh, shit!"

"They got everything, Manny—the load, the truck, everything."

"Fuck the load. I got insurance, and now I don't have to bother selling all that shit to get paid. But your truck?"

"Gone."

"You're insured. You can get another."

"What about our deal?"

"You're a reliable guy. Far as I'm concerned, it's still operative. I'll find someone to fill in 'til you're back. In the meantime, you get better, get another truck, and come see me."

"It might take a little while," Alex said. "I have some business to attend to."

"Don't we all?" Manny said with a short laugh. "Just come in when you can. Oh, and be sure to send me a copy of the police report. I'm gonna need it for the insurance company."

"The cops are coming this afternoon. I'll tell them to send it to you."

"Yeah, fine. Oh, shit, man. Hijacked." Manny gave another short laugh. "Who the hell would want a load of cheap electronics? I'm gonna have to check up on my competitors, see if they're offering any specially good deals."

"Let me know if they are," Alex said. "I'd be interested."

"Yeah, man. Yeah. Well, I gotta go. You take it easy and get well. Give me a call."

He hung up, and Alex cradled the phone, smiling to himself. Well, well, he thought. Manny's human after all.

He called the insurance company, then he lay back and dozed. An hour or so later, he woke about as alert as could be expected with his body semi-sedated with a synthetic opiate. He lay there wishing he had something to do. There wasn't even a TV in the room. About half an hour later, the door opened, and the desert rat and the kid came in.

"How you feeling?" the old man asked.

"Better than I look."

"Well, hell, get on outta bed then."

"Not that good. But I could use something to read."

"Got any preferences?"

"I'm too woozy for Kant, so you'd better make it a mystery. Or science fiction."

"I'll see what I can dig up. Right now, let me have a look under that bandage."

The old man's expert touch and measured gaze as he changed the bandage gave credence to Molly's statement that he'd once been a bona fide doctor. At last the somewhat painful ordeal was over.

"Looking good," the old man said. "Better than I thought it might. You're in good shape, and that helps. The weakness is mostly from blood loss and should be gone in a couple of days. Until then, just take it easy. I'll get you a couple of books to help pass the time."

"Thanks," Alex said. "And thanks for helping me."

"Don't get maudlin on me, boy," the old man said. "Most of the time I'd'a soon help a coyote as a person. But you showed some mettle when you stuck up for the kid and me, and I don't mind returning the favor."

He patted the boy's shoulder and gestured toward the door.

"Let's go rustle up some books for this feller."

The boy nodded and went to the door.

"We'll bring you something for lunch. That stew you had this morning suit your taste?"

"It was good," Alex nodded. "Molly said you made it."

"Hell, boy, caught, skinned, and cooked that rattler myself."

Then they were gone, leaving Alex alone with the hum of the air conditioner.

Sure enough, a couple of cops showed up about two-thirty, one white in a state trooper's uniform and one black in a dark suit, who led off.

"I'm Henry Mitchell, FBI, and this is Captain Jim Reed of the State Police. How are you feeling?"

"I hurt, but that means I'm alive."

"I hear that. Your name is Alex Brant?"

"That's right." Alex pulled his wallet from the drawer in the bedside table, took out his driver's license, and handed it to Mitchell. Mitchell looked it over then passed it to Reed, who jotted down the particulars before handing it back to Alex.

"Tell us what happened to you," Mitchell said

"I was out on U.S. 60, just west of Socorro, heading east," Alex told him. "A car came up beside me, and the woman passenger seemed to be telling me something was wrong with my rig. I pulled over at a rest stop to check, but the only thing wrong was this gang that attacked me."

"Can you give us descriptions?"

"I can even give you names if you want, but I'm not sure they'll do much good."

"Try us," Reed said.

"How about T-Bone?" Alex asked with a wry smile. "He's their leader. A big guy. Lots of muscle. Then there's Blade, Chains, Mallet, and Billy-Bob. Oh, yeah, and Yvonne the Terrible."

"I see what you mean," Mitchell said. "But you can describe them?"

"Pretty well, but it was dark and everything happened fast."

"We'll get an artist up here in the next couple of days to sketch out your descriptions," Reed said.

"Who are these people?" Alex asked.

"I'm afraid we can't...," Reed started, but Alex cut him off.

"That was my rig they stole, and this is my body they shot up and stabbed. The old man said you don't have much, so I've probably given you the best info yet on these jokers. I think you owe me something in return."

Mitchell glanced at Reed, who shrugged.

"Okay," Mitchell said. "But about all I can say for sure is that for the past five or so years an interstate gang of road pirates has been operating all over the Southwest."

"They've been preying on just about anyone with anything worth taking," Reed put in. "Mostly independent truckers like you, but sometimes even families."

"And you can't catch them?" Alex asked.

"Not for lack of trying," Mitchell said. "But this gang is hard to pin down. They strike across state lines like the wind. We don't even know what state they operate out of."

"Besides," Reed admitted, "you're right when you say you've given us the best info we have. You're the only witness they've ever left alive. They're nothing but vicious animals."

"What are they after?"

"Who knows?" Mitchell said. "Some sort of massive chop-shop operation is our best guess. One thing's sure—they're a bad lot. All we've got are vanished vehicles, dead bodies, and dead ends."

TWELVE

LITTLE PARADISE WAS A GAS station and souvenir shop tricked up to look like an old-time Western trading post. But the place had been built in the 1950s, and time had completed the aging of what the original builder probably envisioned as quaint after watching one too many 1950s TV westerns. The unpainted exterior timbers and planks had a silvery patina laid on by more than half a century of sun and wind-blown dust, and the tin roof was mottled with rust. If the climate hadn't been as dry as it was, the place probably would have disintegrated long ago.

In front of the trading post, several cheesy tourist-trap signs, one proclaiming, "See the Petrified Rattlesnake," complemented the three pumps—two gas and one diesel—that poked out of the ancient, crumbling asphalt. Behind the building circled a dusty dirt and gravel drive, and arranged along the drive's rear circumference were Little Paradise's five guest houses, each shaped and painted like an Indian teepee. Incongruously off the back of each teepee jutted the boxy little extension that held the unit's simple bathroom. The tepees' faded paint was peeling from the cement walls, but barring earthquake or a direct nuclear strike, the sturdy little structures might still be standing a couple of centuries hence.

The door to the central unit opened, and Alex stepped into the sunshine for the first time since the day he'd been shot. His left pectoral and shoulder were heavily bandaged, and his arm was in a sling, but his face was flushed with healthy color, and his eyes had lost their glaze of pain.

As his sight adjusted to the late morning glare, he took in the almost surreal look of his surroundings—the fake antique trading post that now was so old it was no longer fake, the cement tepees, the dusty, threadbare earth with a ribbon of blacktop curling in the near distance over rolling hills east and west, and overlaying it all a vast, pale blue sky whose only feature was an immensely burning sun. But the air was clean and fresh, and he was feeling well enough that feeling normal didn't seem that far off.

Wanting to stretch and move after five days of confinement, he circled his teepee and headed toward the copse of cottonwood that he'd seen from his bathroom window. He also felt the need for a little solitude. During the time since he'd awakened, he'd been visited frequently, and he was used to hours alone in his truck, with only the scenery and road for company. Though the old man and the kid and even sour Molly treated him almost like family, he'd begun to feel a bit like a bug under a microscope. As he walked into the shade of the cottonwoods, he relished the brush of crisp desert grass against his jeans and the hiss of the breeze in the leaves above him.

About a mile away, lay a the end of a ridge of hills or low mountains that ran slantwise into the rolling desert. Its tallest peak, another mile or so farther out looked at least a thousand feet high—maybe a little more. About half way to the peak a dark gash, like a tremendous wound, cut upward to the top of the ridge. Below the gash descended an incredible tumble of boulders, huge and tossed at the top and shading to smaller and more compacted toward the bottom. They lay there in the raw sunlight like a huge, frozen cascade.

The angle of the cut didn't look steep, and Alex wondered if it would be possible to scramble over the rock fall and climb up the cut to get on top of the ridge. But not now. Now he was feeling a bit tired and thirsty, and half an hour outside had been enough. Turning from the scene, he returned to the trading post, went around to the front, and mounted the three wide wooden steps to the porch. Tugging open the screen door, he went inside.

It was several degrees cooler inside than out. As his eyes adjusted to the dim light, they took in the rough wooden shelves loaded with assorted cheap factory-made souvenirs liberally mixed with desert junk: interesting rocks, cacti in painted ceramic pots, old bottles purpled by the sun, and small metal artifacts that could have been a century old or a year. But new or old, everything was coated with layers of dust. Judging by the thickness of the dust on some of the objects, they'd been undisturbed for some time.

Hearing a sound toward the back, he came out from between the isles of shelves to find Molly perched on a stool behind a glass counter, half hidden by an ancient cash register. She was reading a book, and she looked up as he approached.

"You shouldn't be out of bed," she said. "But long as you are, get yourself a soda." She punched a button on the cash register, removed dollar bill, and held it out. "On the house," she said when he hesitated.

"Thanks." He took the bill, went over to the soda machine that stood next to several racks of junk food and candy and, a moment later, returned to the counter with a cold can.

The glass case beneath the cash register held an assortment of frontier weapons, including a cavalry sword, in various states of deterioration, but what caught his eye was the largish jar that sat next to the cash register.

Molly saw him staring.

"Yep," she said with a faint smile. "That's our gen-u-wine petrified rattler. Quite an attraction, that little fella."

Alex bent close to examine the exhibit. It was a rattlesnake, all right. Or had been. Now it looked half run over and half cooked by the desert sun.

"Where'd you get it?" he asked.

"Came with the place," she told him. "We just repainted the sign."

"When I was a kid, we used to go down to Galveston every summer," he said, straightening. "On one of the fishing piers off the seawall, I think it was the 61st Street Pier, they used to have a petrified mermaid."

"A mermaid?"

"Yeah. Looked pretty much like somebody had grafted the top half of a hairless monkey corpse to the tail of a fish and glued a phony long black wig to the skull. It was obviously a fake, but I loved to go in and see it."

She chuckled.

"Don't tell Dad about it, or he'll go looking for it."

"What about the rest of this stuff?" Alex waved around at the eclectic junk filling the room. "It come with the place, too?"

"The ambience, as Dad calls it? Yeah, a lot of it, but Dad's brought in his fair share."

"Pretty interesting."

Molly just shrugged.

"Where's your dad?"

"What's it matter?"

"You're pretty hard on the old guy."

"I don't think it's any of your business."

"You're right." He took a swig of his drink. "So, what about you and your dad? What are you doing out here?"

She gave him a hard look.

"You don't know when to give up."

"Guess not."

"We just live," she said.

"It's beautiful out here, but it's a long way from civilization."

"It's hot, dirty, and lonely, but you call what's happening in the cities civilized?"

"Bad stuff happens anywhere. I was out here when I was attacked."

His comment seemed to upset Molly, but it didn't make her angry, only more somber.

"Yeah," she said. "Bad stuff happens everywhere."

She came around the counter and headed for the door.

"I'm not being judgmental," Alex said. "Just an observation."

"Forget it," she replied. "But I got work to do. Customers."

A car had pulled up to the gas pump, and Molly went out to service it, leaving Alex staring after her. While she was gone, he wandered through the isles of shelves, smiling at the oddities lining them. He finished his soda and had just tossed the can into a recycling bin when the desert rat and the kid came in from the back. Alex and the boy exchanged smiles.

"Up and about, I see," the old man said. "How you feeling?"

"Sore, but getting better."

"You look pretty good," the old man said, pulling down Alex's lower eyelid and staring at it. "Getting your color back. Just don't overdo it."

"Molly tells me you really are a doctor."

The old man gave a derisive snort.

"A vet could've done as well for you."

"You still practice medicine?"

"A little," the old man admitted. "But not for anybody who can pay for it. There are plenty of poor people hereabouts—Indians, Mexicans, and other folk who can't afford medical treatment. I help 'em out here and there."

"Well thanks for helping me out."

"I think you'd've done the same for me."

"Not hardly," Alex said. "I don't have a vet's license."

The old man's laugh was broken as Molly reentered from the front. She ignored him, but when the kid ran up and gave her a hug, she smiled and ruffled his hair.

"Hey, kid. You been having a good time?"

The boy nodded, and Molly took a bill from the cash register and handed it to him.

"Get yourself a soda."

The boy hurried over to the soda machine, then, carrying his can, he started wandering around the shop, poking into all the rummage.

"Hope you're having a pleasant stay," the old man said a bit stiffly, obviously uncomfortable in his daughter's presence.

"Fine," Alex said. "I see why you call it Little Paradise."

"Don't give my father any overly sentimental values," Molly said. "The name came with the place just like the petrified rattler."

The desert rat looked wounded by the remark and started to say something, but he noticed that the boy had found a slingshot and was pulling on the rubber band, pretending to shoot it.

"Go on, kid," he said, obviously relieved at the distraction. "You can have it. Let's go out and hunt us up a rabbit for dinner."

The boy grinned and ran out the front door, the old man close on his heels. Molly picked up her book and deliberately ignored Alex, so he followed the other two outside and around the back. There were a couple of chairs in the shade near the back door, and wincing as the edges of his wound pulled, he sat in one of them.

Gazing out over the dusty yard at his rescuers, he watched while the old man gave a pebble to the kid and took the soda. He poured the remaining liquid onto the ground then tossed the can about forty feet away.

"Go on," he urged. "See if you can hit it."

The boy slipped the stone into the leather pouch, gripped the pouch between thumb and forefinger, and drew back on the thick bands of rubber. Squinting at the can, he let go of the pouch. The pebble whizzed between the arms of the forked stick and kicked up dirt a foot and a half away from the can.

"Not bad," the old man said and patted him on the shoulder. "Give it another shot." He tossed the boy another rock.

Alex gingerly touched the bandages covering his chest. It was funny, but though he'd known these people less than a week, most of which he'd spent in bed, he was as relaxed here as he'd been anywhere. Maybe it was the proximity of other losers, like himself. Oh, they hadn't said so, but it was pretty obvious that they'd all lost something. Certainly the kid had lost his parents and his innocence in one fell swoop, and the old man and young woman had lost something, too. Something valuable that had sent them out here together, though it was plain that they desperately wanted to be far apart. Yet here they were, as closely bound by the barren emptiness of their surroundings as by the vacant places in their spirits.

But for Alex, there couldn't be a better place. The old man was right—it was a hell of a lot better than a hospital. The dry air, the stillness, the space—all conspired to lull and soothe. Maybe that was why they were here, each to soothe pain in this environment where the constant breeze blew sorrow into the empty quiet of the desert. He didn't know for sure, and right now, he didn't really care. Sleep crept over him, and he dozed in the chair.

THIRTEEN

THE ROAR, CLATTER, AND GRIND of heavy machinery filled air already thick with dust. Chains, manipulating the controls of the bulldozer, pushed a caved-in hulk of a car into the center of the open space at the rear of the compound. He backed the dozer, spun it on its tracks, and went after another wreck. At the edge of the clearing, Mallet, inside the crane operator's cage, shoved a lever, and the four-foot-diameter disk-shaped electromagnetic head at the end of the cable dropped with a crash onto the car. Glass fragments spit out in all directions as the windows shattered under the impact. Mallet hauled back on the lever, and the crane began to crank the hulk into the air.

Mallet tugged on another lever, and the crane swung the wreck in an airy arc toward the waiting car crusher—an open-topped metal box whose walls could contract and reduce a car to a compact block of metal inside of two minutes. When the car was poised directly over the crusher bin, he punched a button, cutting off the current to the electromagnet. This was his favorite part, watching the car, suddenly released from bondage, hurtle into the crusher's hungry maw.

As soon as the car crashed into the opening, Blade, standing on the crusher operator's platform, threw a safety toggle, and the crusher jaws began closing on the hulk. With a shriek of metallic torment, the jaws bit, squeezing and mashing the automobile.

Blade hated like hell to be out here, working with the junkyard equipment. It wasn't that it was hot and dirty and noisy, though it was all of those. It was just plain boring, and that set Blade's nerves on edge. But T-Bone insisted that the operation maintain its front as a legit working junkyard. He said it kept them from any kind of police scrutiny, and now, in the eleventh hour, wasn't the time to mess things up by fucking around.

Blade knew he was right. They'd all be sitting pretty soon enough. No more work, just play. Not that Blade's life since joining T-Bone had really been much work. In fact, he had to admit that it mostly had been play. And even if there'd been a few boring stints out here fractionally reducing the junkyard's bulk and shipping it out on flatbed trailers, the activity filled in a few empty hours, brought in some extra income, and gave them a way to rid themselves of incriminating evidence.

Blade's life hadn't always been fun and games. A lot of it he'd spent on the run after he'd sliced up Rodney and Jacquelle back in Brunswick, Georgia. Well, hell, it had been their fault, but that didn't matter since he'd been the one to pay for it with four years fleeing from the law. He'd even been featured on *America's Most Wanted*.

Later, when he tried to analyze what had happened, he couldn't really understand. After all, Rodney hadn't been interested in Jacquelle when he'd sort of introduced Blade to her. Rodney was on his way to Jacquelle's to sell her and her roommate, Dashay, some weed. Blade was just along for the ride. Turned out Rodney had known both girls since high school and had been trying to get into Dashay's hot pants ever since.

Rodney never did get Dashay's cherry, but Blade and Jacquelle had hit it off right away. Before two weeks were out, they were a steady item, and a month later she moved in with him. She was good looking enough, but what Blade really appreciated was that she knew what he was like and didn't care. No, it was more than that. She actually got off on it.

What he was like was a boost artist. Cars and light trucks, mostly, though he'd managed a couple of larger jobs, too, including three semis. It was mostly easy pickings, especially in the summer when there were a lot of tourists and rental cars. He'd go out onto one of the barrier islands, like St. Simon's, where the rich and haughty vacationed in huge summer "cottages," and while they were in the store or at the crappy excuse for a beach or sightseeing or whatever, he'd take their Mercedes or Lexus or Volvo or whatever. He could be off the island in minutes and cruising down I-95. In an hour and a half, he'd be over the Florida line and soon after that into Jacksonville, where he had contacts. He was managing three or four cars a week and was making enough cash that he and Jacquelle could even afford to buy something on one of those islands.

If he wasn't black. And if he could have stood being around such assholes for more than the hour it took to scope out a scene and boost one of their cars.

Blade had always been attracted to knives, and by the time he finished high school, he could throw one with fair accuracy and speed. Back then, it had been a sort of hobby—something fun to do to im-press Rodney and the other guys. His parents might have questioned his growing collection of blades, but his father was too busy drinking beer and trying to hump every bitch that came into the dive bar where he hung out with his buddies, and his mother was downed out all the time on tranks. They didn't give a shit what he did. Luckily, he gave enough of a shit about himself to finish high school. But that was about as far as he got since there wasn't much to look forward to on the Georgia coastal plains if you were black and didn't want to go into logging or work at a Home Depot or Wal-Mart or something. And Blade didn't. When Rodney took him along to teach him the ropes of quick and dirty car theft, he was instantly hooked.

Blade got the idea of using the machete after watching some fucking samurai movie—something about an evil samurai who was bad as hell with a sword and who was trying to take over everything. He nearly succeeded, too, and it took half an army to finally cut him down. Man, that mother could move that sword. Blade vowed he'd get good as hell with a sword, too, and even bought himself a pretty good one at a knife and sword store in a rundown local mall. But he'd had to leave that one in Rodney, stuck as it was in some bone.

That'd happened because one of the boosts Rodney had sent him out on had gone wrong. No, not wrong. It just hadn't gone, so he gave up early and went back to the apartment. And there was Rodney with his dick in Jacquelle and her moaning and groaning like a bitch in heat.

Blade didn't know what came over him. He snatched up the sword, and the next thing he knew, Jacquelle was moaning for a different reason as she bled out on the floor, and he was hacking Rodney until the sword stuck.

When he realized what he'd done, he hastily packed his knife collection and about fifty grand in cash—the readily available proceeds from his car heists—and split. As he headed down to Jacksonville for the last time, he vowed never to bother with more than a machete. A good one would slice just as well as anything, and if it stuck in somebody, so what? You could pick up another cheap at any one of thousands of army surplus and sporting good stores all over the country. And if you bought one, no one looked at you twice.

At Jacksonville, he turned right on I-10 and drove on adrenaline until he reached El Paso, where he collapsed for almost a whole day. The day after that, he was deep in the desert states. About three weeks after the episode of *America's Most Wanted* on which Blade made a guest appearance aired, he was hanging out in a podunk town in Nevada. He figured if he got far enough away from anything else, people might be less likely to have TV reception and thus realize who he was. He was right. The TV in the dilapidated motel room he was renting by the week got only the haziest reception on three stations, one of them was Mexican. None carried *America's Most Wanted.*

But though Blade felt somewhat safe out here in the sticks, he hated it, too, because there wasn't shit to do. Only a week, and he was bored stiff. Worse, he was the only black dude in a hick town with no black mamas. But he was ready to give it a shot for six months or whatever it took for things to cool down. All he could do was pray that *AMW* didn't rerun his episode, which might prolong his exile. As soon as it was safe to leave, he was getting the hell outta here and going someplace where there were people he could drink with, women he could fuck, and cars he could boost.

The afternoon he first saw T-Bone, Blade was sitting on a frayed lawn chair in the shade of a tattered umbrella beside the motel's dried-up swimming pool, swigging beers from a Styrofoam cooler at his side. There wasn't shit else to do. He felt like that old movie— what was it? *Raisin in the Sun.* Yeah. He was just a raisin in the sun.

He saw the old Pontiac pull up at the motel office, and he knew when T-Bone emerged and swaggered to the office door that the big man was dangerous. He'd seen the type, though not in this great a measure. About an hour later, when T-Bone and Jojo emerged from the motel room to grab a bite at the diner next door, the big man gave Blade a long, careful stare. And kept staring at him through the diner window. Blade knew the man had recognized him, and Blade took him for a bounty hunter.

Abandoning his cooler, he made for his room to pack his meager belongings, but he hadn't been quick enough. When he came out, T-Bone was sitting on the hood of Blade's car, a big grin plastered over his face. Blade pulled his machete, ready to slice-n-dice before he'd let this big fucker try to take him in, but T-Bone just laughed.

"Put that pig-sticker away, Lamar," the big man said. "I saw you on *America's Most Wanted.* It's one of my favorites. But I'm not here to fuck with you. I'm here to offer you a job."

So here he was, having a hell of a time, even if he did occasionally have to tend the car crusher. And by now, the machine had done its work. Blade opened the jaws, and Mallet dropped the crane head, again magnetized, onto the now-crushed block, lifted it from the crusher, swung it over the bed of a large flat-bed hauler, and released it. It landed next to four similar blocks, bouncing the trailer on its shock absorbers.

In the cage of the crane, just behind Mallet, hunched Phyllis, handcuffed to a stanchion. She watched as the big man manipulated the crane controls. She'd watched him do it enough times she could have done it herself, and she was sick of watching. Unfortunately, from where she was chained, she could see little else besides Mallet's meaty, hairy back, the crane controls, and a slice of the clearing through the cage door that kept shifting repetitively as the crane swung back and forth.

Physically, she was frazzled and worn. She'd never felt so bad. Even worse was that the torment never seemed to relax. During the days, she was chained in some uncomfortable position, usually within Mallet's reach, and at night she was crushed within his mauling grasp, beneath his stinking, sweaty bulk. Strangely enough, the nights were easier to take. Mallet was a crude and ugly lover, unwilling or unable to sustain his passion. She usually managed to put up the shallow front of attention he demanded, giving out the requisite few groans at the appropriate moments, while at the same time retreating into herself.

Although, psychologically, she was as close to the edge as she'd been since these horrible people had killed her husband and dragged her off into the night, she'd found a place deep within that was an unexpected refuge surrounded by an equally unexpected reservoir of strength. From there, she almost could ignore Mallet while he had her body. And then he would invariably pass out, an empty whisky bottle clutched in slack fingers, giving her blessed hours of relief.

Daytimes were different. In the light, there could be no solitude, no chance to phase into her hidden self. And just as she could not hide herself from these people, she was unable to mask the contempt and hatred from them that boiled, it seemed, from her very soul. Usually, she just kept her eyes averted or downcast, never giving the pirates a chance to see into her. But there were times when they were looking elsewhere that she could let her feeling out. Times like now, with Mallet's back to her. She let her eyes blaze, unmasked, with powerful hatred for the big fucking bastard. She wished she had one of Blade's knives.

Mallet, oblivious to her, threw the lever to pick up another car, and she closed her eyes, wishing she could as easily shut out the grinding, splintering racket of the machines.

What bothered her most, now, was not knowing about Heath, not knowing what had happed to him or even if he was still alive. The only thing that gave her hope was that the scum who'd abducted her had never once mentioned her son, even to say that he was dead. Since they often taunted her with memories of Rob's last tormented moments of life, their failure to speak of Heath held out some hope for the boy.

As if anything could have hope in this forsaken hellhole.

From the sound of things, the road pirates had demolished two more cars, and Phyllis, unable to keep her eyes closed against the racket, opened them to see, through her single wedge of sight, the brutal woman, Yvonne, coming down the main aisle. The woman pirate swaggered over to the car crusher, climbed up to Blade, and shouted a few indistinguishable words in his ear. He nodded and waved his arms, first at Mallet in the crane and then at Chains on the bulldozer. The respective operators killed their engines, and silence hung almost painfully over the settling dust.

"T-Bone wants us," Blade yelled at the other two men as he and Yvonne climbed down from the car crusher. They met Chains in the center of the clearing, and the three turned toward the corridor leading to the front of the junkyard.

Mallet unlocked Phyllis's handcuffs from the stanchion, cuffed her wrists together, then roughly pushed her off the crane. She managed to land on her feet, but the force of the shove threw her off balance, and she sprawled on the ground. Mallet's heavy boots landed beside her with a jarring thud. He reached down, grabbed the chain linking her wrists, and dragged her through the dirt after the other three.

By the time they reached the metal building at the front of the compound, Phyllis had managed to struggle to her feet. No sooner had they reached the door than Mallet brutally kicked her through, into the relatively cool interior. It was the first time she'd been inside.

She found herself in some sort of garage and work area. Near the garage doors was a large van painted flat gray. It must be the one they all made such a fuss over, though she didn't know why. Behind that was the work area, where tools and materials were kept. Mallet shoved her into the supply area and cuffed her arms around one of the thick, dull-red metal poles that supported the roof. Then he headed toward the far corner, where a filthy, broken-down sofa and several equally decrepit chairs ringed a TV on a squat packing crate.

Already gathered around the TV were some of the rest of T-Bone's riff-raff—Flix, Slick, Bulge, and Sledge—and the new arrivals joined them. Flix squatted by the TV and slipped a DVD into the player next to it.

"Wanna see it again, Yvonne?" the sleazy cameraman chimed out.

Yvonne leaned attentively forward in her chair, gazing at the screen. She licked her lips, almost nervously.

"My beefcake?"

Flix gave a twisted, toothy grin.

"I edited it just for you."

"Took you long enough," the woman pirate groused.

"Better late than never," Flix temporized nervously. "You know T-Bone's been keeping me busy."

He punched the play button, and the screen flickered to life as the road pirates gathered expectantly around. They all laughed and whooped crude vulgarities as the screen played, complete with sound track, a video of the pirates hijacking a truck. Phyllis didn't know who the poor driver was, but she pitied him almost as much as she pitied herself.

The pirates laughed uproariously as they watched themselves beat the driver. But when he staggered away and turned to face the screen, the bitch, Yvonne, raised her voice.

"Shut the fuck up, you assholes!" She grated harshly. "I want to enjoy this."

Everyone complied as the picture on the TV showed Yvonne, now in slow motion, raise her pistol and take aim at the driver. The scene cut to the driver, also in slow motion. His snarl of defiance almost made Phyllis scream in frustration. Then the driver was staggering back, crimson blossoming from his chest, and he tumbled into the weeds. The camera followed him, still in slow motion, and showed him, bloody and slack-mouthed, lying on the ground. A fly landed on his cheek, then the screen went black.

Yvonne leaned back, sighing lustily and rubbing her groin through her jeans.

"Oh, that slo-mo was good." She looked at Flix. "You're a genius, baby. It was worth the wait."

Flix, grinning broadly, ejected the DVD, slipped it into a case, and handed it to Yvonne with a flourish and an exaggerated bow.

"For your midnight pleasures."

The gathered pirates began stomping on the floor and pounding their chairs and shouting together, "Yvonne! Yvonne! Yvonne the Terrible!"

Yvonne took the disc from Flix and, smiling around at the others, drank in their praise and curtsied crudely.

Just then, T-Bone, Rat, and Jojo entered from a side door.

"All right, cut the shit!" T-Bone barked. "We got work to do."

Instantly, everybody was attentive. T-Bone gestured toward the TV. "Flix, show 'em the shots of the machine shop."

Flix quickly slipped another DVD into the player, and the screen came to life once again, this time showing the outside of a machine shop and the street in front of it.

"Listen up," T-Bone went on commandingly. "I don't want any fuck-ups. Professor Sledge...."

At that moment, T-Bone was interrupted by the sound of his own voice coming from the video sound track. His electronic voice was saying something about the machine shop. The pirate leader looked dangerously at Flix.

"Shut off that fucking sound, you idiot."

The cameraman hastily lowered the volume, and T-Bone continued.

"As I was saying, Professor Sledge needs some specially machined parts to finish the triggering mechanism. He's drawn up the plans, so all we need is someone who can tool them for us. We scoped out this machine shop in Albuquerque a couple of days ago. It looks good. They've got the capabilities and they're an easy jump from I-40. We can hit it, get our parts, and get out quick."

As T-Bone talked, attracting the pirates' full attention, Phyllis tugged at her handcuff chain. That it was securely fastened around the post didn't surprise her. She looked at the boxes, crates, and barrels scattered through the area. They seemed to be filled with assorted parts and supplies. Near her was a small wooden barrel containing large nails. Glancing at the gathered pirates, she noted they were all concentrating on the TV and T-Bone's voice. Surreptitiously, she gathered several of the nails, using her toes to pull them out and transfer them to her hands. In a few minutes, she victoriously clutched a pair of them in each fist. Maybe she could steal one of Mallet's hammers and pound them into his piggish skull.

Meanwhile, T-Bone waved at the TV.

"I want all of you to get a good look at the layout of this joint. Rat can fill you in on the details. Like I said, I don't want any fuck-ups."

Fourteen

Alex emerged from his teepee and stretched in the cooling air of the hour before sunset. His T-shirt was tight against the much-reduced bandage around his shoulder, and the almost-healed edges of the gash beneath pulled and itched, but over the past two weeks, the soreness had nearly disappeared. The real problem was that he was stiff from lack of activity and exercise, and his muscles had lost some of their definition and responsiveness. He needed to get back into a good workout routine, but that would have to wait a little longer until his wounds healed more thoroughly. But he could probably ease into his tai chi form as long as he was careful.

A few steps out in the yard, he found a flat area, and he stretched and flexed for a few minutes, loosening up and testing the limits of his shoulder. Then he began moving through the slow, careful, and measured postures, each motion generated from the center of his body and each melting without perceptible pause into the next. He was completely aware of his surroundings, yet he let nothing disturb his concentration on internal rhythms and balances as he slid gradually and easily into the next movement. Posture transformed slowly into posture in steady succession like the flow of a great river— changing yet unchanging, smooth and relaxed yet powerful and purposeful, without hollows, without projections—just as Captain Selter had taught him. The slow, steadily paced movements fit in with everything else here, seemed harmonious with the still, quiet air, the vast spaces, the cool calm of approaching night.

And then the back screen door burst open with a crash, and the kid raced outside and across the porch. He was carrying a pie, and the mixed look of fear and triumph on his face as he scurried around the side of the house was enough to make Alex stop moving and burst out laughing. He wished he had a camera.

In the blink of an eye, the kid disappeared around the corner, and a couple of seconds later, Molly emerged, looking irate. She quickly glanced one way then the other. Snap! He took another mental photo. The look on her face was too good to forget.

"Which way did he go?" she demanded. Her eyes flashed as if incensed at the mere thought that Alex might not tell her.

Grinning, he jerked a thumb in the direction the kid had disappeared. "He's long gone by now," he commented dryly.

"Wait'll I get my hands on that brat. I made that pie from scratch. It took me all afternoon, and he runs off with it."

"I think your father taught him that."

Molly shot him a flinty look.

"Probably," she admitted. "But I don't want to be reminded." Then the glare in her eyes softened. "I hope he eats the whole damn thing and gets a bellyache."

Suddenly all the anger leaked out of her in a loud sigh of exasperation. She blew back a lock of dark hair that had fallen across her face and peered at Alex. He was still grinning up at her. Her face broke into a doleful smile, and she shook her head in resignation.

"Are all boys as bad as he is?" she wanted to know as she came down the steps and over to Alex.

"Some of us are worse. Your dad, for example."

"He's no example."

"You're pretty hard on him."

"And you're bleeding."

He glanced at his chest and saw that his T-shirt it was tinged with blood.

"You shouldn't be exercising," she said. "It's too soon."

"I'll be careful."

"What's that you were doing?"

"Tai chi chuan."

"Some kind of karate?"

Alex smiled. "Yeah, sort of," he said. "Only karate is Japanese. Tai chi is Chinese. A form of kung fu. The principle is different from karate, too, and a lot of people use it for meditation."

"Kind of slow, isn't it?" the woman asked. "It doesn't look like it would be effective. I mean," she said quickly, "it looks more like dancing than fighting."

"It's as effective as anything and has other dimensions that go beyond the physical."

"Sounds mystical," she said.

"A lot of the legends are, but if they're true, I'm a long way off."

"Dad says you're pretty good."

Alex chuckled. "He said it looks like I'm practicing patience. I guess that's true, in a way."

"Been doing it long?"

"I started martial arts in high school, but tai chi came later."

"Military?" Her tone was flat, but there was a hint of something deeper behind the word.

"Yeah."

"I didn't think they drafted anybody anymore."

"They don't."

"You volunteered."

"Right out of high school. Served three tours."

"I don't much like the military."

"Me, either."

She looked at him with curiosity.

"Funny words for someone who devoted so much time to it."

"I needed an out," he said. "The Marines gave me a home and a life, and it was good for a time. After a while, it was time for a change."

"Were you...were you ever in combat?"

"I saw action."

"Did you kill anybody?"

"That's a hell of a question."

"You're right. It is."

"Yes, I did," he said. "But it's not something I like to think about."

"I know what you mean," Molly said. "The world's an ugly place."

She cast her eyes to the floor, but not before Alex saw them flood with pain. Again he was struck, more powerfully than before, by how familiar she seemed.

"Can be," he agreed, brushing off the feeling.

When she looked back at him, she'd regained control, but he could tell from her eyes that she knew he'd seen her pain.

"So," she said a little defiantly. "What damaged you?"

"What do you mean?"

"What brings you out here? To the desert? Only the damaged like it out here."

"I was shot out here, remember?"

"And you're still here. You could have left weeks ago."

"It's not worth talking about."

"Yeah, right. It's nothing. You said you joined the Marines because it gave you an out. I guess that was an out from a wonderful life."

He laughed, as much at his own negation as at the internally directed sarcasm in her voice. Aw, hell, he thought. The old bastard is dead and buried now. What difference will it make to say a few harsh words over the deceased?

"You've got issues with your father," he shrugged. "Same with me."

"He died, didn't he? I heard you talking to your sister."

"Yeah. He was on his deathbed when I was hijacked. I missed him dying and missed his funeral, but I guess it was poetic justice. He used to miss all my sister's and my special occasions—birthdays, graduation, all that stuff. Hell, he even missed it when Mom packed up and moved us out. He'd say, 'Sorry, boy, but sometimes life gets in the way.' Like a big poker game in Amarillo was something akin to life."

"He was a gambler?"

"That's what he was. Poker, mostly. He didn't like to gamble on games of chance. Said poker gave you an edge on the odds."

"Did it? For him, I mean?"

"I guess you can make educated choices about which cards to keep and which to throw away, but in the end it's still the luck of the draw. He did well enough to keep himself alive for sixty-five years but not well enough to keep his family."

"So you joined the Marines to get away from him?"

"Not really. Mom had already moved Beth and me out while we were in high school, but she didn't have the training to be a household wage-earner all by herself. We barely scraped by. When I graduated, the military seemed to offer some hope. It was an immediate job, and I could get enough money to send home. And they put me through college. Dad really hated the idea of me enlisting. I still remember our last argument. Wanted to know why the hell I wanted to go into the military. 'You know how to take chances like me,' he said. I told him that if I ever took chances, it would be with something more important than just money. Like my whole life." Alex gave a sad, one-note chuckle and shook his head. "All he could say to that was, 'What about our family? Wasn't that taking a chance on life?' I told him it wasn't a chance, just a consequence, and I stormed out. That was the last time I spoke with him."

"How long?"

"More than fifteen years."

Both were silent then, pondering the weight of the past.

At last she said, "But it finally played out. The Marines."

"Let's just say I came to a point where I didn't see eye-to-eye with my superiors, and I knew it was time to leave."

At that moment, a honk sounded from the front of the trading post.

"I gotta go," she said. She started to leave, then turned back and touched Alex's T-shirt. "You better go change that bandage."

Then she was gone, leaving a faint trace of her musk in the dry air.

Alex stared out at the ridge of hills stretching out into the desert. Only their tops remained in the last rays of the sun, like a golden smile spread to the horizon. But he wasn't thinking of the desert's beauty, or even of his father. He was thinking of Molly.

FIFTEEN

BLAM! WENT THE SILVER-PLATED Colt .45. Blam! Blam, blam, blam! Blam! The target's bull's-eye evaporated.

Damn! I sure can shoot, thought Billy-Bob as he twirled the Colt back into its holster. Then he whipped its twin from the left holster and shredded the heart of a second target, though the grouping wasn't quite as tight as the first.

Okay, he admitted to himself. I'm slower with the left and not as accurate. But still damn good. Better than most with their right.

The ersatz cowboy's pride in his marksmanship and speed was justified, but it wasn't luck that gave him an edge. Sure, he had native talent and a love of his work, but practice was what counted. Always had. That was something Yvonne would never understand. Her idea of practice was jerking out her .357 and emptying it in the general direction of her target. She generally hit what she was shooting at with at least one slug out of six, but she barely had the patience to aim, much less practice like Billy-Bob did—at least an hour a day.

Billy-Bob hadn't always been good with guns, nor had he always been a make-believe cowboy. He'd grown up in Pittsburgh in a middle-class neighborhood, and he'd played cowboys like most of his friends. But what he liked about it had been the play, not the props. He could play doctor with the girls just as readily as shoot-em-up with the boys. He went to Penn State and majored in drama, but in his senior year, his parents were killed in a car accident. Billy-Bob didn't inherit much—just about enough to finish college and move to New York to try out for roles.

After a year of practically no work, either conventional or acting, his money was depleted, and he was feeling strung out and desperate. Then he saw the ad in the trade paper. Fullerton, Colorado, had an old U.S. Cavalry post and had resurrected it into a tourist town complete with all the ambience of the Wild West, including a wood-fueled train, saloons, and ten-minute cowboy shootouts on Main Street every hour on the hour between ten and five.

The pay wasn't all that great, but room and board were included, and Billy-Bob figured he could add it to his résumé and claim it was regional theater. Hell, it was better than sitting around in stinking, rude New York and getting nowhere fast except evicted as soon as his money ran out. So before it did, he went to the "audition," which consisted of a fiftyish man and a thirtyish woman who watched him pretend to be in a cowboy gunfight for a couple of minutes. Improv.

"You'll do," the man said, obviously bored with watching gun-fight impersonators. "Wendy, give him the contract."

He didn't have to sign away his life, but he did have to stick around Fullerton through the summer season. He signed and, two days later, he packed his car, skipped out on his lease, and headed west.

Fullerton was a small town, but it wasn't so bad. Not after New York. At first, he thought the gig would be easy—all he'd have to do was wear cowboy clothes, learn to draw a gun with reasonable skill, and not wince when the blanks blasted in the cylinder. But it turned out that it was a bit more involved. It wasn't like being in a play where you had to memorize a bunch of lines, the work lasts a couple of hours tops, and then you became yourself again and went home or to a party or wherever it was that theater people went. Billy-Bob wasn't really sure, since he'd never gotten that far.

Working at Fort Fullerton was more consuming. The whole town was a stage that played all day long, every day. You went on at nine and off at six, and for the entire time, you had to remain in character. To make matters dicier, much of the time, you were right there among the audience who were wandering around, looking at the old buildings and antique furnishings or swaggering into the saloon for a nice cold sarsaparilla or ice-cream sundae. You were under such scrutiny that you had to believe the role somewhat to get by.

But Billy-Bob liked it, even that first season when he played the punk who thought he was faster than the marshal. And hell, nobody was faster than that. Nobody on the Fort Fullerton staff, at least. Tenderfoot that he was, Billy-Bob could see right away that Marshal Bob Dade really knew how to handle his pistol. And daily, right after the high noon shoot out, Dade proved to everybody, staff and visitors alike, why he was number one. That was when he gave his fancy draw exhibition, twirling, whirling, flinging, and slinging the Colt .45 he wore like it had a life of its own.

Even after two weeks, Billy-Bob still caught himself staring open-mouthed at Dade's exhibition of skill. And he saw everyone else looking on with amazement, too, even some of the old-timers who'd worked Fort Fullerton for several seasons. Billy-Bob felt a certain envy of Dade's hold on the crowd, though he couldn't fault the man himself. Dade was top dog at Fullerton, and drew top wages, but he didn't lord it over anyone. He was unfailingly friendly, even to a raw tenderfoot like Billy-Bob.

Billy-Bob started trying to replicate some of Dade's tricks in the evening, after dinner, when everyone else was inside watching TV. He'd go behind the livery stable, where no one could see him, and try a little of this and a little of that. He got to where he could twirl his gun into the holster pretty well, but some of the fancier moves eluded him.

Near the end of the season, one of the other cowboys, a jerk named Jenkins, and a saloon girl heading for the livery stable to make a little hay saw him practicing, and the next day, Jenkins made a wisecrack about it in front of everyone.

Billy-Bob was pissed, but he was the youngest and newest on staff, so all he did was shut up and vow to practice outside of town where nobody could see him.

The next evening, he drove out to a little canyon and was practicing his moves, when he became aware of a presence behind him. He turned to see Bob Dade standing there.

"Been practicing, I see," Dade said.

"Just fooling around," Billy-Bob said, ashamed of his clumsiness.

"That's about all you'll ever do with that gun," Dade said.

"How come?"

"Couple of reasons. Balance for one. Management doesn't believe in forking out the kind of cash you need to do more than fire blanks, so that thing isn't much good for anything else."

"I didn't know."

"Course you didn't. Here, give me that."

Billy-Bob passed over the pistol, and Dade drew his own and handed it to Billy-Bob.

"Give that a try. But don't try anything fancy and drop it."

Dade's gun felt completely different from Billy-Bob's. He held it for a moment, then gave it a tentative twirl, and it spun around his finger with smooth pressure. He twirled it some more, holstered it, drew it, twirled it into the holster.

He thought of his first bike, a little 20″, then of his first mountain bike. It was the same difference between his gun and Dade's. He took out the Colt, handed it back to Dade, and accepted his own pistol in return.

"Thanks," he said. "It feels really different."

"That's partly the balance, Bill, and partly something else."

"Something else?"

"Your gun's a fancy toy; this one's real. It means business, and that means it's more than just a lump of metal with a shape." He eyed Billy-Bob for a moment. "You ever shoot a real gun?"

"Just this." Billy-Bob touched the butt of his pistol.

Dade took out his pistol, opened the cylinder, put in five bullets, closed the cylinder on the empty chamber, and passed the gun to Billy-Bob.

"Careful with that now," he cautioned. "Don't try anything fancy. I don't want to go back to the fort and try to explain how I let you shoot yourself. You just aim at something down that away. Like that tree stump. See if you can hit it."

The pistol slammed in Billy-Bob's hand in an authoritative way that his own, loaded with blanks, never did. Four more shots and the pistol was smoking and empty and the stump unscathed.

"I didn't do too good," Billy-Bob said, handing the pistol back.

"Didn't expect you would," Dade responded nonchalantly. "I just wanted you to see what it really felt like. When you're doing fancy gun work like you see me do in the shows, you have to know all the while that this is what happens when you squeeze the trigger. The way the gun hits your palm and what it does to your wrist and arm. It's all part of it. Even if you never actually fire a shot, you have to understand that every move has to feel like you do."

"How did you get it. I mean, did they give it to you like they did mine? Because you're the marshal?"

"Not a chance," Dade laughed. "This baby's mine."

"You mean I could get my own."

"Yep. And let me tell you, Bill. If you plan on getting good, you have to have the real thing. And you have to learn how to shoot. You can play Fort Fullerton for twenty years and not ever learn, and nobody in the crowd will be the wiser. But if you intend to be marshal, you'd better get cracking."

Billy-Bob went out, spent half his savings on the real thing, and signed on for a second season at Fort Fullerton.

Every once in a while, Dade would come out to the canyon and watch Billy-Bob practice and give him some pointers. And Billy-Bob signed on for a third season. And a fourth. The fifth year, he realized that he wasn't playing summer stock but was living a life that a lot of young boys only dreamed of. And he understood that he wasn't going back to New York anytime soon, though he could hear Hollywood calling.

By now, he'd become Dade's deputy, and his pay had gone up with his billing. And in the sixth year, Dade was struck down by a heart attack. He survived but had to go live with his sister in Atlanta, and the management offered Billy-Bob the role of marshal.

It was the break he'd been looking for, and he played it to the hilt, but Jenkins, the cowboy who'd humiliated him in front of the others all those years ago, wasn't too happy. He'd been at Fort Fullerton longer than anyone else, and he figured he deserved the marshal role more than some upstart kid.

Billy-Bob was too involved in his new role to notice exactly how the harassment started, and by the time he did, it was in full swing. One thing led to another, and finally, Jenkins did the unpardonable—he belittled Dade and Billy-Bob's own proficiency.

There was nothing left to do but shoot it out.

They went out behind the livery stable, the rest of the cast and crew following, and standing next to each other, faced off against the barn wall. At a saloon girl's signal, they drew and shot, the barn wall perforating under the impacts of their slugs. Jenkins, the idiot, refused to believe that his slug had arrived a full second too late. Nor did he understand that Billy-Bob had hit the exact knot he'd aimed at.

Two days later, Jenkins followed Billy-Bob out to the canyon and insisted on a rematch. For real.

When it was over, that was the end of Hollywood. Billy-Bob drove straight to Fort Fullerton, picked up his belongings, and left. Within a few hours he was in New Mexico, heading for the Mexico border. Wasn't that where desperados went after gunning down someone in a shoot-out?

He never made it to Mexico. Down around Las Cruces, he met T-Bone, who caught him practicing in a dry arroyo. The big man was impressed with his abilities and offered him a job.

And that was the end of Mexico.

But none of that mattered. He whipped out his right .45 and emptied it into the next target. He still had the role of a lifetime.

Now the left gun. Blam! Blam, blam, blam, blam! Blam!

In a sheltered aisle in the middle of the junkyard, Bulge could hear Billy-Bob's target practice, but he paid it no mind. He was standing in front of a wrecked car. Its back end was a crumpled mess, but its hood was undamaged though spotted here and there with rust and coated with desert dust. Laid out on the metal were half a dozen pieces of torn and crumpled paper, dimly lit in the light of the last hour before sunset. Bulge smoothed them out and stared at them for a moment. Then he ran a manicured fingertip across the printed nipple on one, the smooth thigh on another. The pieces were parts of the lurid pin-up he and Slick had fought over. About half the pin-up was there.

That mean damn Slick had the other half.

With halting movements, Bulge rearranged the pieces, trying to put them together like a jigsaw puzzle. After a couple of minutes, he had them fitted in roughly the correct way, and he breathed a sigh of relief. A lot of the girl was there—most of her face, one breast, her torso and belly, with the down-fringed crotch showing just above a ragged tear. One entire leg was gone, and the other ended at the knee.

Bulge's lips pulled back from his snaggled teeth as he gurgled a laugh, figuring he'd gotten the best of the deal. He envisioned Slick, angry and disappointed, hiding in the garage somewhere, pulling his pud over one tit, one leg, and a second foot. Oh, yes, and a single lock of crinkly hair.

Laughing again, he drew a roll of electrician's tape from a pouch on his tool belt and, with exaggerated care, began to reassemble the picture, studiously sticking the tape to its back side.

Just as he finished, a shadow fell over the pin-up. Bulge, totally engrossed in his task, was so startled that he jerked back with a gasp and almost fell on his ass. But it was only Sledge.

Bulge grinned stupidly at Professor Sledge then turned his eyes away with embarrassment as Sledge dropped a sodden paper sack on the ground next to the car and bent to examine the pin-up. Sledge eyed the seductive curves for a minute and cocked his head at Bulge. Bulge felt compelled to look at his brother and saw that the wild-haired man was grinning in a way that most men would call mad but that Bulge had come to think of as brilliant because it made his brother's eyes shine like the sun.

"Ah, dear brother," Sledge said in a slow, dreamy voice. "How do you map the body of science?"

Bulge, a foolish simper twitching his lips, bent forward and ran his manicured forefinger along the circumference of a breast. Sledge's eyes followed Bulge's moving finger for a moment, then the scientist laughed mellowly.

"Yes, dear brother," he said. "That is, indeed, one way. But to each his own. I much prefer to trace my finger along the tingling, mysterious lines of printed circuitry, to feel the smooth panels of high-tech cabinetry pulsing warmly beneath my palm."

Sledge straightened and stared into the darkening sky for a long moment. Then he went on, voice breathing the words as if lost in a dream.

"Ah, yes, and to inhale the erotic pheromones of hot wiring, sizzling insulation, and ozone. To nibble electrodes and watch the meters and gauges swing and rise in trembling anticipation." Captivated by his own words, Sledge's voice grew louder as his excitement rose. "To finger the buttons and switches that lead to high voltage release and the purity of spirit married to technical excellence! To be online as the power surges and arcs through me! To know the electric shock of recognition as I insert my screwdriver into the outlet...."

Sledge halted abruptly, panting. He shook his head, bringing himself out of his reverie, then put a sweaty palm to his forehead and smoothed his hair back from his face. His madness diffused for a moment as he looked at Bulge with obvious embarrassment.

"Sorry, Bulge," he said. "You know how it is."

Bulge nodded enthusiastically and flashed his snaggled grin. Sledge smiled back wanly and patted Bulge on the head like a puppy. Then the scientist picked up the paper sack he'd dropped next to the crate. He opened it and reached inside. Bulge was instantly attentive.

"Yes," Sledge said, happily deranged again. "It's dinner time."

He pulled a handful of what looked like table scraps from the bag. Grease mixed with less identifiable liquids slimed his fingers, oozed and dripped to the oily ground.

"Some of the best from T-Bone's own table," Sledge assured Bulge, who now was quivering with excitement.

Sledge separated a chunk of meat from the rest of the slop.

"Here, brother!" he cried. "Catch!"

Sledge tossed the meat high in the air. Bulge bounded forward like a dog, caught it, and crammed it into his mouth. Wolfing the scrap in a single gulp, he capered anxiously in front of Sledge, begging for more. Sledge beamed a kindly smile down at him.

"Was that good?"

Bulge grunted.

"Want more?"

Bulge nodded and gave a gurgling moan as Sledge picked another piece of meat from his handful of slop. "Here!"

Again Sledge tossed a scrap to Bulge, who snatched it out of the air. Sledge, losing interest in the game, passed the whole bag to Bulge, who tore into it with gusto.

As Bulge gulped the food, Sledge wiped his hands on his grimy lab coat then climbed a nearby stack of wrecked cars. At the top, he sat and pulled a silver flask from a pocket of the coat. The warm, rich odor of Chivas Regal wafted into his nose, and he took a hefty slug, gasped, and smacked his lips. Lowering the flask, he stared reflectively out across the surrounding desert as approaching sunset bathed the landscape in red gold.

"It's so lovely out here," he said musingly. "No life to spoil the clean lines. You remember when we were boys?"

Bulge, engrossed in his meal, did not respond as Sledge went on.

"Remember how we used to go to the movies at that old theater in Westwood? How we'd watch all those beautiful people up there on the screen singing songs, winning wars, and falling in love? All those beautiful people." His voice took on a note of anguish. "Where did it all go wrong? How did everything get so twisted?"

This time, he looked at Bulge, who had finished eating and was licking grease off his fingers and staring blankly at him.

"They should pay, brother. They should pay for the way they treated you." He turned back to the landscape. "So beautiful out here. No people smiling falsely to your face and hatching evil conspiracies behind your back. Everything should be as perfect as this land. Clean and unspoiled. Yes. Soon. With T-Bone's help, soon everything will be perfect again."

He took another swallow and grimaced as the liquor bathed his throat with a red gold that matched the desert twilight.

"God," he said, voice filled with longing. "How I wish I was back at Los Alamos."

Below him, Bulge looked up at his brother perched atop the wrecked cars and silhouetted against the desert dusk, drinking from his flask. Love filled his heart.

Sixteen

ALEX SMILED AT THE CHEAP little plastic canteen as he slung it over his shoulder. It was encased in vinyl "leather" complete with Davy Crockett fringe, and he probably would have done a lot to have it when he'd been a kid. Now, it was the best he could find at the trading post, but it would do. With the canteen bumping against his side, he emerged from his teepee into the early morning and struck out away from Little Paradise, toward the ridge that dominated the landscape behind the trading post.

The feel of the ground moving beneath his feet did him good. He needed all the exercise he could get after being laid up so long. But the wound had healed, and he felt like he was ready for anything, even a climb up the ridge. Besides, he needed a little time to himself to collect his thoughts about the future. And about Molly. He'd been thinking a lot about her lately, and if he wasn't mistaken, she'd been thinking about him, too.

And that was the problem. Alex wasn't sure he should be thinking about her because there was something else he couldn't get out of his mind—the muzzle flash from Yvonne's gun and the crashing pain as her bullet tore through his flesh. T-Bone and his gang weighed more heavily on Alex than even his father's death, and he didn't think he could begin something—anything at all—with Molly, when his own future was so uncertain. Because he knew he had to go after T-Bone, had to find him, had to put him and his gang under. It wasn't damaged pride or anger that he felt, or even a need for vengeance, exactly. It was simple, cold certainty.

The height of the ridge grew more impressive the closer he got. The main peak was some thousand feet above him, but about a third of the height was taken up by the talus slope. The dark cleft he'd seen from Little Paradise gouged down the face of the ridge to the top of the talus slope, and below that began the rock fall that spread down the face of the slope like a frozen landslide. Near the bottom, the rocks ranged from gravel to head-sized, but near the top of the talus slope, some of them looked bigger than cars. Obviously the rocks and boulders had come out of the cut during millennia of run-off from the ridge top.

The mile-and-a-half stretch between Little Paradise and the bottom of the rock fall looked relatively flat from the trading post, but the terrain quickly wrinkled into a maze of deep gullies etched by the same waters that had eroded the boulders from the cut. By the time he reached the bottom of the rock fall, he was sweating, but it felt good, and his muscles were tingling with expectation.

After taking a swig of plastic-tasting water from the canteen, he began climbing the rock cascade toward the bottom of the cleft. About half-way up, he skirted a flat-topped boulder to avoid a rattlesnake sunning itself. The snake didn't move, but Alex realized he'd have to watch his step. As he climbed and the boulders got larger, their tumble creating passages and caves of cool breeze carrying a hint of water. It was like some sort of stone wonderland where light alternated with shade in an interplay that was, somehow, profound and moving.

The hint of water grew stronger, and he began to notice there were a lot wasps and bees flitting among the passages. But they ignored him as they went, so he ignored them too. At last, he reached the top of the stone cascade and stood at the bottom of the cleft, and he understood both the scent of water in the air and the insects. Both had the same source—a thin trickle seeping down the cleft to pool shallowly in the sand at the top of the talus slope. The wasps and bees were here for water, and hundreds of them swarmed around the small pool, which was only about a foot in diameter but damped the ground for another foot or so. Even where he stood, some ten feet away in the shadow of a boulder, stinging insects buzzed all around.

Braving the flying squadrons, he stepped into the sunlit area just in front of the pool and tried to peer up the cleft. He could see up it for about forty feet, but after that, it took a turn. From what he could see, though, it looked climbable. All he had to do was step across the water.

Cautiously, he approached until he stood virtually on the lip of the pool. The wasps and bees swarmed around, though none seemed perturbed by his presence. But that didn't mean Alex wasn't feeling strange—a little frightened but definitely exhilarated. The insects flew and dived and buzzed, but he sensed not the least bit of danger, even thought there were enough stingers here to inject a lethal dose.

He slowly and carefully tried to step over the pool but immediately drew back and froze as a current of electric tension galvanized the air. The wasps and bees, until now so docile, abruptly became a potently dangerous force, anger vibrating in the drone of their wings as their flight became an erratic intimidation. Alex forced himself to move back in slow retreat, and almost immediately, the anger subsided, and the wasps and bees settled back into easy flight and untroubled buzz.

"Damn," breathed Alex, shocked that he remained unstung.

"Interesting, huh?"

Startled, Alex turned. Molly stood in the passage from which he'd just emerged. A broad-brimmed straw hat sat on her head and a small but bulky daypack was slung from her shoulders.

"Yeah," Alex said, puzzled by her presence. "I've never experienced anything like this before."

"I know what you mean. I've been up here hundreds of times, but it's always just as exciting." She stepped out of the shadow into the sunlight. "Territory. This water belongs to them, and they're not about to give it up without a fight."

"What about you? Can you cross over it?"

In reply, she slowly stepped forward, and vibrant danger shimmered again in the air. She retracted her foot.

"Dad's the only person I know who can step over them without getting their dander up."

"How's he do that?"

"Got me. He claims it's not territory at all but that the bees and wasps are guardians for an elemental living around here."

"A what?"

"An elemental. An earth or water spirit that dwells in places like this."

"That sounds like something he'd say."

"Yeah. He says he's made friends with the elemental, so it's instructed its guardians to let him pass."

"That's fine for him," Alex said. "But what about us mere mortals?"

"I decided long ago that if Dad can have the protection of an elemental, then I could have some elemental protection myself. So I have these."

She unshouldered the daypack, undid the flap, and drew out a large if somewhat crushed floppy felt hat that she tossed to Alex.

Next out were two pairs of leather work gloves followed by a big wad of mosquito netting that she separated into two sheets, one of which she handed to Alex.

"I saw you heading out here and thought maybe you'd need this stuff." She gave an ironic smile. "Makes it possible for us mere mortals to climb to greater heights." The smile faded. "That is, unless you'd like to go on up alone. I don't want to intrude."

"Is it safe?"

"The climb? Yeah. As soon as you get past the stingers, it's no trouble all the way to the top. You don't need a guide."

"It's all right if you want to come," Alex said.

"Okay," she said. "Just put on that hat and drape yourself with the mosquito netting. Tuck it into your belt, but leave places for your arms. Like a poncho."

When they'd both donned the gloves, she said, "Watch me, but don't follow too close. Give them a chance to settle down. I'll go up to the bend and wait for you. Move quick when you cross—some of these babies can sting through your jeans if you give them half a chance, and you don't want any flying up your pants legs."

He laughed, and then she was gone, stepping briskly over the pool and hurrying through the suddenly angry cloud of insects. But almost as soon as she was past the pool, the bees and wasps settled again as if her passage was but a dim memory.

"Your turn," she called from a perch in the cleft above him. He moved and, in a moment, squatted beside her.

Molly doffed the netting and set it on a rock, and Alex followed suit, but kept on the hat and gloves at her recommendation. Beneath his feet came a gentle trickling sound as water danced down the cleft.

"Does this water run off from the top of the ridge?" he asked.

"Not exactly. When it rains, the water soaks into the dirt and porous rock that make up the top couple hundred feet or so. Then it hits a layer of impenetrable rock. This is a low spot in that layer, so this is where the water ends up seeping out. It's actually a spring. You'll see where it comes out farther up. Come on."

They started upward again, and as Molly promised, the cleft proved an easy climb, never too steep or treacherous to displace enjoyment. And the constant trickle of water underfoot invited green growth and made even direct sunlight refreshing. Fifteen vigorous minutes brought them to the source of the spring, and in another five, they reached the top.

As Alex stood, catching his breath, he thought he'd never seen such a desolate landscape. The top of the ridge was barren of growth except for snatches of sere, brown grass. Molly gestured toward their right.

"Lets go over there."

He followed her, and a few minutes later, they took off their hats as they sat in the shade of a large outcrop of rock that hovered just below the main peak. Beneath them spread the arid rolling plain where Little Paradise squatted beside the road like a toy frontier village set amid desert browns. The view beyond was spectacular. Alex guessed he could see fifty miles, maybe more.

The two of them were silent for a long time as they stared out over the blasted terrain. Alex thought about the layers in the ridge upthrust below him. Looking down, distance equaled time—the farther down, the more layers away, the farther back. Maybe that was why sitting on top brought some kind of peace because up here he felt more in the now, as if he had surmounted the detritus of his past.

But he knew it wasn't so. The young woman sitting next to him was too vital a reminder that the past is not some kind of passive memory that fades but a force that intrudes whether you want it to or not.

"You like it out here," she said, breaking the silence at last.

"How can you tell?"

"You're all healed up and still here."

"Yeah," he smiled. "I think it's...well, beautiful isn't the word exactly. It's got a grace, an elegance, something like that."

"All that," she said, waving, "is called the Jornada del Muerto. Mostly lots of rock and dry dirt and heat and not much else. Walk five or six miles, and you'll come to the fence line of White Sands Missile Range. Trinity Site is just twenty miles inside that."

"Jornada del Muerto," he mused. "Journey of the Dead. It's aptly named. Do you think the government bureaucrat who picked Trinity Site understood the irony?"

"I doubt it," she said. "I don't think bureaucrats, government or otherwise, are aware of irony. If they were, they wouldn't be bureaucrats."

"You may have something there."

"Tell me about truck driving," she said. "What's it like? Isn't it lonely?"

"If you're the lonely sort, I guess it could get that way. But there are basically two types of truckers—those who operate solo and those who are part of a team. If I was the lonely sort, I'd go in for the team, where two or more trucks form sort of a convoy that travels together."

"But you're not the lonely sort?"

"I get lonely, sure. But a person has to live with themselves no matter where they are, whether it's in a crowd or a truck cab. Most of the time, I can stand being alone and not get lonely. Mom died a few years ago, but there's my sister and her family, and I get down to Houston to visit as often as I can."

"You never wanted a family of your own?"

"I'm not opposed," he said. "It just never came up."

"You drive all over?"

"All over?"

"The country. You drive everywhere in the U.S.?"

"I have," he said. "I've been through every state in the contiguous forty-eight, and I've even made short hauls into Canada and Mexico. But not lately. I had a contract with a guy who owns several big electronics outlet stores, and that's kept me in the Southwest for the last couple of years."

"How'd you get started?"

He told her about Simone and their drives across the country. By the time he'd finished, he noticed that Molly's shoulder was pressed up against his.

"I guess we were bound to meet then," she said. "Me standing around by this one road and you driving every one of them."

She turned slightly toward him and stared into his eyes.

"There's only one road that's important," he said after a pause. "It's the one you're on. If you're lucky, it'll take you where you need to go."

She leaned toward him, and he put an arm around her and drew her close enough for their lips to meet.

"It seems like I've known you a long time," she said.

"Me, too."

"Is that what kept you here?" she asked after a long moment.

"It wasn't you at first," he said, then took a breath. "It's still not totally you," he admitted, "though you're certainly enough."

"Is it vengeance?" she asked.

"I harbor something like vengeance," he admitted.

"Me, too. But let's not talk about it now. Let's not talk."

This time it was she who drew him close, down into the shade.

SEVENTEEN

CHAINS WOVE HIS HARLEY-DAVIDSON in and out of the traffic that was the tail end of Albuquerque's morning rush hour. His upper lip curled, partly in sneer, partly because of the stench of hydrocarbon emissions left hanging in the air. How did these assholes live like this, with reek and crowd and rush? The sneer took over as his eyes lashed across the slow but steadily moving traffic. It was like a bunch of cattle happily trotting off to the stockyard. He snorted. He'd been living in the desert too long to enjoy the cheap offerings a city might have.

Chains had been in a biker gang for ten years before he'd hooked up with T-Bone. But the gang hadn't been focused. Sure, the parties and rumbles had been fun, but it all began to seem so hollow. He watched the young squirts come in with their bluster, their characteristic swagger, and their heads up their asses. Stupid turds who were nothing but walking trouble without brains. Trouble for nothing. After a couple of years, he got sick of hauling the dumb shits out of their own stink. It got to the point where all he wanted to do was numb out with alcohol and drugs and fuck whatever was handy, even if it was butt ugly.

Then he met T-Bone. When he'd first seen the big man enter the roadhouse bar, he knew there was going to be trouble, especially from the young squirts who just gotten their colors. But Chains hung back, at the end of the bar, just watching. His experience, and some sixth sense, warned him the big man wasn't to be messed with.

It was in the guy's walk more than his size, though that wasn't inconsiderable. He didn't swagger like the young squirts. No, this big man stalked in the truest sense of the word, like a predator perpetually on the prowl. He reminded Chains of a caged tiger unleashed on the crowded streets of a city.

Danger was there, too, in the way his attention seemed to beam out from him in all directions like an aura. Chains liked that word—

aura. Janie, one of the biker bitches he'd spent time with, was heavy into astrology and Tarot cards. She used to say he had a blue aura. Though she'd turned out to be a real flake, Chains remembered the word. And found a real use for it when he first saw T-Bone.

Yeah, that big guy had an aura all right. Chains couldn't see any color, but he figured if it did have a color it must be black. Pitch black. Maybe shot through with lightning. But even if he couldn't see it, he could feel it like palpable danger.

That was something these young squirt punks couldn't feel, or if they did, they were too stupid to understand what it meant. And sure enough, three of them had to try T-Bone on for size.

Even at the time, Chains couldn't suppress a grin. Yeah, it took three of them to try, and even then, it was a poor fit. Inside of ninety seconds the three were broken, crumpled, and bleeding. A fourth fool stepped in, but T-Bone's terrible gaze halted him in his tracks before he had a chance to join his companions on the floor. He wasn't that much of a fool.

The big man casually ordered a beer and drank it while leaning against the bar, perusing his handiwork. With a pleased eye, Chains thought. Then, just as casually, he walked out.

Chains followed. Outside, the big man wheeled as Chains came out the door.

"Not me, man," Chains protested, holding up his hands. "I'd just like to come along."

"What the fuck use are you?" The voice was surprisingly melodious to carry so much menace.

In reply, Chains, with a corkscrewing movement, unwound his favorite whip chain from around his torso and lashed out at one of the support beams holding up the veranda over the bar's front door. A single jerk, and the four-by-four came loose at its base, the veranda creaking and groaning as it sagged. Another jerk, and the beam clattered to the porch. Chains snaked the chain loose from the beam and wound it again around his body with smooth, economical movements. Only then did he look back at the big man.

When he did, it was one of the highlights of his life. He could see the guy was surprised at the quick efficiency of the whip chain. Surprised, though unafraid. No, never afraid. But still, the surprise, which was now turning to grudging calculation, was enough.

"Why the fuck you want to come with me?"

"You're going someplace, looks like."

"You riding with me?"

"I gotta bike over there." Chains hooked a thumb toward the nearby cluster of Harleys.

"Follow."

That was all the big man had said, and follow Chains had. And that, like T-Bone's command, was enough. Chains left everything he had behind, but what use did he have for any of it, really? Guts was all a man needed. Guts and a prick and a handy weapon. And a heavy machine between his thighs, with the open road stretching out invitingly ahead.

He'd been the first of the gang to join T-Bone, except for Rat, who, it seemed, had known T-Bone from some earlier life when T-Bone had another name. And though none of the other pirates knew what that name had been any more than they knew about that life, they all understood that something had happened then to make T-Bone different from other men. Something to do with Vegas and a debt T-Bone intended to collect one way or another. Whatever it was, Chains intended to be there when it happened.

Hey, he thought, looking over the slow-moving rush hour traffic. Speaking of something happening, there were a couple of fine looking young heifers in a little Ford just a couple of cars ahead of him. He goosed the throttle and whipped up alongside the blue Escort. Inside were two office honeys, both bottle blond with that half-teased hair style that made them look like they'd just gotten out of bed. Or a whorehouse. Made his prick stiffen just to think of it. He eased off the throttle and hovered beside them, taking in the short skirts and the swell of tits beneath tight sweaters.

The passenger in the Escort noticed him leering and poked the woman behind the wheel. The driver shot him a quick glance, then turned away, but not fast enough to avoid seeing Chains flick his tongue like a snake at her. The driver exchanged words with her passenger and looked like she wanted to escape, but the traffic was too densely packed for her to get far. She did change lanes, swerving away from Chains, but he was after her in a flash, swooping down on the wimpy Ford like a hawk on a dove. Did the little bitch think she could escape him in that rinky-dink piece of shit?

The two women began to look nervous, and not a little disgusted. Chains grinned, hoping they'd be clawing and biting fighters, thinking about how he'd like to have the two of them back at the compound, thinking what he'd like to do to them.

He swung up close to the Escort and got the driver's attention. She watched through the window with an expression of horrified fascination as he rubbed his crotch and snaked his tongue again.

"Hey, baby," he shouted at the glass. "Let's me and you and your friend go...."

Panic seized her eyes, and she whipped the wheel of the small Ford, shouldered her way across the remaining lanes of traffic to her right, and squealed down an exit ramp, barely missing the crash barrels. Horns blared in her wake as angry, bleary drivers swerved to avoid her alarmed maneuver.

"Stupid bitch," Chains said to the wind. There was no rancor in his voice, only calm certainty. "Can't drive worth a shit." He shrugged. He couldn't have pursued a hot time with them, anyhow. He had to be at the machine shop in less than half an hour, and that certainly wasn't long enough to service two hot honeys.

He kept to the freeway and tooled past the downtown area then took an exit that dumped him into an area of small office buildings bordered by dilapidated, dried-out neighborhoods. He went through one of the neighborhoods and came to a district of older warehouse-type structures. A couple of minutes later, he found the street he was looking for and leaned into the turn, slowing his bike.

It was the slowing that saved his ass as a powder blue Cadillac Fleetwood lunged uncertainly through the space he would have occupied had he been going any faster. He fought to stop before he crashed into the side of the car, and almost dumped the bike but managed to control it. The Cadillac came to a squealing halt just a moment too soon to let him slide on past the rear bumper without grazing it. The bike wobbled another twenty-five feet before Chains brought it to a standstill.

Hot rage flushed into his head as he wrenched the bike upright and kicked down the stand. He glared at the car and saw that the driver, an older woman with a lavender bouffant, was staring wide-eyed at him. He swung off the saddle and swaggered toward the Cadillac. The woman leaned out of the window, relief blunting the edge of the fear etching her face. He figured she was glad he wasn't hurt. That was her second mistake.

"I'm so sorry, young man," she began as Chains came up to her. "I didn't mean...."

Chains grabbed her by the front of her blouse and half pulled her thick body through the window. He could feel the thin material tear beneath his clawed, callused fingers, and it felt good.

"What's your name?" he snarled into her terrified face.

"Millie," she stammered. "Millie Parker."

"Well, Millie, take a good look at this."

Holding her there with one hand, he reached down, unzipped his fly, and pulled out his cock. Forcing her face down so that she was staring right at his meat, he pissed on the side of her car.

She gasped and tried to turn away, but he wouldn't let her. When he finished flicking the last drops onto the paint, he zipped up and shoved her back inside her car.

"I'll bet you're sorry now," he said with a nasty sneer.

The woman, panic blanching her face, hastily threw the car into gear and pulled off with a squeal of rubber. Chains grinned after her as she peeled around the corner at the end of the block just as T-Bone's Lincoln turned the same corner and came toward him.

The sedan pulled up and stopped alongside the curb across the street from the machine shop. T-Bone was at the wheel. Next to him was Rat, while in the back sat Professor Sledge, clutching a roll of papers in trembling hands.

At that moment, Blade's Pontiac drove into the street at the other end of the block and stopped. With the knifeman were Billy-Bob, Mallet, and Yvonne. Despite their excitement at the impending raid on the machine shop, their usual rowdiness was professionally subdued. This was business, and T-Bone would have it no other way. Heads would roll if anybody fucked up.

The pirates inside the Pontiac saw T-Bone's headlights flicker briefly. Blade slapped Mallet on the arm.

"That's it. Let's go."

The four pirates got out of the car and dispersed toward the big overhead doors at the back of the machine shop.

Inside the Lincoln, T-Bone turned around and said to Sledge, "Okay, Professor, this is where we get your precious parts." He got out, and Rat followed, but Sledge didn't budge. Glaring, T-Bone opened the renegade scientist's door.

"I've been thinking, Mr. T-Bone," Sledge said, glancing sidelong at the pirate leader, eyes twitching nervously. "I'm not certain my presence is required...."

With a derisive snort, T-Bone dragged Sledge from the car.

"Get the fuck in there, Professor," he ordered as he propelled the reluctant scientist toward the machine shop door.

Chains already was beside the door, and he stayed to guard it while T-Bone, Rat, and Sledge entered the building.

Not far inside, they encountered a welder bent over a flaring electric torch. T-Bone tapped the man on the shoulder, and he straightened and levered the welding mask back from his face.

"Yeah?"

T-Bone smiled.

"Where's the foreman?"

Behind the welder, Rat picked up a foot-long bar of metal.

"He's in the office." The welder pointed. "That door over there."

T-Bone followed the pointing finger and saw an office walled with large, grimy windows in the corner of the building.

"Thanks." T-Bone smiled again.

The welder nodded and flipped the welding mask down over his face. At that instant, Rat rapped him on the back of the skull with the metal bar. The welder grunted and collapsed to the floor. T-Bone reached over and flipped off the the welding torch.

"Don't mention it," he said to the fallen man.

The pirates went to the office door and entered unceremoniously. There were two men in the room drinking coffee, a big one behind a cluttered metal desk, the other in a chair. Both looked up as the pirates came in. The man behind the desk sat his cup on the desk.

"Something I can do for you fellows?"

"You the foreman?" T-Bone asked.

"That's right." He eyed the pirates. "But I can tell you right off that we ain't hiring."

"We're not looking for work," Rat snidely informed him.

"We need a couple of parts machined," T-Bone said. "Right away."

The foreman wrinkled his nose and shook his head.

"It'll be at least a week...."

"I said right away," T-Bone interrupted harshly, leaning menacingly over the foreman's desk.

The foreman bristled, shoved back his chair, and got to his feet. Though not as tall or as muscular as T-Bone, he was plenty big and meaty.

"Look here, you...," he began, but stopped as T-Bone snatched across the desk, grabbed him by his shirt, and dragged him halfway across the surface. The other man surged to his feet and took one step toward T-Bone, but Rat reached out and cracked him over the skull with the metal bar. The man crashed to the floor. T-Bone grinned at the sound of the falling body but didn't turn. Instead, he stared deeply into the foreman's eyes. The foreman flinched, glanced quickly at the fallen man, and swallowed heavily.

"Okay. What do you want?"

T-Bone, still grinning, released the foreman, who sank back into his chair. T-Bone swept the desktop clean and motioned for Sledge to come forward.

"Tell him what you want."

Sledge spread the roll of papers on the foreman's desk.

Outside the office, one of the machine shop employees had noticed what transpired through the office windows. As Sledge bent over the desk, the man grasped a heavy wrench and took a step toward the office.

Suddenly, he felt a restraining hand on his arm and a sharp prick just under his right ear. He stopped dead still and rolled his eyes at the man behind him.

"Mighty nice wrench you got there, dude," Blade told him. "Be a shame to get it all messed up with their blood." He motioned with his head toward the pirates in the office. "Or yours."

The machinist let go of the wrench. As it clanged to the floor, Blade stepped back and released him. The machinist turned around and saw that the other five workers in the shop were huddled in a group, surrounded by the armed pirates. One of the welders was stretched out on the floor, blood seeping from a gash in his skull.

Blade jerked a thumb in their direction.

"What say we join 'em?"

The machinist nodded numbly, and the two of them crossed the floor to the others. Just as they reached the group, the office door opened, and the foreman and the three pirates with him emerged. The foreman looked across the space at the captive workers.

"Andy!" he called out.

The machinist who had dropped the wrench looked tensely at Blade. "That's me."

"You heard the man, Andy."

Nervously, Andy headed across the floor to the office. Inside, he bent over the drawings that Sledge had unfurled. While they discussed the schematics, the pirates chained the rest of the employees to heavy machinery. By the time they'd finished, Andy and the foreman were setting up a metal lathe. T-Bone, Rat, and Sledge hovered around, watching their every move.

Once the employees were bound and the lathe in operation, carving the parts for the triggering mechanism, there wasn't much for the pirates to do except wait. Mallet, feeling restless, began rummaging through cases of equipment and tool boxes. While rooting around in one large tool box, he came up with a three-pound maul. A thick leather strap looped from the butt end of the handle. He slipped the strap around his wrist and swung the hammer, testing out its weight and balance.

"Oh, man," he murmured to himself. "Hammer of the gods!"

Meanwhile, the machinist and foreman finished machining the parts, and a lecherously grinning Sledge took them and put them into a foam-lined metal briefcase that Rat had carried in, handling the freshly cut pieces of metal as if they were precious and delicate fossils.

The pirates chained the machinist and foreman to the lathe, then whooping and crowing, they all headed for the doors. A moment later, they emerged into the street and dispersed toward their vehicles, Sledge protectively clutching the case to his chest like a valuable treasure.

In seconds they were gone. Behind them, inside the machine shop, the foreman and employees breathed a collective sigh of relief, not knowing just how lucky they'd been.

EIGHTEEN

BULGE WORKED HIS WAY AROUND the rusted hulk of an old Buick and paused to wipe sweat from his eyes and scope out the pile of scrap metal ten feet away. A snaggled smile split his face. He'd planned it perfectly.

He scuttled from the car to the pile, being careful to raise neither dust nor noise. He arrived panting, but that was more from fear and excitement than exertion. Managing to get control of his breathing, he crouched there, afraid he'd been seen or heard. But as one, then two agonizing minutes passed without another sound, he relaxed a bit, though that did little to abate his thudding heartbeats. His prey was still unaware.

He carefully peeked around the side of the pile, and his breath caught in his throat. This was even better than he'd hoped for.

Jojo lay on a deck lounger in front of the metal building, soaking up the sun's rays. The skimpy bikini did little to hide her luscious curves, particularly since the bikini top was draped over the boom-box next to her. As he watched, she reached for the iced drink sitting on a nearby ice chest, and her sweaty breasts jiggled in a way that tightened his crotch.

He wanted to reach down and stroke himself, but the hot sun poured sweat into his eyes, stinging the sight of Jojo from them. He hastily brushed the back of his sleeve across his face, and her blurred form came into focus just as she set the drink on the ice chest. Then she reached for the bottle of suntan lotion, squirted some into her palms, and began to rub it over her breasts and belly.

Bulge's eyes almost popped from his head, and his prick stiffened uncomfortably. He unzipped, took it out, and began stroking it as he jockeyed for a better vantage behind the pile of junk. He was so intent as he leaned forward, that he failed to notice he'd put his weight on the wrong thing.

Half of the pile of junk toppled with a crash and clatter, and Bulge stumbled forward, propelled by his own lack of balance. He staggered then fell flat on his face in the dirt.

Jojo screeched with surprise and leapt to her feet, clutching her breasts. She watched Bulge wallow frantically in the dirt for a moment then rise to his feet. His face was smeared with grime, and his cock hung out of his fly like a deflated sausage. Rage wiped all shock from her features.

"You stinking perverted freak!"

She turned, dashed toward the metal building, and disappeared through the door, leaving Bulge standing there, looking sheepish. He disappointedly stuffed his cock into his pants then began brushing desultorily at the dirt on his clothes.

Suddenly, Jojo burst through the door, waving a huge chrome-plated .44 Magnum that belonged to T-Bone. Bulge looked up, dumbfounded.

"I'll kill you, you fucking freak!"

The sharpness of her tongue frightened him almost as much as the gun. Almost. Then she ripped off several shots. The pistol was too heavy for her, even using two hands. All the shots went wild, but Bulge was too panicked to notice or care. With the crash of the heavy handgun reverberating in the air, he scurried toward the Buick and ducked around it just as a slug creased the car's roof.

In a second, he was secure behind a wall of junk, and a moment later, he disappeared into the interior of the compound. Behind him, more shots whined through the ragged corridors as Jojo emptied the gun. The ammo may have run out, but her enraged shrieks were endless, and her volleys of curses drove him deeper into the maze of wasted metal.

Poor Bulge, he thought as he sped away as fast as his limping gate could carry him. No toys for poor Bulge.

Phyllis heard the shots and angry yells dimly from where she was in the junkyard maze. She tried to shift position, but it seemed that no matter which way she turned, she was uncomfortable. To say the least. Mallet, the damn bastard, had kept her chained to the inside of this car for so many weeks—or was it months? She'd lost count.

But Phyllis was not without resources. Her strength had helped her husband become a successful businessman, and she'd been an active member of her community. As the junkyard days slipped without reckoning into eternity, her mind and spirit came back from the oblivion of her family's death. She still thought often of them— her husband gunned down and her son either killed or left for the desert to devour—but more often now, her mind gravitated to two paramount considerations: survival and escape.

Unfortunately, there seemed to be no escape from the peril, misery, and horror of her imprisonment. Mallet kept her chained twenty-four hours a day. When she wasn't shackled to the inside of the Cadillac, this filthy hovel Mallet called home, she was chained to the even filthier Mallet; filthier because the car was merely dirty, not brutally degraded and barbarous.

If escape seemed at best a dim and distant hope, survival appeared impossible. She found she was having to fight for her spirit as well as for her body. Mallet fed her enough to sustain her, but only enough. He saw to it that her body would survive, at least until he tired of it. The real problems were his dull viciousness and his disgusting needs and desires. Those sapped her spirit as much as hunger, which the all-too-meager scraps of his own meals that he fed her did so little to assuage.

She looked down at her body with a sort of detached horror. She was naked. That was a recent rule of Mallet's degradation. Not only did he allow her no clothes, he gave her no blanket. That didn't matter during the baking days inside the car, and in truth, she was almost grateful for her lack of clothing during the daylight hours. She kept the car doors open to allow what little breeze that filtered through the junkyard maze to waft through the interior.

But nights were a different matter. Then, even with the car doors shut and the windows rolled up, the chill desert darkness bit into her flesh and kept her teeth chattering. Worse, when Mallet's evening depredations on her body were accomplished and he'd passed out, she was compelled to huddle close to him to eke what little heat she could from his rancid bulk.

Her skin was filthy. Mallet permitted her only enough water to barely satisfy her thirst for the day, never enough to bathe. Her hair was matted and dank with grimy sweat and dirt. Dozens of bruises mottled her flesh with a patina ranging from vivid purple to pallid green, depending on how recently he'd inflicted them. She eyed the chromium ball peen hammer lying on the floorboards. How he loved that hammer. How he loved with that hammer. How he hated….

Bitter scorn tore through her parched throat and past cracked lips in a sudden gale of hysterical laughter. Mallet had to use that hammer, for his real tool was totally inadequate for any job. Then the laughter was gone, torn and oppressed by the blasting desert air, eviscerated by her weakness. She leaned back on the seat as comfortably as possible, staring at the high, thin clouds, envying their freedom.

Her outburst frightened her. Was she so close to madness now, when she'd only just made peace with her past? She didn't want to think so, but with the doors to the future as irrevocably sealed as the metal links around her wrist, what had she to look forward to but madness and death? And the awful thing was that death no longer seemed so bad. Madness, though, that was different. She already felt so debased by her captors that the mere thought of the self-humiliation of derangement made her stomach churn.

But here she was, chained in this foul place, playing the part of a self-lubricating sex doll. She closed her eyes and tried to visualize a nicer place to be in, nicer people to be with. But such dreams were difficult, with neither past nor future. Humanity seemed an eternity away and impossible to reach. Perhaps an endlessly tranquil place in nature, like a small, quiet valley complete with a trickling steam and dappled light falling....

When Bulge heard the shrill, cackling laughter coming from the interior of the junkyard, his ears pricked up. Of course. Mallet's woman. She was older than Jojo but still real good looking. And accessible. He could do more than just watch her. He could touch and play, and there would be no guns or threat of retribution from T-Bone.

Bulge knew the junkyard as well as any of them, which wasn't perfectly. But he knew where Mallet's car was. He was there in minutes. She was lying back on the seat, eyes closed and breathing so softly that he could barely detect the rise and fall of her breasts. Suddenly apprehensive that she might be dead, he reached out to her.

The tentative touch at her ankle shocked Phyllis back to the reality of the car and the handcuffs holding her to its interior. She jerked her foot away, cried out in surprise, and saw Bulge, with his gooney, crooked-toothed grin, in the open doorway of the car. The cry became a groan as she saw the leer on his lips and the glitter of lust in his eyes. It was bad enough to endure Mallet's abuse. There was no telling what Bulge would want of her.

Bulge licked his lips. She would be his. Then he glanced around anxiously. There was no one to stop him. He could take her then kill her and dispose of the body. Mallet would be none the wiser. He'd just think she'd escaped. Bulge looked again at the woman as she cowered away from him. He'd never killed anyone. The road pirates did all the time, but Bulge wasn't sure he really wanted to or could. But her naked helplessness aroused him beyond control. He'd never had a real woman, either, and this was likely to be his only chance.

He dropped his pants to free his erection, though ludicrously, his tool belt remained strapped around his waist. She'll be easy, he thought, chained like she was. He kicked his pants away and crawled through the open door.

Phyllis tugged desperately but without hope at the handcuffs. There was no release, as she knew, for she'd tried a thousand times.

She stared at Bulge as he crept closer. His glowing eyes, the tongue-licked leer, and the drool clinging to the sparse hairs on his unshaven chin were almost as horrible as the knowledge that she probably wouldn't survive his visitation. One more creep, and he was within reach. His eyes dropped to ogle the juncture of her thighs, and he reached a greedy hand toward her.

Phyllis was lying on her back, arm pulled to the full extension her cuffed wrist allowed. When Bulge's limpid hand had almost touched her, she did the only thing her fear-crazed thoughts brought to mind —she stomped him hard in the face with her right heel.

The reaction was like magic. With an incongruous, high-pitched squeal, Bulge threw his arms wide and flew backwards out of the car. He landed on his back in the dirt and lay there stunned for a moment as blood bubbled from his nose. Then he scrabbled to his feet, anger cinching his eyes into tight slits. He wiped at the blood leaking from his fractured face and scuttled out of sight around the car.

Inside, Phyllis slammed the doors then cast around desperately for something to defend herself with. Her eyes fell on the chrome ball peen hammer lying on the floorboards. The torture tool of one predator would be the defensive weapon against another. She reached for it but couldn't get close because of the handcuffs.

Suddenly, the window behind her shattered. Bulge's arm snaked in, and he grabbed a fistful of her hair. Like an animal, she whirled and clamped her teeth deep into his arm. With a yowl, Bulge let go and jerked back.

Phyllis sat up and looked through the broken window at Bulge, whimpering and clutching his masticated arm with one hand and his ruined nose with the other.

"Bulge."

Bulge looked at her, expression a mixture of anger and desire. She rattled the cuffs.

"Let me out of these, Bulge."

Bulge's expression took on the new dimension of fear. He shook his head violently. He didn't dare free her. She was too strong. He touched his nose and winced. She'd kicked him. Bit him.

"Let me out."

She smiled, and though no woman had ever smiled like that at Bulge before, he shook his head again. She tried a more tempting tone.

"Please, Bulge. You be nice to me, and I'll be nice to you. I'll make you feel good. I can't do that chained up like this." She rattled the handcuffs.

Bulge glanced around guiltily. He was going to kill her anyway, and let Mallet think she'd escaped. He could still do that. Nervously, he approached the car.

"Don't be afraid. No one's here, and I won't tell."

No, Bulge thought. You won't tell. He tried an experimental grin, and found his lust intact despite the pain in his face and arm. She was agreeing to let him have her, and she seemed to want to participate. He nodded cautiously then fumbled at his tool belt. In a moment, he had a cordless circular saw in hand, and he leaned in through the window. Another few moments and the handcuff around her wrist fell in two. He dropped the saw and jerked open the car door. Her enticing smile sent blood-pounding delirium slamming through his head, and his cock stood up massively. She wanted him!

Phyllis kept the smile plastered on her face and tried not to cower back on the seat as Bulge crawled in the door toward her. He was more horrible than ever with his blood-smeared face gleaming at the prospect of a willing victim and a penis so huge it looked like it would split her in two.

"I'll be nice to you, Bulge," she managed to get out without throwing up. "Just as nice as I can be."

Her hand felt on the floor for the chrome hammer. Bulge crawled on top of her, groping at her body and dragging his engorged erection into place. Her hand closed on the handle of the hammer.

"Bulge."

He drew back at her commanding tone and looked at her, and she whipped the hammer up and cracked him right between the eyes.

"That feel good?" she snarled.

Bulge moaned and rolled off her onto the floorboards where he writhed and groped with limp fingers at his head. He tried to get up, and she rose over him.

"This is just as nice as I can be to you, Bulge."

She raised the hammer and hit him on the head again, this time on the crown. Bulge slumped to the floor like a sack of concrete and lay still. A huge fart blatted from his relaxed bowels.

Still gripping the hammer, Phyllis scrambled out of the car and disappeared into the junkyard wasteland.

Nineteen

ALEX TOOK A CAREFUL, MEASURED step directly to his left, turned his waist in the same direction and, with that motion leading the rest of his body, slowly swept his left hand across the space in front of him. Gradually, as the hand moved across, he turned the palm to face outward. The movement ended and immediately melted as his waist continued to turn and his right arm swept across his torso, forearm held vertical. His left hand arced in to touch the inside of the right wrist, he stepped forward with his right foot, and he shifted his weight to his right leg. His right arm pivoted around the contact point with the left palm until the forearm was horizontal. The contact broke as the back of the right wrist jutted forward then upward, causing the right hand to wave overhead in a graceful arc, ending with the palm out. At the same time, his left hand dropped in front of his groin, palm parallel to the ground.

His bare chest showed a puckered, crimson scar torn across his left pectoral, but it didn't matter much, for he was healed and nearly back in shape.

In the background sounded a metallic clunking. He was aware of it but didn't let its counterpoint disturb his concentration on internal rhythms as he slid gradually and easily into the next movement. The noise came from the side yard where the kid, coached by the desert rat, was practicing with his slingshot. The boy had gotten damn good with it. The old man tossed a tin can into the air, and the kid quickly slipped a pebble into the leather pouch, drew back on the thick rubber bands, and let fly. The pebble whanged into the can, jolting it before it fell to the ground.

"You could hunt birds with that thing," the old man said, patting the boy on the shoulder. Heath grinned as the desert rat made ready to toss another can.

An impatient horn blared from the front of the trading post, but Alex let the sound go through him. The desert rat and the kid went on with their game, the clang of pebble against can the only sound in the air now.

A muffled crash came from inside the trading post.

Alex was the first one in the back door, the desert rat and the kid right behind him. But he pressed them back when he saw the three men inside. One of them was holding Molly and had a knife at her throat while a second waved a pistol in her face and a third rifled the cash register. Through the front windows, Alex could see a fourth standing by a ratty brown conversion van.

"Recognize them?" Alex whispered and the desert rat and kid both nodded.

"The same four from the Pleasant Haven," the old man said, shaking his head. "Looks like their glorious leader found himself another pistol."

"Wait here," Alex said. "Don't spook them."

He went out through the back door.

Inside the trading post, the thug who'd been rifling the cash register held up a meager sheaf of bills.

"That's it?" the leader asked.

"That's it, Jerry."

"The fuck it is," Jerry said, turning on Molly. "Come on, bitch. There's more than this. Where is it?"

"Want me to cut her?" asked the one holding her, a little too excitedly for her taste. He was pressing a half-hard boner against her buttocks.

"If she don't tell me where the cash is," Jerry said, "we're all gonna cut her." He jammed the barrel of his gun painfully under her jaw, pressed himself against her, and grinned lewdly. "We're gonna cut her more ways than one."

Suddenly the van's horn began a steady blast.

"What the fuck's that idiot doing?" Jerry snarled, jerking around and staring through the windows.

"Maybe someone's coming," said the one holding the bills.

"Get out there, and tell him to shut the fuck up," Jerry ordered.

His crony started around the corner, but Jerry grabbed his arm. "Gimme that shit," he said, snatching the money. The other let go of the bills and went to the door, but he stopped on the threshold.

"You better come see this, Jerry."

The other two joined him, dragging Molly along. Out in the van, the one who'd been on guard was slumped over the wheel, head pressing the horn.

146

"What the fuck?" Jerry said, and he stalked outside, down the steps, and over to the van, where he jerked open the door. The man inside slid off the seat and thudded onto the asphalt, unconscious.

"What the fuck?" Jerry said again.

"Pretty limited vocabulary," said a voice. "Maybe you should have stayed in school."

Jerry whirled and tried to shoot Alex, but the gun was no longer in his hand.

"You!" He jumped at Alex, and his buddies followed, but the three of them were outclassed. Alex quickly put two of them out of commission, but toyed with Jerry, letting the jerk do all the work. Off to the side, one of the other two regained consciousness and began groping for the Jerry's gun, which Alex had tossed beneath the van. He'd just dragged it out when an explosion ripped the air and the tableau froze.

Everyone looked up to see Molly holding a pump shotgun pointed right at the thug with the gun.

"Shoot her, you fuck!" Jerry screamed at his comrade.

"Go on," Molly said, voice deadly serious and as unwavering as the barrel of the shotgun. "Shoot me."

The thug, seeing something he didn't like gleaming in her eyes, dropped the pistol to the pavement.

Alex stared at Molly, as surprised as the thug at the look in her eyes. It was a look he'd seen more often than he cared to remember, a look that had filled his own eyes on occasion.

Jerry, taking advantage of Alex's momentary inattention, tried to stab him, but Alex, with a few swift moves, laid him out next to the van.

At that moment, the desert rat and Heath came racing out of the trading post. Molly scornfully cut her eyes at her father.

"As usual," she said, "you're not around when someone needs you."

Cradling the shotgun, she went back inside, leaving the old man crestfallen.

The cops who showed up half an hour later to take the thugs into custody included the FBI man, Mitchell, and the state cop, Captain Reed.

"These aren't the ones who shot you?" Mitchell asked Alex.

Alex shook his head.

"These are kids playing with dangerous toys. The one's who attacked me are professionals. Do you have any new leads?"

"Nothing," Reed admitted.

"Are you going to be staying here long?" Mitchell asked.

"I'm not sure," Alex told him. "Is there a problem if I leave?"

"Only if you aren't around to ID the suspects when we catch them."

"If you catch them."

"We'll get them," Reed assured Alex. "It's just a matter of time."

"I hope it's sooner than later," Alex said. "If I leave, I'll let you know where I am. I'll be happy to come back and do whatever is necessary."

"I'm not sure I like the way you say that." Mitchell's eyes narrowed appraisingly.

Alex shrugged.

"If the FBI and the state cops from eight states can't track these people down, what could I do?" he asked.

"I did a little checking up on you," the agent said. "I know what you can do. I'm just telling you: Don't. Go back to work and let the law handle this."

"I've got no problem with that," Alex replied.

"I hope not," Mitchell said.

As the cops drove off with the prisoners, Alex went over to the desert rat, who was sitting with the boy on the front steps.

"Why don't you tell me about it," Alex suggested to the old man. "This thing that's between you and Molly."

"She can tell you better than I."

"She won't say anything. Says its none of my business."

"She's probably got something there," the old man said, but his voice held no conviction.

"So it's none of my business," Alex said. "So what? Talk."

"She blames me for her mother's death."

"What happened?"

"It was about five years ago. I was chief medical officer at one of the big hospitals in Albuquerque. I guess I was pretty preoccupied with my work. Molly had just finished her master's in anthropology, and as a present, Molly's mother, Natalie, and I were going to take her on a trip to the Greek isles on one of those cruise ships. At the last minute, we had an outbreak of hantavirus—you know, they call it Four Corners' disease. The really big viral diseases are usually named after the area in which they're discovered, but the people in the Four Corners area didn't want the stigma, so its official name is hantavirus.

"It was a minor outbreak, really—only six cases, and only two of them wound up in our facility. I didn't really have to stay, but I did anyway, rationalizing that we needed to maintain a full staff in the event of a larger outbreak, so I canceled the cruise. Natalie and Molly were disappointed, but they went on without me. The truth is, I could have gone with them, but I wanted the accolade of overseeing a successful outcome. Call it professional greed. Actually, only one of the cases died, and that one wasn't at my hospital, and the crisis peaked just a few days after Natalie and Molly flew out of Albuquerque. The cruise was only in its third day, and I could have joined them, but I decided I'd already missed too much, so I stayed on at the hospital. I thought it would be okay. I thought...well, I didn't think the ship would be hijacked by pirates looking for ransom."

As the old man talked, Alex felt the bottom of his gut open into a pit that left him empty of everything but his personal demons. What imponderable twist of the universe had dropped him here, with these people, at this time? He'd known they were all wounded, and now it seemed that most of them were wounded by the same weapon.

"The M.S. *Markham*?"

"You know about it?" the desert rat asked. "Of course, it was in all the news." He hung his head. "Natalie was killed during the commando raid to free the hostages. Molly saw it happen." He paused, biting his lip to gain control of his emotions. "She's blamed me ever since."

"What could you have done if you'd been there?"

"Died in her place."

"That's Molly's bitterness talking. There's no way to know what might have been," Alex said. "The dynamics of battle can change with the addition or subtraction of the slightest detail." His voice sounded so calm, so rational. So distant to his own ears.

"Easy enough for you or me to say," the desert rat said. "But we weren't there, and Molly was. She killed the man who killed Natalie."

Now Alex understood what it was about Molly that seemed familiar. Paint her face with blood and fear, and she was the young woman whose mother had been murdered in front of her and Alex's eyes.

"How?" he asked, anyway, just to be sure.

"Stabbed him in the inner thigh with a paring knife as he was about to shoot one of the commandos, then she got up and stabbed him in the neck, and when he dropped his gun, she shot him with it."

"I see."

"Do you?" the old man asked, eyes narrowed and staring into Alex's own. "Maybe you do," he said after a moment. "I've seen you fight, and you don't get that good without real-life experience."

"It's worse than that," Alex said, turning away. "Much worse."

TWENTY

"OVER THERE," FLIX MOTIONED WITH his free left hand. "Lean on the motorcycle."

"Like this?" Yvonne asked as she stood by the machine. She put her right foot up onto the seat, and her black leather miniskirt rode up, exposing a considerable length of tanned thigh. Her left hand perched on her left hip, while from her right dangled her chromium .357.

"Great!" Flix praised as he focused on her. "Give me some movement, some drama."

With a repulsive attempt at a sultry smile, Yvonne unbuttoned her leather vest and let her breasts dangle free. Making a moue, she ran the muzzle of her pistol around one aureole, and the nipple hardened to attention.

Yvonne's daddy always said he appreciated having a full-blooded Chiricahua woman like Yvonne's mother. A real warrior woman, he always said. "Get a good woman who'll watch your back, add love, and you've got the best heist partner you can find," he told Yvonne.

But one good woman fell at his side or deserted him right after another. Yvonne's own mother had to've been the one to die out of them all. Couldn't she have been like Martha, who covered for the old man and pulled an eight-to-ten for her efforts? At least the time eventually would be done, and it was better than the alternative. Or like Cathy, who pushed needles into a vein almost as often as she let strange, grimy men stick their cocks inside her so she could pay for the needles.

No, Yvonne believed in watching out for her own ass. In that, the old man had been wrong, and Yvonne assumed his adherence to the love part was equally misguided. Or at least a weakness. Every time one little wifey went down the tubes, she took a piece of Daddy's heart and soul with her, until Cathy, like any determined addict, drained what was left along with his cash and car and even his house.

Daddy died of cardiac arrest during an uproar with Cathy three weeks before Yvonne turned seventeen, and Yvonne took what she could and hit the streets.

Her stint as a hooker didn't last too long. Cathy got her the job, but sweating, stinky men drooling over her tits and pounding their cocks into her wasn't her idea of work. Or fun. But beating the crap out of one dickhead asshole who wanted to play rough—now, that turned out to be fun. Inside of two minutes, she had the asshole bleeding on the floor and whimpering for forgiveness. She kicked him in the head and took his wallet and car keys instead.

Later, in her dingy room, replaying the scene—the white heat that had washed through her, the feeling of his flesh and bones giving beneath her rage, and the pleading cry that emerged from his broken mouth—she felt more than a twinge of satisfaction, and a lot of it came from below the belt.

And damn, was it good—hotter and harder than any cock and so real she could feel it embed itself deep inside her and take up residence.

The incident finished her hooking career—and any other career in Sioux Falls, for that matter—so she split. Wasn't hard; she was free.

Free.

The word had never meant anything to her. It was just a word, short and simple to look at, though oh so difficult to understand. But as she drove the john's car past the city limits and looked at the highway stretched ahead of her, the blatant reality shocked through her. With nothing left at home to hold on to, she could go anywhere. She had the car and not much else, so she headed, like a moth, west. And went that direction as far as the road could take her.

Frisco didn't suit her, and she was smart enough to stay out of LA. She didn't want a pretend life, anyway. So she worked her way down to San Diego. Her father had once said there was a navy base there, and where there was a navy base, there were horny young men. For her, that meant meat on the table.

Within six months, Yvonne had a rock-n-roll operation going and was working half the city. Pick up some dork tourist or sailor in a bar, take him to a motel, conk him on the head, relieve him of his cash, and make a beeline for another bar. The racket was working fine, too, with her pulling in upwards of a couple of grand each week, but it all came to an abrupt end. She hadn't been busted by the cops, who considered muggings of johns just rewards and business as usual, not headline grabbers like smuggling or drugs. Hell, the cops wouldn't have been as bad. What happened to her was Big Bill McKenzie.

Big Bill owned about half the part of the city that wasn't visible to daily commerce, and he didn't like some punk broad picking around the edges of his city and not paying her dues. He sent some of his boys to track her down, and they finally found her. She hurt a couple of them, but not more than they hurt her. It had all been very professional, though, and Big Bill didn't tolerate sexual torture, so she hadn't been raped. And when she'd been dropped to the floor in front of Big Bill, bleeding, exhausted, and half-blind from an eye already swollen shut, he smiled at her and asked if she was willing to give in. She spat bloody mucous on his brown Italian leather shoes, and he took out a gun—a chrome .357, though she didn't know Smith & Wesson from cooking oil at the time, and put it to her head. She closed her eyes, and suddenly the world went out.

When she woke up hours later in a bed in a small, clean, simply furnished room, at first she thought she was dead. Then her bruises and a sore lump on her head told her she was all too alive. But she was dead, too. At least the old her was dead.

She was in Big Bill's house, and after he knew she was awake, he came to see her and lay down the law.

First off was her name. What was it? "No, no, not Janie Watchamacallit," he said matter-of-factly. "I killed that chick last night. Who are you?"

"Yvonne," she said after a moment, thinking of one of Daddy's girlfriends she'd liked best.

"Okay, Yvonne," Big Bill said. "You're a tough woman, and I appreciate that, and I admire the way you didn't give in to me. But I'm tougher than you'll ever be, and smarter. In fact, I'm fucking Zeus ripping children from my brain, and I got bastards all over the place to prove it. And you, tough little Yvonne—who the hell are you?"

She didn't know who Zeus was, but she knew that something was happening here that was beyond violence, so she decided not to kick him in the balls. She probably wouldn't have succeeded, anyhow.

"I don't know."

"That's right. But I do, and I'm going to tell you right now who you are and who I am."

He drew out his pistol—the same .357 he'd used to crack her on the head the night before—and she cringed inside though she didn't allow fear to show on her face or in her eyes. But instead of hitting her with it or pointing it at her, he tossed it onto the bed beside her hand.

"This is who you are, Yvonne, and to know me, you just have to know three things. Number one: I'm boss. Number two: I'm boss. And number three?"

"You're boss."

"Hang out, Yvonne. Heal. Come down to dinner when you're ready." He turned his back and left the room. The gun was loaded, and she could have shot him dead on the spot, but she didn't. It wasn't because he was the boss, though she never forgot that fact. It was because he'd treated her with respect. Like a person with a purpose instead of a young tramp to use and discard.

She worked for McKenzie for two years and proved her salt as well as any of the men he had around. But then a rival mobster blew up Big Bill in his car and went gunning for his loyal henchmen—and henchwoman—and that was the end of the game. Yvonne split as quickly as she could. About three months later, she ran into Chains, who'd been loosely associated with Big Bill on a few drug scores, and Chains introduced her to T-Bone.

And so, here she was, living free and doing what she liked and getting off regularly.

Hell, she even had her own video fan club!

"Great," Flix said again, very quietly, as he tightened the focus on her nipple. A drop of sweat dribbled into the eye glued to the viewfinder. He hastily wiped away the sting, pressed the zoom button to pull back for a nice profile of the whole breast, then stopped as her full body came into view.

"Action," Flix moaned. "Give me action!"

Yvonne grinned and trailed the gun muzzle up the inside her bared right thigh, hiking the edge of the skirt even higher, exposing darker pleasures. Flix felt himself stiffen but kept his attention on the eyepiece.

Chains chose that moment to get behind the motorcycle and Yvonne and ham it up for the camera. He reached toward Yvonne, leering and making squeezing motions with his hands.

"Hey," Flix protested just as Yvonne turned on Chains, anger flaring.

"Get the fuck outta my picture!" She swiped at him, but he danced out of the way.

"It's my bike, bitch," he shot back.

Yvonne struck out and missed again then started around the motorcycle after Chains. Flix stepped to the side to follow the action, and the metal building came into sight in the viewfinder. The door was opening, and T-Bone emerged, followed by Rat. The big man strode purposefully toward his Lincoln, while Rat waved at Flix.

"Scouting party, Flix. Let's go."

Without looking back to see the outcome of the altercation between Yvonne and Chains, Flix hurried over to T-Bone's sedan. T-Bone cranked the engine, barely waiting for Flix and Rat to get settled inside before pulling off. Slick opened the gate, and the sedan roared through in a cloud of dust.

Twenty minutes later, the sedan, with a squeal of tires, spun onto the asphalt of the two-lane highway and sped off through the desert heat.

At the wheel, T-Bone exhibited effortless control of the big car just as his easy, arrogant power held sway over his band of ruffians. Flix, in the seat next to him, shot video of the passing scenery, while in the back, Rat poured over papers and maps. Flix lowered the camera and turned to his boss.

"Where we going, T-Bone?"

"Yuma."

Flix's brow wrinkled for a moment, then he brightened.

"Ain't there a prison there?"

"Shut up, Flix," T-Bone said, and Flix shut up. But he could tell by T-Bone's easy tone that the pirate leader wasn't mad or nothin', just didn't want Flix to disrupt his thinking. So Flix shut up and kept on shooting.

It was what he lived for. He'd started as a kid, though his parents had been too poor to buy him a video camera. Or buy themselves one, for that matter, even if they'd given enough of a shit about their kids to video their parties and graduations and whatnot. What parties and graduations, anyway? Hadn't been many of those among his six brothers and sisters.

Actually, he hadn't intended to shoot video—he'd just wanted to steal Jimmy Reardon's dad's camera. He hated Jimmy, but he'd hated the camera more. It represented all those events that were non-events in Flix's life, and worse, it was capturing them for all time. Jimmy fucking Reardon's own kids would be able to watch them.

So Flix scoped out the Reardon place, and one auspicious weekend night, he broke in, found the camera, and took it away. He would have swiped all the tapes of Jimmy, too, if he thought he had the time. Tape was what video used back then. But Flix wasn't much of a criminal, and he was too scared to hang around trying to figure out which tapes he ought to take, so he just hurried off with the camera.

At first he simply intended to dump it off the bridge into the river, but instead, just before he tossed it, he opened the case to look inside. The camera's black plastic and matte-finish metal looked mysterious in the greenish glow of the streetlight, but there was something about it that seemed accessible in a way that the mysteries of the Reardon household's stability would never be. So instead of throwing it into the water, he took it home.

He had a hell of a time keeping it hidden from his family, but he managed. They would have just sold it, and it was just too precious to convert to mere money that would only go for beer and coke. He began to play with it, and before long, he was shooting just about everything he could. And in the process, he discovered something about himself. His experience in school was shit, and he could barely read, but he'd seen a hell of a lot of TV and movies, and he realized that he knew image in a way he'd never know words. And the more he shot on his own, the more he understood what he saw on TV and the silver screen. By the end of the year, he could critique camera work, and he learned by dissecting the best of what he saw.

When he turned eighteen and his parents tossed him out on his ear without a second glance, he was, he thought, a pretty damn good cameraman. And he might have been, but that didn't mean any of the local TV stations were going to give an illiterate highschool dropout a job toting one of their expensive Betacams. None of them would even let him in the door.

Undaunted, Flix continued his one-man crusade to capture the world on video. It was his unrelenting determination that led to his first break. Late one night, he followed a couple of cop cars to the scene of an accident. Flix caught all the mayhem on tape—the teenage boy hanging dead out of the car, half torn in two, and the dead girl crumpled in the front seat. He sold the footage to the producers of the

Death Knell website, bought a police scanner, and began a lucrative, if increasingly boring, career as a regular *Death Knell* contributor.

But unknown to him, all the while he'd been taping murder and mayhem, someone had been watching him. That someone was T-Bone, who'd deliberately caused three of the accidents that Flix later taped and came back by to rubberneck at the scenes of the crimes. T-Bone was in the process of developing his plan, and seeing Flix at crash scenes on several occasions gave him the idea to use video as a visual planning tool. At the same time, he recognized in the young cameraman a perverse nature that suited his own operation, and he quickly recruited Flix into his growing organization.

The producers of the *Death Knell* site missed Flix's contributions, but Flix was happier with T-Bone's pirates. They gave him what no dead body could: Action!

A whap on his arm jerked his eye from the viewfinder. He looked at T-Bone, who pointed. Ahead was a lone hitchhiker, standing on the shoulder of the road. The hitcher—a young man with longish hair and a backpack—was trying to get what meager shade he could from a highway mileage sign. Flix grinned and raised the camera.

"I got him, T-Bone," he said a heartbeat later. "I got him in focus."

The hitcher stuck out his thumb and hopefully raised a hand-lettered cardboard sign that read, "LA or Bust."

Flix leaned out of the window, shooting video of the hitchhiker. The hitcher, realizing the sedan wasn't going to stop to give him a ride, started to lower his thumb, and just at that moment, T-Bone expertly twitched the steering wheel to the right, and the Lincoln swerved toward him.

The young man's eyes bugged, and he ludicrously thrust the sign out in front of himself with both hands as if the flimsy cardboard could shield him from the heavy automobile. The car struck him a glancing blow, and his body slammed to the hard ground just off the road shoulder. Rebounding with kinetic energy, it hurtled off the ground in a cartwheel that carried it through the air and into the weeds and scrub fifty feet from the blacktop. A squeal of glee wheezed from Flix as he panned after the whirling body until it thudded out of sight.

"Action!" he cried. "Action!" Still chortling, he turned to T-Bone. "Great shot, T-Bone!"

"Shut up, Flix," T-Bone said, but despite his words, the pirate leader looked pleased. He popped a peppermint into his mouth, leaned back, and drove on with one thick hand draped over the wheel.

TWENTY-ONE

ALEX SAT ON ONE OF the chairs in the backyard, watching the shadows creep across the face of the mesa behind Little Paradise. He knew he should be practicing tai chi or doing something, but the welter in his mind wouldn't be still. Nor would the shadows that had been creeping through it since he'd learned that Molly and her mother had been aboard the *Markham*. Worse, that he could personally place them in those final terrible moments in the ballroom.

Why the hell, after all these years of burying the horror, was it reemerging now to spoil the best thing that had happened in maybe his whole life? Twenty-four hours ago, his course, though uncharted, was clear. Today, he was adrift on murky, beclouded seas.

His thoughts, if the bleak state of his mind could be called thought, were interrupted as Molly emerged from the back door. She came slowly down the steps and stood in front of him, but he didn't look up at her. He didn't dare.

"I wanted to thank you," she said after a moment, misreading his mood. "I was mad at Dad but not at you. You saved my ass. All of our asses."

"Don't mention it," Alex managed to say, still not looking at her. "That's what friends are for."

"For a long time, I wasn't so sure you were a friend. You ought to see some of the strays Dad brings in."

"And now I am?"

"You know you are. And more."

At last he let his eyes meet hers. "Sit down."

She caught his pensive mood, and a puzzled expression crossed her face as she settled beside him.

"You ever wonder why he does that?" Alex went on. "Brings in strays?"

"He's an old fool." Bitterness and disappointment tinged her voice.

"You know better than that. It's atonement."

"He told you about the *Markham*, did he?" She tried to sound sarcastic, but the edge was lost in the wound of her sorrow.

Alex didn't respond, but she could tell he knew.

"Well," she said, bitterness back in force. "It doesn't matter. What the hell does he know? He wasn't there."

"That's the point, isn't it?"

"I don't want to talk about it," Molly bridled. She rose abruptly.

"Maybe it's easier not to," Alex said quietly. "Maybe not."

"You think you know a hell of a lot more about it than he does? Why? Because you killed someone? So? I killed someone, too."

Suddenly, she burst into tears. Spinning on her heels, she hurried up the steps, the back door banging behind her.

Alex sat there for long, heavy moments, desires wrestling with conscience, but in the end, he had to face her squarely and honestly. If he held back now, the ugly truth and the uglier lie, even if unknown to her, would always be between them.

He found her sitting on her stool behind the counter, still crying, but trying to control her tears. Alex got a couple of sodas from the machine and came over to the counter and offered her one.

"On the house," he said, and was immediately sorry as she gave a wistful smile. She took the can and lifted it to her lips.

"You don't have to tell me," he said.

She shrugged as she lowered the can and used the other hand to wipe away the last of her tears.

"You told me about yourself. It's only fair." She paused, collecting herself, then went on. "The hijackers had about half of us in the ballroom. When they realized the ship had been boarded by commandos, they started firing. Somehow, they missed me, but Mom was hit right away. She wasn't dead, and I tried to pull her to safety. She'd be alive today if I'd made it, but one of the pirates was standing nearby, firing out into the middle of the room, and he saw us. He killed her right there in front of me, and he would have killed me, too, but he saw one of the commandos coming, and when he looked up, I stabbed him in the leg with a knife I found behind the bar. Then I stabbed him in the neck, got his gun, and killed him. I shot until the gun wouldn't shoot any more."

Alex looked on solemnly as she hung her head.

"He killed your mother," he said at last.

"Yes, but it was the panic when the commandos came aboard that started all the shooting. They never should have attacked the ship. We learned later that they'd been in port twelve hours earlier, and maybe if they'd attacked then it might have been okay. But they hesitated, and they came aboard at exactly the wrong time, when tensions were worst."

"So you blame the commandos?"

"They should have stayed away and let the negotiators handle things. But they came aboard anyway, and then they bungled it. So, yeah, I blame them as much as anybody."

As she spoke, the bleakness in Alex's heart dove into the pit of his stomach.

"Anyway," she went on, "after Mom died, Dad cashed in his pension and sold the house. I guess he couldn't face living there any more. He moved out here and bought this place. Maybe I shouldn't blame him, but I can't help it. It was just so damn selfish of him to stay here with his precious work and not be there when we needed him."

"What could he have done?"

"I don't know," she admitted.

"I can see why your dad might want to live out here, but what about you? If you resent him so much, why are you here with him?"

"I came hoping to forgive him. I guess it didn't work out that way. I didn't plan to stay long. I just wanted to clear my head and finish the grief. But it's quiet out here, and I just sort of stayed. And you know, the grief is never really finished."

"Or the anger?"

"Maybe not. Anyway, Dad used to run the place, but I seem to be doing that lately. Now all he does is mess around in the desert. He's turned his whole life into some silly game. I guess he's spent so much time here, he's gone native." She laughed briefly. "God knows what he does out there."

"He picks up strays," Alex said, and they laughed together. It felt good and brightened the room, but Alex knew darkness was coming again, and he quickly sobered.

She noticed.

"What's wrong?" she asked.

"I haven't told you about the men I killed."

"I don't care," she said, laying a hand on his. "I just know you don't hate me for killing...."

"I killed seven," he interrupted, not willing to give himself the chance of weaseling out of a confession. "Six were the enemy: four with a gun, one with a knife, and one with my bare hands. The seventh was a civilian woman I shot accidentally."

The grip of her hand on his was warm and slightly trembling.

"I'm sure you had a good reason."

"No," he said, voice flat and far away in his own ears. He stared into her eyes, "You aren't sure." He touched his free hand to the side of her face, looked into her eyes, and said, "I'm an American soldier. I'm an American."

He felt her hand atop his stiffen.

"You." The word was flat and heavy as slate.

She pulled away, as if she'd been touching dead flesh.

"It almost seems like it happened to someone else," he said, lowering his gaze from the cold detachment that suddenly filled her eyes. "We got aboard without anyone noticing, and we killed half a dozen terrorists before we were spotted and the shooting started. We lost some of our own, then. Mike, a buddy I'd known six years, died beside me. Twenty of us went in and only eight came out.

"But we killed back. Toward the end, when everyone was numbed with exhaustion, the sound of gunfire, and the sight of blood, I managed to capture two of the pirates. They weren't big cheeses, just troops like me, but they talked later under interrogation, and that eventually led to identifying the masterminds behind the attack."

"Wow, a big hero," Molly said, her upper lip curling. "They shoulda made you general."

"Yeah, they were going to promote me," Alex said, ignoring her sarcasm. "To captain." He snorted. "It was a bribe. Payment for lying at the inquest. I had to say the raid went down the only way it could have. But it didn't, and I couldn't say it did. You're wrong when you say we were too late, though. We were too early. We should have waited another day or two, let them think we were going to negotiate and give them a chance to get lax. But the election was coming up, and the president wanted to look good for the media by bringing the stalemate to a swift conclusion, so he pushed our leadership to order the attack without giving a damn about the situation.

"So, you're wrong about the timing, but you're right about the whole thing being botched. Even our intelligence was lousy, mostly because it was too early to know the facts accurately. We were told that there were about a dozen pirates, when there were three times that many, and we weren't warned they were so heavily armed. We should have had more men, and we should have waited and paved the way. We could have had divers cut into the hull so we could come at them from beneath, but there just wasn't time. Not with the demands from the top.

"At the inquest, my superiors pressured me to say otherwise, but I couldn't back down. Not and live with myself. I'd watched my dad lie his way through life and almost destroy his family as well as himself, and I wasn't going to do that. So, instead of giving me the promotion, they put me into a dead-end job to force me out. Just as well. I couldn't stay."

"You want some kind of sympathy? Nothing's changed. The dead are still dead—Mom's dead—and the living might as well be."

"I know the past is irrevocable," he said. "I was on the way to visit my father on his deathbed, and I missed him, remember? But if we intend the future to be any less terrible than the past, we have to change it, and that has to start inside each of us. I don't want sympathy. I just want the right thing to happen, and I know that the right thing is never founded on lies." He took his soda can to the recycling bin, dumped it in, then came back to the counter.

"I thought we'd started something between us, and I can see now I was wrong. But I want to tell you something. I let my relationship with my dad fester in my soul for fifteen years, and now he's dead. I'll never have a chance to get straight with him. That'll eat at me for the rest of my life. Don't you make the same mistake."

He pulled out his wallet, extracted a credit card, and laid it on the counter.

"Total my bill through tomorrow. I'll be leaving right away."

The hot desert air seemed unusually stultifying as he left the trading post and went to his teepee. But even the air conditioning inside didn't do much to refresh him, though it made breathing easier. His mind was a confused roil beneath a pall of darkness, and he practiced a few deep breathing exercises to calm himself. Then he propped himself on the bed to plan what he was going to do. Where he was going to go. He could get the desert rat to drive him to Socorro, and from there he could catch a bus to Lubbock. Beth was back in Houston, but his dad wouldn't be leaving, and Alex still owed him that one last visit.

A knock on his door interrupted his thoughts. He called out, "Come in," and it opened. The desert rat and kid were there, silhouetted in brilliant sunshine.

"Molly said to give you this." He handed over Alex's credit card. "She also told me you were on the *Markham*."

"One more dastard."

"In her eyes. She said you're leaving."

"Yeah. Mind driving me to Socorro?"

"What's in Socorro?"

"Time alone."

"What about after?"

"I'm not sure. Beth has already gone back to Houston, but I still need to pay my respects to Dad. I owe him that much."

"And T-Bone?"

"I don't know."

"The desert rat nodded. "Okay," he said. "I'm sorry to see you go, but I can't blame you for leaving. Get your gear together, and me and the kid'll drive you in."

They left, and Alex looked around the spare, odd-shaped room, noting just how little he had to take and how much he had to leave behind.

Twenty-two

Luke Air Force Base stretched 150 miles across the dust and rock east of Yuma, Arizona. The base's drab buildings clustered toward the Yuma end, and most of the rest was arid test range, where high-dollar ordnance regularly blasted the crap out of lizards, snakes, and cacti. The high chain-link fence and perimeter guards could keep out just about anything but the heat. And so, the two guards arming the kiosk at the southeast corner gate had capitulated and beat a hasty retreat to the cool confines of the booth sitting beside one of the base's rear gates.

Hell, they were well out of the city and could see for a mile in either direction along the fence. Anyway, nothing was cooking except any fool who stayed out there. One of them eyed the burger shack that hunkered next to the dilapidated gas station just across the highway from the booth, but he knew better than to even try. Soon as he'd get out, some smart-ass officer'd come by and write him up. He glanced at his watch. Two hours to go. He could wait.

Across the road, T-Bone waited also, though his mind was more purposefully patient than the guard's. He was sitting behind the wheel of his Lincoln, watching the gate and the two bored men in the kiosk. On the seat next to him, Flix kept his camera low as he shot surreptitious footage of the gate, booth, and surrounding area.

Out of the corner of his eye, T-Bone saw Rat hurry from the burger joint carrying a couple of sacks and a cardboard tray holding drinks.

"Yuma," Rat spat as he slid into the back seat, making the word sound nasty. "I hate this place. And to top it off, they got to park their fucking Air Force base right across from the worst eats in the state. This is the third time we've had to eat this shit. It's enough to rot your guts."

"Quit grousing, Rat," T-Bone said, taking the bag. "You haven't got any guts to rot."

Rat didn't let T-Bone's words get under his skin. He'd known T-Bone too long, and besides, he was man enough to admit they were all too true. At least Flix and Slick were more cowardly than he. But Rat had something none of the rest of the pirates had—a calculating mind that jived well with T-Bone's schemes. No, there was something else he had that none of the others could touch, and that was T-Bone's trust. Even Jojo couldn't compete in that area.

He and T-Bone went back to high school in Minneapolis. It had sort of been like the fable of the lion and the mouse. T-Bone hadn't been T-Bone back then but a big punk teenager named Walter. Walter had a burgeoning criminal career that consisted mainly of breaking into houses of the parents of fellow students he knew were on vacation because the kids blabbed proudly at school about going out of town. Nobody suspected Walter of perpetrating the string of holiday-time burglaries, but Rat knew because he'd accidentally seen Walter in action one night.

Rat had been sleeping out in the back yard in a mildewy old army pup tent because his father thought it would toughen him up. Or rather, hadn't been sleeping because every nighttime sound sent something akin to the Tingler creeping up his spine. One noise, though, coming about two in the morning, didn't sound like a monster prowling in the darkness—it was the tinkle of breaking glass. Peeking through the pup tent flaps, Rat saw Walter entering the neighbors' back door. Rat, like Walter, knew the neighbors were in the Smoky Mountains for two weeks, though it hadn't occurred to him that their absence left their house and belongings vulnerable.

Rat could have done the right thing by waking his parents, alerting them to the felony taking place next door. But Rat didn't. It wasn't that he was afraid of Walter, though he was because he tended to be afraid of just about everybody, especially toughs like Walter. Anyway, he knew that if Walter was caught, he'd go to jail without knowing it was Rat who fingered him. No, the reason was at once simpler and more complex than that. Rat was intrigued by Walter's courage and determination—by his sheer audacity in entering a stranger's home and taking what he wanted. It was a courage Rat thought he could never possess but only wonder at in others.

So he kept quiet and lay there on his sleeping bag, peering from the pup tent and keeping an eye on his watch. A little less than an hour later, Walter emerged, toting a couple of bulging pillow cases, and promptly melted into the darkness at the corner of the house. When he was sure Walter was gone, Rat lay back on his sleeping bag, exhausted, and within seconds fell into a deep sleep.

After that, he began to observe Walter more closely, though he rarely saw him until school began again a month later. And though Walter came from a modest home, he always seemed to have what he wanted, including a car.

Before long, Rat could tell when Walter was going to do a heist, though that happened nearly every weekend, so there wasn't much prescience involved. Rat followed Walter almost every time, and watched him work and timed him, marveling at the big teen's growing proficiency. That went on until well into March, which was when Walter caught him.

It came as a complete surprise. Rat, who thought he'd become as silent and unseen as a shadow, suddenly found himself grabbed by his jacket and yanked into a crevasse between two huge bushes.

"What the fuck you following me for, you little rat?" Walter snarled, shaking the smaller boy. Or was it Rat's trembling that shook Walter's arm?

Somehow, Rat convinced Walter that his being there was coincidence, and that if he let him go, he'd help Walter out when Walter needed help.

"Sure," Walter said with a contemptuous shove that sent Rat sprawling. "You help me out some day. In the meantime, beat it. And if I catch you sneaking around behind me again, I'll beat the shit outta you."

And then he was gone. Rat got to his feet and went home. That night. But other nights he kept following Walter. He couldn't help himself, even with the refrain of Walter's threat constantly ringing in his thoughts. But Rat was, in the end, more fascinated than afraid, and that meant his fascination was a powerful thing. Though not powerful enough to negate caution. Rat just made sure he was as invisible as a ghost since he didn't want to become one himself.

About six weeks after Walter caught him, Rat saw Walter get caught himself by a store owner who had a gun and a bad attitude about punks trying to rip him off. He'd forced Walter into a storage shed, bolted the door, and gone to call the cops when Rat heaved a brick through his front plate glass window. While the store owner was distracted, Rat opened the storage shed door and saw Walter standing defiantly at the back of the shed.

On realizing it was Rat, not the store owner, Walter's defiant look was erased by a bright grin. "Well, if it isn't the little rat who's been following me."

"Come on," Rat said urgently. "He'll be back in a minute."

"Sure, Rat," Walter said, and they ran until Rat couldn't run any more, though Walter was barely winded.

When they stopped, Walter said, "I thought I told you not to follow me."

"Yes," Rat gasped, knowing better than to lie. "I couldn't help it."

The big teen looked down on him with a calculating expression, then said, "I guess that's a good thing for me." He slapped Rat on the shoulder. "All right, let's go."

And so they went from high school larceny to small-time burglary, and things had gone just fine, even when Walter had fallen for Gwen and married her. She hadn't been the possessive sort, and she'd taken a real liking to her husband's apprehensive friend. For his part, Rat adored her the way a kid brother adores his older sister.

Then things changed. Walter, wanting to be more than just a small-time operator, had come under the influence of the local mob. That was good for him, but not so good for Rat. Walter tried to get him a position, but Walter's new bosses had just laughed at the idea. Walter did manage to get him some flunky work, and he supposed that was better than nothing, but it sure wasn't the same as the old days.

What hadn't changed was their friendship. Even though they no longer worked as a team, Rat was a regular visitor to Walter and Gwen's home. And when little Andy was born, they'd named Rat his godfather. Rat was happy, and life could have gone on like that forever.

But the mob had different ideas. They sent Walter to Vegas, and Rat was left in the lurch.

"I'll find a place for you," Walter had promised before he left. "Just give me some time."

Rat said a tearful farewell to Gwen and Andy, little knowing it was goodbye for good. For the next year and a half, he had sporadic phone calls from Walter, who said the time was getting close for him to send for Rat. Then suddenly there Walter was, in person, standing at Rat's door, looking like hell but mad deep down inside in a way that made everything else trivial. Did Rat want a job helping fuck the fuckers who'd murdered Gwen and Andy?

Rat had agreed instantly, but even after the shock of the news had lost its edge and he could think about it more rationally, he knew there was nothing else he could do. Or wanted to do. He'd loved Gwen and Andy better than his own family. Walter could rely on him, and he knew Walter knew it too. He could rely on Rat like he did no one else, and Rat wouldn't have it any other way.

Even if he occasionally had to eat shitty cheeseburgers from dives in places like Yuma.

He handed one of the bags of food to T-Bone then opened his own bag and started to dig into it. Hearing the rustling of paper, Flix abruptly swung around, carelessly panning the interior of the car with his camera.

"Hey, Rat...," he began, almost hitting T-Bone with the camera lens. T-Bone slapped the camera down.

"Get that goddamn thing outta my face, fool," the big man growled at the cameraman. Flix flinched and dropped his eyes.

"Sorry, T-Bone. Sorry."

T-Bone ignored him and bit into his hamburger. Flix grabbed the respite to turn off the camera and set it aside. Then he looked at Rat.

"Hey, Rat, You get my Coke and onion rings?"

"Yeah." Rat carelessly tossed a bag to Flix, who greedily tore into it.

Across the road, the two guards felt the rumble of the convoy before they heard it. But they knew the trucks were coming, anyway. The radio in the booth had just announced the fact. A moment before the lead vehicle came into view around a nearby hillock, one of the guards emerged from the refrigerated closet of the kiosk into the blast furnace of the desert. He stepped toward the highway, lightly caressing the machine gun slung from his shoulder, and glanced up and down the road.

The other guard, still in the kiosk, put a hand to the gate controls and watched through the window as the convoy, a Chevy Suburban in the lead, followed by three eighteen-wheelers, and trailed by a second Suburban, rolled toward the gate in a cloud of dust. All the vehicles were tan, unmarked, and unremarkable except for the long whip antennas swaying on the Suburbans' bumpers. Those and the U.S. government license plates.

"Look." Rat pointed through the windshield.

"It's them!" Flix bounced excitedly. "It's them!"

T-Bone shot Flix a contemptuous look. "Shut up and get your camera ready," he commanded, starting the car.

T-Bone waited until the convoy roared through the gate, inundating the guard outside in a tsunami of dust. Then, as the gates rolled shut and the guard returned to the booth, slapping dust from his uniform, T-Bone wheeled the big sedan around the parking lot. He let the three trucks and two escort vehicles accelerate down the highway for half a minute, before pulling out onto the road behind them. As he did, bags of garbage from the meals flew from windows on both sides of the car.

T-Bone drove with cool steadiness in the wake of the convoy. Next to him, Flix shot video of the trucks and the escort vehicles. Behind him, in the back seat, Rat made notes on a pad of paper then pulled out a map and began to check it.

They followed the convoy for several miles, when ahead of them, it turned off the road, onto an interstate entrance ramp.

"They're taking I-8," T-Bone told Rat, who made a note on his pad then further perused the map.

Flick, eye still glued to his eyepiece, spoke out of the side of his mouth. "Where we gonna do it, T-Bone?"

"If they're trying to get to I-40 quick as possible," Rat said, thoughtfully looking over the map, "they'll probably leave I-8 at state highway 85 and take that north to I-10. That'll take them on into Phoenix, where they can pick up I-17, and that'll take them to 40."

"Shit!" said T-Bone, grinding his teeth. "That's interstate almost all the way. No chance." He rubbed his jaw, and sharp stubble rasped under the thick skin of his palm.

"Hey, T-Bone," Rat said, thoughtful look turning to a grin. "You remember that abandoned motel where we hijacked that load of coke last year?"

T-Bone's eyes met his in the rearview mirror. "Yeah, I remember it."

"Isn't that on 85?"

"You just might be right, Rat. Let's check it out."

The big man accelerated the sedan down the road.

A moment later, it began to pass the slower convoy. As it did, Flix draped a jacket over the video camera and let only the exposed muzzle of the lens poke over the window sill. He couldn't see the eyepiece, but he knew he got a hell of a pan of the convoy's entire length. Cool angle, too.

Then the sedan pulled into the lane ahead of the lead Suburban. Flix undraped the camera and leaned over the back seat, shooting through the back windshield. He grinned as he saw the convoy dwindling in the tiny viewfinder image.

"Smile, suckers."

The Tradewinds Motel squatted beside Arizona 85, almost smack dab between the towns of Gila Bend and Buckeye. It had been abandoned a good fifteen years, and that probably had been ten years too late. If the name was incongruous for the desert, the motel was not. The three crumbling buildings were simply constructed, mostly of cement blocks, two-by-fours, and plywood, and arranged in a U-shape around a parking lot that opened onto the road. Wild grasses poked through myriad cracks and potholes in asphalt that had baked and softened beneath too many years of hot desert sun and been torn and gnarled by too much harsh traffic.

The roadside end of the southern wing held the meager restaurant, and the facing end of the northern wing had housed the office. The rest of the three buildings were occupied by boxy, drab little rooms, some still littered with the smashed and dusty remains of generic motel furniture.

The Tradewinds might once have done a fair amount of business when the pace of life and travel had been slower, but life had caught up with it, and the government had built the interstates, and now most travelers just saw the fast, big blue lines on the map and forgot the red and orange lines that marked the smaller roads. It seemed like modern people couldn't bring themselves to steer off the bustle and magnetic rush of the interstates. But the locals hadn't forgotten the older routes, and they were still good roads, and you could make good time on them.

The military tractor-trailer jockeys driving the convoy out of Yuma hadn't forgotten, either, as Rat had predicted.

T-Bone kept the Lincoln just ahead of the convoy, and the pirates watched as the three trucks and two escort vehicles followed them off I-8 onto Arizona 85. The cat was in the bag, then, and the pirates in the Lincoln knew it. T-Bone punched the gas, and the sedan quickly rocketed out of sight of the convoy.

Now the Lincoln was sitting in the parking lot of the Tradewinds Motel, close against the south wing so that it wouldn't be spotted by the convoy drivers when they passed. T-Bone and Rat lounged around the car, drinking sodas they'd bought at a tiny gas station about twenty miles down the road. Rat glanced at his watch then up at T-Bone.

"Any time now, boss."

T-Bone nodded and, without looking, called, "Flix, get over here."

Flix, who'd been shooting footage of the motel layout, hurried over.

"They're coming. Get where I showed you."

"Right, T-Bone." Flix hurried scurried to the corner of the restaurant and poked the snout of his camera around, being careful to remain hidden himself.

Rat, standing inside the restaurant and staring through the broken-out southern windows, perked up.

"Here they come!" he called as he crouched out of sight.

T-Bone, still in front of the building, remained standing, leaning casually on the wall beside the restaurant door, watching the road.

The lead Suburban whooshed past the restaurant. Just as it disappeared beyond the north wing of the motel, the first semi rumbled on by, raising a cloud of dust. Rat risked a glance out the window. The southern road was empty.

"Where are the others?" he wanted to know.

"Straggling," T-Bone said casually. "They've gotten lazy. This run's been candy for them every week. Until now. Next Thursday, we're gonna take their candy away."

"You're right, boss," Rat said. "Here comes number two. Without the others." He ducked, and the second truck rumbled past, with the third truck and the second escort vehicle nowhere in sight.

T-Bone nodded and smiled.

"We got it, Rat. If number two is alone in the middle, we'll cut it out, and the others won't be any the wiser until they get to Phoenix."

"What if number three and the second escort vehicle aren't so far behind?"

T-Bone popped a peppermint into his mouth, slapped Rat on the shoulder, and grinned.

"Hey! The more the merrier! You know how Yvonne likes to party!"

The three pirates laughed.

TWENTY-THREE

THE DESERT RAT HAD LEFT Alex at a pretty decent hotel where the rooms were cool, dark, and quiet and the beds firm. But Alex spent a fitful night. The *Markham* sailed, large and malignant, across his thoughts, his heart felt heavy, and his gut was hollow. At last, he managed to get a few hours' sleep, and if he didn't wake refreshed, at least he wasn't exhausted. After breakfast, he carried his second cup of coffee out to the pool and found a plastic deck chair to settle into. On this weekday morning, there wasn't much activity, and he was alone as he sat there, staring moodily at the water.

After a time of blankness, he noticed that a single large leaf was floating on the surface. Over the course of about ten minutes, the wind or water currents gradually carried it around the edge of the pool. Around and around, always moving but never going anywhere it hadn't already been. Like a boat. Like a cruise liner plying the same ports of call time and again.

God how he wanted that ship to take its final berth. But he suspected that it never would, for the rust and mechanical failure of time would never affect it. In fact, time seemed to bring only a perverse intensification, transforming the *Markham* into a *Flying Dutchman* forever haunting the Sargasso Sea of his mind and never finding rest.

Life sure takes some weird shifts, he thought. He'd fled a screwed-up childhood to the safety of the military, only to find there an even more devastating outcome. And then he'd fled to the road, which had first brought him consolation from that grief and, finally, even love. But now, the disparate conspiracies of his screwed-up childhood and the circumstances of the *Markham* incident had blended in an ugly cocktail that was poison without the surcease of intoxication.

What kind of karma was he playing out, he wondered, that had the power to turn his best efforts to complete waste?

And where could he turn now?

Well, he'd visit his dad's grave first then head down to Houston and spend some time with his sister. The insurance company had paid off on his truck, meaning he could buy a new one. Maybe Manny would live up to his promise to take Alex back, and he could get back to some kind of normalcy.

Back on the road.

The thought gave him pause. The occupation that had once brought him so many rewards now looked like useless preoccupation. Could he ever again take the same pleasure he once had in driving now that T-Bone's pirates had, in one fell and casual swoop, so completely destroyed his equanimity as well as the comfort he felt as miles of pavement spun out beneath his wheels? Driving had once given him some control over a world gone mad; now even the thought of it felt unsafe.

At last, as much because his butt was tired of the plastic chair as to quell the turmoil in his mind, he got up, went to his room, and changed into workout clothes. A few minutes later he was in the hotel gym. Here he felt somewhat better because his body was something over which he had some minor measure of control, and the effort gave him something productive to concentrate on. He spent a good hour at the machines then returned to the poolside and did a set of tai chi, eliciting curious stares from the housekeeping staff as they pushed their carts from room to room.

After the workout, he cooled off with a quick swim, then he went back to his room, called the airport in Albuquerque, and made several other phone calls. Half an hour was all it took him to decide that renting a car and driving to Lubbock would be the most expedient route, and he made a reservation to pick up a rental in the morning.

At loose ends and feeling both restless and emotionally paralyzed, he decided to stay in the room and read and watch TV. He planned to hit the hay early since he hadn't slept well the night before, and he wanted to get an early start.

About an hour later, a knock sounded on the door. Thinking it would be a housekeeper here to straighten up, he padded to the door and opened it.

It was Molly, expression bleak, shoulders tense and angular, hands thrust into the pockets of her jeans.

"Dad told me where you were," she said.

Alex didn't know what to say, so he said, "You want to come in?" If she had more harsh words for his participation in the *Markham* disaster, he just as soon have them said in private, not out where everyone could hear.

She came into the room, but if he expected a lambasting, it wasn't forthcoming.

"Dad said you might be going to Lubbock to visit your father's grave." She looked at the floor. "I thought I might have missed you."

"Tonight's my last night here," he said. "I'm leaving in the morning."

"What then? After Lubbock?"

"I don't know. I might come back out here for a while."

"Are you going after the gang who shot you?"

"Yes," he said after a moment, not seeing any need for subterfuge.

"Because of the *Markham*?"

"Because this is where my life has led me. Because I can, and because it's the right thing to do."

"When you said to settle your bill before you left, I didn't ring it up." He looked at her, an unspoken question in his eyes. "There's only one way to settle your bill with me," she said. "Show me there's something real between us that doesn't lie."

Alex was afraid, but he reached out anyway, brushed her left cheek with his fingertips, and stared deeply into her eyes. In a moment, she was in his arms.

By mid afternoon, they were back at Little Paradise. They didn't say much but just sat together on chairs on the front porch, watching the sparse traffic drift by and the day wane. About five, the desert rat and kid drove up in the desert rat's Jeep Cherokee. As the two came over to the front porch, the old man's only response at seeing Alex back and Molly so close to him was a gruff grunt.

"We've went into town," he said. "Wanted to check on those fellows from the other day. Seems like the law's been looking for them for a couple of other holdups, so they won't be back on the road any time soon."

"Any word on the others?" asked Alex.

"None. No new leads, though it looks like the bunch raided a machine shop in Albuquerque a few days ago. Had the foreman make some special kind of part, some spring-loaded gizmo."

"I'm thinking of trying to find them myself," Alex said.

"You sure you want to do that? These are dangerous people."

"I've seen what they're capable of."

"You were a mercy killing," the old man said. "They've done things that would curdle your blood."

"I can't sit around here all day doing nothing."

The old man eyed Alex and Molly with a mildly amused expression.

"Doesn't look to me like you've been doing nothing."

"I'm going with him, Dad."

"You think you can make up for the past by doing this now? You'll just get killed. And even if you do succeed, there isn't anything that can change the past. The *Markham* still happened."

"Maybe you're right," Alex said. "But I know one thing for sure —these people have to be stopped." He looked at the boy, then back at the desert rat, and said, "I can't bring back the dead, and I can't make up for what's already happened, but maybe I can save the next kid out there from going through what he's had to."

"Okay," the old man said. "Where do we start?"

"I thought I'd go back to the rest stop where you found me," Alex replied.

"What do you expect to find there?"

"Blood."

TWENTY-FOUR

PULLING HIS RAGGED CLOTHES ABOUT himself as if he was a Tibetan lama adjusting his robes, Bulge turned his back to the steady desert breeze and hunkered down atop his own private Everest. This was the highest pile of wrecked cars in the junkyard, and from it, the compound spread out in multicolored shades of auto paint and rust. Sunlight glittered everywhere off broken glass and mashed chrome.

In his hands was the object of this morning's contemplation—a cone-shaped side view mirror, its patina of chrome barely rusting around the edges of the glass. He held the cone in one hand while he caressed it with the other. As he ran a forefinger around the point of the cone, he didn't see the manicured nail, or the chrome, for that matter. He saw a nice, coffee-colored nipple. He heard, instead of the wind moaning through ragged heaps of cars, the breath of desire.

He cupped the metal tit in one hand, but then he could see himself in the mirror, and he didn't like what he saw. The vista of heavy brows and lopsided features was bad enough most days, but today the view was even worse. His nose was a raw, swollen mass, and his forehead sported a large, purple bruise hovering around a nasty lump. The other lump, the one on his scalp, wasn't visible, but it felt the size of an egg and was sore as hell.

He grinned in spite of the pain that lanced through his face. It almost had been worth it. If the woman hadn't produced that hammer, he'd have had her. He stroked convulsively at the chrome surrogate breast in his palm, but his mind was on the jiggle of Mallet's woman's tits and the slash between her thighs. All that almost had been his, and perhaps still would be. He knew she hadn't left the compound. He'd checked the perimeter too thoroughly. Nothing had been in or out for weeks, except for the pirates themselves.

Besides, she'd die out there in the open desert. She must know that. If she stayed in the compound, she'd at least be able to scavenge food, water, and shelter. She *had* to still be here, and if she was, sooner or later he'd find her. It was only a matter of time. The junk-yard was big, but not so big he couldn't thoroughly search it all in a couple of weeks. That is, he reminded himself as he saw a bulky figure move through the corridors of metal below him, if Mallet didn't find her first.

Bulge enfolded the chrome cone in his rags, then flattened him-self as much as possible against the car, hoping that the hammer wielder hadn't seen him.

Mallet was pissed as hell. He stalked along, peering into nooks and crannies in the stacks of junk cars, and at the next junction, he looked both ways, expression a scowling storm of frustration and wrath. A gargling roar suddenly wrenched from his throat, and he slammed his new maul against a junk car, adding to its plethora of dents with a loud bang.

"Shit! Where is that fucking bitch? When I catch her, I'm gonna...."

And that was the whole point, really, for Mallet—that here he could do what he wanted to do. And not only did no one give a shit, most of them enjoyed watching him do whatever it was he did.

Mallet had always been as impulsive as he was large, and he'd been large the day he was born. His mama took him off the tit at three days, claiming he bit her, and two months later, she dumped him along with his old man. The new arrangement lasted until the infant Mallet got hungry again and his whining interfered with the old man's drunken stupor. By nightfall, the old man had taken the boy to his sister. She agreed to baby-sit while the old man went out on the town, and unfortunately for her, he never came back.

She could have turned the boy over to child protective services, but while she harbored no love for Mallet, she did possess a sense of familial duty that kept her working two and sometimes three jobs to support her mother who was slowly and painfully succumbing to liver cancer. The cancerous Mrs. Mallet passed on soon enough, leaving the boy Miss Mallet's sole charge, and she tried her best, she really did.

She raised him as her own, but as soon as the boy began school, nothing seemed to work out for him. He was big and clumsy and dyslexic to boot, and fighting quickly became his favorite occupa-tion. When he was fourteen, he clobbered a schoolmate with a baseball bat, breaking the boy's left humerus, collar bone, and several ribs. Mallet went home, stole everything of value his aunt had handy, rode his bicycle to the bus station, and left the state.

Although he was only fourteen, he was big enough to pass for eighteen, and he managed to find odd jobs as a construction worker and roughneck where the pay wasn't necessarily great but came in cash. Usually these jobs ended in a fight of some sort, and Mallet was usually the one left standing, which was fortunate for him since he usually had to flee the scene. And so passed twenty years of crappy construction jobs that never lasted long enough for Mallet to develop a skill greater than bashing people unconscious. And he never found a way to exploit that since his temperament was too volatile to take orders for very long, and no one could make him do other than he pleased.

Until he met T-Bone.

That happened one cold-as-shit day outside of Farmington, New Mexico. Mallet was between jobs—between states, really, having had to leave Colorado as quickly as possible after cracking the skull of an ironworker, right through his hard hat, forty-eight hours earlier. About mid-afternoon, he'd stopped in at some dive Indian burger joint, and being low on cash, decided to bully the tiny brown old woman behind the counter into filling his belly at no charge. He was just in the midst of looming over her, when a shadow in a booth at the back said, "Is that any way to treat the oppressed underclass?"

Mallet wasn't sure what that meant, but he didn't like the tone. Leaving the old woman, he stalked toward the back to express his wrath and further whet his appetite. Then the shadow rose from the booth, giving Mallet pause since it was fully as tall as he was. But the pause was only momentary. Mallet had destroyed men as big as he was and larger, and as the man from the booth stepped into the light, Mallet could see he had fifty or sixty pounds on the guy. Piece of cake, he thought, wading in.

That was his last thought for some time. He wasn't sure what hit him, but it hit him hard, fast, and in just the right place. The next thing he knew, it was night, he was lying on the ground expertly roped and tied, his head ringing and smoke stinging his nostrils. The smoke came from a campfire. Next to the campfire sat the big man who'd emerged from the shadows at the back of the burger joint.

"Lemme outta these," Mallet had growled, straining at the ropes.

"Promise to be a good boy?" the big man asked.

"Sure," Mallet lied.

The big man cut the ropes, and Mallet shrugged them off and charged. The next thing he knew it was morning, he was lying on the ground expertly roped and tied, his head ringing and smoke stinging his nostrils. The big man sat by the campfire, drinking coffee from a blue-enameled cup.

"Promise to be a good boy?" the man asked as Mallet squinted at him through the smoke.

"Yeah."

This time, he was, as much from curiosity as from fear. No one man had ever bested him once, much less twice, and he was impressed. The fear came later, when he learned that T-Bone's heart was granite and his soul dead.

And when T-Bone offered him a job, he accepted, knowing he would have to obey always or face the big man's final wrath. So here he was, where he could do as he pleased as long as he pleased T-Bone first, and life had been great and gone as it should until now—until that bitch escaped.

But he'd find her, and when he did....

Mallet halted suddenly and whirled, scrutinizing the cars around him. He felt eyes watching. Another moment, and he spied Bulge on top of a nearby heap of cars, looking down on him.

"Come down here, you filthy little fucker!"

Bulge flinched and violently shook his head. Mallet let it go, mostly because he couldn't climb up there to get the freak and pull him down.

"You seen that bitch I had chained in my car?"

Bulge shook his head again, even more vehemently. By now, his armpits were stinking with the sweat of guilt, and his nose and bruises ached and flared as if they were neon letters spelling "liar."

Mallet's eyes narrowed.

"You sure?"

Bulge nodded.

"You see her," Mallet grated, "you tell me right away. You hear?" Bulge nodded emphatically. Mallet peered closely at him. "What happened to your face?"

The heat from Bulge's bruises hiked itself another few degrees, and his head felt like it was going to catch on fire. Stupidly, he put fingers to his nose and tentatively touched the contusion there. All he could think was, thank God the woman hadn't scratched him.

Then he noticed, as if for the first time, the side view mirror in his other hand, and he knew a way out of his present predicament. Abruptly, he slammed the chrome tit against his forehead, and a rainbow coruscated though his brain.

When his sight came back, he looked with dizzy, watering eyes at Mallet to see if Mallet believed him. The big man was just standing, staring agape at him. Bulge banged his head again, then a third time.

Mallet shook his head in contemptuous disbelief.

"Fuck," was all he could say. He turned away from Bulge and resumed his march through the junkyard, searching for the woman.

Behind him, Bulge winced, gripped his head with his free hand, and rocked back and forth in pain. As he did, he caught a glimpse of himself in the mirror. Blood was streaking out of his hair and running beside one blackened eye and down beside his swollen nose. He could taste it as it dripped over his lips.

Women, he thought forlornly. They're just not worth the effort. It was true what those songs said, that love only leads to ugliness, humiliation, and misery. At least, he suddenly realized, it always would be that way for him. Without a second thought, he flung away the chrome tit, and it clattered off into a pile of junk and disappeared. Where didn't matter because he would never need it again. Women were out. All that was real was here and now and his love for Sledge. That would never bring pain, only joy and fruition. Suddenly he felt clear inside, as if a fog of confusion had vanished beneath cleansing sunshine.

Bulge gazed out over the desert, a new determination gleaming in his eyes. Let people like Mallet pursue inevitable grief, he thought, watching the hammer man enter another corridor in the junkyard. From now on, I'm done with all that.

"Come on out, little lady," Mallet called in his best attempt at a cajoling tone. "Come on out to Mallet. I won't hurt you. I promise."

She didn't come out, and he continued on down the aisle, calling and wheedling but at the same time ominously slapping the head of his maul into the palm of his hand. He walked on through several more corridors, staring into crevasses and between cars, but seeing them less than the visions of mayhem he would wreck on that bitch when he caught her. So it was that, as he passed by a particular wall of junk cars, he missed the two eyes staring at him through a chink in the ragged wall. He went on, out of sight, his wheedling calls punctuated by the slap of the heavy hammerhead on his rough palm.

From the other side of the wall, Phyllis peered through the chink, watching until Mallet was both out of sight and out of earshot. Only then did she breathe more easily and step away from the metal wall.

She was in the clearing where T-Bone performed his exercises. It looked much the same as it had when she'd seen the huge man work out. The main difference was that the car he'd mangled was gone, replaced by another. Somehow, she didn't think the new model would hold up any better than the last one. She glanced hastily around, and her eyes fell on the pile of boards lying next to the exercise machine. She picked up one and hurried from the clearing.

Twenty-five

THE BLOOD STAINING THE MASHED weeds was a crusty brown that could have passed for mud from the local red sediment. In a less dry climate, the stain would have washed away months ago. Most passersby at this lonely rest stop wouldn't even notice it. But to Alex, that stained nest crushed in the weeds was both grave and cradle of rebirth.

The kid was at Alex's side, clinging to his arm, staring up at his face, eyes wide and filled with anguish. But for the moment, as the man contemplated the encrusted weeds, he was oblivious to the boy and the others around him.

Instead, each blink of his unfocused eyes conjured forth another picture of the scene that had played itself out that fateful night these long months ago. First, he had been alone, pounding the tires with his crowbar and shining his flashlight under the trailer, looking for what was wrong. Blink, he turned, and what was wrong was right behind him in the form of a man, quick as a lash and with the sting of a scorpion. And then the rattle of the chain snaking out to rip the crowbar from his hands, followed so quickly by the scorpion's sting as the man's knife bit into his abdomen.

Blink, blink, and each moment revealed another agonizing detail, though everything looked preternaturally dark and distorted, as if time already was at work on his memories, taking even these from him. But no, it was only the edges that were blurring. The center, that core of horror at what had happened to him, remained without alteration, without misrepresentation. The shock of the blade entering his flesh may have turned into a scar and a dull souvenir of ache, but the fear of looming, sudden, and painful death remained sharp and immediate.

Blink, and the other road pirates issued from the darkness, loving his fear as the wolf loves the hunt and relishing his death as the wolf relishes hot flesh between his teeth. Then, blink! And there was T-Bone—imposing pillar of steel-corded flesh, will as implacable as his marble-eyed scrutiny.

Alex's eyes. T-Bone's eyes. Alex's eyes.

A sharp and ratty little man stepped up to T-Bone and spoke. "Check this out, boss. Electronics. Just like the man said."

Alex's eyes remained locked with T-Bone's. In the almost palpable flow of the pirate leader's glower, the ratty man's words sounded thin and distant, and they evaporated on the next minty breath of words from T-Bone's lips.

"I'm the only thing between you and ten thousand lifetimes of emptiness and pain." The big man said it with such knowing beyond conviction that Alex had absolutely no doubts, then or now, only perfect certainty.

Alex's eyes. T-Bone's eyes.

"Give him to the darkness," T-Bone finished.

Alex tried to get away. It was all he could do. But there were too many of them, and he was injured. They jostled him with a glee that was both fraternal and casual, somehow in the process getting a grip on his mortality that they might rip it from him. Then it was over, and he stared into the small round maw of Yvonne's gun—the small hole that would open into eternity. And as the darkness there flared with light, darkness flooded his memories.

"Alex! Alex!" It was Molly's voice, dim and far away but urgent with worry. He dragged his consciousness toward the sound and opened his eyes with effort, blinking. Her face came into focus, her own eyes dark wounds in a pale and shaken face.

"Alex. Are you all right?"

He looked at her and nodded with sober reflection.

"Yeah. Just remembering."

The others clustered consolingly around him.

"Anything of help?" the desert rat wanted to know, voice softer than Alex had ever heard it.

Alex shook his head.

"Sorry. It's all too fragmented. They didn't say much. It's just that...." Alex paused pensively, and Molly gripped his shoulder.

"What?"

Alex shook his head again. "I don't know. I can't get it."

He rubbed his face as if to cleanse himself of the memories.

"Let's move on," he suggested.

"Where to?" asked the old man.

"I'm not sure. I guess the Pleasant Haven. That's the last place I stopped before here."

With one last glance at the blood-crusted grass, he turned and strode toward the Jeep.

An hour and a half later, the afternoon sun gleamed from the plate glass windows of the Pleasant Haven Truck Stop as Alex and his friends pulled into the parking lot. They got out, stretched wearily, and entered the restaurant, where they ate in tired silence.

"This was my last stop before I was hit," Alex said when they were finished.

"You don't remember anything unusual?" Molly asked.

"Not really. I was going to spend the night, but my sister called and told me Dad had collapsed, so all I did was make a phone call, eat, and refuel."

"You don't count kicking some scum ass unusual?" the desert rat asked dryly.

"Well, I did meet your father and the kid," Alex said to Molly.

The boy, grinning, pulled the two $50 bills out of his pocket and waved them toward Alex. Alex gave a short laugh, then looked sheepishly at the desert rat.

"Yeah, I gave the kid the money to buy his gramps a decent meal."

They all laughed, then the desert rat went on more seriously, "This gang hits independent truckers, but why you? What made your load worth the taking?"

"I was hauling electronics. That's always worth something."

"But how did the hijackers know that?"

"I don't know."

"What about the phone call?" the old man asked. "Who was that to?"

"Manny Casper. He's the owner of Max Electronics. The electronics were his."

"That guy on TV?" the desert rat asked. "The one who has all those electronics equipment blowouts all over the place?"

"That's him."

"What a sleaze. That guy's a Zen huckster if I ever saw one."

"Could he have set you up?" Molly asked.

Alex thought for a moment then shook his head.

"Not likely. I've known Manny for three years. He may be a cheap crook in his own way, but that's not his style. If he was going to hijack his own load, he would just have me bring it in, and he'd warehouse it, claim it was stolen, and collect the insurance."

"It had to be someone who knew your load and where you were," the desert rat said.

"Yeah," Alex said, "But there wasn't anybody who knew...."

Then he was remembering again. As before, the recollection was dark and distorted. He was at the rest stop, stabbed and surrounded, facing the huge T-Bone. From all around came the jeers and curses of the other road pirates. Then the ratty little man came up to T-Bone, carrying Alex's manifest, saying, "Check this out, boss. Electronics. Just like the man said."

"Just like the man said."

Alex squeezed his eyes shut and tried to stuff the memory back into the mental closet it had emerged from. Then his eyes opened, focused, and narrowed in calculation.

"Yes, they were expecting me. They knew my truck and they knew my load."

"Then it had to be Manny," Molly said.

"No," Alex said. "Even if he was that low—and he isn't—he didn't have any idea where I was or what route I was taking."

The memory came again, more insistent. "Just like the man said," Rat intoned. "Just like the man said.... Just like the man said."

And then Rat disappeared and the rest stop disappeared and another face and location filled Alex's memory—the trooper at the weigh station. The trooper was standing on the scales, saying, "Yep, just about two-sixty over. Looks like it might be just about the weight of one of them video games you got." A video game box dropped to the pavement, followed by a VCR. The trooper smiled and said, "Won't nobody miss it.... Won't nobody miss it.... Won't nobody miss it."

Alex shut off the memory and stood up abruptly, startling the others, who stared at him. A hard smile spread over his face.

"I've got it," he said. "Let's go."

He spun on his heel and stalked toward the door.

The desert rat gestured to the remains of the meal.

"Who's picking up the tab for this?"

At that, Heath, grinning broadly, tossed the two fifties onto the table. The others chuckled, got up, and followed Alex outside.

TWENTY-SIX

THE SKY STILL GLIMMERED IN the west with the last rays of the sun, but dusk had settled and gone an hour before, and the darkness that had fallen shrouded the Cherokee where it sat on the shoulder of the highway. But the same darkness had brought lights to the weigh station across the road, and in their glare, the activities of the trooper on duty were clear to the friends in the SUV. While they watched, an eighteen-wheeler pulled into the station and stopped. The trooper came up to the cab just as the truck driver stepped down.

"That's him," Alex said. "Watch."

The trooper, who had been inspecting the driver's manifest, was now waving the driver toward the back of the van. The driver was obviously irate, but following the trooper's directions, he opened the van doors, climbed inside, and tossed out a couple of boxes.

"Bastard," Alex hissed under his breath. "That's what he did to me."

The truck driver now shut the truck doors and, waving angrily again, returned to his cab, got in, and started the truck. As the truck pulled out of the weigh station, the trooper carried the boxes to his car, opened the trunk, and put them inside. Then he picked up something smaller from the trunk and brought it close to his mouth.

Alex raised a pair of binoculars and focused on the trooper.

"What's he doing?" Molly asked.

"Using a radio," Alex answered. "I wonder...."

He handed her the binoculars, started the Cherokee, pulled off the shoulder, and began following the truck.

The trucker stopped at the Pleasant Haven to refuel and eat, then he pressed on into the night, driving the same road that Alex had the night of his hijacking.

After an hour, the kid and the old man were both asleep in the back, propping each other up. In the front, though, both Alex and Molly were alert.

Past them, through the windshield, they could see the taillights of the truck they were trailing, about a quarter of a mile ahead.

"The rest stop is only a few miles from here," Alex said. Abruptly, he reached out and killed the headlights. Molly shot him a quick look.

"I hope you know what you're doing," she said.

"The moon's almost full and there isn't any traffic. Maybe we'll see more night life this way." He jerked his head toward the back seat. "Better wake them up."

The desert rat and the boy were just sitting forward attentively when a lone car sitting on a dirt side road, its lights off, whipped into motion. It pulled out onto the highway between the truck and the Cherokee, spitting dust and gravel. It's lights flared on.

Molly put her hand on Alex's arm. "Night life," she said.

As soon as the eighteen-wheeler passed the mouth of the dirt road, Blade whipped the big Pontiac into motion. It's tires grated across the shoulder then bit into the pavement with a squeal as Blade stomped on the gas and sped after the truck.

Beside him on the front seat, Yvonne adjusted the top half of her clothes, which resembled a wedding gown. Below the waistline, though, she sported tight short-shorts in her favorite material, denim, and black leather cowboy boots with chrome toe tips.

It took only a few moments for the powerful sedan to catch up with the cruising truck. For the sake of authenticity in the deception, Blade waited for the legitimate passing zone he knew was there before swinging into the opposite lane. As the car pulled abreast of the truck cab, Yvonne leaned out of the car window, a worried look plastered on her face. She gestured toward the back of the truck.

The driver, face hazily illuminated by his dash lights, stared quizzically through his window at her. Yvonne waved again and stabbed her finger toward the back of the truck. This time, the driver threw a quick glance in his side view mirror before returning his eyes to her. Yvonne rolled her eyes in overt frustration, shrugged, and slipped back into the Pontiac as Blade passed the truck and sped off down the road.

Less than three minutes later, the truck slowed and pulled into the roadside park that conveniently appeared ahead. He emerged and walked around the back of his truck and trailer, flashing a light on the tires.

Suddenly, a chain whipped out of the gloom, entangled his legs, and sent him tumbling to the earth. He barely managed to break his fall with his hands, but before he could rise, Chains, Mallet, Billy-Bob, and Flix surrounded him, grinning malevolently.

Flix switched on his camera and shined the light right in the driver's face just as Blade and Yvonne drove up and parked near the front of the truck. Blade left the engine running. This was going to be short and sweet, he thought as he got out of the car. Short for the driver and sweet for Yvonne. She'd stripped off the wedding top to reveal her leather vest and chrome .357.

"What do you want?" the driver cringed nervously away from the light, but Blade noticed that his eyes strayed inadvertently to the all too flimsy restraint of Yvonne's vest. Yeah, he grinned inwardly. Sweet for Yvonne.

"Everything, babycakes," the woman said, unbuttoning the vest and letting her breasts bobble free.

The other pirates laughed, and Mallet kicked the fallen driver. The man cried out and flinched away, but with his feet tangled in the chain, there was no place for him to go. The pirates began tormenting him in earnest, poking and prodding and kicking him, spitting curses and phlegm on him.

Flix shot some footage of them for a few moments, but he soon tired. It was always the same. The story never varied. Terrify them, beat them, then Yvonne shoots them and gets her rocks off. Besides, nothing could top that beefy trucker Yvonne had wasted a few months back. The way that guy fought, even when he was wounded, showed real drama.

While Flix didn't particularly mind the violence of the other pirates, it wasn't really his thing. Not like the camera was. He was an artist, always looking for shades of light and dark. Flix believed in the camera, in the image. What went on in the little viewfinder was more real to him than the occasional pain he suffered at the hands of the other pirates or the transitory pleasures he'd had with women on three occasions in his life.

After all, he thought, you couldn't record the feeling and save it for later replay. You just lived it once and grabbed what little you could and then moved on. With the camera, it was different. Capture the image once, and you captured it for all time. It was always there to go back to and savor. And others could enjoy it as well.

He aimed the lens at the truck and noticed there was a nice angle along its length, lit with a slash of illumination from the Pontiac's headlights, with the melee around the fallen driver as its focal point. He got that for a few moments, the sound track picking up the driver's escalating agony. He wondered if there would be other good angles and tones elsewhere on the vehicle. Still looking through the viewfinder and shooting footage, he began to wander around the front of the cab.

As he started down the other side of the trailer, something moved in the dimness just beyond the range of his camera-top light. He peered intently into the eyepiece, wondering if it was a trick of the light or something was wrong with the camera. A second later, he realized it was no trick. Something was wrong, but not with the camera. Staring back at Flix through the viewfinder was a big man whose expression radiated cold anger.

Psychologically tied as he was to the ersatz reality of TV, Flix took several seconds to realize he might actually be in physical danger from this image in his viewfinder.

"Oh, man," he murmured in a preoccupied voice as he twisted the focus ring to sharpen the approaching image. "Will you look at this! Man, oh, man! What a shot! T-Bone'll never believe it...."

"He'll never see it," the image assured Flix, reaching for him. It didn't even occur to the cameraman to try to run.

"Oh, shit! It's comin' outta the camera! It's comin' right outta the camera!"

Alex grabbed Flix. The little cameraman, with a sudden flash of insight into the nature of reality, tried to kick Alex, all the while shooting footage of him, but Alex easily evaded the foot. He lashed out with a lightning move, and Flix collapsed with a groan. The camera fell from his stunned fingers, and the light on top gave a hissing pop as it went out.

"It came outta the camera," Flix moaned groggily from his supine position. "The TV's alive. It grabbed me."

As Flix lay there, Alex's friends stepped quietly up. Molly cradled her shotgun, and the desert rat, like Alex, was armed with a 9mm. They'd left the kid back in the Cherokee.

With silent gestures, Alex directed Molly and the desert rat around the front end of the truck, while he headed toward the rear, where the pirates were still beating the downed driver.

The trucker, dazed and weak with shock and defeat, just lay on the ground, barely conscious. The pirates encircling him were totally oblivious to anything but their victim and their pleasure at his pain. For the moment, a sort of quiet had fallen as Yvonne squatted over the driver and caressed his broken face with the barrel of her pistol, whispering obscenities into his ear. Mallet absently slapped the bloody head of his maul into the palm of his hand, while Blade wiped a knife on the driver's pants leg. Chains simply stood by. He'd untangled the length of whip chain from the driver's legs. One end was looped and clipped around his wrist so it wouldn't slip on blood and be pulled free, and he'd snaked the rest of the chain along the ground toward the back of Blade's Pontiac so it would be out of the way but ready to whip forward in an instant.

Unseen by the pirates, a small arm edged out from under the car. The fingers snared the end of the chain and gently dragged it out of sight beneath the bumper.

Underneath the car, Heath looped the chain around the rear axle then dug a coil of cord and a pocketknife from all the other junk in his pocket. He wasn't about to stay in the car while the adults had all the fun. In a trice, he'd looped the chain twice around the axel and tied the free end to the main length of chain with several sturdy twists of cord. A second after, he squirmed out from under the other side of the car.

At that moment, Alex stepped into view of the pirates, pistol leveled.

"Old friends and good times," he boomed sarcastically.

The pirates turned with a unanimous jerk from the fallen driver and stared at Alex. Yvonne's eyes widened in amazement. "You!"

Alex locked eyes with her.

"I hate to break up the party," he said mockingly.

Suddenly, from the side, Mallet flung a small ball-peen hammer, knocking the gun from Alex's hand.

"You didn't," Yvonne said. "We just get to dance again." She lifted the barrel of her gun, but before she could aim, Molly stepped in from the shadows, shotgun pointed at her belly.

"Mind if I cut in, bitch?"

Yvonne froze, the triumphant sneer on her face turning sour.

"Throw it away."

She did, and Billy-Bob, partially obscured by her, looked like he was getting ready to draw.

"Forget it, bub," said the desert rat, moving into view, his own pistol trained on the cowboy. "Take off that ridiculous belt and throw it out there, too." He indicated the dark weeds that hid Yvonne's gun. "Now!"

Billy-Bob complied.

"Now, get back," Molly ordered.

As Yvonne stepped back, there was a sudden flash of motion at the edge of the group. Blade's arm whipped up underhanded, releasing the knife he'd been cleaning on the trucker's pants right at Molly. She twisted at the movement, and the knife seared along her right shoulder and spun off behind her. She staggered back, and her finger convulsed on the trigger of the shotgun. The muzzle belched fire and pellets into the night air.

The scene erupted as wildly as the shotgun. Chains tried to whip up his chain and found it fastened. But he had enough reach to kick the desert rat's gun out of his hands. Yvonne and Billy-Bob dashed into the weeds and started thrashing around, searching for their guns, and Molly tried to aim her shotgun at them again, but Mallet, swinging his maul, split the stock and knocked the weapon from her hands then backhanded her. As she fell to the ground, stunned, he loomed over her, raising the maul.

"You're my kind of meat, baby," he said then found himself blinded as Heath leapt onto his back, ripping at his hair, clawing his eyes, and pummeling his head. The desert rat danced in and kicked the big man's shins and popped him on the face. Mallet swung at him but, blinded by the boy, couldn't find a target.

Meanwhile, Blade's machete hissed from its sheath, and he moved in on Alex.

"We're back to square one, trucker," Blade said. "Only you don't got no crowbar this time."

"And you don't have Chains to help you."

A quick glance told Blade that Alex spoke the truth. He could see Chains jerking at the chain, which seemed stuck beneath the Pontiac. He turned back to Alex and slashed viciously half a dozen times.

Alex leapt back, avoiding the hissing steel, but he knew this couldn't go on for long. Blade was too expert with his weapon, and barehanded, Alex didn't stand a chance.

Then he saw something long and metallic lying on the ground. It was Molly's shotgun. He dove toward it and came up in a crouch.

The gun was ruined by Mallet's smashing blow, but he could use the barrel to parry Blade's slashing steel.

Twenty feet away, Mallet's maul finally found the old man's shoulder and slammed him to the ground. He ripped the kicking and struggling boy off his back, cuffed him into submission, tucked him under one arm, and lumbered toward the Pontiac.

Alex, unable to get the better of Blade with the unwieldy remains of the shotgun, was slowly being backed toward the truck when Yvonne and Billy-Bob found their weapons almost simultaneously and started shooting.

Two rounds hissed by Blade, making him lose his concentration and giving Alex a chance to smash him on the arm and make him drop the machete. Blade ducked as more bullets slammed into the truck. He saw Mallet heading toward the car and dashed after him.

By now, Molly had found Alex's automatic, and she opened fire on Yvonne and Billy-Bob. The cowboy dove for cover, but Yvonne just stood there, ignoring Molly's bullets and shooting wildly at Alex.

"You fuckin' bastard!" she shrieked. "I'll get you!"

Alex had ducked under the eighteen-wheeler as soon as he disarmed Blade, and the desert rat grabbed Molly and dragged her around the front of the rig a split second before Billy-Bob's bullets bit the air where she'd been.

Just then, Flix staggered around the corner of the truck.

"It's alive," he muttered. "The TV's alive. It hit me."

Suddenly, a hole appeared completely through his head where his right eye had been, opened by the last round in Yvonne's cylinder. As he collapsed to the ground, she stopped to reload. Billy-Bob fired too, but Molly and the desert rat were both shooting now, and he gave up and dashed after Blade and Mallet, snatching at Yvonne as he rushed past.

"There's too many of them!" he yelled. "Let's get out of here!"

"Let go of me, you bastard," she bellowed, but she allowed him to drag her toward the car. Mallet had already tossed the kid inside, and Blade was revving the engine when they jumped in.

"Where's Chains?" Mallet yelled.

Yvonne and Billy-Bob turned. Through the back windshield, they could see Chains out there pulling at his wrist.

"What the fuck's he doing?" Billy-Bob asked.

"Fuck him!" Blade yelled over the roar of the engine. "He's got his motorcycle! I'm getting out of here!"

Alex rolled out from under to the truck just in time to see Chains look up, panic washing over his face.

"Shit!" the biker yelled as the Pontiac peeled out, and an instant later, he was jerked off his feet as the car squealed out onto the road. His gurgling screams faded quickly in the darkness.

"They got the kid!" yelled the desert rat in a stricken voice.

The three of them rushed toward their car, which was parked a hundred yards down the shoulder, the desert rat pausing only to scoop up Flix's camera and fanny pack and the remains of Molly's shotgun.

After they were in the Cherokee, Alex at the wheel, chasing through the darkness in the wake of the pirates' Pontiac, the desert rat took out a cell phone and punched buttons.

"State police," said a tiny voice.

"Better get some officers and an ambulance out to the rest stop on U.S. 60, about halfway between Oatil and Magdalena," the desert rat snapped before disconnecting. He took out the phone's sim card, bent it in half, wiped it and the phone clean of prints, and tossed them out the window.

"Where the hell are they?" Molly asked.

"We're still on the right track, at least," Alex said, and the others could see he was right—a broad, wet-looking swath ran down the blacktop.

But after a couple of miles, that vanished, and with it went any trace of the pirates.

"They could have taken any of a dozen turns," Alex said at last, slowing. "We're just chasing around blind in the dark."

"We've got to find him," Molly moaned. "We've got to get him back."

"We'll find him," Alex said, though he wasn't sure how he'd keep that promise.

Twenty-seven

SLICK NERVOUSLY FIDDLED WITH THE carburetor, even though he could barely see it in the light from the arc lamps in front of the metal building. At last, frustrated, he set it down. But his jittery fingers couldn't stay still. He dug a greasy pack of cigarettes from one pocket, a worn Zippo lighter from another, and a moment later breathed smoke into the night air.

Where the hell were they?

He was perched on the lookout platform by the compound's front gate, and he'd been staring into the darkness so long it felt like his eyeballs were gonna to pop. But he didn't dare abandon his post. Not when T-Bone had assigned the duty. He'd have to stay up here until dawn if T-Bone said so.

He always did what T-Bone said, though unlike most of the others who obeyed their leader out of respect, fear, or love, Slick did what he was told because T-Bone let him do what he loved to do most. Not that he didn't respect T-Bone or that T-Bone didn't scare him shitless. Hell, even Rat scared him, and Rat wasn't known for his courage. But T-Bone—now that man could make Slick tremble just with a glance. In fact, Slick had trembled the first time he'd seen the big man a couple of years ago.

Slick had been working in a roadside garage outside of Winslow, Arizona. He pretty much couldn't stand the place he was working, but it was the best job to be had outside of the big cities, and he hated big cities even more than he hated his job. Actually, it wasn't his job he hated but his boss, George McGill, a pigshit of a man fond of Philly cheesesteak sandwiches and wearing suspenders over his greasy white T-shirt because they didn't make belts long enough to wrap effectively around his middle. The nasty thing was, the grease on his shirt wasn't honest thirty-weight but cheese-and-meat drippings from his perpetual cheesesteak sandwich that dribbled onto his hands, which he then wiped onto the shirt. It was fucking sick.

Slick had gone out after work, as he often did, to a local titty bar. None of the girls would let him touch them because he was always greasy from his job. Some wouldn't even get close enough to give him a table dance. But he was a regular, and the bouncers let him hang around as long as he bought a drink or two and stayed away from the stage. This particular night, there was a fight over a redhead dancer named Toni, who could put both her feet behind her head and....

But Slick didn't like to think about that. He'd had a couple of women in his life—not many, but enough to know what he was missing—and thinking about what Toni did with her feet behind her head made him miss all that even more. Not enough to quit being a mechanic, of course, but a whole lot, just the same.

The two men fighting over Toni slammed around for a few minutes, and when the bouncer tried to break it up, one of the combatants bashed him over the head with a chair before tangling with the other again. About thirty seconds later, they flung themselves into a dim booth at the back.

Because of all the people standing around, Slick couldn't see exactly what happened, but he saw the effect, and that was impressive enough. Both the fighters flung backwards out of the booth, hit the floor, and remained there.

Then two men stood up back there. One was a motorcycle gang member wearing a leather jacket dangling loops and coils of chain, and the other...well, he was damn big and mean looking. The two of them stepped calmly over the unconscious fighters and left the bar as if nothing had happened.

Slick was hiding near the door as the fight progressed, and the two men passed right by him on their way out, but neither noticed that he was alive. He let the front door close behind them, waited for a count of twenty, then followed. Outside, he saw the motorcycle gang member mount a Harley and roar off down the highway, while the big man got into an old Pontiac, started the engine, and headed off in the opposite direction.

Slick was intrigued, as much by the sound of precision tuning coming from the Pontiac's engine as by the way the two men had laid out the fighters and calmly exited. But they were gone now, so he went back inside and bought another drink. By then, the bartender had dragged the two fighters out the back, the bouncer was propped blearily in a chair, and Toni was shaking her stuff as if nothing had happened.

Two months later, Slick was out north of town in George's wrecker, looking for a stranded motorist who'd called in for a tow, when he stopped at Meade's gas station to fill up and get a cold soda. Just as he emerged into the sunlight, an old Pontiac with a sweet-sounding engine pulled up to the pumps. Slick recognized the car instantly, and the big man, too, who got out and walked into the station.

Slick couldn't help himself. He had to get a look under that hood. And there was only one way he could do that. On the way back to the wrecker, he crouched beside the Pontiac, reached up underneath the engine, and let his nimble fingers play for a moment. Then he was in the wrecker, driving off the way the Pontiac had come.

As soon as Slick was out of sight of Meade's, he stopped and waited. He reckoned that the big man would take five minutes or so at the station and he'd probably make ten or fifteen miles at the most before the Pontiac quit on him. Give him another half an hour to stew in the hot sun, and he'd be glad as hell when Slick came along.

After half an hour, Slick pulled onto the road and headed in the direction the Pontiac was going, making an effort to keep his speed under sixty. Sure enough, about fifteen miles past Meade's, there was the Pontiac, sitting beside the road with its hood up and the big man bent over the engine looking pissed and puzzled at the same time.

"Need some help, mister?" he'd asked as he walked up to the Pontiac. He noticed that his voice was trembling.

"Depends on if you can fix it or not," the big man replied.

"I can fix anything on wheels," Slick said.

He eased beneath the hood and made a show of looking at all the obvious things that could go wrong but hadn't.

"Could you crank 'er up?"

Wordlessly, the big man got into the car and twisted the key. The engine ground but didn't catch.

"Hold it, a sec," Slick called as his fingers undid what they'd done at Meade's. "Okay, try 'er again."

This time the engine caught immediately, and a moment later the big man was standing beside Slick.

"Nice car, mister."

"What do I owe you?" the big man asked, ignoring the compliment.

"Oh, wasn't nothin'," Slick said. "I ain't gonna charge you."

"Good thing," said the big man.

"Huh?" Slick said involuntarily, though he instantly knew better.

"If you'd charged me, I'd have to think you were fucking with me back at that gas station so you could take advantage of me out here."

"Gas station?"

"Gas station."

"Honest, mister. I wasn't messin' you around."

The big man snorted and twisted his upper lip in a cross between a snarl and a grin as his eyes bored into Slick. Then he laughed.

"I must say, that was pretty good work. It takes a real pro to do what you did. What'd you have—ten second or less? I'll bet you even knew just how far I'd get before the engine stopped."

Slick didn't know what to say, but something in the eyes staring down at him warned him to abandon all pretense.

"I figured about right," he said, unable to keep a trace of pride out of his voice.

"So why'd you do it if you didn't plan on gouging me?"

"I got curious." He told the big man about witnessing the fight at the titty bar. "I never forget a good car," he finished, "and when you come along, I just hadda get a closer look. Don't hurt me, mister. I didn't mean nothin.'"

"What're you doing?" the big man asked. "Working for...." He glanced at the lettering on the side of the wrecker. "Working for George?"

"Yep."

"Like it?"

"Not much."

"Want a new job?"

"Doing what?"

"What you do best. Fixing things with engines on wheels."

"I don't know...."

"What's George paying you?"

"Twelve an hour."

"I'll triple that and throw in food and housing."

"No shit?"

"There's a condition."

"A condition?"

"Yes." Like a predator pouncing, the big man grabbed Slick by the throat and hoisted him off the ground. "If you ever try to fuck with me again, I'll pop your head off like a filthy pimple. Understand?"

Slick couldn't really nod, strangling and dangling as he was in the big man's hands, but his acquiescence must have showed in his eyes because the big man dropped him.

"Good. Just so we understand one another. Get in your truck and follow me."

"But," Slick gasped through his bruised throat. "It's not my truck. It's George's."

"Fuck George," the big man spat. He slammed the Pontiac's hood, turned on his heel, and slid behind the wheel. "Coming?"

Slick thought about the Philly cheesesteak grease all over George's T-shirt, and that's what got him into the wrecker. As he followed the Pontiac, he worried the sparse hairs on his chin, trying to figure out just what the hell he was doing.

Shit, he thought as he paced the catwalk by the compound's gate. I'm still trying to figure that out sometimes. Playin' lookout ain't my job. I gotta finish stripping that semi they brought in a few months ago, not to mention fixin' the brakes on the *Granola Gray*. He shouldn't be makin' me stand guard. He's got the warriors for that.

Trouble was, the warriors weren't home, and that's why he was up here, peering into the darkness. They were overdue. Where the hell were they?

As if in answer, the ladder next to him rattled. Slick shook as well, knowing that what climbed the ladder was only more unanswerable questions. T-Bone's head appeared, and a moment later, the huge man towered over the grease monkey. He scanned the empty night, radiating tension. Slick was afraid to look him in the face, so he missed the angry but somewhat worried look in his chief's eyes.

"Nothing?" T-Bone demanded after a prolonged, heavy silence.

Slick hesitated slightly, afraid of T-Bone's reaction, then thought better of remaining mute.

"No, sir," he blurted. "I ain't seen nothin' yet."

"Damn!" T-Bone hammered a fist against the rail. Slick noted that the pressure-treated two-by-four cracked. "Those assholes were supposed to be here hours ago. You tell them to get their butts into the briefing room as soon as they get here, or they'll answer to me."

"Yes, sir," Slick quavered.

T-Bone climbed down the ladder, leaving the cowering Slick to watch the empty blackness. Striding across the greasy earth toward the metal building, he entered and went straight to the briefing room. Inside, near the dark and silent TV, clustered Professor Sledge, Bulge, and Rat. Jojo sat off to one side, painting her nails and pointedly ignoring the freaks and losers.

"I don't like it," Sledge was saying. "They should be here. It's too close. No room for slip-ups."

"Look, Professor," Rat temporized. "They've been cooped up here for a week. You can't keep people like that confined. They needed a little R&R is all."

"It's no good, Rat," Sledge shook his head.

Suddenly T-Bone loomed at Sledge's shoulder.

"Relax, Sledge," the big man said in a voice that was anything but relaxing. "We'll get your reactive material for you."

"They should be here, Mr. T-Bone," Sledge said, peering owlishly at the big man. "Nothing must go wrong. Nothing must keep me from getting that reactive material." His eyes misted and lit with unnatural light, and he clutched convulsively at T-Bone's arm. "I must have it, T-Bone! It's all I live for!"

T-Bone stared contemptuously at Sledge and cuffed away the clutching grasp.

"Are all you sci-fi brains warped, Sledge, or is it just you?"

"I crave it, T-Bone," Sledge said, voice subdued but madness still gleaming behind his thick spectacles. "I can't help it."

At that moment, the door burst open.

"They're here!" Slick yelled shrilly.

He stepped back as T-Bone strode for the door, everyone crowding outside behind him. As they emerged, the Pontiac slewed to a stop beneath the arc lights. T-Bone jerked open the driver's door, dragged Blade out of the seat, and held him eighteen inches off the ground.

"Where the fuck were you assholes," he grated, face just inches from Blade's flinching features.

"Oh, man, you wouldn't believe it...," Blade began.

"I'd better," the pirate leader snarled, then he tossed Blade aside as he saw Mallet pull the kid from the car.

"What the fuck is that?"

"A hostage," Mallet said.

T-Bone snorted derisively.

"What the fuck we need a hostage for?"

"He was there, T-Bone," Blade said. "He just came outta nowhere. We hadda take back roads...."

"Who was there?"

"That beefcake, T-Bone," Yvonne said. "The driver of that electronics shipment. The one I shot."

"The one you missed, you mean?" T-Bone asked, angrily facing her.

"I didn't miss the motherfucker," she yelled, angry herself. "You saw it. I hit him right in the heart. We got video!"

"You figure he's got a spare heart, Yvonne?" T-Bone asked, voice heavy with dangerous sarcasm.

"Maybe a heart of stone," she said quietly.

T-Bone turned on Blade. "How did this guy find you?"

"I don't know," Blade said, cowering away from his boss. "We was taking care of this truck driver, you know, at that rest stop on 60, when all of a sudden this guy comes outta the darkness. He had some friends. Two or three. They had guns, and that trucker is a real good fighter. You saw that yourself."

T-Bone scanned the returned pirates, contempt in his eyes.

"Obviously better than you jackasses." Suddenly he realized that someone was missing, and he looked around. "Speaking of video, where the fuck is Flix? And Chains?"

"I don't know about Chains," Mallet said. "I thought he was right behind us. But Flix...he's gone."

"Gone!" T-Bone bellowed, tendons and veins standing out on his neck. "What the fuck do you mean gone?"

While they were talking, Slick had been moving around the Pontiac, looking for damage, and he tripped over something that went clink. Puzzled, he reached down and found a length of chain protruding from the rear of the car. Curious, he pulled on the chain, lifting it into the light from the metal shed. When he got to the end, he found himself holding hands with the gruesome remains of an arm clad in shredded and bloody leather. Shocked, he dropped the mangled limb and jumped back with a choked cry.

The others, hurrying to see what happened, found Slick cringing against the trunk of the car, pointing to the ground. Bulge pulled a flashlight from his tool belt and shone it where Slick pointed, illuminating the dismembered appendage.

"Well." T-Bone spit to one side. "Now we know what happened to Chains." He looked around at the others. "But what happened to Flix?"

Yvonne hung her head, but no one spoke.

Twenty-eight

AT THE WEIGH STATION, HOBBS was still on duty. Though there wasn't much traffic at this late hour, he liked the night shift because it was cooler and gave him a greater opportunity to fleece the drivers who stopped. His superiors were in bed and unlikely to drop by, and the drivers tended to stop one at a time, allowing him to have his way with them. At the moment, he had no victims, so he had a couple of chairs set up outside, his big ass in one and his scuffed size twelve cowboy boots in the other. The night was balmy, and he blew a puff of cigarette smoke into it in appreciation and watched a shooting star graze the sky. Damn, he loved his job.

What he didn't see was that out on the highway, a pair of hands were, at that moment, reaching up to turn the weigh station sign from "Open" to "Closed."

Hobbs took another puff from his cigarette and blew the smoke at a moth hovering too close to his face. Suddenly he heard a slight sound behind him. Heaving himself out of his chairs, he spun around to see a man standing seven or eight feet away.

"You lost or something?" Hobbs asked gruffly, puffing out his chest and assuming his best cop tone. The truth was, he was a little rattled at having the guy sneak up on him like that.

"You don't remember me?"

Hobbs did, then, and his features hardened. The bastard was one of the truckers he'd set up for T-Bone. He drew his gun.

Or tried to. The distance between them vanished, and Hobbs's gun went skittering across the pavement. Undaunted, Hobbs aimed a haymaker at the guy's head. It missed, and so did the followup gut punch, but not Alex's open palm strike to the trooper's chest. Suddenly Hobbs couldn't breathe, and he sat heavily on the asphalt. He tried for his backup .32 in the holster at his ankle, but Alex kicked it out of his hand, stepped in and levered his arm into a painful joint lock.

Hobbs groaned and tried to writhe away, but that only made the lock wrench more painfully at his elbow and shoulder.

A beautiful woman and a scraggly old man stepped around the kiosk and came over to them. The woman bent close. She really was a looker.

"We'd like some information, officer," she said in a too-sweet voice.

"You folks better watch what you're doing," Hobbs spat. "You're assaulting a police officer."

In reply, Alex levered the joint lock a couple of more degrees, and Hobbs groaned, face twisting.

"I doubt if you're going to be a police officer much longer," Alex said. "In fact, I think the police are going to be looking for you by tomorrow morning."

"I don't know what you're talking about," Hobbs said.

"Don't fuck with us, asshole," said the old man, squatting and digging Hobbs's car keys from his pocket. "Play nice, and we'll give these back and give you a twenty-four-hour head start. Play dumb, and we leave you tied in the booth and put in a call to your head-quarters. It might take them a little time to get to you, though, since right now they're busy taking the statement of that last trucker you handed over to T-Bone. By the way, he's still alive, as is our friend who has your arm in a sling, and I think both of them would like to relate just how you treated them."

"I don't know nothing," Hobbs insisted, a bit less vehemently.

"You know T-Bone," Alex said. "You set up drivers for him using that little radio you got in the trunk of your car. Right next to all that stuff you've ripped off tonight. Now you're going to set him up for us."

"I can't help you," the trooper whined. "I never seen where they live. I just talk to them on the radio."

"How do they pay you?" asked the woman.

"They bring it to me. I never go to them. I don't even know where they are."

Alex looked at Molly and the desert rat. "Think we can believe this scumbag?" he asked.

"He set you up to die," the old man said. "And no telling how many more. The devil wouldn't trust him."

"You gotta believe me," pleaded Hobbs.

Alex twisted the joint harder, and Hobbs groaned.

"It's the truth!"

Alex dropped Hobbs's arm and stood up.

"Maybe he's...," Molly began, but as Alex looked at her, Hobbs lashed out and kicked Alex behind the knee. As Alex lurched, the trooper, with a surge that belied his weight, was on his feet and running.

Molly, quickly followed by Alex and the desert rat, took off after him as he raced away from them. The fugitive had just reached the highway when he threw a frightened look over his shoulder and saw his pursuers close behind. Blinded by panic, he turned, took two steps out into the road, and was instantly tumbled beneath an eighteen-wheeler barreling past what the driver thought was a closed weigh station.

Alex, Molly, and the desert rat stopped short, staring with disgust at the mangled remains lit by the lurid red glare of the truck's taillights as the truck screeched to a halt fifty yards down the road.

"Poetic justice," the desert rat commented dryly as the driver of the truck that mashed the trooper, panting with fear, hurried toward them. He tossed Hobbs's keys to Alex. "You two check out his car. I'll take care of this guy."

In moments, Alex and Molly were opening the trooper's trunk. Molly shone a flashlight into the interior, where several crates of cured ham sat next to a shortwave radio. Alex turned on the radio and picked up the microphone.

"Hello," he said. "This is the weigh station."

After a moment of silence, he tried again.

This time a voice came back, crackly with static but plainly puzzled. "That you, Hobbs?"

Alex exchanged a glance with Molly and said, "Yeah, its Hobbs."

"It sure don't sound like...."

In the metal building in the compound, T-Bone quickly stepped over to Slick, who was talking on the radio.

"That's not Hobbs, you idiot," he snarled. "Gimme that mike!" Snatching the microphone from Slick's hand, he roughly shoved the mechanic aside. "Who the fuck is this?"

"Remember me, T-Bone?" asked the voice on the other end of the connection. "The one you spared ten thousand lifetimes of emptiness and pain?"

"I remember. You killed some of my people."

"There's another one, T-Bone. He's fresh road pizza right now."

"Hobbs always had shit for brains. The buzzards won't pick his bones if they know what's good for them."

"I'm getting close, T-Bone," said the voice. "Pretty soon I'm going to find you and your gang of cutthroats. Then the cops'll be down on you like a runaway diesel."

"You better hope not. I got your kid here, and he'll be buzzard bait the first time I get a whiff of cops."

"I'll keep the cops out, but I'm coming after that boy personally, and if you've hurt him, you're the one who'll see ten thousand lifetimes of emptiness and pain."

"Looking forward to it, trucker. I'll keep the brat alive just to be sure you show up."

Back at the weigh station, the desert rat came over to them.

"I've got the driver calmed down, but we'd better skedaddle, or we'll be tied up here all through tomorrow explaining to the cops what happened. And since it's one of their own plastered all over the road, they won't be inclined to be polite, even if he was crooked."

Alex nodded, and said into the mike, "Be seeing you, T-Bone."

"Come on and die," the speaker crackled roughly. Then Alex dropped the microphone, and he and Molly followed the desert rat back to the Cherokee parked just off the highway.

In the compound, T-Bone shut off the radio and looked at Rat. "It's only a matter of time before that guy figures out where we are." "No way," Rat replied. "We're locked up tighter than a steel drum. Even the cops and feds don't know where we are."

T-Bone chuckled. "Rat," he said, "I wish it was that simple. But this guy is different."

"How do you know?"

"Look around you. We're two less than we were this morning. Two and a half, if you count Hobbs."

T-Bone turned from the little man and strode over to the *Granola Gray*, where Professor Sledge and Bulge were at work. Bulge stood by with his tools as Sledge, half inside the large, open panel in the base of the black console inside the van, made some connections and adjustments.

"We're running out of time, Sledge. How much longer you gonna jack with that thing?"

Grunting, Sledge pulled himself out of the opening, straightened, and peered like an insane owl through his thick lenses.

"It goes well, Sir T-Bone. By the time you obtain the reactive materials, we will be ready to insert them. Then we will be—how do you say?" He grinned lopsidedly. "Ready to roll."

TWENTY-NINE

IN THE COMPOUND, HEATH WAS ready for something to happen, too, but he wasn't sure what. He only knew that he was locked in a tiny wooden shed with only a stingy, stinky old army blanket to keep him warm at night. He also knew he was in a junkyard, and if he hadn't been in such dire straits, he'd have been jumping to go exploring. As it was, he was just ready to leave.

That was easier said than done. So far, his captors had fed him a few times and let him out to go to the bathroom, but someone was always with him when he wasn't locked up tight. That someone was usually a skinky little man covered with grease, but once it had been the woman called Yvonne. The one who'd slapped his dad. She'd led him out of the shed, joking about his age and size and boyhood until he kicked her in the knee and tried to bite her.

She'd knocked him to the ground and drawn her pistol, face red with rage, but then she laughed, holstered the gun, and said, "Do that again, kid, and I'll break your fucking arm."

He believed her.

Sitting in the shed quickly grew boring, and he tried to figure some way out, but the wood planks defied his young fingers. He wished he had his pocketknife, but the big bald man named Mallet had held him upside down and shaken everything out of his pockets. Without tools, he was stuck here. He knew he couldn't allow that. He was alive, and that could only mean the pirates hoped to use him to deter Alex, Molly, and the old man. He had to get out. Even if it wasn't far or for long, he'd make sure it was far and long enough to give his friends a chance to find him.

And they would, he told himself. He had faith. They would find him. They were looking for him right now.

They had to be.

At that moment, however, Alex and Molly were sitting despondently on the porch of Little Paradise, staring at the gas pumps and wondering what the hell they *could* do. But there didn't seem to be anything. There wasn't a clue, only a million square miles of empty desert and an equally empty ache in their hearts knowing that the pirate gang had snatched the kid right out of their hands and probably sent him the way of his parents. Or would all too soon, since they wouldn't keep a troublesome brat around for very long.

A state police car materialized down the sizzling, shimmering pavement, approached Little Paradise, and pulled up in front. Out got Captain Reed and Agent Mitchell. The two men ascended the steps to the shaded porch and came over to where Alex and Molly sat.

"How you folks doing?" Mitchell asked, mopping sweat from his dark face with a handkerchief. His tone indicated he thought they'd been doing something they shouldn't.

"Fine, Mr. Mitchell," Alex replied. "Care for a cool soda?"

"If you'd asked me yesterday, I'd've said yes," Mitchell said. "But I don't think we can be that sociable today."

"Why the sudden change?"

Mitchell wrinkled his face and stared out across the gas pumps into the desert beyond the road. "Little incident just across the Arizona line," he said. "Arizona state trooper manning a weigh station got himself run over by a truck."

"You think the road pirates did it?" Molly asked.

"I'm not sure," Mitchell said, looking at her from behind his sunglasses. "What do you think?"

Molly shrugged. "Arizona's a long way from here. First we heard of it."

"Is that right, Mr. Brant?" Reed asked, staring at Alex. "First you heard of it?"

Alex shrugged. "We don't get much news out here."

"No?" Mitchell said, focusing on Alex. "And here I thought you might have something to tell me."

"Such as?"

"Such as why an Arizona state trooper who got himself squashed running away from an old man and two other people might have a load of contraband in the trunk of his car."

"You mean the trooper was dishonest?" Alex asked, tone astonished.

"It appears he had goods that belonged to a truck driver who'd been hijacked earlier in the evening. The hijackers match the descriptions you gave of the bunch that hit you. The driver said he was rescued by several people, but that it was too dark and he was too dazed to tell who they were. And just up the road a few miles, we found the shredded body of.... Well, somebody. It looked like he'd been dragged behind a car. I don't suppose you know anything about that, either."

"All that took place in Arizona...," Alex began, but Reed cut him off.

"Nobody said the hijacking was in Arizona. That happened in my jurisdiction."

"Funny thing was," Mitchell said, "the hijacking happened at the same rest stop where you were shot and robbed." He stared hard at Alex. "You didn't happen to stop at that weigh station, did you?"

"Probably did, if it was on the same route." Alex shrugged. "I stop at a lot of weigh stations. I can't remember them all."

"I think differently. Besides, it doesn't matter to me if the trooper was killed in Arizona or New Mexico," Mitchell said. "This is a federal case. I could take you two in right now."

"On what grounds?"

"I don't need grounds."

"You will to keep us."

"Withholding information."

"We don't know anything more than we've told you," Molly said. "Alex is one of the victims, remember?"

"I saw how victimized he was by those punks that tried to rob this place last week," Reed commented dryly. He didn't sound particularly upset—more like he appreciated the fact that Alex had demolished the bandits.

"Look," Alex temporized. "I promise you we don't know any more about the pirates now than we did before...."

"Before what?" Mitchell pressed.

"Before today. I've told you what I can, and that's all I have."

"I hope so," Mitchell said. "You've already been hurt by this bunch, and I'd hate to see you hurt again."

"That's not going to happen," Alex said.

"It better not. You let us do our job, and you get on with your life." He turned and stepped off the porch, Reed following. He stopped, then, in the sun, and squinted back up at Alex and Molly. "Be thankful you have a life to carry on with."

Then they were in the car and pulling out of Little Paradise, heading back the way they'd come.

"Shit," said Molly.

"They're just doing their job," Alex said, squeezing her knee.

A large brown UPS panel truck passed the highway patrol car going the other way, pulled into the Little Paradise parking lot, and stopped.

"Hey, Dad," Molly called out. "You expecting a package?"

"I think it's for me," Alex said, rising.

"Mr. Brant?" the driver said, stepping out of the truck.

"That's right."

"Sign right here." The driver passed over a hand-held invoice computer, and Alex signed in the space.

"Want some help with that?" he asked as the driver opened the back doors. "It's probably heavy."

"Sure."

They hauled a four-foot long wooden case out of the back of the truck and lugged it onto the porch.

"Let's take it inside."

After Alex and the driver had deposited the case on the floor behind the counter, Molly handed the driver a soda.

"Thanks," she said.

"Ma'am," he replied lifting the soda and taking a drink. A moment later, he was in his truck, heading back toward Socorro. As soon as he'd gone, Alex unlocked the padlocks fastening the chest's lid and opened it. Most of the case was taken up by a Steyer AUG and several cases of ammo, but there was a Beretta 9mm and several cases of ammo for that and magazine slings, too.

"Damn," Molly breathed.

"Called in a favor," Alex said.

The desert rat poked his head out from the back of the trading post and cast a jaundiced eye on the case's contents.

"I assume those cops are gone, the way you're parading that hardware around."

"Yeah," Molly replied. "Not that we had anything new to tell them."

"Maybe you don't, but they didn't ask me."

"What do you mean?"

"Come in. I want to show you something."

They followed him into the back rooms. The TV was playing a fuzzy picture of a talk show where a couple of hundred yelling people were watching a hairy man in lace panties and a bra argue with a chubby young woman in a suit.

"Not that," he said, going to Flix's camera, which trailed wires to the set's inputs. "This. It's one of the video cards from the camera I took off that dead pirate." He punched the camera's play button. "I warn you, though, some of it isn't pleasant."

The fuzzy talk show vanished, replaced by clear footage that showed the road pirates laughing, joking around, and hamming it up for the camera. It looked like they were in some kind of junkyard. Then the camera focused on Yvonne as she leaned against a motorcycle, dangling her pistol. Chains stepped into the picture behind her, mugging and making what he thought were comical gestures. An argument ensued between the two, then the camera panned across the clearing to show T-Bone and Rat emerging from a metal building.

Rat signaled the camera and said, "Let's go, Flix. Scouting party."

The picture changed, now showing desert scenery with an occasional flash of the inside of T-Bone's car as the vehicle emerged from a dirt road onto a two-lane blacktop. A sign came into view not long after, and standing in its shade was a hitchhiker. Suddenly, the sedan swerved toward the hitchhiker, who barely had time to react before his body was tossed into the air, the camera following its arc until it disappeared into the scrub a dozen yards off the road.

Molly gasped as the hitchhiker was flung into the brush.

"Those bastards," Alex grated.

"There's more," the desert rat said grimly. "Not as bad, but more interesting."

The picture changed again as the camera focused on a kiosk next to a gate in a high chain-link fence. There came the sound of footsteps and a car door opening and closing.

"Yuma," said a reedy voice. "I hate this place. And to top it off, they've got to park their fucking Air Force base right across from the worst eats in the state. This is the third time we've had to eat this shit. It's enough to rot your guts."

There was a rustling sound like paper, then another voice, deep and harsh but oddly melodious, said, "Quit grousing, Rat. You haven't got any guts to rot."

"T-Bone," Alex said.

They watched as the camera focused on a convoy emerging from the Air Force base, and the sedan followed the convoy. Rat's comments about the convoy's route were clearly audible, as was his recollection of the Tradewinds Motel. Soon after, scenes of an abandoned motel appeared on the screen, and the three clustered around the TV heard T-Bone's plot to hijack one of the convoy trucks on Thursday.

As the video ended, Alex and the desert rat exchanged a meaningful glance.

"I don't get it," Molly said. "What's it about?"

"Those trucks on the video are a military convoy," Alex told her. "They transport munitions and such. They're unmarked, so most people don't recognize them, though truckers can spot them. Sometimes, they carry radioactive materials and bomb and missile components."

"What would they want with radioactive material?"

"Alex said his truck was hauling electronics," her father pointed out. "And Mitchell said something about the gang having a fancy, spring-loaded mechanism fabricated at that machine shop."

"And don't forget they mentioned some kind of scientist—a professor of some kind," Alex said.

Molly's eyes grew wide with understanding. "You don't think...?"

"Yeah, I do think. These bastards are trying to build some sort of nuclear bomb."

"Is that possible?"

"Very possible," the desert rat affirmed.

"Shit!" said Alex. "Tomorrow's Thursday!" He gave the others a significant look. "Looks like we've got some traveling to do."

Molly nodded and said, "I'll get the Jeep ready."

THIRTY

HATLESS, BILLY-BOB CROUCHED BEHIND an outcrop of rock. Below him, some fifty feet in elevation, the asphalt ribbon of Arizona 85 curved within a hundred feet of his hiding place. The southern end of the curve disappeared half a mile away around a nearly barren hillside, and it was at this juncture that Billy-Bob trained the binoculars he held to his eyes. So far, the road was devoid of significant activity. He set the binoculars on a rock and picked up a walkie-talkie.

Two miles north, at the Tradewinds, T-Bone stood in the entrance to the motel parking area, cradling an M-60 .308 assault rifle in one arm and holding a walkie-talkie in the other hand. A rivulet of sweat rolled down his cheek. He absently wiped at it with the back of the hand holding the radio as he looked down the road toward the south. Next to him, Rat nervously consulted his wristwatch. Suddenly, the walkie-talkie came to life with Billy-Bob's tinny voice.

"Hey, boss. You there?"

"Yeah," T-Bone said, raising the radio.

"I'm in position," Billy-Bob came back.

"Good. Keep your eyes peeled."

"Right. Out."

T-Bone lowered the radio and turned to inspect the motel behind him.

Yvonne and Mallet lounged on some steps, talking and laughing. Parked alongside the north wing, near the highway, was Alex's tractor trailer rig, idling with its front end pointed toward the road. Blade leaned against the fender next to the driver's door, methodically running a whetstone down the blade of a new machete.

The walkie-talkie crackled to life again.

"Here they come, boss," said Billy-Bob.

The gunslinger, still hidden behind the outcrop, was watching the lead Suburban and the first truck round the bend just south of him.

"Take care of things," came T-Bone's voice.

Billy-Bob lowered the binoculars and raised the radio.

"Right, boss. Out."

He propped the walkie-talkie against a rock and picked up a high-power sniper rifle. A large scope hugged the top of the weapon, and the silencer on the barrel gave a cancerous look to its sleek lines. Billy-Bob chambered a round then rested the barrel on a pad he'd placed on the boulder. His eyes narrowed as he squinted through the scope, tracking the lead Suburban and the first truck as they trundled up the highway.

At the motel, T-Bone turned to Rat, simultaneously waving toward Yvonne and Mallet.

"Get them in position," he ordered the small man.

As Rat hurried to obey, T-Bone walked over to Blade where he lounged by the truck. Blade stopped sharpening the machete and looked up expectantly.

"Time?"

"You know what to do." T-Bone waved toward the truck cab.

Blade nodded, sheathed the machete, tossed it up onto the seat, and climbed up after it. He shut the door and looked down through the open window at T-Bone. The big man stared back with deadly seriousness.

"Don't jump the gun, Blade. Wait for my signal. Understand?"

"I won't move until you give the say-so, T-Bone."

While Blade hunkered down in the cab so he couldn't be seen, T-Bone spun and stalked away from the truck. He raised the walkie-talkie.

"Status."

Billy-Bob had stopped peering through the scope because the lead escort vehicle and the first truck had disappeared around the hill at the northern bend of the curve. He heard the query and lifted his radio.

"The first two are by me, boss, and coming your way. Nothing yet on the others." He paused to stare at the southern end of the curve. "No, wait. Here's the second truck."

"What about the others?"

Billy-Bob squinted through his rifle scope at the truck as it moved along the curve, then he scanned the road behind it.

"Can't see 'em."

At the Tradewinds, T-Bone strode toward the gutted restaurant in the end of the motel's southern wing.

"Do the deed, and keep watching for the others," T-Bone said into the radio.

"Right, boss," Billy-Bob came back.

T-Bone spoke into the radio again. "Blade, you read that?"

Inside the cab of Alex's truck, Blade picked up his radio.

"Loud and clear," he said.

T-Bone entered the restaurant. Ignoring the trash and graffiti, he went to a window overlooking the road, his feet crunching on shards of glass broken from the empty frame. Through the gap, he could see the lead escort vehicle and the first truck drawing near.

"First two vehicles approaching," he said into the radio.

Inside the truck cab, Blade peeked over the dash and watched as the Suburban and the truck passed. He chortled.

"They're by," T-Bone's voice crackled over the radio. "Target vehicle should approach in a few minutes. Billy-Bob. Status."

"Target vehicle coming into range now," Billy-Bob said. He set the radio down and quickly took a bead on the truck through the rifle scope. His finger tightened on the trigger as he tracked the target for several seconds. Then a single shot spat out, muffled by the silencer and desert emptiness.

Billy-Bob's accuracy with a rifle was even more phenomenal than with a pistol. The truck's roof-top antenna snapped off cleanly.

In the cab, the truck's driver was tooling along, bored and restless. On the seat beside him lay an AR-15. He heard the whang of the antenna as Billy-Bob's bullet decapitated it, and puzzled at the sound, glanced out of the window. But there was nothing unusual for him to see, the antenna stub being on the roof of the cab above him. He shrugged, figuring he'd unknowingly run over something that had been thrown up into the truck's undercarriage, and settled back in restless boredom.

Billy-Bob lowered the rifle, smiling with satisfaction. He picked up the radio.

"He's deaf and dumb, boss."

In the restaurant, T-Bone, smiling grimly, raised his own radio.

"Good work. Stay in position. If the rear vehicles come on too fast, take care of them.

"Right. Out."

T-Bone looked out the window. Another minute, and the second truck rolled into view. He lifted the radio.

"Okay, Blade. Target vehicle approaching. Get ready."

Inside Alex's truck, Blade sat up and shifted the truck into gear. Concentrating his attention on the portion of the road he could see through his windows, he revved the engine, a nervous grin spreading across his features.

"Keep it cool, Blade," came T-Bone's voice. "Wait for my signal."

The truck was only a hundred yards away, now.

"Get ready, Blade. Ready…."

Blade revved the engine and hunched over the wheel, grin tightening into a grimace. Even he could see the oncoming truck. T-Bone watched the truck rumble up to the motel's southern wing, concentrating on its movement. Suddenly his eyes lit, and he shouted into the radio.

"Now!"

Blade gunned the engine, and Alex's truck lurched forward, rolling out onto the highway, completely blocking it.

The convoy driver's eyes jerked wide as he saw the truck wallow from the motel parking lot, right into his path. He slammed on his brakes. Blade stared out his side window, eyes widening, as the semi bore down on him all too fast.

"Turn, you mother!" Blade shouted, waving frantically. "Turn! Turn!"

For a moment, it looked like the driver wouldn't be able to keep from smashing his vehicle right into Alex's truck. Eyes bugging, Blade raised his hands across his face.

"Oh, shit!" he wailed lamely.

The driver of the convoy truck, in a desperate attempt to avoid a collision, swung his wheel and swerved the careening vehicle into the motel parking lot. The truck sheared across the asphalt, tortured rubber howling, trailer leaning dangerously into the turn.

As the shriek of frantic tires passed, Blade lowered his hands, and his rictus grin of fear vanished in triumphant glee as he stared after the truck that had just missed him.

In the convoy truck, the driver's own look of grim concentration spasmed to horror as he saw the line of motel units strung across his path. He cried out and tried to shield his face as his truck barreled toward the building.

T-Bone rushed out of the restaurant and stared at the truck closing in on the units. There was awe even in *his* heart. This was the kind of action he lived for! Not much else could move him.

The careening truck smashed into the wall of the motel. Shattered cement blocks and boards exploded from the impact site as the eighteen-wheeler went crashing halfway through the narrow building. Momentum finally halted, the truck groaned to a stop in a hiss of steam and clatter of falling boards, its cab protruding through the back wall. A pall of dust rode into the air on the turbulence of the collision. A final board thudded to the ground.

T-Bone's radio crackled to life in air left preternaturally still after the violent wreckage of the moment before.

"Third truck and tail escort in view," came Billy-Bob's voice.

"Let them pass, then get your ass over here!" T-Bone said. He waved at Blade and bellowed into the radio, "Get that truck into position!"

Blade, relieved and not a little surprised to be alive, shakily threw the truck into reverse, backed it up, then pulled forward across the entrance to the parking lot, blocking the lot from the view of anyone passing by on the highway. It now looked just another eighteen-wheeler stopped at a convenient spot to give the driver a chance to nap. Behind it, the cloud of dust began to settle slowly in the heat.

Inside their motel room, Rat, Yvonne, and Mallet crouched by a window overlooking the parking lot, staring at the wreckage of the truck.

"Look at that shit," was all Yvonne could say.

Mallet nodded approvingly. "Hammer of the gods," he agreed.

"Get ready, you two," Rat told them. "The other vehicles are due any minute. If they suspect anything, the shit's gonna fly."

Outside, T-Bone hurried over to Alex's truck and stood beside one of the wheels. In the cab, Blade crouched out of sight.

On the road, the third truck and the tail Suburban approached the motel. The road pirates waited, their weapons ready, as the truck rumbled by Alex's parked eighteen-wheeler. Seconds later, the Suburban passed the motel, its personnel not suspecting that violence to one of their own lay just fifty feet away.

The pirates relaxed and lowered their weapons as T-Bone stepped out into the middle of the parking lot. "All right!" he bellowed. "Let's crack that truck!"

They all swarmed out of their hiding places and over to the wreckage. Yvonne and Mallet went right to the cab to finish off the driver, only to find, to their disappointment, that the job already had been done. The driver was dead, impaled on a jagged piece of lumber that pinned him to the seat like a bug on display.

"Party pooper," Yvonne said, turning away and holstering her .357.

T-Bone shot the locks off the cargo doors at the rear of the trailer with a short burst from his machine gun, and in a moment, he and Rat had the trailer doors open. T-Bone, hefting a crowbar, climbed up inside, followed by Rat.

The two of them rummaged among the tumbled crates for a few moments, until Rat called out from beside a crate, "Here it is, boss."

T-Bone came over and used the crowbar to pop off the wooden lid. Inside were two cradled metal canisters painted yellow and marked with radioactive insignia. The pirates removed the canisters and, carrying one apiece, left the truck.

"Back to the compound!" T-Bone shouted as he hopped to the pavement.

While the other pirates began to move toward their hidden vehicles, T-Bone and Rat set the metal canisters in the trunk of T-Bone's Lincoln. T-Bone tossed his M-60 in after the canisters, and shut the lid. He liked the finality of the thud of the trunk thumping down, but when he turned to get inside, he didn't like what he saw at all.

That fucking trucker who should be dead was standing near the cab of his truck, and it looked like he was holding a Steyer AUG in his hands.

The two men locked eyes for a deadly moment. Then a snarl twisted T-Bone's lips. He whipped the .45 dfrom the holster at his hip and ripped off several shots at Alex.

Alex ducked behind the truck when T-Bone lifted the barrel of the pistol. As the shots split the air, Yvonne and Rat began shooting, too. Bullets peppered the cab of the truck.

From his position behind the cab, Alex couldn't see where all the shots were coming from, but it seemed that only two other pirates besides T-Bone had guns. He risked a quick glance beneath the truck and almost took a flurry of bullets for his trouble. But he'd seen what he needed to see. He'd spotted the positions of the other two shooters, and he'd seen T-Bone opening the trunk of the Lincoln, no doubt to get the M-60 he'd just tossed in there. Alex knew he'd have to do something quickly before T-Bone could bring the heavy machine gun to bear, for slugs from it could tear completely through the cab.

But not the engine block.

Using the big front tire and wheel as steps, he climbed up onto the wheel cover and crouched there a split second before popping up and firing two quick bursts. The first drove T-Bone behind the Lincoln and the second splintered the doorway from which one of the other shooters was firing.

Alex ducked as bullets scored the hood where he'd just been. The shots sounded like they'd come from a heavy handgun, and he knew that it must be Yvonne pulling the trigger. Then he could do little more than crouch and pray as heavy rounds from T-Bone's machine gun hammered the truck cab. Glass shattered, and fragments of metal and plastic flew.

T-Bone was standing erect behind the Lincoln, feet braced against the jackhammer recoil of the M-60. He was determined to tear the truck to shreds if he had to to get at the trucker hiding behind it. But something changed his mind. That something was a shotgun blast that peppered the Lincoln's rear windshield. He ducked behind the sedan as another shotgun blast slammed into the doorway from which Yvonne was shooting.

That goddamn trucker had at least two friends, one at the end of each motel wing and both with scatterguns.

"Fuck!" he said as he groped for another magazine for the M-60 and realized his extra ammo was still in the trunk, which he'd never make without taking a shotgun blast or a burst from that fucking trucker's Steyer.

"You fucker!" he screamed at Alex in impotent fury.

Alex heard the pirate leader's cry of rage. He popped up, saw T-Bone looking toward the southern wing, then caught a movement out of the corner of his eye. The little man known as Rat was leveling a gun at him from inside the doorway where he'd been hiding.

Alex whipped up the Steyer barrel and squeezed off a burst. The bullets caught the man in the chest. Blood and bone flew, and the shattered body tumbled backwards into the room.

Alex ducked as Yvonne fired at him, but a blast from Molly at the north wing made the pirate woman jerk back into her room.

So far, so good, Alex thought. We've got them pinned down. He hopped off the wheel cover, but stayed behind the wheel itself. Poking the snout of the Steyer around the rubber, he snapped off a quick burst into the wall of the room where Yvonne was hidden and was rewarded by a shriek of surprise.

Then it was his turn to be surprised as a slug whanged into the bumper inches from his head. He whipped around to see the pudgy cowboy, Billy-Bob, racing up the road in the pirates' Pontiac, shooting one of his silver-plated .45s left-handed from the driver's window.

Alex rolled behind the wheel as another bullet kicked up dirt, and he saw the desert rat dive through a window into the restaurant as Billy-Bob's bullets crunched cement block near him, sending chips zinging out.

Then the Pontiac spun into the parking lot and stopped near the room where Yvonne and Mallet crouched. In a second, Billy-Bob was out of the car, fast-firing at Alex's position and yelling for the other pirates to get in.

They didn't need urging. T-Bone, throwing a final glimpse toward Rat's body, leapt into the Lincoln, started it, and peeled out across the bruised asphalt, barely pausing to pick up Blade before fishtailing south down the highway. Yvonne and Mallet raced for the Pontiac and dove inside, Mallet in the back and Yvonne shotgun. With Billy-Bob and Yvonne's guns blazing out of the windows, the Pontiac chased the Lincoln down the blacktop. A moment later, all that was left was the diminishing sounds of their engines hanging in air thick with dust and the smell of gunpowder.

Alex, Molly, and the desert rat ran for the Cherokee, which was parked just south of the restaurant, then slowed as they came up to it. One of its tires was shot out.

Alex just stood there, knuckles whitening on the Steyer, watching the pirates' cars vanish around a distant curve to the south.

Thirty-one

Phyllis crouched in the interior of a wrecked car. Her "home." This den with metal walls had been a lucky find. Though not large, it was long enough for her to stretch out and high enough to sit up. Buried in the midst a large pile of wrecks, it was completely invisible from either of the nearby corridors. The bulk of metal around her kept the temperature relatively cool in the daytime and, at night, retained some warmth from the heat of day, making the chill desert darkness tolerable. Even better, she could get to it through a tunnel in the wrecks, so she didn't have to leave a telltale trail on the ground that would lead Mallet to her. He was the only one actually looking for her—even Bulge had given up, and the rest of the pirates didn't care. Most probably thought she was dead or that Mallet would eventually find her.

In the dim light filtering through chinks in the pile of rumpled metal around her car, Phyllis was pounding a nail through the board she'd taken from T-Bone's exercise machine. Mallet's ball peen hammer rose and fell on the head. Two other nails already pierced the board. She missed a stroke and smacked her finger. It was a measure of how much she'd changed during the past few months that she merely jerked and grunted before going right back to work. A few more strokes, and she was finished. She set the board aside and slipped the hammer into a looped thong tied around her waist. Then she ducked through the opening to her den, crawled through the cramped, twisting corridor into the daylight, and peered around suspiciously. Seeing and hearing no one, she hurried off into the maze of corridors.

A week of living on her own in the metal labyrinth had set its pattern in her brain. She knew every twist and turn and a few bolt holes that only a rabbit, or a desperate human, might find. At first, she'd thought about leaving the junkyard and striking out across the desert, but prudence had halted immediate flight. She knew she'd need food and, more importantly, water in order to escape across the burning earth and rock. So she'd spent the next few days laying aside a travel bag.

Water was easy enough to come by. There was a spigot at the rear clearing used for servicing the heavy equipment, and she'd found and rinsed out a pair of plastic gallon jugs and filled them from it.

Food was harder to come by, but she made do. There was garbage from the pirates' meals tossed in a dump over the junk-yard's back fence, and a couple of times she'd found bird eggs in nests hidden in the warp and woof of twisted wreckage. She fried them on sun-blasted metal. Once she caught a large lizard, intending to eat it, but its helpless captivity reminded her too much of her own, and in pity, she let it go.

She'd even managed to get hold of some cast-off clothing and no longer had to go around naked. A ragged pair of pants with its legs tied shut made an admirable pack to carry the provisions that she'd acquired for a short journey. Why she hesitated as she stood on the top rung of the makeshift ladder she'd built to get over the corrugated metal wall she wasn't sure. She just looked over the expanse of desert and the short, rocky mountains in the middle distance, then descended back into the junkyard.

For one thing, she had no idea where she was, which direction to go, or how far help might be. For all she knew, she'd have to go hundreds of miles before she found someone, and she didn't think she'd make it that far. Her feet had callused, but not enough to withstand days on end of ragged rock. Of course, she could always go down the dirt road that led to the junkyard. It had to connect to another road and that to civilization. But the pirates were always coming and going, and that way lead only to recapture.

She wasn't sorry for her decision to stay. The desert would be certain death, though she realized that if she stayed, sooner or later she was bound to be caught. There were too many pirates, and she couldn't maintain a constant vigil. She doubted that Mallet would be the one to find her. He was such a rude, noisy clod that she invariably heard him coming a hundred feet away. But some of the others weren't so loud. And when she was caught, by whomever managed it, she would quickly end up in Mallet's embrace. She suspected that this time that embrace would be all too tight and all too short.

So it was that she resolved to do as much damage to the pirates as she could before Mallet's hands and hammers tore the life from her. It was the least she could do for Rob and Heath.

A few minutes after emerging from her den, she came on the bulldozer squatting silently in a corridor. She circled it, eyeing it appraisingly, then found the oil filler cap and unscrewed it. Bending, she scooped up a handful of dirt and dumped it into the opening. A second handful followed the first. She was bending for a third when a small scuffing noise startled her. Her hand automatically dropped to the hammer at her waist, and she crouched behind the bulldozer and peered under it at the mouth of a corridor that opened on the clearing.

A second later, Jojo came into view, toting the chrome-plated .44. She walked into the center of the clearing while Phyllis crouched behind the bulldozer, keeping it between them. As Jojo passed the bulldozer, she paused and looked around suspiciously.

"Where are you, you stinking freak?" she muttered.

Her eyes passed over the small open mouth of the oil fill hole, but while Jojo knew a lot about servicing T-Bone, she knew nothing about servicing machinery, and the fact that the oil filler cap was off meant nothing to her.

Besides, even the compound's working machinery looked like junk to her, whether it was running or not. That's all there was around this shitty place—junk, junk, and more junk. Jojo was sick of all this shitty junk. In fact, the only reason she stuck around was T-Bone, with his promise of the good life just around the corner and the feel of his big cock between her legs any time she wanted it.

Jojo had had her fair share of cock growing up in Kansas City. She was, after all, beautiful, which meant that there was no end to the men desiring to possess her. But the good life had never been around any corner in her neighborhood. It had always seemed to be on the other side of town. Somehow, though, she'd never been taken in by the self-waste of gangs, prostitution, and drugs that masqueraded as the good life on her side of the tracks. She wanted the real thing—the kind lived by movie stars and celebrities. That's why she split for LA as soon as she turned eighteen, carrying a single suitcase and packing a couple of grand in cash that she'd earned at the local burger shack.

She never made it.

At the bus station in Amarillo, she noticed a big man talking to a couple of Mexicans. Hell, who wouldn't have noticed T-Bone? But there was something hauntingly familiar about him. Had she been a little more self-aware, she'd have realized that he could have posed for the cover of any of the cheap bodice rippers she constantly read, but even with one in her hand, she didn't notice. All she saw was that the Mexicans looked rough, but T-Bone's whole way of holding himself said he didn't give a shit how rough they were.

Not that there was any hint of trouble. They seemed to be just talking over cups of coffee in the bus station lounge. Pretending to read her paperback, she tried to figure out what they were discussing, knowing that it had to be dangerous or illegal or both. She knew about bad boys—she'd dated enough of them, hadn't she?

Suddenly, she realized that the big man was staring right at her. His gaze speared through her like she was a rodent transfixed by a cobra. It seemed like a long time before she managed to lift the book like a dead weight to block him out. When she had the courage to peek again, he was facing the Mexicans.

She got up and went to the ladies room, surprised to find that her knees felt weak. When she came out a few minutes later, the big man and Mexicans were gone. Sitting down, she opened her book and began to read, but after she'd gone through most of the rest of the chapter, she felt a presence beside her.

And there he was, two seats away, staring at her like she was naked or something.

"Going to LA," he said without a trace of question in his voice.

"That's right. Not that it's any of your business."

"Gonna be the next big thing. Make the scene. Be rich and famous."

"I can do it."

"Maybe you can. But I have a better suggestion."

"What's that?"

"Leave with me."

"Yeah, right." She meant it to come out heavily laced with sarcasm, but it sounded shaky instead.

"You'll be better off."

"What could be better than being rich and famous?"

"Rich and anonymous."

"You don't look rich, but you sure look anonymous," she said, wrinkling her nose.

"Looks can be deceiving," he said, but she didn't believe him. His looks could never deceive anyone.

"I have to catch my bus," she said.

"Why don't you let me drive you?"

"Drive me?" She laughed in spite of herself. "To LA?"

"Sure."

"You going there?"

"I wasn't," he shrugged. "But I can if you want."

"Yeah, like I'm going to get in the car with a strange man who says he'll drive two thousand miles out of his way just for the heck of it."

"I won't hurt you," he said. "I promise."

And the hell of it was, she believed him. And he didn't. He was the perfect gentleman until they reached Flagstaff, where he rented two rooms for the night—one for her and one for him—in a pretty decent motel. About two o'clock, she couldn't stand it any more. She knocked on his door, and after he let her in, he fucked her brains out. And he never did hurt her. Ever.

And the longer they were together, the more she believed that he really would be rich and anonymous.

But that didn't mean she wasn't bored with this junkyard in the sun. She wanted to be with T-Bone, sure, but she wanted them to be together on some exotic beach somewhere. She understood, though, that she'd have to be patient a little longer. T-Bone had business to take care of, and that was fine, since she had some un-finished business of her own.

Bulge.

That freak had to be around here somewhere. All she had to do was catch him alone. Hefting the heavy revolver and walking on, she entered the mouth of another corridor across the clearing.

As soon as Jojo disappeared, Phyllis quickly tried to replace the oil filler cap, but in her haste, she got it on crooked. Instead of struggling with it and taking a chance that Jojo might come back, she left the cap skewed and scurried out of the clearing in the op-posite direction from the way the pirate woman had gone. She was going back to her den to wait for dusk and its relative protection, but she might have gone a different direction and taken a risk had she realized her son was locked in the shed where she'd been kept when she'd first been taken prisoner.

Heath was alone and afraid, though no one had really hurt him. Yet. But he knew they were keeping him in this bare, hot little room for a reason that couldn't be pleasant.

He heard a clatter as someone unlocked the door, and he crouched against the back wall, shielding his eyes from the glare as the greasy man they called Slick came in, carrying a plate of food and a spoon.

"Here," the mechanic said, setting the plate of food on the wooden floor. "The boss told me to feed you."

He leaned against the door frame and watched as the boy picked up the spoon and took a tentative bite.

The food—some kind of stew—was awful.

"Good, ain't it?" Slick asked conversationally. "Made it myself."

Heath forced himself to take another bite. He was too hungry not to.

Several miles away, dust billowed in the late afternoon air as T-Bone's Lincoln spun off the blacktop into the entrance of the dirt track leading to the compound. Billy-Bob followed as best as he could, but after a momentary clatter of gravel on the Pontiac's windshield, the Lincoln was too far in the lead to try to close on it. Billy-Bob let off the gas, and the jouncing of the car along the dirt road eased.

"What the fuck you slowing down for?" Mallet shot from the back seat.

"Because I want to get to the compound in one piece," Billy-Bob said.

"Fuck peace," Mallet ground out. "Step on it."

Yvonne, riding shotgun, glanced over her shoulder at the hammer man. "No need killing ourselves." she said. "Besides, you want to catch up with T-Bone when he's so pissed? Personally, I want to keep as far away from him as I can until he cools off."

Mallet barked thick laughter.

"He ain't gonna cool off until that trucker's on ice."

Inside the Lincoln, now nearly half a mile in front of the Pontiac, T-Bone drove with maniacal intensity, jaw muscles bunching, eyes burning with insane anger. The heavy car jolted down the ruts as the big man hunched over the jerking, twisting wheel.

Next to him on the seat, Blade ground his teeth and hung on as the car swerved around a huge boulder that nearly blocked the road and soared down an incline. He glanced over at T-Bone, a touch of panic at his reckless speed and abandon overlaying the anger in his own eyes. But the anger overcame the fear, flaring to match his leader's glare.

"It was him, T-Bone. It was that bastard beefcake Yvonne shot."

"I recognized him," the pirate leader grated.

"How the fuck did he know we were there?"

T-Bone hadn't heard him, or he simply ignored the question.

"Goddamn bastard," T-Bone snarled. "I'm gonna catch him and shred his guts in front of his own eyes."

T-Bone slowed, but only barely, as the car approached the entrance to the junkyard.

"Goddamn that Slick!" T-Bone thundered as he saw the gates were closed.

He hit the brake, and the car skidded to a halt a bare two feet from the chain-link. He laid on the horn, and as the sound blared into the darkening air, he jabbed the electric window button. When the glass dropped into the door, the pirate chief leaned out and bellowed angrily.

"Slick, you fucker! Open this goddamn gate!"

The kid had nearly finished eating when Slick heard the horn and T-Bone's yell. Without a second thought, he hurried from the shed, pausing only to lock the door before he ran to the front gate.

In the shed's dimness, Heath pushed away the plate and, gripping the spoon tightly, turned to the floor at the back corner.

Outside the gate, T-Bone slammed a fist onto the horn again, and the sound cut through the still desert air. A second later, Slick's face peeked timidly over the wall.

"Open this gate, Slick, or I'll pop your head like a greasy pimple!"

The look of terror on Slick's face was his only reply. His head jerked behind the wall, and a moment later, the gate rolled aside.

T-Bone, peeling out in a cloud of dust, whipped his sedan into the compound. By now, the Pontiac had caught up, and it followed. The gate closed behind the two cars, but even as it did, T-Bone was out of his car and slamming the door.

Professor Sledge and Bulge emerged from the metal building and came over to the Lincoln.

"Ah, my dear Mr. T-Bone," Sledge said jovially. "Did you get my reactive materials?"

T-Bone grabbed the renegade scientist by the lapels and hoisted him off the ground, bringing them eye-to-eye.

"This bomb better work, old man," T-Bone snarled, "or there'll be shit to pay. Your shit."

As he spoke, Jojo hurried from the junkyard and came over.

"I assure you, Mr. T-Bone," Sledge said in a mollifying tone. "It will work most eminently."

"It better. We almost blew the whole thing getting your radioactive junk, and I lost another man."

"Rat...?" Jojo asked, looking around, voice shocked.

"Yeah. The little fucker finally gets the guts to shoot at something and gets a bellyful of lead for his trouble." T-Bone released Sledge and dropped the car keys into his hand. "The stuff's in the trunk."

Roughly shouldering Sledge aside, T-Bone gestured to Jojo.

"Come inside," T-Bone said, boiling with subdued ferocity. "I want to dictate a letter to the Vegas mob. They're either gonna come up with five hundred million cash, or they're gonna host the biggest barbecue in history."

With that, he stalked off toward the metal building, Jojo hurrying primly along in his wake.

After the pirate leader disappeared inside, Sledge and Bulge went to the rear of the Lincoln and opened the trunk. Inside lay the canisters marked with radioactive warning signs. Sledge, eyes glowing, gently lifted one and cradled it like an infant in his arms.

"My baby." He looked at Bulge. "Our dreams are about to be realized, dear brother."

Bulge, grinning, nodded vigorously and caressed the tools on his belt. Sledge held the canister up and squinted intently through his thick glasses at it, reading the label.

"'Low-grade fissionable material,'" he quoted, and a broad, pale smile smeared across his face. He cradled the canister once more and rocked it back and forth, his eyes staring skyward, gleaming madly. "Ah," he chortled. "It's going to be such a *dirty* little bomb!"

THIRTY-TWO

IT WAS EARLY MORNING AT Little Paradise. In the backyard, Alex and Molly were working out, both grim-faced as he showed her some martial arts moves.

It would have been difficult for her to believe that these soft, gentle, flowing movements could impart deadly skill, but she'd seen the results with her own eyes.

"It's harder than it looks," she had to admit. "To make it go so slow and yet be yielding and graceful."

"There are a couple of factors involved," he said. "You go slow to train your body to do each movement as precisely and thoroughly as possible. You also go slow to increase strength and stamina. Lift your arm like you normally would."

She did.

"Now, lift it as slowly as possible."

She did that, too, and found it much more difficult.

"It's harder when you go slow," she admitted. "But its harder in ways other than just physical. It's harder to concentrate on the movement all the way through and make it smooth."

He nodded.

"Yeah. That's the other aspect of going slow. Concentration's the key. It's like a coin. There's *attention*, which is the passive side, and *intention*, which is the active side. For most people, the intention part's easy. It's the attention that's more difficult. But they really have to work together."

She looked puzzled.

"Try this," he said, smiling. "Look at the cut in the mesa."

She stared across the flats behind Little Paradise to the dark cut that climbed the mesa wall.

"Now, focus on the top of the rock fall, just at the base of the cut. What do you see?"

"I see the cut and the big boulders at the top of the rock fall."

"Now look at me."

She faced him, eyes curious.

"Now," he said, waving expansively toward the desert behind Little Paradise. "What's out there?" She turned.

"The mesa. Sand and rock. Scrub. The mesa and cut. A few high clouds."

"What's the difference between the two times you looked?"

"The action's the same, but what's happening inside is totally opposite. Like giving and taking. But no matter which one I'm doing, the other is still there."

"The yin and yang," Alex said. "Intention is yang and attention is yin. The Chinese equivalents to positive and negative force or any other sets of polar opposites. The theory says that when positive force reaches its peak, it turns into negative force, and when negative force reaches its nadir, it turns into positive force. That's the theory behind tai chi."

"So, if you practice softly and gently," she said, "when the time comes to use it, it automatically can become hard and not so gentle."

"You got it."

The back screen door opened, and the desert rat emerged, followed by Henry Mitchell, the FBI agent. Mitchell's tie was loosened, and he carried his jacket draped over his arm.

"How you folks doing," Mitchell asked.

"I tried to tell him I was watching a cheap action adventure movie on TV," said the desert rat, "but he insisted on coming in."

"Where's Captain Reed?" Alex asked.

"This is New Mexico," Mitchell said. "As you keep pointing out, and everything keeps happening in Arizona."

"Something new?"

"What if I told you we found your truck?"

"Great," Alex said. "When can I pick it up?"

Mitchell eyed him for a long moment, then he shook his head.

"You look like a strong fellow, but not that strong. Besides being in impound, it isn't worth the salvage. Keep on working with your insurance company. I'm sure they'll do right by you."

"Yeah, sure," quipped the desert rat. "You filed any claims, lately, Mr. Mitchell?"

"No," Mitchell said. "I'm usually a little more careful who I deal with, and my vehicles don't usually get shot to hell with an M-60.

The cab looks like it was made of Swiss cheese, and the engine block is full of lead. Oh, and there were a couple of bodies nearby."

"Well, damn," Alex said. "Anybody know who they are?"

"One of them's a mystery, but we're working on it. The other was a U.S. Air Force driver. He was dead at the wheel of his truck from which two canisters of low-grade fissionable material were stolen."

"You wouldn't be accusing...," began the desert rat, but Mitchell cut him off.

"Save it," the agent snapped. He looked at Alex. "I did a background check on you, and I know what you're capable of."

"I'm just a vet trying to get along."

"I know what you're doing," Mitchell went on, ignoring the remark. "And there's only one thing worse than me catching you doing it—that's seeing some innocent person get hurt because you think you can do this better than we can."

"Seeing innocent people hurt is the last thing on our minds," Alex said. "In fact, we're studiously avoiding it."

"Shit," Mitchell spat, then he stared hard at Alex. "You better call me if you get anything definite. I mean it." He pivoted and strode toward the corner of the trading post, but about half way there, he paused and turned. "Or at least have the courtesy to call me to wipe up the mess when it's all over."

Then he was gone.

"And I had to interrupt my show for that," the desert rat said.

"You're watching some crappy movie?" Molly demanded. "At a time like this?"

"A rerun," the desert rat said with a sly grin. "Come on in. I think you'll like it too."

They followed him inside to the TV.

"We've seen this," Alex said as the road pirate footage began playing on the screen.

"Maybe," the desert rat replied. "But we haven't really looked."

The camera followed the pirates around the compound as they joked and hammed it up for the camera.

"I still don't see," Alex said. "It's the pirates, but...."

"I'm beginning to get the picture," Molly said, and she poked Alex. "You're looking with intention. Try attention.

"Okay," he said. "That's got to be where they live, right? But what good does it do us? There's nothing to identify where they are. It's just out in the desert somewhere."

"Desert schmesert," the desert rat said scornfully. "It all looks the same, right? Wrong. It doesn't all look the same. See?"

He froze the picture. On the screen, beyond the fence, was a mountain. Not a peculiar-looking mountain, just a mountain as unlike other mountains as it was similar. As the camera panned to cover the pirates, other physical features of the terrain showed themselves. Alex perked up and smiled.

"I see. That mountain. If we could find it, we can find them. But how can we narrow it down? There's a lot of square miles out there. It'll be impossible to find that particular valley without help."

"Keep watching," said the desert rat.

The screen showed the scenery as the car emerged from the dirt road. Then the hitchhiker appeared, standing in the shade of a mileage sign.

"Look's like we've got help," Molly said, pointing to the sign. "I'll get a map."

THIRTY-THREE

SLICK FIDGETED, MOVING ONE WAY then the other as he tried to see around T-Bone's broad back. The pirate leader was standing in the open side door of the *Granola Gray*, casually leaning on a meaty forearm draped across the top of the opening.

T-Bone was watching Professor Sledge and Bulge work on the large angular black console that occupied most of the van's interior. The renegade scientist certainly cut a comical figure. Dressed in a heavy apron of lead shielding, thick gloves, and a bizarre tube-shaped helmet with a thick, square faceplate tinted silver, he looked like some whacked scientist in a low-budget 1950s sci-fi movie. T-Bone nearly burst out laughing, but he caught himself—not out of courtesy but because he didn't want to break Sledge's concentration.

Sledge turned to Bulge and held out his gauntlet-clad hands.

"The reactive materials, dear brother," he said in a muffled voice.

As Bulge unscrewed the end of the first canister, Sledge leaned close. "Careful, now," he warned.

He was so bound up in his protective clothing that he couldn't see what he was doing, and he jostled his brother's elbow. Bulge promptly dropped the canister lid, and it hit the van floor with a ringing bang.

"You stupid klutz!" Sledge snatched the canister from his brother's hands and cuffed him on the ear, nearly spilling the canister's contents in the process.

Bulge whined and backed away as Sledge fumbled to regain control of the canister with his thick gauntlets.

"Get the other canister, fool," Sledge snarled. "And be careful this time."

T-Bone laughed, then, unable to contain himself.

"Why don't you take off all that shit, Sledge? You're gonna drop it yourself."

"This is reactive material, dear Mr. T-Bone." The silver face plate turned in T-Bone's direction. "One must exercise caution."

"Caution!" T-Bone snorted. "You afraid it's gonna mess up your chromosomes?" He guffawed loudly and slapped Slick on the back. Slick winced and gave a weak grin. He didn't know what a chromosome was, but it must be something funny.

"This is my child," Sledge said, waving around the interior of the van. "And this is the seed that will give my child life." He held up the canister. "I simply wish to live long enough to see my child blossom into full adulthood."

"Just get on with it," T-Bone said curtly, all humor gone.

Wordlessly, Sledge picked up a pair of tongs, reached inside the canister, and drew out a chromium cylinder. He put the canister aside and, grunting, crawled into an open panel in the side of the angular console. Just in front of him was a lead casing, and inside the casing was a small cradle to hold the cylinder. Sledge slipped the cylinder into place and closed the casing panel.

"The second canister, Bulge," he ordered, reaching out of the console. Bulge handed him the second canister, and Sledge removed the second cylinder and placed it into another cradle inside the other end of the lead casing. He twisted a final pair of wires together, then stuck his hand out of the panel.

"Wire cutters."

Bulge slapped the cutters into his hand like a surgical nurse handing a doctor a hemostat. Sledge clipped the ragged ends of the wires then set the wire cutters aside.

"Tape."

Bulge handed over a coil of black electrician's tape, and Sledge taped over the bare wire ends then crawled out of the bomb casing and shut the panel. As he removed his helmet, Bulge plucked at his sleeve, trying to mouth the words, "Wire cutters," but failing. He pointed to the empty slot in his tool belt, but Sledge just shrugged him off and turned to T-Bone.

"We have done it, Mr. T-Bone," Sledge said, voice tinged with awe.

"It'll work?"

"Shall we test it?"

Grinning insanely, Sledge reached toward a switch on the control panel. Slick and Bulge cringed, but T-Bone just laughed.

"We'll test it, Professor. In Las Vegas."

"I wish you'd reconsider your choice of cities, Mr. T-Bone. LA is a much more rational choice…."

"I know you got some sort of negative thing for LA, Sledge," T-Bone said. "And I appreciate that. But for this first effort, we have to go for the big money. Do you know how much cash is in Vegas?"

"There is much gambling there."

"Gambling isn't the half of it. The place is the world's largest money laundering operation. The mob, drug lords, Internet scam artists—they all use Vegas. If we ask LA for five hundred million, they'd bring in the feds and aircraft surveillance and the whole nine yards. Vegas, though, they don't want to lose their gravy train, which couldn't really exist anywhere else. There'll be enough dirty cash lying around to easily make our ransom. The city fathers—namely the mob—won't like it, but they'll call it the price of doing business. But don't worry, Sledge, LA's a ripe target. If Vegas works out, we'll do LA next."

"But what if we have to detonate Vegas?" the professor asked, creases forming between his wild eyebrows. "Our bomb will be gone."

"You built one, didn't you?" T-Bone waved at the *Granola Gray*. "I'll make it possible for you to build another."

"Why, yes," Sledge said, brightening. "I suppose I could."

T-Bone turned to Slick.

"Tell the others to get ready. We travel at first light."

THIRTY-FOUR

THE ASPHALT SPUN BENEATH THE Cherokee's tires as the vehicle cruised slowly down the two-lane blacktop. Molly was at the wheel, steering casually with one hand while she lifted a covered cup of coffee to her lips. Next to her sat Alex, also drinking coffee and scanning the surrounding countryside. The sun was just peeping over the low mountain ridge to the east, bathing the landscape in red-gold light.

A rustle of paper came from the back seat as the desert rat held the map closer to his eyes.

"I think we're getting pretty close," he said.

"We must be," Alex said, "since we're getting about as far from anything else as possible."

"Look!" the desert rat said, pointing. The Jeep had just rounded a bend, and ahead on the right was a mountain with a familiar shape.

"The mountain on the video," Alex said.

"Yeah," Molly agreed. "We're close."

A moment later, the Cherokee passed a dirt road on the right leading out into the desert. It was like thousands of other dirt roads they'd seen and ignored, but here and now, they stared suspiciously at it as they drove by. A weather-worn wooden sign, completely devoid of paint, was crumbling into a nearby patch of creosote and prickly pear.

"Think that's it?" Alex asked.

"Could be," the desert rat said. "Let's go on a little farther."

They didn't have to go too much farther.

"The sign," Alex said simply.

Molly parked the Jeep on the shoulder next to a sign that looked exactly like the one they'd seen in the footage of the hitchhiker being killed. They got out and began rummaging around in the scrub. That didn't take long, either.

"He's over here," Alex said.

There wasn't much left of the hitchhiker, just a grisly, caved-in skeleton stripped of flesh. The backpack was on its back, the sign, "LA or Bust," lay face up across the crushed ribs, and the right hand was still extended in the classic hitchhiking gesture, thumb stuck out.

"Nothing lasts long out here," said the desert rat.

"Nothing soft," Alex said. "Come on. It has to be that dirt road back there."

In the Jeep, Molly made a U-turn and sped back to the insignificant intersection. Pulling into the dirt road, she proceeded at a cautious pace.

"How far do you figure it is?" she asked.

"Your guess is as good as mine," Alex said. "Eustace, better get armed." The desert rat, wincing at Alex's use of his name, unzipped a duffel bag and a couple of day packs on the floor behind Molly and began removing weapons: the Steyer and 9mm for Alex, shotguns and pistols for Molly and himself.

The condition of the road was much worse at its mouth than it was farther into the desert, but Molly maintained a relatively slow speed. They drove along the road for several minutes, watching for signs of the pirates and keeping an eye on the telltale mountain. After nearly five miles, the road took a sharp twist around a large boulder, and Molly downshifted and started to steer around the outcrop. Suddenly, with a curse, she whipped the wheel hard to the side, just barely avoiding a collision with three vehicles that roared around the bend and raced toward the highway in a cloud of dust.

In the lead vehicle, the Lincoln, T-Bone barely flinched when the Jeep veered out of his path, though his jaw muscles bunched as he glanced in the rearview mirror. But Jojo beside him and Billy-Bob in the back both swung around and stared as first the *Granola Gray*, with Blade at the wheel, then the Pontiac, driven by Mallet, sped by the Cherokee.

"It's that fucking trucker!" Billy-Bob yelled. He drew his pistols and checked the chambers.

"I want to shoot him, T-Bone," Jojo pleaded.

With a grin, T-Bone thrust his M-60 at her.

"Here, baby," he said with grim humor. "Knock yourself out."

Jojo took the weapon. Though it was far too big for her, she drew the bolt and cradled it like she knew what she was doing.

Inside the *Granola Gray*, Blade hadn't had to swerve to avoid hitting the Jeep, which already had gone off the road, but he had to pound his brakes to avoid rear-ending the Lincoln. An instant before impact, the Lincoln, spewing dirt and rocks, accelerated away.

"Goddamn!" he commented. "Oh, shit!"

Sledge, gasping as the overloaded van jolted and swayed on its springs, held on to the bomb casing for dear life. Next to him, Bulge gaped wild-eyed at the near miss.

"What is it?" Sledge asked.

"It's that trucker and his friends. The ones who've been giving us all that trouble." He looked out his own rearview mirror just in time to see Yvonne, face distorted with rage, hang out of the Pontiac's window.

"You're mine, beefcake! Mine!" she shrieked.

"Get the fucker!" Mallet yelled from beside her, fighting to keep from ramming into the back of the *Granola Gray*.

Yvonne fired a couple of convulsive shots at the Jeep, whose occupants crouched as her gun barked. Then the Pontiac was gone around the outcrop, and Molly spun the wheel, gunned the engine, and fishtailed back onto the dirt road.

"The bomb must be in that van" she said.

"Yeah," Alex said. "We've got to stop it."

He leaned out the window and fired at the pirate vehicles, his bullets stitching the trunk of the Pontiac. The desert rat fired, too, but his shotgun had little effect except to pepper the rear windshield. Yvonne, screaming curses, emptied her gun at them then ducked back into the car, still cursing, to reload.

As her enraged fingers fumbled ammo into the cylinder, Mallet threw a quick glance at her.

"Get the fucker, Yvonne!"

"Keep your eyes on the road," she snapped.

Mallet looked ahead just in time to see a large mass of rock looming just ahead. He wrenched the wheel, and the Pontiac slewed sideways, just missing the boulder. He spun the wheel again and mashed on the gas. The Pontiac growled back onto the road, churning a new rut in the desert floor. As soon as Mallet regained control, Yvonne popped out of the window, pistol in her hand.

Alex let loose another burst as Yvonne fired back. One of her bullets starred the Jeep's windshield, forcing its occupants to duck. Then, as Yvonne plunged back inside to reload, Alex ripped off two more bursts, and the Pontiac's rear windshield frosted with myriad cracks and holes. One of the bullets punched through the windshield right in front of Mallet, and he jerked instinctively, sending the car swerving off the road and plowing into a hillock sixty feet away. As the Jeep roared by in a cloud of dust, Yvonne flung open her door and jumped out, gun blazing.

Two of her shots pierced the Jeep but missed those inside. Then the Jeep was past the Pontiac, accelerating after the *Granola Gray*.

Billy-Bob had been watching the action through the rear window of T-Bone's sedan.

"They're by Mallet and Yvonne!" he shouted.

"Shit!" T-Bone yelled. "Shoot the fuckers!"

"I can't see around the van."

"There's a curve coming up. You'll have a clear shot then. We gotta shake 'em before we hit the highway."

As the three vehicles scrambled down the road toward the curve, Sledge hung onto the bomb and peered through the back windows at the Jeep as it closed in on the *Granola Gray*.

"They're approaching, Blade," he whined, voice tinged with panic.

"I know! I know!" Blade yelled, struggling with the wheel. The *Granola Gray* was heavy with lead shielding and sluggish on springs not quite strong enough for the load, making it difficult to control at any sort of high speed over the ruts in the dirt road. "And we don't have a gun!"

Alex fired a couple of bursts at the *Granola Gray*, and bullet holes etched the van's rear door panels. One of the slugs gouged a chunk out of the bomb casing not two feet from Sledge's face. Sledge stared at the scar with wide eyes then threw himself onto the casing, stroking the hot slash with frantic fingers.

"My baby," he moaned. "They're trying to kill my baby."

Bulge cowered on the floor.

At that moment, the Lincoln bore into the curve. Both Billy-Bob and Jojo leaned out of their windows, and as the Jeep came into sight, they blasted away at it. The three in the Jeep threw themselves down as bullets shattered the windshield and whined through the vehicle. Molly almost lost control but kept the Jeep from going off the road. T-Bone glanced back and saw the Jeep still fast on his tail.

"Kill the fuckers!" he bellowed insanely. "Shoot 'em! Shoot 'em!"

Jojo and Billy-Bob leaned out again, looking for an opening. Billy-Bob, quicker with his lighter weapon, fired a couple of shots. Jojo, seeing a chance, raised the M-60, and her finger tightened on the trigger just as the three vehicles careened into another curve. Bullets sprayed from the machine gun's muzzle, churning dirt then metal and plastic as they plowed across the front of the Jeep. But T-Bone's sedan had arced into view of the Cherokee, too, and Alex fired an extended burst, his bullets trailing holes across the back of T-Bone's sedan. The last two slugs shredded the left rear tire.

The sedan lurched and swerved wildly as T-Bone fought to retain control. Billy-Bob was thrown back into the car, but Jojo, burdened by the weight of the heavy M-60 and overbalanced by the lurching of the sedan, couldn't get back in. The Lincoln slewed sharply toward a boulder and sideswiped it, battering JoJo against the rock, leaving gore spread across its face.

T-Bone reached over and dragged Jojo back inside even as he was regaining control of the car. What flopped onto the seat beside him was a nearly headless ruin with one perfect breast protruding from a torn top.

Face contorting first in disbelief then in utter rage, T-Bone roared and tromped on the accelerator.

Billy-Bob, his own face a mask of fear and disgust, was thrown back into his seat as the sedan sped dangerously along the dirt road, wobbling and jouncing on its blown tire.

Inside the *Granola Gray*, Blade stared in disbelief as T-Bone's sedan roared off. Bulge, who'd gotten of the floor, frantically jabbed a finger at the retreating car and mouthed incoherent, panicked babble.

"What the fuck's he *doing?*" Blade shouted.

"He's running away, Blade!" Sledge screamed. "He's abandoning us! Catch him!"

"I can't! This crate's too heavy!"

Alex, Molly, and the desert rat watched the Lincoln disappear over a rise then threw curious glances at each other.

"What gives?" asked the desert rat.

Alex shrugged as he fitted a fresh magazine into his Steyer. "Who cares, as long as we get that van."

Now far in front, T-Bone's sedan roared out of the desert, onto the two-lane blacktop, and spun to a stop across the road. T-Bone looked wordlessly for a moment at Jojo's battered and bloody body before prying the M-60 from her fingers.

Billy-Bob was afraid to say anything and afraid not to. "T-Bone...," he began hesitantly, but T-Bone, jaw clenched, silenced him with a curt wave of his hand and got out of the car.

Billy-Bob followed, and they stood next to the sedan, facing the entrance to the dirt road. T-Bone slammed a fresh magazine into the machine gun and cocked it, his upper lip twitching in an otherwise lock-jawed scowl.

Bare moments passed before the two vehicles appeared. T-Bone stared at them, his cold expression giving way to a maniacal rage that erupted in a roar that might have come from an insane tiger.

As the *Granola Gray* hit the intersection, Blade and Bulge stared through the windshield in awed disbelief at T-Bone's horrendous mask of wrath. Then T-Bone lifted the snout of the machine gun and pointed it right at them.

"Shit!" Blade grated as he jerked the wheel, sending the *Granola Gray* wallowing onto the highway. As the van swerved out of the way, almost overturning, the Cherokee was totally exposed to T-Bone, his fury, and his M-60.

The Jeep's occupants had no warning because the *Granola Gray* had blocked their view, but when the van swerved unexpectedly onto the road, they saw the terrible figure in front of them. Before they could do more than throw themselves down, T-Bone, legs solidly planted, roaring in rage, hosed slugs at them.

The front of the Jeep exploded as lead from the machine gun tore it apart. Billy-Bob leapt frantically to one side as the Cherokee hit a dip just as it reached the pavement and bounced out of control toward T-Bone and the Lincoln. T-Bone, still bellowing and blasting away, seemed oblivious to the danger. But suddenly, his gun clicked on empty. He dropped it and threw himself to the side as the Jeep careened through the space where he'd just been.

Inside the Cherokee, Molly fought for control, and found just enough to miss the Lincoln. But the effort flipped the Cherokee onto its side, and it slid across the pavement in a crashing grind of tortured metal and shattering glass. At the far side of the road, it went off the shoulder and rolled and slid another couple of dozen yards, stopping at last, on its side, dust boiling around it.

Blade brought the *Granola Gray* to a halt a hundred feet from the intersection. He and the other occupants of the van gaped at the wreck of the Jeep as dust settled around it. Blade, threw the *Granola*

Gray's transmission into park, emerged, and looked from the wreckage to T-Bone.

The pirate leader was glaring with unvarnished hatred at the wrecked Jeep. He unholstered his .45 automatic and took a deliberate step toward the wreck. Billy-Bob and Blade drew their weapons as well and started to follow T-Bone as he closed in on the Jeep, but he aimed his weapon at them threateningly.

"Back!" he snarled.

Billy-Bob and Blade stopped as T-Bone stalked toward the Jeep. Inside it, Alex, Molly, and the desert rat were just coming to.

Sledge and Bulge watched the proceedings through the windows of the *Granola Gray*. Sledge glanced down at the keys dangling from the van ignition, and a calculating smile suffused his features. He clambered into the driver's seat. Bulge shot him a surprised look, and Sledge grinned back.

"The *Granola Gray* is ours now, dear brother. All ours. I knew all along that providence would deliver this small token of the Big Bang into our worthy hands."

A grin lit up Bulge's face, and he nodded enthusiastically as Sledge put the van into gear.

Out on the pavement, T-Bone continued to advance on the wrecked Jeep when the *Granola Gray* suddenly pulled off. Billy-Bob and Blade reacted instantly and raced after the van, shouting and cursing.

"Shoot!" Blade yelled at Billy-Bob. "Shoot!"

"Are you insane?" Billy-Bob stopped and stared after the shrinking van. "There's an A-bomb in there!"

T-Bone, intent on the Jeep, didn't seem to notice his big plans driving off down the highway without him. Grinning fiendishly, he raised his pistol and fired steadily spaced shots into the Jeep.

"Ten thousand lifetimes, trucker!" he bellowed. "Of pain!"

The occupants of the Jeep, groggily struggling to extricate themselves from the wreckage, ducked as the bullets ripped through the floor and seats, barely missing them. Still grinning, T-Bone ejected the empty magazine from his pistol and groped at his belt for a fresh one. He found it and was just about to ram it home in the gun, when Alex's hand fell on the Steyer. He poked its snout out of the window and squeezed the trigger.

Dirt gouted a few feet from T-Bone, and he ducked and fired back, but now Molly and the desert rat had recovered their own guns. Billy-Bob, ignoring T-Bone's orders, joined in, but the pirates' pistols were no match for a machine gun and two shotguns. Pellets rattled off the pavement near Blade and Billy-Bob, and Blade slapped the other's arm.

"Let's get the hell outta here!" he yelled.

They ran to T-Bone's sedan, shouting at T-Bone to join them. As they got in, T-Bone realized he was outgunned and, with a look of impotent rage, joined them in the Lincoln, pausing only to retrieve the M-60. He had plenty more ammo back at the compound, and he was going to use it all on that fucking trucker, starting at his feet. Gunning the engine, he raced as fast as the flat tire permitted back down the dirt road toward the compound.

Alex, Molly, and the desert rat emerged from behind the Jeep. Alex checked his Steyer, found it was empty, and lowered it.

"Alex!" Molly said urgently. "The van!"

They stared down the road in the direction the *Granola Gray* had gone, then at the wreckage of the Jeep.

"Maybe it's time to call in Mitchell," the desert rat said, and at Alex's nod, he reached for his cell phone. But a trickle of broken plastic met his fingers.

"Dead," he said. "There's nothing we can do."

"We can get the bastards and get the kid back," Alex said.

Molly nodded. "Let's go."

Several miles west, the *Granola Gray* tooled along, the blacktop sizzling beneath its overloaded tires. At the wheel, Sledge was grinning fiendishly.

"We did it, Bulge!" he chortled. "The technology is ours!"

Bulge bobbled his head enthusiastically.

"Isn't this a blast, dear brother?" Sledge went on. "I'm so happy I could burst! You remember how Mama used to sing that song to us when we were little. 'Shortnin' Bread?'"

Bulge nodded.

"Well, I've composed my own version." He began singing, his voice off key but lively. "Mama's little baby loves short little, short little, Mama's little baby loves short little fuse!"

The two of them erupted into laughter, Bulge's voice a strained, gasping grunt. As the *Granola Gray* whizzed off down the road, Sledge resumed the ditty, Bulge humming in happy accompaniment.

THIRTY-FIVE

"I'M GONNA TAKE THIS HARDWARE," Yvonne gestured with her .357, "and ram it where the sun don't shine. Then I'm gonna...." She viciously twisted the barrel, demonstrating what she would do.

"You get the beefcake," Mallet agreed, "long as I get his bitch."

"Maybe," Yvonne said. "Long as they're still alive, which I doubt."

They'd heard the sound of gunfire coming from the highway, and figured the heavy hammering of T-Bone's M-60 had left them little to play with.

"What about the old man?" Yvonne asked.

"Blade can use him for target practice."

The two of them laughed. Having failed in their half-hearted attempt to free the Pontiac from the hillock it had plowed into, they were trudging down the dirt road toward the highway. T-Bone would be waiting for them there, impatient as hell.

Suddenly, T-Bone's Lincoln jolted into view, the back left wheel riding on rim and shreds of rubber. Yvonne slapped Mallet's arm.

"What gives?"

The car rocked to a stop, but even the cloud of dust that rose around it couldn't obscure the human wreckage that slumped on the seat next to T-Bone.

"Jojo," Yvonne said in a low voice.

"Get in," T-Bone ordered, voice dead ice.

They squeezed into the back with Blade and Billy-Bob, and T-Bone tromped on the accelerator.

"What about the beefcake and the others?" Yvonne asked.

"Don't worry, Yvonne," T-Bone said. "They'll be along. They didn't come this far to stop at the highway. Besides, that trucker and I have a score to settle." He shot her a hard look. "You got that, Yvonne? Him and me. This time, the trucker is mine."

Yvonne didn't have to look at Jojo's body to get the picture.

"I got it, T-Bone," she said demurely. "He's all yours."

Without another word from the occupants, the car lurched off toward the compound.

Half an hour later, Alex and his friends, carrying their weapons and day packs full of ammo, came on the pirates' abandoned Pontiac. With the desert rat at the wheel and Alex and Molly pushing and shoving, they managed to work it free. The desert rat looked out of the window at the other two.

"I'm going after the van."

Wordlessly, Alex nodded, and the desert rat put the car into gear. Suddenly Molly rushed forward and embraced him through the window.

"Be careful, Dad."

"You take care of yourself," he replied, stony-faced. "Both of you. And bring the kid back. I can't afford to lose anyone else."

He sped off in a cloud of dust.

Just as he topped a rise and was gone, Alex noticed something and pointed to the earth where the car had rammed up against the hillock. A wet spot was quickly drying in the hot air.

"His radiator," Molly said, looking down the road where her father had disappeared.

A few minutes later, the desert rat emerged from the dirt road and turned down the blacktop after the van. The old man couldn't see it, but steam was hissing from a sprung weld along the bottom of the radiator.

Atop the compound walls, Slick was watching the road. He'd heard the sound of gunfire crackling faintly on the desert breeze, and he knew something was amiss. Nearly forty minutes went by before he saw T-Bone's sedan approaching the compound, wobbling on one blown rear tire. Slick slapped the button to open the gates.

As the Lincoln came to a rocking halt, T-Bone slammed out of it and stalked toward the shed where the boy was held captive.

"I'm going to gut that fucking kid and hang him to dry on the front gate," he muttered to himself, pulling a heavy-bladed hunting knife from his boot. "Just in case that fucker ain't got incentive enough to face me down."

Not bothering with the bolt, he jerked the door open, ripping the latch from the wood. Light spilled into the little room and across the hole in the floor where two boards had been removed. Next to the opening lay a bent spoon and several nails to show how the kid had managed to get loose.

Of course the kid's gone, T-Bone thought. Everything was fucking going fucking wrong. Jojo, Rat, the bomb, everyfuckingthing!

"Fucking shit!" he yelled as rage flared in his brain. He slammed a palm against the open door, and the panel, torn right off its hinges, flung into the dirt.

T-Bone stalked back to the Lincoln, scooped up Jojo's remains, and carried her off into the corridors of twisted metal.

By noon, the day had turned into a scorcher, but T-Bone didn't notice. His own internal temperature was at the boiling point, and he was ready to kill. His gang—what was left of it—knew him well enough to stay out of his way in the hours since they'd returned from the firefight on the dirt road, or he might have picked one of them to fuck up. What he really wanted, though, was that asshole trucker, though he'd have settled temporarily for the brat. But the little fucker had gotten out. The kid's spunk deserved a nod, but that wouldn't stop T-Bone from ripping the little shit to pieces as soon as he laid hands on him.

Actually, it hadn't been too difficult for T-Bone's gang to keep out of his path. He'd spent most of the morning in his exercise clearing, digging a grave in the hard, rocky soil. And now it was done, the freshly mounded earth to one side of the clearing mute testimony to the irrevocable absence of one more thing T-Bone had cared about. The image of that one perfect breast protruding beneath the raw mass of what had been left of Jojo's head made lightning flash in his brain. He thought of the pleasure he'd taken from that body, only to have it torn from him and mutilated before his very eyes on the eve of his victory. Then to have that victory snatched and tossed to the uncaring desert winds.

It pissed him that Sledge had gotten away with the *Granola Gray*, but Sledge's theft of the van was only to be expected. The insane scientist was a fuckup, but T-Bone didn't doubt for one second that he would detonate the bomb. Or that it would work. T-Bone figured he'd be hearing about the vaporization of LA in a couple of days at the most.

You fuck, T-Bone thought, snarling aloud as he visualized Alex's face. If it wasn't for you, everything would be in my pocket—Sledge, the bomb, Las Vegas. Hell! The whole fucking country!

And Jojo.

That was what hurt. Jojo and Rat. The only two fucking people he cared about, and that goddamn bastard had fucked them up along with everything else. And now all that was left was to finish off the fucker himself. Well, he'd do that in spades, starting with his scum-sucking buddies and that brat.

"That bastard'll pay for what he did to you, babe," he said to the grave. "I promise."

T-Bone turned to his exercise equipment, features taut, eyes seething with controlled rage. He had only one thing on his mind—to prepare his body and mind for the confrontation he knew would come sometime after nightfall.

He picked up a board from the pile, jammed it into the holder in the exercise machine, then began his workout, going at it with vicious intensity. When he finished with the machine, he went to the axle, doing slow, tortuous repetitions relishing the powerful bunching muscles in his arms and shoulders. And finally, there was the old car sitting nearby, waiting. He put a face on the old hulk, the face of the trucker, and he attacked.

After he'd torn off both doors, shattered all the glass, and ripped off and crumpled the fenders, T-Bone squatted, gripped the bottom of the car's frame, and strained upward. Giving a grating cry that sounded more animal than human, he lifted the side of the car off the ground. Groaning, he bore the car upward then gave a tremendous shove that sent the hulk rolling over its side and onto its top. With the crash of the toppling car still reverberating in the clearing, the giant whirled toward his exercise machine, whipping the ham of his back fist toward the bracketed board in a brutal, smashing blow.

So intent was he on the action and his fury that he didn't notice the three protruding nails until he had struck, driving the nails completely through his balled fist. One nail impaled his middle finger, lodging in the bone. The skewed angles of the nails impeded his blow, and the board failed to break.

For a second after the strike, T-Bone stared in shock at his pinioned hand, face a mixture of pain, rage, and bewilderment.

Peering through a gap in the wall surrounding T-Bone's clearing, Phyllis saw the look, and triumphant satisfaction lit her own face.

Then the rapid exchange of expressions on T-Bone's face was washed away by a tsunami of pure rage. Jerking his hand off the nails, he vented a howl of insane wrath that echoed like a knell of doom through the aisles of twisted and torn metal.

THIRTY-SIX

AS THE SUN SANK BEHIND the ridge on which Alex and Molly spent the day, the ridge's shadow inched across the valley floor below them and finally engulfed the ragged walls of the junkyard, throwing the interior into jumbled twilight.

The two stirred from their uneasy wait, and Alex checked his watch. It read after eight.

"Let's give it another hour," he suggested.

"Fine with me," Molly said. "The darker the better. I don't want them picking us off while we go over the wall."

At the appointed time and in wordless agreement, Alex and Molly hefted their day packs and began carefully climbing down the darkened ridge to the desert floor. They arrived there twenty minutes later and hurried across it toward the junkyard, pausing occasionally behind creosote bushes to scan the walls for watchers.

By the time they arrived at the junkyard's corrugated sheet metal walls, night had completely darkened the desert. Their approach had been unseen as far as they could tell. At least, no alarm had been raised or shots fired. Above them, the ragged spikes cut along the top and the drapery of coiled razor wire were silhouetted against the light coming from the sodium vapor lamps inside the junkyard.

Alex tapped Molly and pointed to the spikes. He shrugged off his pack, removed the contents, tossed the empty bag to Molly, then hoisted her onto his shoulders. Molly slung the pack over two adjacent spikes and their coils of wire and leaned hard on the pack. The spikes bent, trapping coils of wire and leaving a gap in the wall's ragged top.

While she perched in the gap, Alex tossed up the contents of the emptied pack. Molly caught the items, mostly spare ammo clips in a pocketed harness and a bandoleer of shotgun shells, and one by one, carefully dropped them over the wall into the interior of the junkyard. The last item was a coil of rope. She looped the rope around the spikes adjacent to the gap and dropped one end to Alex and the other end into the junkyard.

Then she quietly went down the rope into the junkyard. While she gathered the dropped ammo, Alex climbed up the other side and pulled himself to the top of the wall. Squatting there, he unsnagged the pack strap, leaned out, and dropped the bag beside Molly. Then he slid down the rope. After gathering their weapons and ammo, they moved off warily into the interior of the junkyard.

Nearly five hundred miles west, the desert rat pulled the shuddering Pontiac up to the curb in front of a darkened furniture store in some podunk little town. Steam hissed from the bottom of the radiator, and the temperature gauge had been in the red for so long, the desert rat was sure the block must be cracked. He'd had to fill it at every opportunity as he blindly chased the van across the desert. At each stop, he'd asked about the van, and it hadn't been long before he'd had his first hit. Sledge and Bulge weren't easily forgotten, and they seemed oblivious that there might be any kind of pursuit.

Now, there the van was, half a block behind him at the pumps of a convenience store. He could see two figures moving around in the store who fit the descriptions of the van's occupants, and a third person standing behind the counter.

The desert rat got out, held his wrist up to the light, and checked the time. Just after nine, and he was dead tired. Just about asleep on his feet. Feeling his age, he supposed, though when he thought about it, he'd been awake nearly twenty four hours, and that time included a car chase, a wreck, and a protracted gunfight, not to mention a hell of a lot of driving. What he really needed was a nap.

He was ready for all this to be over, but he didn't dare confront the two oddballs, at least here in town. He didn't know how dangerous they might be, and he didn't want the clerk, who looked like just a kid, to get hurt. Nor did he particularly want to be at ground zero of an atomic explosion. They might have some sort of remote control that they were going to use when they got to their destination, and he figured they might set off the bomb in a tiny town rather than be completely deprived of it.

His first thought was that he'd have to wait until they were out in the desert somewhere before he approached them. He still might go up in a fireball, but at least the bomb would detonate in the middle of nowhere.

Trouble was, the middle of nowhere was getting harder and harder to find. They'd already crossed into California, and the direction they were heading eventually would take them right into Los Angeles. That had to be their destination, and he figured he'd have to come up with something real soon, or it would be too late.

And he knew the Pontiac wouldn't last much longer. He opened the hood, and a thin billow of smelly steam wafted by his face and vanished in the dry air. Not much left in the radiator, he mused. He'd have to cool it down enough to open the cap then fill it before the two oddballs came out and drove off. He also needed to pee. Seeing the restroom doors in the side of the gas station, he headed toward them, carrying an empty gallon milk jug and trying to think of some safe way to stop the van's contents from making mincemeat out of this town, LA, or any place in between.

Inside the store, the clerk was doing a lot of wondering, himself. He was just out of high school, and this was his first real job. Mostly, he was wondering if it might not be his last job. Today there'd been the after-school kids trying to steal any and everything they could get their hands on, then there'd been a trio of bikers, smelly, intimidating, and frightening. They'd paid and left quietly enough, but not until the clerk had just about shit himself. Now there were these two weirdos. He couldn't decide which was worse, the hunchback who acted retarded or the other one, who looked more normal but who was obviously crazy as a horse on locoweed. He surreptitiously watched the two, expression a mixture of disbelief, disgust, and anxiety.

Sledge didn't notice the teenager's stare. He was too busy plucking items of junk food off the shelves and piling them into Bulge's arms. Bulge grunted and nodded excitedly toward a rack of cellophane-wrapped cupcakes.

"You have such a sweet tooth, brother." Sledge clucked. He pinched Bulge's cheek. "A sweet tooth for a sweet boy." He piled several packages of cupcakes on top of Bulge's burden. "I suppose you want some candy bars too."

Bulge nodded excitedly.

"Ah, well. It's not as if you'll have to worry about cavities, eh?"

They both laughed and walked toward the clerk. Bulge dumped the stuff onto the counter while Sledge dug in his pocket. Pulling out a wad of grungy, crumpled bills, he separated a twenty from the rest and handed it to the clerk. The boy took it gingerly between forefinger and thumb, as if it might infect him. Doing little more than ascertaining its denomination, he dropped it beneath the cash drawer, made change, and put the money on the counter. The brothers grinned at him in their own inimitable styles as Sledge raked the money into one of the lab coat pockets.

A moment later, they left the store, Bulge carrying the sack. Behind them, the clerk plucked a newspaper from the rack beside the counter and began looking for the want ads. Those two were it. No more. He was looking for another job starting right now.

Outside, Sledge and Bulge got into the *Granola Gray*, and Sledge started the engine. As the van pulled out from under the lights and drove off into the night, it passed by the Pontiac, hood still up but otherwise looking deserted on the street. Neither Sledge nor Bulge noticed the car or that, behind them, light shone from beneath the restroom door.

THIRTY-SEVEN

ALEX PACED CAREFULLY ALONG THE junk-strewn ground, Steyer loose and mobile in his grip. Across the aisle, shotgun at port arms, Molly shadowed him. The piles of wrecked cars loomed over them with hidden threat, and the aisles between the ragged metal walls were dark and menacing. Alex took the lead as they worked their way deeper into the junkyard, and before long, he couldn't have easily found his way back to their point of entry.

Suddenly a sharp whistle pierced the air, and from the other side of the wall next to them reverberated the roar of an engine. In the adjacent corridor, Slick had just cranked over the bulldozer. He ground the gears into place, levered the mechanical beast around on its treads to point at the wall of junk cars, and gunned the engine. He was so intent on the wall as he ran the dozer toward it, that he didn't notice the grating sound that came from the engine or the black pall of smoke that belched from the stack and quickly blended into the night. Three seconds later, the dozer blade smashed into the wall, sending it toppling.

With a clash and grind of grating metal, the wall of junk cars heaved inward toward Alex and Molly. They both leap aside as half a dozen rusted hulks crashed into the aisle where they'd just been, blocking the passage with a jumble of wreckage.

When the crashing din stopped, Alex picked himself up and peered through shadows and the cloud of dust raised by the falling junk, looking for Molly.

He couldn't see her because she was on the other side of the jumbled pile. She, too, scanned the wreckage, and Slick pranced out onto it, cackling and cavorting madly and looking down on her. She watched the greasy mechanic for a couple of seconds then took a step toward him.

On the other side of the barrier, Alex was searching for his Steyer, which he'd dropped as he leapt back from the collapsing wall of junk. He heard Slick cackling, and he drew his 9mm. A second later, he spotted Slick and shot at him, but the grease monkey, practically the same color as the junkyard itself, blended in like a chameleon.

A carburetor, then a side view mirror, then a really old AM radio sailed out of the sky like mortar shells from a junk gun, making Alex duck. He fired again and again in the direction from which the junk was flying but didn't seem to hit anything but old cars.

Out of bullets, he ejected his magazine and groped at his belt for a fresh one. But before his fingers found it, a ghostly figure materialized out of the gloom and settling dust. The sinuously waving machete identified the ghost a moment before his face was revealed in the glare of an arc lamp.

As Blade's machete sang through its expert arcs, Alex dropped the 9mm and grabbed a length of pipe from the junk, and the two men circled warily. Meanwhile, Molly reached the pile of junk where Slick was dancing and grabbed for a handhold when a bullet whanged from the metal next to her and whined off into the darkness. Molly threw herself behind a fallen wreck, ducking more bullets.

"Fuck," Billy-Bob muttered in the little hidey-hole he'd found. The angle was wrong for a clear shot and the light was bad and the air full of dust. Plus, for the first time in his gunslinging career, he was nervous. None of the other pirate victims had put up anything close to this much of a fight.

As the shots shook the air, Blade leapt at Alex, swinging his machete in scything slashes. The blade and pipe clashed as the combatants thrust and parried, slashed and blocked.

With the barks of the shots dying into stillness, Molly stared into the darkness, trying to pick out where they'd come from. Several more shots slammed in out of the shadows, and she spotted the muzzle flare in a small gap in the wall about a hundred feet down the aisle. Well, two could play this game. She sent a blast toward the dark gap.

Billy-Bob jerked back as shotgun pellets rattled into the metal around his hidey-hole, then he popped out and ripped off twelve shots nearly as fast as a machine gun, shooting simultaneously with both guns. One of the bullets ricocheting off the hulk protecting Molly spun close enough to Slick's face that he could feel the breath of its flight. Howling in fear, the grease monkey flung himself to the other side of the pile where he was out of range of the gun battle. From his new vantage, though, he could see Alex and Blade.

He saw Alex's 9mm lying on the ground, and he hopped down, picked it up, and aimed it at Alex. But nothing happened. The damn thing was out of bullets. Slick threw the gun into the junk heap and scrambled back up to watch as the two men swung, slashed, and stabbed in a ferocious, eye-boggling whirl of gleaming arcs and thrusts.

Suddenly they were apart. Blade was panting. Alex, though not winded, felt a hot flush along his left forearm. He threw a quick glance and saw blood slowly welling from a shallow gash. His opponent was proficient, no doubt about it. At least as good as Alex with a sword, maybe better. The only reason he'd won before, he realized, was that Blade hadn't been expecting any sort of expertise in his victim, and Alex had been armed with a heavy crowbar with its conveniently hooked end. Now, though, Blade was ready, and that made the pirate as dangerous as a double-edged sword.

Alex's momentary reflection was cut off as Blade sprang at him again. They fought furiously for several minutes, Alex taking another minor slash and returning the favor by pounding Blade across the rib cage. Alex felt as if his personality was strangely isolated inside of himself, as if his consciousness was separated from the actions and reactions of his body, and he was merely a spectator to his sport. He had little time to do more than marvel that one of the movements he had practiced for so long actually worked before another movement came along at precisely the correct moment to protect and counter. Exhilaration surged through him as if, instead of being in the midst of whipping, slashing edges and deadly points, he was, like Pecos Bill, riding a whirlwind and taming it to his will.

And suddenly, just like that, there it was, like a stab of light in the darkness. He saw, he reacted, he drew the madman with the machete in, and then he acted. A quick twist of the pipe, a sudden wrench, and Blade's machete was sailing through the air to clatter against a rusted hulk and thud to the ground.

Surprised at the loss of his weapon, Blade retreated a step. But Alex had only enough time to contemplate his alternatives when a chunk of metal struck his arm, jarring the pipe from his hand. Above him, Slick howled in delight and groped around for something else to hurl.

Instantly, a throwing knife appeared in Blade's hand. With a movement like a snake striking, he threw it at Alex. Alex ducked in a spasm of pure instinct as the knife hissed by. Alex was just straightening as Blade made a peculiar twisting motion with his wrist. A switchblade slid into the knifeman's palm. It's nasty tongue flicked open, and Blade charged, catching Alex off balance. Alex barely managed to ward off the strike, and the two men fell to the ground, wrestling for the knife.

On the other side of the barricade, Molly continued to trade shots with Billy-Bob. The cowboy gunman quickly discovered he'd picked a poor spot to hide in for someone facing a shotgun. His hole was fairly shallow, and while slugs would have buried themselves in the crushed car bodies, the buckshot swarmed into it and bounced around, stinging him like angry hornets. Worse, there was no retreat. He was bleeding from dozens of shallow punctures, he'd almost lost one of his eyes, and his fancy cowboy suit was ruined. He stuck a muzzle around the corner and emptied the gun in the woman's direction.

But Molly wasn't there. While Billy-Bob had been contemplating his mangled condition, she'd managed to work her way around the junk car she was using for cover to a better vantage. She was about to flush the gunman out into the open, when slugs from another direction perforated the metal beside her. She dove and rolled, seeking protection from the crossfire. As she scrambled under the ruin of another car canted against the pile, she heard Yvonne's voice crack like a round from her gun.

"Looks like I got the drop on *you* this time, bitch!" She sent more shots at Molly.

Across of the pile of junk, Blade had managed to separate himself from Alex, and the two men rose and warily circled each other.

"You're pretty good," Blade admitted. "But I'm better. And I've got this." He waved the knife in a small circle then leapt at Alex, slashing and jabbing. In a furious flurry of blocks and parries, Alex kept the knife out of his flesh, and suddenly Blade overstepped. Alex knocked the knife from his hand and, with a rapid set of strikes and kicks, drove Blade back into the wall of metal. The knifeman drew another sliver of steel, but Alex caught the thrusting hand and twisted it in a bone-crunching joint lock. The knife dropped to the ground.

"Now you don't" Alex said.

With a movement almost too quick to see, he drove a rigid hand edge against the side of Blade's neck. Vertebrae snapped, and surprise filled Blade's eyes before they glassed over. He toppled into the dirt.

As Blade's battered and bloody body collapsed, Alex heard the gunfire from the other side of the barrier and looked up at Slick staring wide-eyed at him. The greasy mechanic scuttled off the pile and disappeared.

On the other side of the barrier, Molly was in a precarious position as Yvonne pinned her down, allowing Billy-Bob to duck out of the alcove he'd been trapped in. He dodged toward an up-turned car as Yvonne's pistol shattered the night. When he reached the hulk, he crouched, catching his breath, then raised up and peered over the hood. He could see the woman lying low beneath Yvonne's bullets. The bitch wasn't even aware that he was here with a clear shot at her. Payback for his raw flesh and his ruined clothes, he thought, raising one of his pistols.

Suddenly a knife hissed through the air, whisking off his hat. Billy-Bob ducked without firing, trying to see where the knife came from, when another whizzed by his head. In desperation, he ripped off a couple of shots into the darkness and jumped behind the up-turned car. All he could see was his hat lying in the dirt, knife piercing it through.

Molly, given an opportunity now that Billy-Bob wasn't shooting, waited until Yvonne had to reload then fired three blasts at the pirate woman's position. The flurries of ricocheting pellets drove Yvonne back, down the aisle.

Alex, on top of the pile of junk, threw Blade's last knife at Billy-Bob then turned as he heard a roar of heavy machinery. It was the bulldozer, driven by Slick, rounding the corner of the aisle. Slick gunned the engine, lifted the dozer blade, and headed right for the pile of junk Alex was on. Alex, out of knives, turned and threw Blade's machete like a spear at Slick. The blade went between the heavy mesh protecting the cab, but the handle halted the blade bare inches from Slick's face.

The mechanic, gaping stupidly at the blade, rammed the dozer into the pile of junk, nearly knocking Alex off. Alex hung on and scrambled to regain his feet as Slick backed up the dozer for the killing blow. All of a sudden, the dozer engine shuddered and grated, and thick oily smoke spewed from the stack. In amazement, Slick watched the oil pressure gauge bounce wildly. The engine missed, then ground to a complete stop. Slick stared down at the dead dozer with complete disbelief, only then noticing the oil filler cap was on crooked. Fuck, was that dirt around the hole? But he didn't have time to find out because the trucker looked mad as hell. Slick jumped to the ground and raced out of sight.

Billy-Bob peeked cautiously over the upturned car. He saw Alex rise atop the pile and drew a bead on him. Molly saw Billy-Bob aiming at Alex and fired at him. Throwing himself to one side, Billy-Bob rolled his rotund body sluggishly out in a crouch and aimed his pistol at Molly, but she'd tracked him as he moved, and her next blast sent him staggering back, against a junk car. Chest torn, Billy-Bob fell to the ground, leaking the last of his life onto the oily ground.

Alex dropped to the ground, and Molly came out from behind the car. She discarded her empty shotgun and took out her pistol, while Alex picked up both of Billy-Bob's pistols and reloaded them from the dead man's belt.

"We'd better split up," he said. "We're too much of a target together." Molly nodded, and at the next intersection, they went separate ways.

Thirty-eight

ALEX MOVED CAUTIOUSLY DOWN A narrow corridor, keeping to one side. He was following Yvonne. Moments later, he spotted her and barely had time to duck before she sent two slugs through the air where he'd just been. Without exposing his body, he shoved the muzzle of one of Billy-Bob's .45s around the corner and emptied it in her general direction. Risking a quick glance, he saw that she was not in sight, so he tossed the empty gun aside and advanced into the corridor again, second .45 sniffing for a target.

He had no time to react as a length of metal pipe slashed out of a dark alcove and smashed down on top of the pistol, sending the weapon skittering beneath a car. Grunting, Alex jumped back as Slick popped out of the shadowed nook, holding the pipe like a baseball bat ready to swing. Alex took a step toward him, then stopped as Yvonne, grinning triumphantly, stepped around the next corner, her gun pointed at his chest.

"Ah, my beautiful beefcake with his heart of stone. You saved the last dance for me." She cocked her pistol.

"You're supposed to wait for T-Bone," Slick stammered nervously. Yvonne paused, but just for a heartbeat.

"The hell with T-Bone," she said. "This beefcake is mine. He's always been mine."

Her finger tightened on the trigger when a rock whizzed through the air and smacked the back of her gun hand. She yelped in pain and jerked the trigger, the shot losing itself in the dark air. A second rock gouging her knuckles made her drop the .357, and a third thudded into the side of her jaw, raising an angry welt.

Alex pounced on Slick, easily avoiding the swinging pipe, and grabbed him. But Slick's strata of lubrication was too slippery to hold. He wriggled out of Alex's grasp like a greased pig and dashed off.

Ducking another rock, Yvonne snatched up her pistol and fired at Alex, but he dove after Slick, and almost instantly, another rock smashed into her head. Vision swimming, she whipped around to face the aisle of junk, covering it with her gun. She couldn't see anyone, but another rock gouged her arm, and another hit her shoulder, and she shot wildly down the aisle. Her bullets ricocheted into the night as more rocks cut at her and thudded into her body. She cried out and tried to seek cover, but wherever she turned, the pebbles stung and tormented her. She emptied her gun and managed to fumble a single bullet into the cylinder, but then gun was knocked from her shaking hands, and this time she couldn't get it.

Stumbling down the aisle, pursued by a barrage of whizzing stones, Yvonne managed to make it to the front gate. She pounded the button to open it, and while the mechanism slid the gate back, she raced to the old battered pickup with the party-colored fenders, parked near the metal building, and started the engine. But as she sped toward the front gate, a stone flew in through the side window, sliced across her cheek, and smashed into her nose, instantly flooding her eyes with tears and blood. The shock made her jerk the steering wheel, and she lost control of the speeding vehicle. For a precarious moment, it seemed as if she might bring it back on course, but the truck flipped over, slid fifty feet across the oily earth, and crashed into the wall next to the gate.

As she tried to crawl out of the wreck, she saw a strange, small figure approaching. She blinked blood and tears from her eyes, unbelieving. It was that brat kid. Then she noticed the slingshot, made from a bent piece of metal and inner tube rubber, dangling from his hand just as the wreck burst into flames. She yelled and struggled frantically to free herself, but the fire reached the ruptured gas tank first, and the wreck exploded.

The detonation flung Heath to the ground, and he scrambled to his feet and backed off, shielding his face from the inferno as the wreckage burned. Inside, a macabre scarecrow of flame danced for several moments then was still.

Abruptly, Heath bumped into something solid. He whirled, and towering over him, T-Bone grinned wolfishly.

"Imagine that," he said. "Yvonne done in by a boy."

Heath tried to run, but T-Bone snatched him, wrenched the slingshot from his hand, flung the puny weapon aside, and smacked him on the side of the head with the flat of a hand wrapped in bloody bandages. Tucking the still form under one arm, the big man disappeared into the junkyard.

A hundred yards away, Alex was trailing Slick through the junkyard, but Slick, on his own territory, easily evaded him. When the explosion shook the metal walls and lit the night, Alex could only hope that Molly hadn't been too close.

She wasn't. In another part of the junkyard, still armed with her pistol, she moved soundlessly down a corridor. But no matter how quiet she was, someone had seen her coming; hidden in a shadowed niche, Mallet waited in ambush. As Molly passed, he threw a small hammer, jarring the gun from her grip. She jumped into the center of the aisle as Mallet moved in. Instead of swinging his maul, Mallet hooked it onto his belt.

"I don't need this for sweetmeat like you."

He moved in on Molly and tried to grab her, but she warded off his arm with a defensive move Alex had taught her, taking Mallet by surprise. He went after her again, but he was so big and clumsy that she managed to keep out of his reach.

"Come here, you slippery bitch!" he shouted.

The longer he pursued her, the more enraged he got, until he was charging and bellowing like a maddened bull. At last, he stopped, panting and staring at her out of bloodshot eyes, and he pulled a hammer from a pouch and threw it at her. She dodged, but he quickly threw another, a third, and a fourth. All of the last three hit Molly, one on the head, bringing grunts of pain. Face a twisted grimace, Mallet moved in, unhooking his maul and smacking it into his palm. He closed, swinging the maul, and Molly dodged the blows, but now found it was difficult to do more than barely keep out of his reach. And then even that wasn't possible.

One of his swings slammed into her shoulder, sending her spinning in wrenching pain. It felt like her arm was broken. Uttering a gloating laugh, Mallet moved in for the kill. In desperation, Molly kicked him in the knee, and he gave a whining gasp and staggered back, giving her time to scramble painfully to the top of a nearby pile of junk.

Mallet sucked in a moaning breath, aimed the hammer at her but missed. Then he grabbed onto the junk wall and tried to climb up after her, but she was now in a superior position and could easily use her feet to keep him from gaining the summit. Mallet, knee throbbing, gave up after several attempts and limped off into a dark aisle.

Molly watched him go then looked longingly at the gun she'd dropped. But she was afraid to go down to get it. The monster with the mallet might be watching and waiting, and she might not be so lucky in getting away a second time. Putting the gun out of her mind, she gingerly moved off, keeping to the top of the junk piles as much as she could.

Alex, still following Slick, chased the greasy pirate toward the back of the compound, into a clearing where a crane and a car crusher stood. There he stopped stock still, grim rage hardening his eyes.

Across the clearing, Slick scurried behind T-Bone, and Alex could see that the big man had the kid tucked under one arm and the M-60 under the other. A moment later, Mallet stepped into the clearing and stood near the crane.

T-Bone, face a dead, gaunt mask, pointed the M-60 at Alex.

"Well, well, Mr. Trucker Fucker," he said with a rotten snarl. "We meet again—for the last time."

At that exact moment, the *Granola Gray* passed a sign that read, "Los Angeles City Limits."

Inside the van, Sledge's sly look was illuminated by the dash lights. "We're here, Bulge. The City of Angels."

Bulge grinned.

"Many, many angels, eh?" the scientist went on.

Bulge choked out a laugh and nodded heartily.

"Where and when shall we detonate, dear brother?" Sledge mused. Bulge looked blank, then his eyes brightened. He held up his right hand with the first two fingers extended and his left with forefinger and thumb circled. Sledge brightened and patted his brother on the shoulder.

"Excellent suggestion, dear brother. The old 20th-Century Fox theater in Westwood. It has such pleasant memories. We'll set ourselves off at dawn, right in front. How does that sound?"

Bulge leaned back in his seat, sublime satisfaction on his face.

"Yes. It will be a new dawn for the movies," Sledge said as he eased into the city traffic. Behind them were a lot of cars, but not the old Pontiac.

The city had expanded considerably since Sledge had last been here, and his sense of direction had never been strong, anyway. It took him almost an hour to orient himself and maneuver the sluggish van through the impatient faster traffic before he found the old theater. He parked across the street, about half a block away.

A city is never truly quiet, but for the moment an aura of almost preternatural stillness settled around the *Granola Gray* where it sat in the shadows. Inside the van, Sledge eased his aching bones out of the driver's seat and into the back. There he caressed the control panel for the bomb, touching switches and readouts as if they were precious jewels.

"Oh, my baby," he crooned. "About to be born."

Bulge looked on like a proud new uncle. Sledge gave him a sly glance. "And now it is time, dear brother. I shall arm the mechanism like this."

He flipped several switches. "And set the time like this." He punched buttons, and an LCD clock lit up, showing a little over two hours. Sledge glanced at his watch, then at Bulge.

"It won't be long now, dear brother. We shall ride eternity at dawn." He punched a button.

As the LCD started counting down, the demented brothers smiled brightly at each other.

Thirty-nine

"I'LL BET THAT MAKES YOU nervous," Alex's voice was just as cold as T-Bone's. "Every time you see me, you lose something."

"I've still got my life, and that's something you're about to lose." T-Bone's eyes blazed as he raised his machine gun.

"Yeah, a coward as well as a loser."

It wasn't false bravado or even desperation that prompted Alex's quiet words. They were a truth that illuminated the big pirate with clarity, and they rang like a bell in the still air.

Though the muzzle of the weapon didn't waver a millimeter, T-Bone shook with rage and hatred, muscles tight and jaw clenched. He hated to admit it, but the fucking trucker's words struck deeper than even Rat and Jojo's deaths. They took him back to that dark rendezvous where he had crept away rather than confront Brooks and his men, though they'd used him and butchered his family. And then he'd retreated to this barren oasis and tormented his enemies from the safety of distance, always picking on victims weaker than himself. But now, all it seemed like he'd done was pick at the edges of a scab, keeping the wound festering and unhealed. Now where was his revenge, when all his schemes looked like little more than grandiose dreams born of desert heat, no more substantial than a mirage. And with Sledge's defection with the bomb, the mirage had evaporated as instantly as if the bomb had gone off in T-Bone's heart.

So even if he did not want to acknowledge the trucker's words, he knew that the past five years had been as much evasion as carefully planned revenge.

But, goddammit! The plan would have worked, and it would have been proper punishment for the mob and Brooks. Would have except for this fucker standing in front of him, unarmed yet defiant.

"Come on, T-Bone," Alex taunted. "You got me. There's the kid and the gun to hide behind. And I'm unarmed." He showed his empty hands and shrugged dramatically. "Go on. Shoot. There's no one but these two geeks to see you crap out. No one to see your fear."

T-Bone snarled and tossed the kid aside like a sack of meal. Slick scuttled forward and grabbed the boy before he could get away as T-Bone stalked toward Alex, the assault rifle still centered.

"Yeah," Alex said. "I guess you got a right to be afraid."

T-Bone looked like he was going to explode. His face flushed hotly, and his lips drew back from his clenched teeth in a skeletal snarl. He no longer thought, just envisioned. And what he saw was himself ripping that stone heart right out of the trucker's chest and holding it up to his dying eyes.

"Ten thousand lifetimes, trucker! Of pain!"

With a roar, T-Bone threw the M-60 aside and erupted right at Alex. Alex expected the big man to be strong but not so blindingly fast. The leap was like a tiger's spring, and Alex evaded it, though T-Bone's out-stretched arm slammed into him, and the shock bounced him backward two yards. Alex managed to remain on his feet as T-Bone rushed again and, this time, caught him with one vise-like hand and tried to slug him repeatedly with the other. Alex blocked and used a twisting maneuver to lever himself out of T-Bone's grasp.

T-Bone's blinding fury subsided into a steady boil. His initial rush had almost immediately given him the upper hand, but with skill and cunning, the trucker had kept him at bay. There may have been desperation fueling that skill, but T-Bone wasn't going to let that make him complacent. This bastard was good. If he expected to rip out the guy's heart, he'd have to be careful. Warily the two men circled each other.

Off to the side, Mallet hurried forward to grab T-Bone's discarded rifle, but a shot shattered the weapon and sent it spinning. He jerked back and saw Molly on top of a nearby junk pile, cocking Yvonne's .357. Aiming right at the center of Mallet's massive body, she squeezed the trigger. Mallet had only time enough to gasp, but the gasp turned to a rasping chuckle as the hammer clicked on empty. Mallet lumbered toward the crane, climbed to the cab, and started the engine.

With the crane's diesel roaring in the background, Alex and T-Bone traded punches and kicks, for the moment testing each other's limits but not inflicting much damage. Alex needed a good opening, but T-Bone's rage was under control now, and he wasn't committing any blunders that Alex could take advantage of. That was bad. T-Bone, inches taller and thirty pounds heavier than Alex, would eventually wear down Alex and give him the opening to use those huge fists. A couple of direct hits with those would inflict serious damage, though Alex noticed that one was wrapped with a crude, crimson-stained bandage. Maybe he'd been hit during the firefight. Whatever had happened, it was a weakness, and Alex would have to exploit every weakness he could find on this seemingly impregnable giant. Striking, kicking, and blocking, the two fought across the clearing.

Inside the crane cab, Mallet manipulated the controls, sending the crane arm swaying back and forth, causing the electromagnet on the end of the cable to arc like a huge hammer.

"Hammer of the gods!" he bellowed as he swung the heavy magnet right at Molly.

She leapt to the side barely in time, but stumbled on the precarious footing atop the pile. Hampered by her injured shoulder, she scrambled to keep from falling. Mallet swung the electromagnet again. It slammed into the car Molly perched on, almost knocking her off the pile.

Below, Slick tried to drag the kid away from the center of the clearing, but the boy kicked the mechanic in the knee, and the greasy man yowled and dropped him. The boy scurried away, around the circumference of the clearing.

By now, Alex and T-Bone were both showing some blood but little sign of weakening. Alex dodged a roundhouse and came back with a shoulder strike against T-Bone's back. Off balance, T-Bone stumbled. Then he lashed out with a chopping side kick that caught Alex behind the thigh. Alex almost went down, but he was able to rise before T-Bone could gain his own equilibrium and take advantage. Even as he rose, though, he could tell that the kick had taken a toll on his leg as the muscles bunched painfully at the strike point.

T-Bone immediately noticed Alex's limp, and his lips twisted in satisfaction. He went at Alex again, pressing the side with the wounded leg, and with a flurry of kicks and punches, drove Alex backward across the clearing. Alex, hands and feet moving as if they had minds of their own, blocked and back-pedaled, hoping to find a break in T-Bone's momentum that would allow him to disengage. The big man's arms and legs were like concrete, and the only thing that saved Alex's own limbs were the circular blocks he employed that redirected T-Bone's force rather than confronted it.

But the break didn't come, and suddenly Alex's back slammed into the solid side of the car crusher. Then T-Bone was on him, hammering him with fists and knees. Now, though, T-Bone's relative size was a disadvantage. Alex's tai chi training had included not only close-quarters blocking that used every part of the body but techniques to deliver penetrating blows from distances of less than six inches, while the big man needed at least eighteen inches to launch an effective strike. Alex fended off the pirate's fists for a dozen seconds then snaked a hand up between them with all of his weight coming up behind it and slammed the open palm against T-Bone's jaw. The big man grunted and lurched backward, but he didn't fall, though the blow could have broken a lesser man's neck. Instead, he just shook his head once and glowered at Alex.

"No wonder you got this far," the pirate said. "Too bad for you you did."

"You gave me no choice," Alex pointed out. "So shut the fuck up and fight."

T-Bone came at him.

Mallet, at the crane controls, swung the electromagnet again. It slammed into the car Molly was on, and she lost her grip, slid off, and fell to the ground, stunned.

As Mallet clambered to the ground, Slick chased after the kid, but the brat eluded him. All the greasy mechanic got for his pains were several more kicks, one all too close to his gonads. At last, he managed to grab onto the boy, and the two fell onto the ground. Although Slick was bigger and stronger, the kid, squirming and writhing, fought like a cat. It was all Slick could do to keep from being mutilated by the boy's gouging fingers and churning knees and elbows.

Mallet lumbered over to Molly, and loomed over her, gloating, as he unhooked the maul from his belt and looped the thick leather strap around his wrist. There was going to be blood—lots of blood —and he didn't want his grip to slip on the hammer's haft until he was completely satisfied.

By the car crusher, Alex's training was again showing its advantage over T-Bone's brute strength and speed. A rapid series of punches and kicks sent the big pirate slamming backward into the crusher. But in an instant, he rolled up onto the crusher platform and, in the same maneuver, kicked Alex in the side of the head. Alex fell to his hands and knees. Dimly knowing that he had to get to his feet, he staggered erect and saw that T-Bone had risen also and was crouched, ready to spring. Before he could, Alex swung up onto the platform in a low crouch, sweeping T-Bone's legs from under him. The big man crashed down, but he was up in an instant.

Straddling the fallen Molly, Mallet raised the maul, anticipating the solid thud of its weight into tender flesh.

As he lifted the hammer high over his head, there was a sudden throaty hum. Surprise washed over Mallet's face as his maul was jerked upward. Looking up, he saw the huge electromagnet poised over him. Kicking, he was jerked bodily upward as the magnet attracted the hammer with irresistible force.

Unable to slip out of the thick leather strap because of his own weight, Mallet dangled there, twirling slowly, hand turning to fire as the thong bit into his wrist. At last, his turning brought him far enough around to see the crane cab and the woman at the controls.

Sneering at him, Phyllis threw a lever, and Mallet was hoisted aloft, kicking and screaming, to the very peak of the crane. Slick, seeing what was going on, dropped the squirmy brat and dashed toward the crane.

He climbed over the caterpillar treads to gain access to the cab, but when he reached for Phyllis, she whipped out a ball peen hammer from the loop at her waist and pounded him on the hand. Slick jerked back with a cry of pain, stumbling backward onto the crane's treads. Phyllis threw another lever, starting the crane moving forward. She'd watched Mallet operate the machine so often, she could have done it in her sleep.

Slick staggered, lost his footing, and grabbed a stanchion as his feet dragged over the moving treads. At the top of the crane, Mallet shrieked, his body swinging back and forth with the machine's jerking motion. Blood ran profusely down his arm as the leather strap cut into his wrist.

Up on the car crusher platform, T-Bone was at Alex again. But having learned his lesson on the ground, he stayed off Alex and kept to a more effective range where his power was at maximum and his reach an advantage. Tiring, Alex had taken a couple of blows, one that temporarily numbed his arm and another than might have cracked a rib. He blocked a savage kick to his groin then a follow-up to his head and caught T-Bone's foot before the big man could withdraw it, wrenching the ankle around. T-Bone flipped onto his side but immediately reacted with a kick to the back of Alex's already-injured knee. Alex's leg gave way, and he collapsed on the brink of the crusher's open maw. He barely had time to roll over before T-Bone was on him, hammering with massive fists and trying to shove him inside the opening.

Slick, dangling over the moving treads, tried to hold onto the stanchion, but his hands were so greasy that he couldn't keep his grip. Howling, he fell onto the moving tread, was dragged along them, and in a wink, was cycled beneath them. His final gasping cry cut off abruptly in a crackling crunch as he was ground to greasy pulp.

Phyllis stopped the crane's forward movement, and Mallet bellowed weakly from his height. The strap had literally cut him to the bone, and each swaying jerk sent agonizing jolts of pain down his arm. Phyllis flipped a switch, turning off the power to the electromagnet, and with a strangely feminine squeal, Mallet plunged thirty feet to the ground. He struck with an audible crack as both his legs snapped at the knees, and he lay there on his back, spread-eagled, stunned, and broken. Opening his eyes, he saw the heavy weight of the electromagnet poised high above him. His eyes turned, panic-stricken, toward the crane cab, where Phyllis smiled.

"Hammer of Phyllis!" she yelled. With a flourish, she threw a lever.

"Nooooo!" Mallet shrieked as the heavy electromagnet dropped with dead weight right onto him. The cry was ended in a large, squishy thud as the weight squashed him like a bug beneath a heel, leaving only his twitching arms and legs protruding around its edges.

Straddling Alex, T-Bone rose, both fists balled into a solid ham of bone and gristle that he slammed at Alex's head. Alex heaved to the side, and T-Bone's fists caught him on the shoulder. There was a moment of blinding pain, and in that moment, the big man was off him and following the blow with a kick to Alex's side that sent him pitching into the crusher.

A second later, T-Bone was at the controls, and with a grind and scrape of heavy metal, the crusher's jaws began levering shut. Alex realized that he'd have only a minute or two to get out before he was smashed, but T-Bone was too quick, stomping at his fingers and kicking at his head, keeping him trapped.

It was impossible to tell what warned the pirate—some sound or instinct. Whatever it was, he ducked just as the crane's head whooshed by him. But the momentary distraction was all Alex needed. He surged out of the crusher, and nearly made it upright before T-Bone was back on him. They swayed there on the brink for a moment then toppled together into the narrowing space.

As the metal walls closed in, they fought with renewed desperation. Suddenly, eyes alight with mad intensity, T-Bone jerked the heavy-bladed hunting knife from his boot and slashed at Alex. Alex leapt back, and T-Bone slashed again. With his back against a moving wall, there was no way for Alex to evade, and he took a gash across his chest, not far from the ragged scar left by Yvonne's bullet. Blood gushed hotly over his skin.

T-Bone, eyes gleaming with triumph, stabbed at Alex, but Alex, acting out of pure, exhausted instinct, knocked the lunging blade aside. The knife clattered into a narrowing corner where its blade was trapped and shattered beneath the edge of the closing wall. Then T-Bone jumped him, and there was nowhere for Alex to go. The fight grew hopeless as the narrowing steel walls restricted the space, promising to defeat both men. T-Bone seemed oblivious to the danger, but Alex was all too aware that bare moments of life remained. With a bold and desperate flurry of strikes and parries, he beat back T-Bone, turned, and tried to climb out of the crusher.

He was half way out when T-Bone grabbed onto his leg with a grip of iron. With brutal strength, he tried to haul Alex back into the crusher, at the same time trying to crawl over him to escape before the crusher swallowed him, too, in its iron jaws. For an intense moment there was stasis as Alex and T-Bone struggled on the brink of the crusher, neither able to get out.

Alex's panicking vision saw the bandage around T-Bone's hand, and he cruelly ground his thumb into the middle of the blood spot, feeling the digit sink up to the knuckle in the wound. T-Bone howled in pain, and as his grip loosened, Alex kicked free and clambered out, into free air. T-Bone tried to follow, but the blood now flowing from his wound caused his hand to slip on the greasy metal. Then it was too late. He tumbled back into the crusher, staring with intense hatred at Alex through the narrowing gap.

"Ten thousand lifetimes, T-Bone," Alex said, staring into the big man's eyes. "Of emptiness."

T-Bone's bellow of rage and pain blended with the mechanical grinding as the iron jaws irrevocably finished their work with a symphony of wet snapping sounds.

Alex climbed painfully off the crusher and looked around the clearing. Phyllis cut the crane's engine, and silence hung palpably in the air. Molly staggered to her feet, and Phyllis came out of the crane cab and hopped to the ground. The three of them stared at one another for a long moment before the kid emerged from behind a pile of junk across the clearing. When Phyllis first saw the boy gaping at her in disbelief, his identity didn't register, but then her eyes widened in shock that quickly turned to emotional relief.

"Heath!"

Reaching out, she took a halting step toward the boy.

"Mom!" he yelled. "Mom!"

With open arms, he rushed across the clearing, into her embrace.

FORTY

DAWN WAS JUST LIGHTING THE sky above the old 20th Century Fox theater and the *Granola Gray* parked down the block. As the sky brightened, a few early pedestrians and cars passed by the van.

Inside, Sledge and Bulge were crouched over the bomb console, watching with fascinated expressions as the LCD clock counted down. The clock read one minute.

A couple of joggers loped by, and an older woman walking her dog paused next to the van to scoop her pet's poop into a plastic bag. While she did, the dog peed on the tire.

Inside the van, Sledge and Bulge continued to watch expectantly as the clock counted down. It read twenty-seven seconds, and by the time it reached fifteen, the brothers looked positively ecstatic. There were now numerous people and cars passing by, and the sun's rays began to creep across the tree tops. The waking city went about its business, not realizing the day would end before it even started in a dawn more brilliant and polluted than any it had ever seen. The clock counted from eleven to ten to nine. Bulge was practically jumping with joy, and Sledge beamed with beatific radiance. The clock counted from six to four. Sledge and Bulge looked at each other with brotherly love.

"Apotheosis now, dear brother," Sledge pronounced.

They both looked at the clock as it descended from two to one. "Now!"

Bulge tightly squinched his eyes and held his breath. As the clock hit zero, Sledge's face split with an insane grin.

Nothing happened.

Realizing something had gone wrong, Bulge opened his eyes, a blank look in them. He glanced at Sledge and saw dazed surprise covered his brother's features.

At that instant, the large panel in the base of the console burst open with a crash. The two brothers leapt back in shock as an old man popped out of the bomb like a maniac jack-in-the-box. In one hand he held a shotgun and in the other the wire cutters Sledge had left inside the console. Behind him was a spaghetti tangle of severed wires.

"Boom!" yelled the old man.

Bulge's eyes rolled up in his head, and he fainted. Sledge stared blankly at the old man for a moment, mouth hanging open. Then his mouth snapped shut as realization hit him.

"You must be God," he said. "I'm so pleased to meet you."

"Jeez," the desert rat said, rubbing his eyes. "I must have fallen asleep in there."

FORTY-ONE

IT WAS HOT AS HELL, and FBI agent Henry Mitchell was not in a good mood. He'd just been out in the middle of nowhere, where a huge junkyard baked under the desert sun. And stank to high heaven with the bloated and rotting remains of at least seven bodies, including one buried in a shallow grave. Well, seven that could be identified as bodies at this point, though several more skeletons and a lone, recently detached arm wrapped up in a piece of chain were discovered in a dumpsite not far behind the junkyard's rear wall.

The one burned in the wreck near the front gate, the one smashed beneath the electromagnet, and the one ground beneath the treads of the crane were bad enough. Those could at least be identified as bodies. But the most problematic was the gory block of pulped meat and bone they found when they opened the car crusher. One of the forensics team speculated that it belonged with the arm found out back, but Mitchell thought the limb more likely matched the leather and chain-clad, road-burned torso discovered up the road from the rest stop. Only DNA analysis could tell for sure.

It was late afternoon when he pulled into the parking lot of Little Paradise. As he emerged, he noticed that the heat had dropped a little. He also noticed that, despite the "closed" sign on the front door, music and savory smells wafted over and around the trading post. He followed them both around to the back of the building, where he saw a small but lively party in full swing.

He immediately spotted Alex and Molly dancing to the music, which issued from a portable stereo. One of the woman's arms was in a sling, and Alex limped and looked somewhat battered. Not far off, the desert rat, wearing a stained apron, stood in front of a barbecue grill, poking at its contents with a big fork. Next to him was a woman Mitchell didn't recognize, though there was no mistaking the way she stayed extra close to the old man and glanced at him now and then with an adoring eye.

Alex saw Mitchell, stopped dancing, and turned down the stereo.

"Agent Mitchell," he said. "Come by on business, or is this a social call?"

"Business," Mitchell said flatly, not particularly in the mood for anything lighthearted.

"Have you found our perpetrators yet?"

"From the look of you, you know damn well I found them."

"Oh?"

"You don't deny it?"

"Don't admit anything," the desert rat called out jovially over the barbecue pit.

"Deny what?" Alex asked, a twinkle in his eye.

"Look," Mitchell said shortly. "I didn't come here to play games."

"Then you'll have to come back tomorrow," Molly said firmly. "Because today we're playing."

"How do you like your steak, Agent Mitchell?" the desert rat asked. "Rare, medium, or well done?"

"Skip the steak," Mitchell said. "And the small talk. I'm about one inch from hauling all of you in."

"For unlicensed barbecuing?" asked the desert rat.

"I'll start with murder."

"And who are we supposed to have murdered?"

"I'll bet forensics'll be able to answer that one in another day or two."

"But for right now," Alex said, "you've got the bodies of a gang of cutthroat murderers, kidnappers, and rapists. No telling what they might have tried to do if someone hadn't made sure they wouldn't— like blow up a major U.S. city with a homemade atomic bomb."

Mitchell's eyes widened.

"So that's what...." He stopped and glared at Alex. "If there was a bomb, what happened to it?"

Alex shrugged.

"I'm just speculating, understand. I wouldn't recognize an A-bomb if one dropped in my lap. But I'd say that anything that can be put together can be taken apart. Maybe someone took it apart."

"You think that makes what you did any better?"

"I think," the desert rat said, "that makes us and everybody happy to be alive."

Mitchell took off his sunglasses and passed a hand across his dark face. It came away wet with sweat. He tucked the glasses into his jacket pocket.

"Christ," he said. "You could have let me know something."

"No," Molly replied. "We couldn't."

"The ways of justice are mysterious, eh, Mitchell?" the desert rat asked. Mitchell sighed, and the last of his anger vented with it. What the hell could he do? Arrest them? Okay, maybe forensics could come up with something to link some of them to the scene of the crime, but maybe not. So far, the only fingerprints found on shell casings belonged to the dead pirates, and there were many without fingerprints. Obviously whoever loaded those into weapons had used gloves. And the whole crime scene was a junkyard, for Christ's sake. It was going to be hell telling evidence from anything else in that sea of refuse.

Besides, were the deaths of the pirates a crime, really, or just retribution? A bunch of deadly scumbags dead and a bunch of friendly lunatics alive. He had to admit that it was a pretty fair trade.

"How about that steak?" the desert rat asked.

"I have to leave," Mitchell said. "You can party, but I've got a report to fill out."

"The report can wait until tomorrow," Alex said. "Celebrate with us. The insurance company paid off on my rig, and I'm getting a new one next week." He put his arm around Molly's shoulders. "But I think I'll be basing myself out of Little Paradise from now on."

"I really can't," Mitchell said. "It's a long drive to Albuquerque, and I've been on the road all day as it is."

"All the more reason to relax," Molly said. "You can even stay here overnight." She waved toward the teepee motel units. "On the house."

Oh, hell, Mitchell thought, the savory smell from the barbecue pit making his mouth water and stomach rumble. "Okay," he said. He loosened his tie and sat as Molly offered him a chair.

That's when he saw the others. The kid he'd seen before, though at present, he looked a little scuffed up. The other two he was sure he'd never seen before. They weren't the sort to forget. Or be prepared for. The kid was with one, showing him how to shoot a slingshot. The guy was a hunchback and had the blank face of a child. He couldn't seem to get the hang of the slingshot, and all his rocks were flying wild of the target, but the kid didn't seem to mind as he patiently told the man he was doing good and handed him another pebble.

The second man was sitting in a chair about fifty feet away. His back was turned to Mitchell, and all the agent could see was a long white jacket of some sort and a head surrounded by a halo of wild white hair. He seemed to be just staring out over the desert at a ridge that lay a mile or so behind the trading post.

A loony bunch, Mitchell thought, looking around, but there was no rancor in his mind. And then Alex pressed a cold beer into his hand, and he forgot about all the craziness of the past several years. The case was finished, if not actually solved. He'd write his report and say that either a rival gang or factions within the gang were responsible. There'd be no mention of atomic bombs, renegade truck drivers, or desert rats.

"Hey, Mitchell," the desert rat called. "Come and get it."

Mitchell went over to the pit, and the woman with the desert rat smiled and handed him two plates heaped with steak, baked potato, and corn on the cob.

"Take one to him, please," she said sweetly, nodding in the direction of the man with the wild white hair.

Mitchell nodded and headed over to the man. When he got there, the man looked up at Mitchell. His eyes, magnified by thick spectacles, looked demented, but there was peacefulness in them, too.

"Molly asked me to bring your dinner." Mitchell handed over the plate, and the man took it and set it in his lap. The jacket, he saw now, was a sparkling white lab coat.

"Isn't it beautiful?" the man asked, gesturing out across the desert.

"Yes," Mitchell agreed, not because he thought so, but because it seemed the easiest thing to do.

"They told me it's Little Paradise," the man said.

"Yes. That's what it's called."

"And what do you do, young man?"

"I'm with the FBI."

"Could I doubt that this is paradise if the FBI affirms it?" The man's eyes opened wider than before, though Mitchell would have thought it impossible. "Did you know that God brought me here? He gave me this new lab coat, too."

Mitchell looked around, wondering if the man might be dangerous, wondering who could help him. But the kid was with his uncouth playmate, the unknown woman was snuggling up to the desert rat, and just around the corner, Alex was kissing Molly.

"Yes," he said. "Well, I've got to go...."

The man with the wild hair reached up, caught his arm, and stared into his eyes with a fervent stare brightly magnified by his thick lenses.

"Don't go," he said earnestly, "Seek. Seek and ye shall find."

Phosphene Publishing Company
publishes books and DVDs relating to literature,
history, the paranormal, film, spirituality, and the
martial arts.

For other great titles, visit
phosphenepublishing.com